THE DEED

Robert

My best wishes

Gene

THE DEED

EUGENE R. BOFFA, JR.

For

My wife
Patricia Lytle Boffa

My children
Eugene III, Kevin, Jessica & Michael

In memory of
My Dad
Gene Sr.
and
My father-in-law
James R. Lytle

Acknowledgments

Without Bob Cavalero this labor of love would not have come to fruition. His support and more importantly his friendship are responsible for this book being published. I am honored to have him as my friend. His staff worked wonders, especially Chris Buono an editor's editor who made me crazy with rewrites and Emilie Cerar for putting everything together and always taking my calls. Thank you.

Tony Seidl who guided me along the way, and made enough suggestions to fill a book.

Joe Winterberger, a man without a watch who thankfully is a better fisherman than a literary critic.

CHAPTER 1

When death knocks the door opens.

— Old Chinese proverb

❦

THE temperature was hovering around a hundred-and-five degrees and the humidity was off the charts as MacKenzie Daniels lay in a clearing about seventy-five yards from a thick stand of Colombian jungle.

God, he thought, it's hotter than hell. He wanted to be back in his hotel room with the air conditioner running full blast and a cold beer in his hand. This was no place for a sane man, not even for a crazy man, he thought, and he swore he would speak to Admiral Charko about these bullshit assignments.

"*No mas,*" he whispered.

Less than fifty yards away, three men were patrolling the grounds at one of the largest cocaine processing operations in South America. They stopped for a moment and lit up. Shouldering their AK-47 assault rifles with thirty-round clips, they stood around for a few minutes inhaling lungfuls of smoke and humid air. Until they moved on, all Daniels could do was to lie there and wait. The sweat pooled in the small of his back, attracting a swarm of biting insects.

The guards were professionals. Except for smoke breaks, they kept moving around the perimeter at irregular times, keeping in radio contact with central control. High in the trees, Daniels spotted the motion sensors and surveillance cameras. For an outdoor operation, security was tight and first class; Daniels wasn't sure he could get much closer without being discovered. Maybe it was the heat, but he felt it was time to get out of there. He had what he came for—the proof, the photos, just what the Admiral had ordered. As soon as the Three Stooges moved on, he decided to make his retreat.

Daniels knew he had to be quiet because, basically, he was unarmed. His 9 mm Glock was of little use against automatic rifles. To add to his discomfort, he was dragging along a camera with a damn telephoto lens—a lens that looked like a baseball bat and probably weighed about the same. But it was hardly lethal. He smiled, picturing himself swinging the lens at the guards while they blasted away at him with their AK-47s.

God, how I hate recon missions, he thought, feeling the sweat pour off his body and the insects eating him alive. This was an R-and-R mission, not rest and recreation, but retrieve and report. All he had to do, Admiral Charko had told him, was to get the pictures and report back. What a snow job that was, he thought. He would much rather have lined up a few local operatives and destroyed the damn processing plant. But that was not the way Charko ran the Special Operations Division of the CIA.

To get into Colombia, Daniels's cover had been that of a photojournalist—a cover he had used so frequently. He was actually getting good with a camera. Before that, he mused, the only time he had used a camera was back at Princeton University. Then it had been a cheap Polaroid and his models were beautiful and willing young women, not aging drug lords. The quantity had gone up, but the quality had come way down.

Using his false press credentials, he had managed to get into and out of some pretty hot spots. But in the Colombian jungle, he wasn't sure that the cartel would appreciate being photographed or interviewed. Years ago he had had Saddam Hussein in his sights; later, he knew he should have shot the bastard and not with his camera. That was one time MacKenzie Daniels admitted he blew it.

Recon missions were as dangerous as they were useless. He could have passed on the assignment; Admiral Charko would have understood. But he and the Admiral were at the mercy of Washington politics. The State Department had been satisfied that the Colombian government had cleaned up the drug manufacturing trade, but the DEA and Justice wanted proof. The vice president had pressured Charko to send someone to look around, to see what they could find, to document it, and to get out. Charko told Daniels that the official word was not to look too closely. Hearing that, Daniels had doubled his efforts to find the evidence. Now that he had it, he would deliver the proof to the CIA section chief in Bogotá, who would turn it over to the field desk at Langley, who would pass it onto Sam Bergen at the National Security Agency, who would turn it over to the Assistant Secretary of State for Latin and South American Affairs, who would give it to the Colombian ambassador, who would give it to the Colombian officials, who would throw it away. What bullshit, he thought. Why not just blow up the place? The answer, of course, was politics.

Suddenly, one of the guards, "Curly," the bald one with the scar going from his ear to the side of his mouth, stopped talking to his comrades.

He looked directly at Daniels as if he had heard him thinking, and started walking in his direction. Daniels didn't move; he didn't want to breathe. He hunkered down in the tall grass, sweat running down his face, his black hair plastered to his skull.

He was not sure whether he heard it or saw it, but from the corner of his eye Daniels spotted a brown snake with light stripes and dark diamond markings. He hoped he was wrong, but it looked like a highly poisonous pit viper, the fer-de-lance. He tried wishing it away. The snake stopped; Daniels exhaled softly. Then the snake picked up its head revealing a yellow throat. No doubt about it, Daniels thought, it was a fer-de-lance. One bite and he would be history.

Curly came closer and now there were two reasons Daniels couldn't move. If he did, either the man or the snake would get him. The viper started to slither over his extended arms, surprising him by how warm and dry it felt. It stopped, turning its head toward Daniels. The snake's tongue darted in and out of its mouth as if it were trying to lick the moisture off Daniels's face. The sweat filled his eyes, but he didn't dare to move or even blink. The snake tensed its body, staring at Daniels. The guard moved closer, his footsteps growing louder as he tramped through the undergrowth.

When Curly was only a foot or two away, Daniels knew he had to act. The vibrations of the guard's footsteps were enough to spook the snake. The fer-de-lance opened its mouth and prepared to strike. With lightning speed, Daniels's left hand intercepted the snake just behind its head and, in one fluid motion, he flung it into the air. The viper landed on the guard's neck, sinking its fangs deep into the exposed flesh. Curly never got off a shot. He was dead before he hit the ground.

Daniels was up and running. The other two guards weren't sure what had happened and hesitated, giving Daniels a break, not a big break, but a break. They chased after him, but they made the mistake of firing at him while running. Bullets went everywhere, whizzing by his head, as he ran for the cover of the jungle. Slightly over six feet tall, Daniels seemed to be all legs as he sprinted ahead. He thought his football coach would have been proud of this run. Maybe he should have taken the coach's advice and tried for a career in the NFL. But to Daniels, a deal was a deal and, when he had accepted the ROTC college grant, he had promised a four-year commitment to the Navy, not the NFL.

Once in the jungle, his odds improved and Daniels stopped running. It was time to go on the offensive. The two guards had separated, trying to cut him off. The first guard was talking on his radio, while the second started to search the area. Daniels knew he had to get them quickly if he were to have any chance at all. In a few minutes the jungle would be crawling with heavily armed men.

Flanked by the two guards, Daniels chose to take on the one on the radio first and he moved in for the attack. Unsnapping his camera strap and fastening one end to a stick, he crouched low and moved closer to the guard. As he got within a few feet of his target, the guard clicked off his radio. Springing forward, Daniels pulled the strap around the guard's neck. The loop tightened as Daniels's knee went into the guard's back, snapping the strap and breaking the cartilage in the man's throat. The guard dropped his gun, opened his mouth as if he were about to scream and died.

Picking up the AK-47, Daniels pressed his body into the cavity of a tree, listening, waiting for his prey. The other guard was moving toward the spot where his partner had been. The dead man's radio gave away his position. The metallic voice coming through the speaker was a sound beacon to the second guard, who was following his own voice. Finding the body of his friend, he bent down to examine the lifeless form. He never got up. Daniels flew out from behind the tree, slamming the rifle butt into the head of the unsuspecting guard, crushing his skull.

By now, armed men were everywhere. Daniels, clutching his camera under one arm, the rifle in the other, ran north, deeper into the jungle; then he moved west and finally back to the south. He decided that the best place to hide was back at the cocaine camp, the last place they would look for him. Most of the men had gone past him, searching the northern area as Daniels worked his way to a clearing at the western edge of the jungle. He had a good view of the compound, close to the processing tables and the drying racks. Quickly raising the camera, he snapped off several shots, focusing in on the storage facility, which was packed to the rafters with cocaine. On the other side of the camp Daniels saw two airplanes parked at the edge of a small airstrip. They were Cessna 182s, single-engine planes, good at short field take offs and landings. Outnumbered a hundred to one, Daniels knew he couldn't fight his way across the camp without creating a diversion. He had to get to one of the planes if he were to get out of there alive. With a little luck he might be able to get around the far side of the camp making it to the planes. But it was bad luck he had. One of the young women working the cutting tables was coming back from a break and suddenly appeared out of the bush. She was startled to see Daniels. She opened her mouth to scream, but he swung the camera, hitting her in the jaw with the oversize lens. It made a terrible crunching sound and knocked her unconscious. That was the best use of the camera all day, he thought, popping out the film.

"Here," he said, dropping the camera. "Enjoy your Kodak moment."

As she hit the ground, a hand grenade rolled from the pocket of her apron. Spotting the grenade, Daniels bent down to retrieve it. He also grabbed the kerchief she wore around her neck.

Quickly pulling several of the bullets from the AK-47's magazine, he pried them open and poured the gunpowder into the kerchief along with a dozen cartridges. He tied the kerchief off in a knot and used some straw as a makeshift fuse. The gunpowder would burn, igniting the kerchief, causing the cartridges to explode. He hoped the noise would distract the guards while he cut across the camp. Lighting the fuse, he threw the homemade bomb toward the processing table; it landed near a jar containing clear liquid—ether. Not paying much attention to it, Daniels started to move around the camp's perimeter. At the sound of the bullets going off, Daniels would make a dash for the plane. The bullets started to pop just as a group of guards were coming back from the jungle, having abandoned their search.

At first, everybody ducked for cover as the bullets exploded, giving Daniels a chance. He ran, firing the AK-47. When he emptied the clip, he used the rifle as a club, hitting prone guards with the butt to keep them down. Passing within throwing range of the storage facility, he pulled the pin on the grenade. It was a good throw, right at the gasoline tanks.

He was twenty-five yards from the planes when he heard a massive explosion and saw a fireball erupt like a volcano from the storage facility. The concussion leveled almost everything, knocking Daniels to the ground, flat on his face. Spitting out the dirt, he was up immediately and running again.

What the hell was in there? he wondered. But he didn't dare turn around to look. The whizzing of bullets became a familiar sound again as Daniels kept running for his life. Twenty-five yards soon became ten, then five, but his luck was about to run out again. An old-timer propped his ancient 30-06 bolt action on the processing table and took careful aim, putting Daniels square in his scope. The shooter was grinning as he was about to squeeze off a round. That's when another explosion shook the ground, blowing the shooter's head off. The grenade had set off the gasoline tanks in the storage facility, while one of the exploding rounds had pierced a bottle of ether, which had run onto the burning kerchief, causing the various chemicals to combust. Daniels never knew what had caused the second explosion—or how lucky he was to be alive.

Jumping into the nearest Cessna, Daniels hit the starter and played with the choke. The engine coughed to life.

"Come on, come on," Daniels urged the engine.

The prop made a few turns, a few more coughs, and finally caught. The noxious fumes smelled good to Daniels and he pushed in the throttle to the dashboard wall. Dropping the flaps, he guided the plane down the grassy runway. At the base of the runway, he turned the plane into the wind—and into an army of blazing rifles. Bullets were jumping around the cabin as the windshield was shot out. Racing toward the shooters, the plane picking up speed, Daniels pulled back on the stick, starting to climb. The bullets were coming through the underside of the fuselage and a few tore into the overhead wing fuel tank. Once out of range, he checked the gauges, glanced around the cabin, realizing he was piloting a flying Swiss cheese.

Miraculously, he wasn't hit and the engine was running smoothly. At last some good luck, he thought, until he noticed the fuel pouring from the left wing tank. The right wing tank was undamaged and the gauges indicated it was full. Daniels turned the fuel selector lever to the left tank, using what fuel he could before it ran dry. Then, he would switch to the right tank. Daniels didn't know how far he would get, but he knew it wouldn't be long before he would have to ditch the plane.

The radio and the navigation system were gone, but fortunately the compass still worked. Heading northeast at five thousand feet, Daniels was beginning to relax when bullets suddenly ripped through the side door, passing by him, and out the other side of the cabin. Looking left he saw the other Cessna off the port side of the aircraft. He opened up with the Glock, knowing that he hadn't a prayer of doing any damage. But he fired as fast as he could anyway. After five shots, the gun jammed, a shell lodged in the ejection port.

"Oh, fuck," he yelled, throwing the Glock down.

Banking the plane hard to the right, he pushed the nose down. The Cessna dropped screaming toward Earth, the other plane following close behind. Picking up air speed, he started to execute an Immelmann roll, a maneuver invented by a German fighter pilot during World War I. The maneuver was a way of turning the plane around and rolling it over at the same time. It wasn't designed for a Cessna, but Daniels didn't really care. He had no other choice against the barrage of automatic fire.

Coming out of the Immelmann, Daniels headed straight for the other plane. If he had been in a fighter, he would have been able to take a perfect shot. The other pilot was startled by the maneuver and pushed the nose of his plane down, giving way to the crazy gringo. The pilot called Daniels a few other choice names as he pulled the nose of his plane up, scanning the sky. The gunner opened the door of the cabin, looking down. The Cessna's wing was positioned over the body of the plane, giving good visibility for a ground view, but it prevented a pilot from seeing up and over the aircraft, only what was in front or down. Daniels had looped his Cessna, flying upside down over the other plane.

The two planes were wing to wing, about two feet apart. Flipping on the automatic pilot and unbuckling his seat belt, Daniels opened the cabin door. He crawled out onto the wingtop of the Cessna beneath him. The gunner was still leaning out of the cabin searching the sky for his target. Daniels reached down and gave the gunner a quick hard shove, knocking him from the plane. The pilot turned toward the scream and saw Daniels sitting in the shooter's seat. Daniels punched the pilot, who released the wheel to fight back, causing the plane to dive. Both men were exchanging punches as the ground raced closer. It was a question who was going to reach for the wheel first.

Daniels managed to get in a good right uppercut that snapped the pilot's head back. That gave him a chance to unsnap the pilot's seat belt and pull him out of the seat. As the pilot came toward Daniels, his foot hit the controls sending the plane into a ninety-degree bank. Both men were tossed from the plane. The Colombian fell head first, bounced off the wing strut, and dropped to his death.

Daniels went out the door, hitting the strut with his shoulder. He grabbed it. Holding on with all his strength, his legs dangling off the wing, he managed to get his feet on the landing gear. As the plane was getting closer to impact, Daniels reached up for the loose seat belt flapping in the wind and pulled himself into the plane. He pushed the wheel to the left and he pulled back hard. The Cessna seemed to hang there for a moment, destined for impact, when the nose suddenly lifted up—but not soon enough. The wheels hit the ground knocking off the landing gear. Daniels let the plane climb back to five thousand feet before leveling off. Then he set a course for the ocean.

"This is Bird Dog. Are you there, Sky Bird?" he said into the radio. "Repeat, Bird Dog calling Sky Bird. Come in, please."

Sky Bird was a high-altitude navy reconnaissance aircraft that flew early warning for a battle group. Often they lent support to special operations like the one Daniels was on. Over the speaker, a metallic voice crackled: "You okay, Bird Dog? We picked up explosions on the ground. Pretty big fireball. Thought you were on a surveillance mission. What happened back there?"

"I'm fine, but I need a ride out of here. To tell you the truth, I don't know what happened back there. I guess death knocked and someone opened the door," Daniels said.

"Can you make it to Cartagena?" the metallic voice came back.

"Negative. I lost my landing gear. And somehow I don't think I would be welcomed there. I have some interesting photos. If I dump this crate in the ocean, can you get me out?" Daniels asked.

After a few minutes, Sky Bird gave him a set of coordinates for a rendezvous with the USS *Adams*, the destroyer that would pick him up.

As Daniels cruised toward his ditching spot, he scanned the horizon for a sign of the *Adams*. Shipboard life wasn't so bad, he thought. He was still on the navy roster as an officer on assignment to the CIA's Special Operations Division. After graduating from Princeton, Daniels had announced to his family that he was going into the navy. That came as a shock to his father who was a retired air force general. Training at the San Diego naval base, Daniels learned to fly, then he became a member of the Navy SEALs, seeing plenty of action in the Gulf War, Bosnia, and a few other places. He thought of making a career in the navy when the Admiral approached him to join the agency's Special Ops team. Daniels would still be listed as a naval officer, on special assignment, drawing full pay, and receiving his hazardous duty supplement. He would be entitled to normal promotions and had a promise that he could see the world—and not just from the deck of a ship. The offer was tempting and after a long deliberation, which lasted about thirty seconds, Daniels joined the Special Operations Division of the CIA. That had been eight years ago.

It took about an hour before the little plane was over the ocean, a good thirty minutes from the *Adams*.

Daniels was ten minutes from international waters when he heard a voice in bad English calling on the radio: "Cessna 710 Zulu, return to San Martin Airport."

Deciding not to answer, Daniels hoped that if he got far enough away they wouldn't bother sending a chase plane after him. He was wrong.

"If you don't turn around and fly back to San Martin, we will shoot you down," the heavily accented voice said.

Pushing the throttle all the way, Daniels tried to gain more air speed. He wasn't trying to outrun them. He knew he couldn't. He was flying the slowest craft and he just wanted to put as much distance as he could from land, hoping to deter them from causing an international incident by shooting down an American journalist. But he was wrong again.

Off the starboard and port sides of the Cessna were two Mirage Vs, bought by the Colombians from the French. The jet jockeys flew in close, so close Daniels could see their names painted on the sides of their planes. The pilot on the port side made a motion for Daniels to turn around by pointing back over his shoulder. Daniels started to lower the nose of his plane slightly, trying to get close to the water for ditching. The two jets broke off, coming at Daniels, while firing bursts across the front of the Cessna from their 20mm cannons.

"Listen, gringo, if you don't turn around, you're dead."

The pilots moved their jets alongside Daniels, closing the distance, their wings almost touching.

Looking at the pilot closest to him on the port side, Daniels gave him a big smile and a little wave; then he pointed to himself as if to say "who me?"

"You, on my port wing, if you don't mind, it's Mr. Gringo, you dumb sack of shit," Daniels said into his radio mike.

With that, he pushed the nose of the plane down, racing toward the ocean. The two jet pilots were momentarily stunned by the death maneuver and dropped back to get a missile lock on the small plane.

Daniels was getting close to the water, but not close enough to jump.

The radio crackled to life.

"Mr. Gringo, this is Lieutenant O'Connor, United States Navy. If you would please pull up, we would be happy to escort you to the USS *Adams*."

Picking up the microphone, Daniels replied: "My pleasure, Lieutenant, what kept you?"

Daniels overheard the exchange between O'Connor and the Colombian pilots. O'Connor told them they were in the no fly zone of the United States aircraft carrier *Kennedy*, and would they please turn around. The Colombians protested that they wanted the stolen Cessna returned, along with the thief. O'Connor was polite, telling the Colombians he didn't see any Cessna.

"Anybody see a Cessna?" O'Connor asked his wing man over the radio.

"What Cessna?" came the reply.

O'Connor's weapons officer flipped on his radar-seeking guidance system. Inside the Colombian jets, the pilots' screens started to blink alert. A few seconds later, the radar had a lock.

The screens in the Colombian jets screamed their warning. The alert had given way to danger. The pilots wished they could turn off the noise that sounded like fingernails across a blackboard.

"You are now in the target practice area. Firing in five, four, three," O'Connor said.

Not wanting to die that day, the two Colombian pilots turned around and headed for home, leaving behind a string of anti-American epithets relating to someone's mother and sister.

The USS *Adams* was now in sight.

"Good luck, Mr. Gringo. Hope you enjoy your swim. If you ever get over to the *Kennedy*, I'll buy you a cup of coffee," O'Connor said.

Daniels extended the plane's flaps. The engine sputtered as the last of the fuel ran out. Suddenly, it became quiet in the cabin. The only noise Daniels could hear was the whistle of the wind. Flying parallel to the *Adams*, he pulled the wheel back into his lap, making the nose pick up, and slowing the plane down even more. Then it stalled and hit the water, bouncing like a stone skipping across a pond, before it came to rest, flipping over onto its wings. As the plane began to sink slowly, Daniels stepped casually out onto the wing. Before he was waist deep in the water, a rubber raft came alongside, picked him up, and took him to the *Adams*.

CHAPTER 2

Rumors fly faster than the wind.

— Old Chinese proverb

✿

GOVERNOR Christopher Patten opened his daily diary to Friday, June 19, 1997. Only eleven more days to go, he thought. Eleven days until he became a trivia question: Who was the last Governor of Her Majesty's Royal Colony of Hong Kong?

Patten had spent his entire life working for Her Majesty's government, rising through the ranks through sheer hard work and determination. He was considered one of the best and he was highly regarded by his peers, the queen, and the prime minister. Working with former Prime Minister Margaret Thatcher, Patten had been the guiding hand, the voice of reason, and the driving force behind the talks that had led to the 1984 accord, whereby Great Britain agreed to turn over Hong Kong to China on July 1, 1997.

Patten didn't want to leave Hong Kong with an uncertain future. He had realized early on that unless there was some degree of continuity, the economy would collapse, leaving seven million refugees who were by law British subjects. In his heart, Patten believed that the agreement in which the Royal Colony would become the Hong Kong Special Administrative Region of China was the best of a bad deal. China had promised that Hong Kong would not be under its "one country, two systems" formula, basically a socialist system, but rather it would be allowed to be independent in all matters except foreign affairs and defense.

The turnover of the Royal Colony, however, would be the hardest thing Patten ever had to do. And, like Cinderella, he dreaded the stroke of midnight on June 30th. Would it all be lost? he wondered.

His eyes drifted back to his diary. Winston Williams was his first appointment of the day. As commissioner of foreign affairs, Williams reported directly to Patten on all matters. If there was a disagreement on the foreign policy, however, Williams had the right to go directly to the prime minister. That didn't bother Patten excessively because Williams was a professional who didn't abuse his discretionary powers. He had never before gone over the governor's head to call Downing Street.

Patten knew why Williams wanted to see him. The commissioner had some crazy notion that the island of Hong Kong was owned by the British government, not leased. Patten wished he could believe Williams, but it was more a Don Quixote windmill tilt than a real possibility. He was sorry for the many civil servants who, like Williams, felt that the island belonged to them and to Britain. Patten could not afford to entertain such fantasies. It was his duty to be off the island on July 1, when the Chinese flag went up.

At 9 a.m., the governor's secretary announced Williams.

"Good morning, Winston," Patten said, extending his hand.

Winston Williams had been born in Hong Kong, educated in England and, after completing his studies at Oxford, had taken a position with the Foreign Office. A tall, handsome man with charm to match, he traveled in the right circles. His wife, Ashley, was the only daughter of Lord and Lady Bristol, powerful supporters of the Conservatives in England. After his marriage, Williams's rise in the foreign service was meteoric. When the post of foreign affairs commissioner in Hong Kong became vacant, it was Williams's if he wanted it. He did.

Because he spoke several Chinese dialects, Williams was highly regarded by the local politicians and businessmen. He thought of himself as a citizen of Hong Kong first and as a British subject second. He didn't want Hong Kong to revert to China.

"Are you and Ashley going to return home to England?" Patten asked when they had both been seated.

"Mr. Governor, with all due respect, this is my home," Williams said gravely. "I hope to spend the rest of my life here. My children were born here; they speak Chinese. This, sir, is their home, too. If I am required to, then I shall return to England. But we shall all be very sad to leave. That is why I am here, sir. As I have told you previously, we need not turn over the island to the Chinese. All we need are the original land grant papers."

"Winston, you are wasting your time talking about these mysterious documents. Ever since it became apparent that England could not buy Hong Kong or extend the term of lease, stories about a land grant, a deed of some type, have sprung up all over Hong Kong and throughout mainland China. It is the wishful thinking of those who hope that the turnover will not happen. Rumors fly like the wind, but where's the proof? There is no deed, Winston, no land grant papers. It is only wishful thinking," Patten said.

"Nevertheless, sir, I believe—"

"A belief, yes," Patten said. "Not a fact. Besides, if there were some document granting Hong Kong to Great Britain, do you think the Chinese would stand for it? Good Lord, man, they have three divisions of troops at the border right now and that's just for the parade. They could have three armies here in hours. Then what?"

"Mr. Governor, I am asking you for permission to call the prime minister," Williams said, knowing the governor would not budge.

"You don't need my permission, but I appreciate the courtesy of your request. Whatever you do, Winston, I wish you the best."

Back in his office, Williams glanced at his collection of eight wall clocks that gave the time in major cities of the world. It was eleven in the evening in London, a little late, but the prime minister would still be up. He hit the automatic dial.

The phone at the prime minister's office didn't ring, it buzzed—a horrible nerve-wracking buzz that set a light on top of the handset flashing. That immediately got the attention of the prime minister's assistant who answered before the second buzz.

Williams announced himself and requested to speak with the prime minister. The assistant knew that any call on the hot line had to go directly to his boss, although he didn't like to break in on the prime minister, who was in his private library drinking cognac and smoking cigars with President Clark of the United States and his highness the Prince of England. Still, duty was duty.

"Sir, would you please step outside for a special call on the hot line from Commissioner Williams?" the aide said discreetly from the doorway of the library.

"Take your call, John. Believe me, I understand when the hot line goes off it's never good news," the president said.

Excusing himself, the prime minister left the president with the Prince and entered his office. He picked up the phone.

"Prime Minister here. Are you there, Williams?"

"Yes, sir."

"Please go ahead. I have only a few minutes."

Taking a deep breath and realizing that a lifetime of credibility could be lost with the next few sentences, Williams quickly outlined the story of the land grant.

"As it happens, I am familiar with the deed," the prime minister said to Williams's surprise.

"My undercover sources inside China believe the deed is real. The Free China Society has the land grant and they are trying to get it out of China," Williams said.

"But do you have any hard evidence, Williams?"

"No, sir. No hard evidence except my sources, which have been reliable in the past."

"What is Patten's position on this?" the prime minister asked.

"He thinks I'm tilting at windmills, sir."

"You may well be, but I think we shall have a go at this anyway. What do you need?"

"For the Secret Intelligence Service to get involved."

"Very well. Call the director and tell him I've approved this. I'll ring you in the morning. Goodnight, and by the way, my love to Ashley."

The president and the prince stopped talking as the prime minister entered the room. Both men turned toward him, looking at his face for a sign, hoping for the best but expecting the worst. The Prince spoke first, "Well, John, anything seriously wrong?"

"Possibly," Major said. "Probably."

"Anything I can do?" the president asked, hoping he wouldn't have to do anything.

"Do you have time to hear a story?" the prime minister asked.

"Sure," the president said. "I like a good story."

"This one is not so good," Major said. "In fact, it is a shameful chapter in the history of Britain."

CHAPTER 3

History is written by the victors.

— Old Chinese Proverb

THE British had been engaged in the opium trade, doing a thriving business, and causing widespread addiction in China. Attempting to stop the flow of drugs, the Chinese government had closed their ports to the British and destroyed British-owned opium warehouses. Tensions rose as British sailors and marines, assigned to protect English property, were fired upon and killed. The British used the deaths of their men, the closing of the Chinese ports, and the seizing of its opium, as their excuse to wage war.

The Opium War was an opportunity for the British Navy to show the world it was still the master of the seas. From the start of the war in 1839, the navy freely sailed the Chinese rivers and seas, using their gunboats to pound the Chinese positions unmercifully. But the real destruction was caused by the Royal Marines.

No match for the superior British forces, the Chinese were systematically butchered by the marines, who were fighting a war not only for pride and satisfaction, but to inflict as much punishment on the Chinese as possible. They thought it was important to bring China to the bargaining table humbled and bloody.

On January 8, 1842, the headline in the London *Herald* read simply: *It's Over!* The bells of Saint Paul's Cathedral peeled the joyous tones of martial triumph. After three long years of bloody fighting, the war had ended with a British victory over their under-armed, ill-trained enemy. The Chinese never really had a chance: Surrender or defeat was their only option. Her Majesty, Queen Victoria, had sent her tidings to Prime Minister Robert Peel for a job well done. Prime Minister Peel, pleased that the Opium War had been brought to a smashing conclusion by the Royal Marines, immediately sent Sir James Lytle of the British Foreign Office to prepare a treaty for a fair and just peace. World opinion did not look favorably upon the British actions in China, and Peel wanted to end the matter quickly. The man for the job was Sir James, who was well-respected by the Chinese.

On August 15, 1842, the peace treaty negotiations began in the Kowloon Province of China. Major General H. R. Powell, leader of the victorious British forces, sat on his favorite horse, Lance, a large bay, almost seventeen hands high, waiting for the noon hour to enter the Chinese camp to begin negotiations. Standing slightly over six-foot-three, Powell seemed even bigger sitting atop of his mount. His head was adorned with the traditional marine officer's shako, which added another foot to his already gigantic stature; the sun glistening off his numerous medals made him shine like fire. The Chinese called him the "Red Devil," a name he well deserved.

It was exactly noon when Powell gave the order to draw sabers. The sound of the steel swishing against metal sheaths made Powell smile. At the command of "present arms," twelve sabers rose straight up, then smartly down, in a perfectly choreographed fashion. Returning the salute, Powell heard the officer call: "Order arms; carry sabers." Powell's big bay pranced excitedly; seemingly anxious to gallop into the fray as he had done so many times before.

"At a trot, forward," Powell ordered.

Lance shook his head as if to question what he had just heard. Powell whispered to his horse: "Easy, Lance, easy, boy," giving him a reassuring pat.

With his aides in tow, Powell approached the tents the Chinese had erected for the negotiations. When he got close enough, the general deliberately spurred Lance into a fast trot to create a dust storm; then, before dismounting, Powell reined in the bay, while spurring him on, causing the animal to rear up on his hind legs, his forelegs furiously kicking the air. It was a frightening sight for the diminutive Chinese. They knew that this man was truly a demon.

Had Gen. Powell had his way, there would be no peace until he had marched into the forbidden city of Peking. Despite his protests in favor of continuing the war, an order from Prime Minister Peel was an order— an order he had to follow, but he didn't have to like it. Dismounting, he threw the reins to a Chinese guard who tried to hold the excited mount. Unable to hold the horse, the man was dragged into the dirt. Powell sneered at him with contempt, turning to an aide, barking: "Get me a real man to hold my horse."

Powell was a leader who would never ask his men to do something that he wouldn't do himself. He didn't fear battle. In fact, he loved it because it made him feel alive. The sound of the small arms, the roar of cannons, and the screams of horses brought him to life. Each night before a battle Powell would pace the ground, constantly looking at his watch, counting the moments until it would begin. His men held him in great reverence, and each would have gladly followed him into hell.

Because they were heathens, the general considered the Chinese unworthy enemies. But if they wanted war, then war it would be. War on Powell's terms meant death, no prisoners, no rules, and his men could rape and loot as they pleased. His victories looked impressive in the London *Herald*, but Powell knew his opponents were not a formidable foe. Even so, he asked for and granted no quarter.

Inside the tent was the assistant minister of the Foreign Office, Sir James Lytle. His mission was to negotiate a peace treaty giving the British the right to use the Kowloon Peninsula and the New Territories. Sir James was an intelligent man who appreciated the art of diplomacy, spoke several Chinese dialects, and even read some Mandarin. Married to an Oriental woman of mixed ethnic heritage, Sir James wanted a peace that would satisfy all parties, thus ensuring that Great Britain would have a foothold in the Far East without having to shed more blood.

Sir James did not like Gen. Powell because he considered his tactics and actions repulsive. Knowing of the atrocities committed by Powell's troops, he thought the general should be court-martialed, not honored. Unfortunately, the sentiment in England was too strong in Powell's favor. The British loved their heroes.

"Good morning, Sir James," Powell said, extending his hand.

In order to avoid taking the general's hand, Lytle gave him a sloppy, half-hearted salute.

"Please be seated," Sir James said in perfect Cantonese to the Chinese delegation. "Perhaps we may take some tea before we begin our talks."

China was under the rule of the Ching Dynasty, descendants of the Tartars, who had been in power since 1633. The country was divided into thirty provinces, each ruled by a governor. Hong Kong Island, Kowloon Peninsula, and the New Territories were a part of the Kwangtung province, under the governance of Ti Lu Chou. Chou was a scholarly man, who spoke English fluently. He knew Sir James well, and trusted him, believing that together they could achieve a lasting peace.

Chou had never wanted war and he had tried his best to persuade the central government not to fight the British. But they had not listened to him and the results were disastrous. The peace, he knew, could be as ruinous as the war if Gen. Powell had his way. Powell wanted the war to continue, and he was a man who would stop at nothing to get what he wanted. Chou's only hope for an honorable peace was Sir James Lytle, sitting across from him, sipping tea.

Sir James and Chou carried on the negotiations in Chinese. Powell, not knowing a word of the language, just glowered.

The meetings eventually dragged on for several days, causing Powell to grow impatient, and finally to stop attending the peace talks sessions. Sir James, who was a man of infinite patience, was comfortable with the slow deliberations and was pleased with the progress.

Every evening after the day's session, Powell would inquire of Sir James as to the status of the negotiations. When Sir James told Powell they had almost worked out the terms of the settlement, Powell asked what lands Great Britain would receive as war reparations. He was stunned when Sir James told him: "None."

"For God's sake and love of country, man, what do you mean?" he asked, outraged.

Lytle, realizing he had made a mistake in being honest with Powell, tried to explain.

"Prime Minister Peel wants a lasting peace and the right to use the Kowloon Province and the New Territories. I have secured a lease for these lands—a lease with a term of one hundred and fifty years. I don't think either of us will be around when it expires, General."

Powell, his face as red as his dress tunic, stormed out of Sir James's tent. He leaped onto Lance's back and galloped out of the camp with his entourage racing behind him. He swore he would fight this stupid decision.

At the end of August 1842, the Treaty of Nanking was signed by Sir James Lytle, on behalf of Her Majesty's government, and by Ti Lu Chou, representing the Ching Emperor of China.

A furious Powell did not return to England, but stayed on in Hong Kong for another year, waging a letter-writing campaign, pleading with the members of parliament and Prime Minister Peel almost daily. He claimed that China had started the war and should pay heavy reparations for the death and suffering they had caused and for the millions of pounds lost when trade was suspended. What he didn't say overtly was that he and his men stood to gain substantially if China were forced to pay dearly, for it was customary for the Queen to grant some of the conquered land to Powell and his officers as a reward. Powell wanted that reward and he also wanted Great Britain to gain territory in China as it had in India.

The British press picked up on the story and, with public support growing in favor of Powell's position, Prime Minister Peel was forced to order Sir James back to the bargaining table. Vindicated, Powell swore he wasn't going to allow Sir James to give up what belonged to him and to England.

This time, Powell had a plan, a simple plan. He was going to kill Sir James and blame the murder on the Chinese. That would give him the pretext to start the war again. When he had annihilated the enemy,

Powell would negotiate the next peace treaty and he would extract a harsh penalty from the Chinese.

Sir James was sitting outside his tent, enjoying the view, waiting for the arrival of the Chinese emissary, his old friend Ti Lu Chou. From high on Victoria's Peak, on Hong Kong Island, Sir James had a magnificent view of the harbor and of Kowloon. Sitting back, enjoying the afternoon, he took out his favorite pipe, one that he brought back from the United States. The Americans called it a corncob pipe. He was impressed with the simple ingenuity and packed the pipe with a Virginia tobacco blend, which he reluctantly admitted was the finest tobacco in the world. Placing his feet on a stool and striking a match, Sir James drew in the smoke. The taste of the tobacco was good. Blowing out the smoke in a long slow exhale, he forced himself to relax, just enjoying the moment. Of course, any moment was enjoyable when Gen. Powell was not around.

The peace and tranquility was suddenly broken by a shot. A musket ball smashed his pipe, causing Sir James to fall to the ground. The shattered corncob pipe splintered, sending fragments into his face, and making him bleed. The wounds were not serious, but Sir James was stunned. There were several more shots, but he couldn't tell where they were coming from.

Gen. Powell came riding into the camp, dismounting from his horse while Lance was still in motion, and ran over to Sir James. He saw the blood on Sir James's face, but he was disappointed his man had missed.

"Are you all right, sir," Powell asked with pretended concern.

"Yes, General, I'm fine," said Sir James, as he got up and dusted himself off. "What happened? Who did this?"

Powell didn't answer. He was trying to decide his next course of action. By now Sir James was surrounded by a score of aides tending to him. With so many witnesses, Powell decided he would try again later when a better opportunity presented itself. From over the rise, two of Powell's marines came into view, dragging something behind them. As they got closer, it was apparent they were pulling a dead Chinese solider. Powell's men threw the red-stained body at the feet of Sir James.

"What was the meaning of this?" Sir James asked, horrified by the sight of the bullet-ridden corpse.

The two men waited for permission to speak. When Powell nodded, the senior man reported: "Sir, we saw this man take a shot at Sir James. We went after him, but when he refused to surrender we had no choice but to shoot him."

Powell thought this was good thinking on the part of his men. They may have missed Sir James, but this could give him a wonderful opportunity.

"Sir James, you can't trust these people. I will place guards here for you and put the troops on alert," Powell said.

Then, without waiting for an answer from Sir James, Powell left with his men.

Ti Lu Chou, arriving at the camp amidst the confusion, heard Powell's words to Sir James. Powell, rushing past Chou, almost knocked the emissary down and gave him a contemptuous glance. Chou looked at Sir James's bruised and reddened face; then at the dead Chinese soldier, a cook. He asked Sir James what had happened.

"This man tried to kill me. He was shot by Gen. Powell's men, who tried to apprehend him, but he refused to surrender. What do you know of this Lord Chou?" Sir James asked.

"Nothing, Sir James, I give you my word on that. I promise I will find out who did this and they will be punished. May I beg your forgiveness and request that we start the talks tomorrow? You should have those cuts attended to and I shall arrange to have this man buried. I will find out who had ordered this."

"I shall take you at your word, Lord Chou," Sir James said, still optimistic. "Shall we meet here tomorrow at ten?"

A worried Chou returned to his advisors telling them that someone had tried to kill Sir James Lytle. From the looks of shock and concern on their faces, he knew they were innocent of this crime.

"Who would want to harm Sir James?" one advisor asked.

"The British caught and killed the man who supposedly tried to shoot Sir James," Chou said. "It was one of the cooks."

They knew then why Chou was so anxious. Cooks were not armed and seldom carried weapons. Chou doubted that the man had ever fired a gun. He knew it was the general who was trying to kill Sir James blaming it on the Chinese. Powell wanted war.

At midnight, a messenger carrying a white flag rode into Powell's camp. A sentry dragged the Chinese messenger to Powell, who had been with some of his senior officers plotting their next attempt against Sir James.

"Sir, an envoy from Chou," the sentry said, standing at the entrance of the tent.

"Envoy? You mean a lap dog. Throw him in here, sentry," Powell ordered.

The sentry shoved the envoy through the entrance of the tent. The man fell on his hands and knees, making Powell smile.

"How appropriate," the general said. "Stay down."

The messenger made no attempt to rise and, without looking up, he handed Powell a parchment scroll. Powell gave it to his adjutant who could read Chinese.

"Sir, Ti Lu Chou begs an audience with you," the adjutant said.

"Tell Chou to report here now," Powell said, dismissing the frightened messenger with a kick.

"This, gentleman," Powell said, "is an unexpected blessing. I know exactly what we are going to do when Chou gets here. We're going to provoke war."

Chou entered the camp later that night with several of his advisors. They were all unarmed and dressed in sleeping clothes.

"I have come unarmed," Chou said, looking up at the Red Devil. "In fact, as you can see, General, we are not dressed for war, but for bed. The men with me are my advisors, all of whom are too old to fight. But I see that does not matter to you. You will probably lay arms upon us, telling the world we came here to attack you. We will be dead, so there will be no one to tell the truth. After all, history is written by the victors."

Powell was impressed with Chou's candor, knowing he was right.

"What do you want of me?" the general asked.

Chou wanted to plunge a knife deep into Powell's chest, but instead he said: "What is the price of peace? Please, there is no reason for you to kill Sir James. Do not try it again. Just tell me what you want."

Powell's face reddened, showing his anger. His men stepped back, drawing their muskets, waiting for the command to shoot. Then for the first time in his career, Powell spoke almost softly.

"Hong Kong," he whispered. "I want Hong Kong or I want war."

Chou showed no emotion. He had known the price of peace would be high, but he thought it would have cost him gold not land.

"So be it," Chou said. "The land is yours. When we sign the treaty, we will bring you your land grant."

Without another word, he left Powell standing there, not knowing whether to be glad or sad with Chou's decision. Powell was almost disappointed; he had hoped for another war.

* * *

The peace talks moved swiftly, and the final papers were prepared with due pomp and ceremony. Lord Chou and Sir James Lytle signed the Treaty of Boque on October 8, 1843, providing payment of an indemnity by China and the cession of five ports for British use. It wasn't much in tribute, but enough to appease parliament. Sir James never knew the real cost of the peace.

After the treaty signing, Chou handed Powell a brown glass vase.

"The inside is protected by the sands of time," he said.

Powell didn't deign to answer and immediately rode away. Several miles from the camp, he reined in Lance and removed a rolled parchment from the vase. He passed the document to his adjutant.

After a moment, the adjutant smiled and said: "This is it, sir."

Powell nodded as the adjutant rolled the parchment up and placed it back in the brown, sand-filled vase.

Later that evening, Powell and his officers raised their glasses in a toast to their new land, Hong Kong.

CHAPTER 4

Reality may be like a slap in the face.

— Old Chinese proverb

A FTER speaking with the prime minister, Winston Williams placed a call to the Secret Intelligence Service, Britain's equivalent of the CIA. Within a few minutes the director himself was on the line.

"Get on with it, Williams, it's late here in London," the director said gruffly. "I'm getting too old for this middle-of-the-night nonsense. What's so important?"

Taking his time, Williams told the director a more detailed story than he had with Prime Minister Major. After thirty minutes, he finished the tale of the land grant.

Bored and annoyed by what he considered a pipe dream, the director asked Williams, what he needed.

"Montgomery," Williams said without hesitation.

"He's one of our best men," the director said.

"I know," Williams said.

"Montgomery will be on the next plane out of Australia," the director said with a sigh. "You may expect him in Hong Kong at around five in the evening your time. My office will contact you. Anything else?"

"No," Williams said. "And thank you."

"Best of luck," the director said, hanging up the receiver.

He swirled the whiskey in his glass for a few seconds; then took a big swig. He held his glass up to a portrait of the queen and said: "Your Majesty, where do you get such idiots?"

Shaking his head in disgust, the director downed the rest of his drink and picked up the phone. He placed a call to his operations officer. In a few minutes Michael Anthony Montgomery, the best field agent in the SIS, would receive orders to report directly to Mr. Winston Williams in Hong Kong. A navy jet would soon be waiting for him at the airport in Sydney.

Williams placed a quick call to his wife to tell her he would not be home for dinner; then he called Col. Leslie Adams. The phone rang a few times before Adams answered it.

"Adams, here," said the commander of the British garrison in Hong Kong. Like Williams, he too had been born in Hong Kong. Adams had married a Chinese woman, Lu An Chi, and he was the third musketeer in the trio of Williams, Montgomery, and Adams. They had all been at university together and Williams was looking forward to the reunion, wishing it was under better circumstances.

"Could I entice you for lunch at the club today? Say noon?" Williams asked.

"Noon it shall be. And don't be too late. You know how I hate to drink by myself. See you there, Winston," Adams said.

At twelve sharp, Col. Leslie Adams made his way across the back patio of the Victoria Club, which was at the top of Victoria Peak, one of the highest points on Hong Kong Island. The view was spectacular, always eliciting mandatory "wows" from the tourists. But for Col. Adams, who was charged with the defense of Hong Kong, the view was much more than scenic. It was a military nightmare. As garrison commander, he was in charge of a small but highly trained division of Royal Marines and a wing of the Royal Air Force. But he had to protect about two hundred islands covering more than four hundred square miles. He felt he was defending the indefensible.

Spread out before him in the blue waters of the South China Sea were some of those islands, each one a possible target for the Chinese Army. His eyes dropped toward Hong Kong Island's waterfront, which was covered with high-rise buildings—eleven of the fifteen tallest buildings in the world were in Hong Kong and ten of the eleven were on Hong Kong Island.

Spotting the Star Line ferry, he smiled, remembering when he had been a young officer dating Lu An before she became his wife. They used to ride back and forth on the ferry as an evening's entertainment. Now they were always rushing, never taking the ferry, never enjoying the ten-minute boat ride with the tourists. When they came over from the Kowloon Peninsula, where they lived, they always drove through the Cross-Harbour Tunnel. He made a promise to himself that the next time he and Lu An went to Hong Kong Island, they would take the Star Line ferry.

Looking across the harbor, Adams could clearly see the old clock tower by the Kowloon public pier. It was overshadowed by the thirty-story tower of the famous Peninsula Hotel. Although the Kowloon Peninsula was only four miles square, it contained most of the tourist attractions, hotels, and shops. In the Tsimshatsui District, at the tip of the peninsula, the pace was frenetic. North of Kowloon was the New

Territories, which shared a northern border with the People's Republic of China.

The drone of a 747 Jumbo Jet caused him to look up. Ever since the new airport had been built on Chek Lap Kok Island, the planes passed over the central district of Hong Kong—the "downtown" where the offices, shops, and government buildings were. A lot of the businesses complained, but because the airport was a government-sponsored project, he kept his mouth shut, although at times he could not hear himself think with the roar of the jets overhead. The only people who didn't seem to notice or care were the bar and club owners on Hong Kong Island, in the Wanchai area.

Chek Lap Kok Island was to the northwest of Hong Kong, where the airport was located. Adams could see planes taking off, landing, and circling, waiting to land. Because the airport took up the entire island, and nobody lived there, the name of the island had been lost except to old timers like Adams. To most people, it was just the airport.

The flapping of the Union Jack overhead brought Adams back to reality like a slap on the face. In a few days the flag would be lowered forever.

Taking a seat at a table that was reserved for Williams, Adams waved to the waiter, holding up two fingers. The waiter, seeing the colonel, bowed his head in acknowledgment, knowing the order was for two very dry vodka martinis.

Dressed in civilian clothes, Adams was wearing a lightweight tan suit, a blue shirt, and his regimental tie. He looked more like a business executive than a soldier.

The waiter approached with the drinks at the same time that Williams appeared. He sat down just as the waiter placed a drink in front of him.

"Good show, old man. I'd say my timing is perfect," Williams said.

"Perfect for a politician, Winny. You're ten minutes late," Adams said looking at his watch.

They toasted the queen, as was their custom, and then got down to business.

"Les, this is very important and most serious," Williams said.

Adams put his drink down and leaned closer so as not to miss a word.

Williams went right into his tale about the possibility of Hong Kong being owned outright by Great Britain.

There was a silence for a moment. Then, Adams spoke: "Winny, if we find this deed, this land grant, and Hong Kong stays free, this could—"

"Yes, this could lead to war," a pensive Williams said solemnly.

CHAPTER 5

A secret is best kept by a dead man.

— Old Chinese proverb

G EN. Alexis Zimkeroff, the former director of the KGB, sank into his
favorite chair, put his size fourteen boots up on a foot stool, and
yelled in his thunderous voice to his longtime personal aide to bring him
some vodka. The well-worn leather chair had long ago surrendered to
Zimkeroff's massive hulk, its cushions permanently formed to his two-
hundred-fifty pounds. Standing at six-feet-five inches, Zimkeroff had a
full head of wavy salt and pepper hair that was combed straight back.

Zimkeroff was the Moses of the Red Army, leading them from a second rate, second-class mob to a real fighting force. His popularity with
the army personnel caused concern at the Kremlin, prompting them to
promote him to the KGB, and getting him away from the armed forces.

Sergeant Major Yuri Petroff came in carrying two bottles of vodka in
one hand and three glasses in the other. He was wearing his Soviet
army boots, his American cowboy pants, blue jeans, and his old army
shirt without the many stripes he had earned. Petroff, too, was a large
man, but not quite the size of Zimkeroff. As a young man, Petroff lost
most of his hair, so rather than fight a losing battle, he had decided to
shave his head. His deep-set eyes were guarded by thick bushy eyebrows, making them appear as two dark spots on a bald melon.

Petroff put the bottles and glasses on a table; then he poured a tum-
bler for Zimkeroff. After that, he served the other two men in the room.
Petroff took a seat next to the general, saying nothing, just sitting ramrod straight in a wooden chair, his eyes watchful. He looked and listened, but had anyone made a move toward the general, he would have
attacked without hesitation. He knew the other two men in the room,
but he trusted no one but Zimkeroff. Petroff was as cold and heartless
as he looked.

Sitting across from Zimkeroff was a tall slender man with black hair
and a small mustache. He was Col. Boris Kertrinkoff, Zimkeroff's for-

mer head of Far Eastern Operations at the KGB. Next to Kertrinkoff was a shorter, overweight man, with a closely cropped military haircut. Maj. Joseph Bresneyev was the former head of intelligence gathering. Both men were forced into retirement when Zimkeroff left the KGB. They barely survived on their meager pensions. Zimkeroff, in contrast, enjoyed a large pension and unbeknownst to most people, he had a sizable account safe in a Swiss bank.

President Yeltsin wanted to keep his generals happy, especially Zimkeroff. The mere presence of Zimkeroff made emotions run high within the military establishment. Yeltsin knew if anyone could or would start a civil war, it would be Zimkeroff. President Yeltsin and Zimkeroff had served in the army together, and both men were devoted to their country. But Yeltsin was now president and Zimkeroff, the once well-respected leader of one of the world's great armies, the former head of the most dangerous and notorious espionage agency in the world, was consigned to a small house on the outskirts of Moscow—his reward for a lifetime of devoted service to his country. Longing for the old days, Zimkeroff was sure that democracy was not the best thing for Mother Russia.

After a few rounds and the requisite toasts, the general asked the men if they would like to take a trip to Hong Kong. The room was silent.

"Come on, come on," he said, in his booming voice. "It's an enjoyable place to visit, especially in light of the upcoming turnover by the British."

The men, except Petroff, looked at the general blankly.

"It's time for a holiday," Zimkeroff said. "Time for some fun."

Maj. Bresneyev spoke first: "When do we leave?"

"First thing tomorrow morning," Zimkeroff answered. "We will be away for two weeks—or perhaps for all eternity. Prepare yourselves accordingly."

Neither man flinched and the general was pleased that they still followed his orders without question.

"We are with you, but what is this all about?" Kertrinkoff asked.

The general leaned forward in his chair; instinctively, his men leaned toward him, as if he were about to reveal the secrets of the universe. He was.

"What I am about to tell you may change the course of history," Zimkeroff said. "And it will make you rich beyond your dreams."

He waited for their reaction, but both men's faces were cryptic.

"For the past several months," the general continued, "I have been in contact with some of my old friends in China. They have told me two interesting things. First, Hong Kong is not going back to China."

The two officers sat back as if the words had some magical power to repel them. They both knew that war was a real possibility.

"At first, I wasn't sure myself," Zimkeroff continued. "But yesterday I received a call. The SIS is sending Montgomery to Hong Kong. If this were just a rumor, Montgomery would not be involved."

Zimkeroff then told them about the land grant.

"The Chinese are very concerned. They believe the deed exists. More important, I know that the Inspector General of Hong Kong believes it exists," Zimkeroff said.

"Do you believe this land grant exists?" Kertrinkoff asked the general.

Zimkeroff nodded.

"The deed won't leave China without our agents knowing about it. All we have to do is intercept the document when it comes across the border. Then we sell it back to the Chinese for their BCV."

"BCV?" Kertrinkoff asked.

"That is the second secret I learned about. It is the key to riches, power—and the restoration of the Soviet Union," Zimkeroff said.

The men sat in silence, not sure what to think. But they knew that Zimkeroff was not a madman and, if he had a plan, they would follow it.

"Tell us more about this BCV," Bresneyev asked.

"Not now," Zimkeroff said. "Wait, and I will tell you. But I'll tell you this, it is a weapon of mass destruction, a weapon that could destroy the world."

After his men had left, Zimkeroff thought about his next move. He had a plan, but it was a difficult and dangerous one. He was sure he could turn the BCV into a billion dollars for himself and his men. But there was something else in it for him, something even sweeter— revenge against the United States.

* * *

Kertrinkoff and Bresneyev were up all night. They would not sleep until the general's orders had been fulfilled. Kertrinkoff was contacting all the Russian agents in the Far East. By the time he arrived in Hong Kong there would be a network of listening posts, passing on information. The Hong Kong team would be in place, ready to intercept and kill if necessary.

Bresneyev also had a busy night downloading the data he had managed to steal after hacking into the British security files. He would have all the information for Kertrinkoff to coordinate the field force. Both men were glad to be working with Zimkeroff again. Most of the field agents were not getting paid, but they too were pleased to be a part of the KGB once again. No one knew why Zimkeroff was doing this, but they followed and obeyed.

Petroff knocked on the general's bedroom door.

"Yes, Sergeant Major, what is it?"

"General, will it work?" Petroff said, opening the door. "Do you really trust...?"

Zimkeroff raised his hand as if he were stopping traffic, cutting off Petroff in mid-sentence.

"I don't know. But we have to try. And Yuri, I only trust you."

"Goodnight, sir," Petroff said, closing the door.

In his own room, the Sergeant Major stripped to his underwear and got into bed. The last thought that passed through his mind before he fell asleep was one of bodies lining the streets where they fell. Like leaves in autumn, he thought, all over the ground.

CHAPTER 6

The light of love blinds the eye.

— Old Chinese proverb

L EAVING his office in downtown Hong Kong, Col. Lesley Adams drove through the Cross-Harbour Tunnel onto Hong Kong Road. He went past the Hong Kong Coliseum toward the Kwun Tong area of Kowloon where he lived. Knowing it was going to be a late night, he decided to stop by his home to see his wife and children for a few minutes. Williams had arranged to pick him up on the way to the airport to meet Montgomery.

Adams and his wife Lu An lived in a small two-story house owned by the British government. It wasn't palatial by any standards, but for the Adamses it had two extravagances that made it a palace: a backyard and a garage.

In Kowloon, most of the houses shared common walls, offered no yards, either front or rear, and only a handful had garages. Parking in Kowloon was impossible, so having a place to park was luxury, second only to having a place to be buried. Many times when tourists passed a cemetery they assumed they were witnessing a burial, but more often than not, it was an exhumation. In Hong Kong, after seven years one set of remains was exhumed so another could be laid to rest. Adams had his garage and his wife a backyard. They didn't plan to be buried anytime soon.

Approaching his house, Adams pressed the remote control button and the garage door rose upward. Hearing the garage door open, Lu An glanced at her watch, surprised to see that her husband was home so early. A petite woman, just over five feet tall, she had hair that was so black it looked blue. She wore it piled high on her head and held there with what looked liked colored chopsticks. Her dark eyes reflecting her happiness with her life and family.

35

Parking his car, Adams came through the side door into the kitchen.

"You're home early," Lu An said.

"Just to say hello. I'm going to the airport with Winston to pick up your boyfriend," he said.

"Which one?" she asked smiling.

"Montgomery."

Her joy was apparent at hearing Montgomery's name.

"Are you bringing Michael home for dinner?" she asked.

"Not tonight, but I'm sure we will get together. We are going back to the office, so you can get me on Winston's extension. I have a feeling it's going to be a long night," he said.

His voice had an edge to it and Lu An immediately became concerned.

"Is there anything wrong?" she asked.

Thoughts of what could happen if Williams was right about the deed went through his mind. His life, Lu An's life, could be gone with the push of a button. He didn't believe Williams's story. He didn't doubt his friend's sincerity, but he believed that some Chinese group had made up the whole story because they couldn't stand the pain of reunification. It was all wishful thinking, he thought. There was no land grant, no deed— but that was why Montgomery was here: to find the truth. If anyone could solve this puzzle, he was sure Montgomery could.

"Les," she said. "What's wrong? You seemed troubled."

Adams sat at a kitchen stool and took one of his wife's hands in his. She waited sympathetically, looking directly into his eyes. Against his better judgement Adams told Lu An the story of the land grant. She listened intently, never interrupting. Finishing his tale, Adams's sad eyes explored her face.

"Darling," she said, searching for the right English word to describe her feelings about what she had just heard. Then she said it: "Pooh!"

"Pooh! That's all, just pooh?" he asked.

Pooh was the password used by the children when they had to go to the bathroom. Lu An never used vulgar or obscene language.

"Yes," she said. "Winston's dream, I'm sorry to say, is pooh."

"Could you say that Winston is full of pooh? That's it, Winnie the Pooh," he said, laughing.

It was his first laugh since lunch and it made him feel good.

"Bu. Ni gua re xiatian feng," Lu An said.

"Which means?" Adams asked.

Before she could answer, their son Winston chimed in.

"It means you blow like the hot summer wind, Daddy."

"In other words, I'm full of hot air? I give up," he said, shaking his head.

Like many Chinese women, Lu An had no use for politics. She would let her husband worry about the politics. She had more important things to do. Her father, who still lived in mainland China, would talk about politics all the time. She hated it then and she hated it now.

Her father hadn't approved of her marriage at first, but when he realized how much Adams cared for his daughter, he blessed the union. After the children were born, he even grew to like his son-in-law. Lu An's brother Sang Chi was the problem.

Trained and schooled in Beijing, her brother had no use for any Westerner, even his brother-in-law. Contemptuous of the Western way of life, Chi worked for the People's Republic of China's Airline as an aeronautical engineer. He traveled frequently all over the world, but despite the places he had seen, he believed that China was the best place on Earth to live. When he was in Hong Kong, Chi always visited his sister. He didn't like his brother-in-law, but for his sister's sake he was invariably polite. Adams never felt his brother-in-law's secret hostility.

Adams heard a car horn. Looking through the lace curtain that covered the window, he saw the waiting limousine. Lu An was right behind him offering her soft cheek for a quick kiss, and Adams was out the door. She waved to Williams, who was standing by the car waving back. Before the limo was out of sight, Lu An was back in her kitchen preparing dinner for the children. She didn't give the conversation with her husband another thought.

* * *

The Royal Navy Falcon was cruising at forty thousand feet. Michael Montgomery, who was enjoying the smooth ride, stretched out on the couch nursing a drink. His blue blazer was thrown over the chair, his Gucci loafers were off, and his feet were up on the couch's arm rest. His red rep tie was pulled down from his open shirt collar, exposing the black hair on his chest. He was wondering what kind of mission this would be. Would it be important or just another jaunt? It was odd, though, starting off with no briefing, just orders to report directly to Williams. He wasn't complaining, but the whole mission was highly unusual.

For the past month he had been wasting his time in Australia, supervising the installation of a relay station for SIS satellite communications. Montgomery had no idea what it did or how it worked, but it was supposed to make the calls on his cell phone go anywhere in the world in complete privacy.

An assignment in Hong Kong was a vacation for Montgomery: A time to see his old friends, their wives, and their children. He was the godfather to both Williams's and Adams's little girls. Ashley Williams had given birth the day before Lu An Adams and the families had a friendly argument over the naming of their daughters. Adams had insisted he wanted to name his little girl Michele after Montgomery. Williams wanted the same. In the end, they had tossed a coin. Michele Williams and Jessica Lee Adams were the final selections.

Montgomery was the only one of the three musketeers who hadn't married. His bachelorhood seemed to be part of his job description—he was never in one place long enough to put down roots. Lu An and Ashley were always trying to match him up with their friends, but to no avail. Montgomery had a stock answer for his untiring matchmakers: They had broken his heart by marrying, dooming him to a life of solitude.

The whine of the jet engines was making him sleepy or perhaps it was the whiskey. Fighting off the urge to nap, he picked up a copy of the *South China Morning Post,* Hong Kong's leading English newspaper. The impending turnover was history in the making and reading about the planned festivities he realized that he enjoyed seeing history being made instead of making it himself.

Montgomery had spent his whole career with the SIS. Before the Americans brought down the Soviet Union, the spy business had been pretty exciting. He had spent years traveling the globe as a member of the foreign office, doing his part on undercover teams in the Gulf, in Bosnia, in the Middle East, and in Cuba. He didn't look like the movie version of a spy. To the contrary, he was of medium build, five-feet-ten inches tall, and he wore wire rim glasses. His hair was light brown, thinning on the top, gray at the temples. Beneath his mild manner, however, was the heart of the lion. The Director called him a pit bull, never letting up once he had sunk his teeth into something.

After clearing customs, Montgomery met his two friends. The three of them climbed into the limo that took them across the small bridge connecting the airport to Lantau Island. Then they drove onto the North Lantau Expressway toward the Tsing-Ma Bridge, which connected Lantau Island with Tsing Yi Island, and finally onto Kowloon Peninsula. Montgomery inquired about their families and made fun of his friends' expanding waistlines. Once on the Tsing-Ma Bridge, Williams busting with pride asked: "What do you think of this modern marvel?"

The bridge had opened that year and was the longest suspension bridge in the world—three hundred and seventeen feet longer than the Golden Gate Bridge.

"It's beautiful, Winston. You should be proud it was built under your watch."

Williams flashed a sad smile. It pained him to think that this would soon be just a part of China.

The driver skillfully maneuvered the limo through the heavy evening traffic, driving through the Cross-Harbour Tunnel, past the Royal Hong Kong Yacht Club, turning west onto Gloucester Road, and heading toward the downtown district. Coming to Gardner Road, he turned left, driving past Saint John's Cathedral; then he turned into the government office building. Pulling past the security guard and into the underground parking lot, the driver managed to get into the building without having to blow the horn once—a feat for the *Guinness Book of World Records,* because in Hong Kong, it was said, drivers used their horns instead of their brakes.

They entered Williams's conference room and began what was to be a long night.

*   *   *

Lu An Adams ran to the door and answered the bell. Peeking through the side glass, she smiled at her brother and opened the door for him.

"What a pleasant surprise," she said, giving him a hug and kiss. "Come on in I'll fix you dinner. I'm alone tonight. Les is at a late meeting with Commissioner Williams."

"I would love that. How have you been? You certainly look wonderful. I'm sorry the colonel is not here," Chi said, lying about the last part. "Where are the little dragons?"

"Upstairs, playing video games," Lu An said. "How long can you stay?"

"Not long. I am leaving for China on the last flight tonight," he said.

"I hoped you could stay for a few days. Les would love to see you. We can have a nice family meal together. Les's friend from the university came to town this evening. You remember him? Michael Montgomery, Jessica's godfather," she said.

Chi knew Montgomery only too well. If the SIS agent was in Hong Kong, that meant trouble.

"I've got food on the stove," Lu An said. "The children are upstairs. Why don't you go play with them while I finish dinner?"

Chi bounded upstairs to see his niece and nephew. Lu An watched him disappear onto the second floor landing, before she returned to the kitchen.

The children looked up from their game for just a second, acknowledging their uncle. Chi greeted them in Chinese, refusing to speak with them in English. The three of them played video games until Lu An called them.

After dinner, Chi and Lu An sat in the living room talking over tea. After the usual conversation about the family, she asked him if he heard anything about the land grant, the deed.

"What land grant?"

"You know, the deed to Hong Kong that the British have."

"What are you talking about Lu An?"

She repeated the story that her husband had told her. Chi sat there with the look of disbelief on his face. That must be why Montgomery was here, he thought.

"This must be some kind of ploy by the British," he said. "They don't want to hand over Hong Kong. We must drive them from our country."

"Enough," she scolded him. "My husband is British. Your niece and nephew have his blood. Britain is not the evil empire these days. Why don't you move here permanently and live free?"

"I may live here when my flag flies from every building and tower, but not until then."

Chi was breathing deeply, his chest was heaving, but he apologized for the outburst.

"I have to go now, Lu An. I have to meet someone before I leave. I'll call you later."

"Have a safe trip, brother," Lu An said, walking him to the door.

Chi looked at her, touching her cheek with his hand.

* * *

"Is it your love of Hong Kong making you believe in this, this deed?" Montgomery asked Williams after hearing the history of the land grant. "Are you thinking with your heart and not your head? The light of love blinds the eye."

"No," Williams said, after a pause. But he knew there was some truth in what Montgomery said.

"I have orders to cooperate fully with you—to do whatever needs to be done," Montgomery said. "So where do we begin?"

"You're the expert. What do you want? What can we do to help? My office is yours. This conference room could be the center for operations. There is a secure line to London."

By the time they had examined the subject of the deed thoroughly, Williams was dead tired, Adams was fading, but Montgomery was going strong. At five in the morning, Montgomery finally had a plan that he believed would give them a fair chance. First, he would contact all the operatives working in China and put them on alert to gather intelligence about the land grant. Montgomery also had a few good contacts in the Chinese government who might be able to help. Second, he wanted the names of any diplomats or government officials arriving from Russia or China delivered to him daily. Who arrived and who departed the city could be telling. Third, he would pay a visit to the Free China Society, an underground organization that was trying to cause a revolt in China. The society had been around for years, but it hadn't achieved much. Yet if anyone would want to prevent the turnover of Hong Kong to China, they would be the ones. Their program was not ideological, but practical. They wanted to line their pockets.

The SIS believed that support for the Free China Society came from the heads of the Chinese crime families. The Chinese government has been fighting them for years. These crime families reached deep into Chinese history and would be a valuable source of information.

"You had better be careful when you call on the Lengs—old man Johnny and his American educated grandson, Jeffery, would kill you for the fun of it,"Williams said wearily."They run the largest family outside of China—probably the largest in Southeast Asia. Drugs, gambling, smuggling, you name it.The old man runs a bunch of whorehouses and works out of a strip club in the Wanchai district. I'll get you the name of the place."

"Where is the grandson now?"Montgomery asked."He may be easier to deal with."

"I'll get the address. Anything else?"Williams asked.

"One more thing, Les,"Montgomery said to Adams."Can a squad or two from the regiment be available to do some bar hopping?"

"I would be happy to bar hop for you. I'm sure that more than enough men will volunteer for such an assignment,"Adams said, laughing.

Montgomery told Adams that he wanted the men to hit the bars and hot spots that served the clerks from the Chinese and Russian consulates. He wanted the men to complain about the preparations for all the VIPs who were coming for the turnover and listen to their counterparts to find out who was arriving. If there was a land grant, there would be quite a few interested parties showing up for this event.

"What about the Americans?"Williams asked.

"That is a tough call. I'll take the direct approach. I'll pay a visit to a friend of mine at the American Consulate,"Montgomery said, glancing out the window. The American Consulate was on Lower Albert Road directly across the street.

"Harry Saltzman may be of some help,"he continued."Winston, have your staff ready for a briefing later this morning. It's going to be a long couple of days."

When the other two men had left, Montgomery picked up the phone and called London to speak with the Director; then he collapsed on the couch to get what sleep he could.

Funny, he thought, he had arrived in Hong Kong expecting to watch history, but now he would be making history—or maybe war.

CHAPTER 7

History is prologue.

— Old Chinese proverb

ⱷⳆⱷ

S ANG Chi drove toward the airport faster than he should have: head-
lights, taillights, street lights, traffic lights, neon signs, all blended in
a kaleidoscope of colors. His mind was in a frenzy as he forced his foot
down harder on the accelerator. What Chi had heard from his sister was
not possible. He wanted to scream it out at the top of his lungs.

He drove without thinking, racing along the North Lantau
Expressway toward the airport, where he had his office at the old
People's Republic of China's Airline hangar on Perimeter Road. But he
didn't have time to stop there. If he hurried, he could make the next
flight to Beijing.

Chi pressed a preset key code on his cell phone. When the ringing
stopped, he heard a click, but no voice came on the line to acknowledge
the call. Chi knew they were there. They were always there, listening.

"Meet me at the airport," he said into the phone.

Chi didn't wait for an answer. The other end of the line was always
silent, nothing was ever said, but it didn't matter, the message always
got through. To any unwelcome ears there would be no way of knowing
if the message was received or not, or what it meant. Slipping the phone
back into his pocket, he continued the race to the airport.

At Hong Kong International the traffic forced Chi to slow down. He
inched his way around the airport, pulling up to the curbside loading
area for the People's Republic of China's Airline—the government
owned and operated facility by the Civil Air Administration of China.
Jumping out of the car, he flipped the keys of his car to a young man
who was standing there. Navigating through the crowd with the skill of
a broken field runner, Chi twisted, turned, bobbed, and weaved until he
was at the desk facing a strikingly beautiful CAAC agent. Without a
word he handed her his ticket and passport.

Finding a seat in the waiting area Chi spotted a boy carrying a shoeshine box. In English, then in Chinese, the boy called out, "Shine! Shine!" Glancing down at his shoes Chi called the boy over.

"*Ni hao*," the boy said.

"*Hao, xiexie*," Chi responded.

"Is there anything else you need?" the boy asked, polishing Chi's shoes.

"*Duoshao*," Chi said.

Before the boy could answer, Chi handed him several yuan.

"A car, no delays at the airport, and a meeting with the Inspector General, tonight," Chi said.

The boy pocketed the Chinese currency before disappearing into the crowd. Chi knew that the message would be delivered to the contact person; then relayed to Beijing. His request for a late night meeting with the Inspector General was not out of the ordinary. Chi usually reported in whenever he landed in China, but this time he wanted an immediate meeting. His plane wasn't scheduled to land in Beijing until one-thirty in the morning, but by the time he arrived at the Ministry of State Security, it would be almost two. The Inspector General, he knew, had odd working habits. Often he was at the ministry until very late. It was widely rumored that he even slept there, a rumor confirmed by many a janitor who found him reading reports at three and four in the morning. Chi hoped the stories about the Inspector General were true. More important, he hoped that the Inspector General would believe the story he was going to tell him.

Even though Chi held several degrees in aeronautical engineering, his passion was reserved for his country. He worked tirelessly for the Chinese Ministry of State Security, an ultra secret organization, the counterpart of the FBI and CIA combined. Inside of China, State Security was the secret police; outside of China, it was an intelligence gathering organization; in Hong Kong, it was both. Indoctrinated in the true Chinese Communist tradition, Chi believed that the meaning of life was in service to the state. That left him no time for marriage or children. He worked hard for the state and lived alone—all was for the good of the state. An excellent student, Chi had received the best education People's Republic could offer and, after graduating from the university, he had entered the Ministry of State Security, where he learned his trade as a spy.

Walking down the jet way to board the Airbus 300, Chi blended right in. He was just slightly under five-feet-six inches in height. His thick black hair, which showed no signs of graying, was close cropped. At thirty years old, he had a promising future with the ministry. His was a rising star.

By the time he settled his compact frame into the small airplane seat he had convinced himself that the deed was a British trick to keep Hong

Kong. If the Brits really had a land grant, he thought, they would never have agreed to the Hong Kong Accords of 1984. He knew the British. They would not want to start an all-out war. The deed was simply a delaying tactic designed to tie the matter up in the World Court for another hundred years. Chi swore this would never happen, promising himself that if there was such a land grant, he would find it. Anyone who got in his way would die, even his brother-in-law, Leslie Adams. The thought of killing Adams brought a sadistic smile to his face. With Adams dead, perhaps his sister would come to her senses and return home to China.

Putting Adams out of his mind, Chi knew he had to come up with a plan for the Inspector General. He had several hours to think of something before the plane landed in Beijing.

* * *

High over the Atlantic, Air Force One was on the way back to Washington. President Clark sat comfortably in his mile-high office enjoying a private lunch. Alone with his thoughts, he found something was nagging at him. On his desk was a humidor filled with fine cigars. He took one, held it to his nose, and turned it slowly, inhaling the aroma. Cutting the end off the cigar, he picked up a box of matches adorned with the crest of the House of Windsor. The president studied the matches, realizing he had picked them up when he was with the prime minister. Then it hit him.

He picked up the phone.

The National Security Advisor Sam Bergen answered on the first ring.

"Yes, Mr. President."

Bergen was on the job at 5:30 a.m. most days, spending many a night in the little bedroom off his office in the basement of the White House. Bergen was the man who advised the president on matters relating to national security. He was one of the president's closest and most trusted advisors, the one person who always told the president the truth. That in itself would qualify him for hazardous duty pay.

"How are you, Sam?" drawled the president.

Like most politicians, he didn't want an answer nor did he wait for one.

"I'd like to see you all this afternoon when I land. Call Betty," he said, referring to his secretary, "and tell her you're comin' up."

"Is there anything wrong, Mr. President?"

"No, Sam, this is, uh, a prophylactic meeting. See what you all can find out about a land grant for Hong Kong that was supposedly given to Britain around 1843," the president said.

"A land grant?"

"Yes, a land grant. The deed to Hong Kong."

With that, the president hung up. Kicking off his shoes, leaning back in his chair, putting his feet up on the desk, lighting the cigar, he was going to enjoy the smoke, take it easy, and maybe nap. He wanted to be fresh when he met with Bergen, and more important, he didn't want to face the traveling press corp. They were a royal pain in the ass, always asking him about his private life and not about the real issues. He would let his wife deal with the press on board. She could handle them.

He closed his eyes to relax, but the thought of the British having a land grant was going through his mind. There was something about this that bothered him and he was going to play it safe. If there was a land grant, he thought, the repercussions could have a worldwide effect, even spark a war.

When he had hung up, Bergen wondered what the hell the president had been smoking. A land grant for Hong Kong was the craziest thing Bergen ever heard of. Calling in his chief of staff, Bob Caruso, for a meeting, he repeated what the president had said.

"Bob, find out what you can. When the president gets back, he will want a full briefing."

Deep under the White House, Caruso wasted no time. He had the NSA's computers abuzz. All branches of the government were on line: FBI, CIA, Secret Service, Military Intelligence, the Library of Congress, and the National Archives. If there was anything, Caruso's people would find it. While he thought the assignment was nuts, Caruso knew that if he kept track of all the little things, it often led to something big.

Reasoning that if the president had asked for this information, then the other world leaders might also be looking for it; soon his people were tapping into the foreign data banks around the world. As a back-up he had sent a request to the Department of State to put all American embassies on alert for anything to do with Hong Kong. He had been with the National Security Agency for twenty years, but it still amazed him how much information was available at the push of a button.

* * *

Chi's plane landed in Beijing, late as usual. Two men were there to greet him: the Inspector General and his bodyguard chauffeur. Chi was taken aback by the sight of the elderly Inspector General, the man who ran the Ministry of State Security. He had never personally met Chi at the airport.

"Good morning, Sang. I trust you had a pleasant flight."

Sang Chi took the Inspector General's hand, giving it a hearty shake along with the traditional bow. The Inspector General's bodyguard took Chi's bag.

"I am honored you came to meet me, sir."

"The honor is mine. It is late—come, come."

The Inspector General took Chi by the arm and led him away, as the bodyguard followed. Chi had to slow his usual fast pace out of respect for the Inspector General, who was in his seventies. Neither man spoke until they were in the car. As they drove away from the airport, the Inspector General listened to what Chi had to say about the land grant. While Chi spoke the Inspector General sat back listening intently, nodding his head occasionally. When Chi finished, he turned to his superior, waiting for a reply. There was nothing but silence. It was difficult to see in the dark interior of the car. The Inspector General's head was back against the seat, his eyes closed.

"What is most interesting," the Inspector General said at last, "is that your information came from your brother-in-law, Adams, who is very close to Williams. The arrival of Montgomery in Hong Kong is not a coincidence. Did you know that Montgomery, Williams, and Adams have been meeting all night at the central government building?"

Chi never understood how the Inspector General knew so much so fast.

"No, sir."

"Moscow is onto the story of the land grant, too," the Inspector General said. "Gen. Zimkeroff himself will be in Hong Kong soon. All of a sudden, the Russians in China have come awake. We've seen more activity in the last two days than in years. The story of the land grant has been around for many years, Chi. Long before my time. But no one paid much attention to it. Now maybe we should. This could be very interesting Chi, very interesting."

The Inspector General stared off into space, collecting his thoughts. Finally, he said: "The Americans are the only ones not yet involved in this, but give them time. I'm sure they will also wish to play this game. Thank you, Sang Chi, your information is good and I appreciate your efforts. I will carry on from here."

"Sir, I beg that I may be of assistance to you. Please allow me help you," Chi said.

"This is a little out of your line, Chi. You are good at gathering information. Do what you do best. Let the others handle this."

"Please let me help you in the research."

"Your determination is admirable. You may help me, but we must proceed very carefully."

The Inspector General had the car stop in front of the National Archives building.

"The answer to this puzzle may be in the past. Remember history is prologue. Go read what the elders say in their writings. For you the building shall be opened."

Entering the National Archives through a side door, Chi was led down a long hallway by a night attendant to the special rooms reserved for ancient volumes. The humming of dehumidifiers was the only sound Chi heard. The attendant told him that the door to the room must stay shut. If Chi needed anything, he was instructed to press the button on the desk.

Alone, Chi appreciated the power of the Inspector General. These rooms, these records, were almost sacred, yet with one call it was available to him. He would show the old man his trust was justified; he swore he would find the evidence.

The Inspector General didn't go home that night either, but he returned to his office. He took off his coat and made a pot of tea, resigning himself to another sleepless night. He had been working on the land grant for some time, but now his instincts told him it was all true.

Chi had confirmed his worst fears, he thought; taking a sip of tea, his eyes danced around the pile of books on his desk. They were written in dialectic form, making them difficult for the nonspecialist to read. Pulling on his glasses, he picked the writings of the Ching Dynasty about the invasion of 1842. The ancient warlords had their scribes record the events as they happened. But no provincial governor or warlord was pleased to write about a lost battle. The account was written as a reminder for future generations, not to forget, to do honor, to seek revenge.

Two pots of tea later, he was reading about the peace talks with Sir James Lytle. Page after page, chapter after chapter, he devoured the material like a starving man. Turning a page, taking a sip of tea, the process repeated itself all night long. It was almost eight in the morning when his secretary came in and brewed him a fresh pot of Hangchow tea, green tea, his favorite.

She was quietly closing the door to his office when the Inspector General startled her.

"I found it!" the old man shouted.

CHAPTER 8

Victory is like the wind, easy to feel, hard to hold.

— Old Chinese proverb

IN the back of the official car the Inspector General had sent for him, Chi tried to relax. This was a treat for him. He enjoyed being chauffeured around Beijing, for most people in China did not own a car or feel the need for one. Those in a hurry took buses and subways, but the common means of transportation was the bicycle—and the foot. Only government officials had cars, something Chi never questioned. Like all good Communists, he was prepared to walk or ride the bus to the Great Hall, where he had been summoned by the Inspector General. But the official car made him feel almost important; then he remembered that wasn't allowed.

Chi sat forward as the car passed through Tienanmen Gate, one of his favorite places in Beijing. On the top of the gate was a pavilion with the large red columns which, on important occasions, was transformed into a reviewing stand for government dignitaries and their guests—all fifteen to twenty thousand of them. Chi was as proud as if he had helped build the structure, though it was begun some seven hundred years ago during the Ming Dynasty. He was convinced that there was nothing like it anywhere else in the world and, to him, it was a symbol of the greatness of China.

The driver turned west through Tienanmen Square to the Great Hall of the People. He pulled into the parking area reserved for official visitors and Chi was out of the car before it came to a full stop. As a schoolboy he had once taken a tour of the Great Hall with his classmates. The size and the majesty of the buildings had impressed him then. He was still impressed. Like that schoolboy, his mouth open in wonderment, Chi approached the entrance of the Great Hall, a building larger than the Forbidden City itself. The Great Hall was where the head of state, the President of China, the Supreme Leader, Jiang Zemin, had his offices, as did the other high officials.

At the front entrance a guard was waiting to escort him. Following the guard past the meeting hall where the People's Congress met, he saw the plaque honoring the first American President, Mr. Nixon, who had visited there. The guard led him down the marble corridors, past the Hall of Heroes, past the great banquet hall, where as a boy he had had lunch with five thousand other children. As they went past the Great Theater, he had to stop and look at its cavernous interior. Ten thousand people could attend a show there. He lingered by the theater, his heart bursting with pride, until the guard grabbed him and pulled him along, saying: "Hurry up, the meeting with Mr. Tung is about to begin."

Chi wasn't sure he had heard the guard correctly, Mr. Tung, the new chief executive of Hong Kong after the turnover? Why had the Inspector General ordered him here, he wondered. But as usual he did as he was told and obeyed. The guard opened the door to the reception area outside of the executive office wing. Stepping in, Chi saw several uniformed men. Recognizing their insignias, he knew they were all high-ranking generals of the People's Liberation Army. In the midst of the crowd was the Inspector General in military dress. His chest was covered with medals, the Red Star hung from his neck, and his shoulders carried the stars of a full general. The Inspector General's round face was accented by thick, dark-rimmed glasses.

Chi stood in the doorway not moving until the Inspector General beckoned to him. Bowing deeply, Chi thought he was in the presence of the gods. Putting his arm around Chi's shoulder, the Inspector General walked him away from the others.

"We are meeting with the chief executive, the head of the new Hong Kong government, Tung Chee-Hwa, who takes office officially on July 1. We will also be in the company of the Chairman of the Central Military Commission, Gen. Xi, and Gen. Wu Ti, the head of the Guangzhou Military Region, which includes Hong Kong," the Inspector General said.

When they were far enough away from the others, he stopped walking, and stared directly at Chi, who was just a bit taller than he was.

"What did you find?" he asked.

"I am not sure, sir," Chi said. "I believe there was a land grant given to the British. As you have told me many times, it is good to read the past, and I have. I believe, I've found references in the ancient books to a land grant. I think that we should spend the time to find this land grant, this deed. There are references to it. I need more time, but I'll find it."

A small grin came over the Inspector General's face.

"You're right. There was a land grant and I found it," he whispered.

"Do you have it? Where is it? May I see it? This is wonderful," Chi said, excited.

"Not yet. Listen as I report to the chief executive. You will have the task of protecting what is ours. Be careful. The eyes of your country will be upon you and so will the eyes of Gen. Xi."

Rejoining the group, the Inspector General nodded toward a wooden door that opened into the waiting room of the chief executive. The generals, trailed by their aides, entered; they were followed by the Inspector General, then Chi, as if he were the Inspector General's shadow. A secretary stood at perfect attention as the group entered, bowing her head. Barely looking up from her bow, she asked them to be seated. Generals Xi and Wu Ti took the couch; their aides stood beside them. The Inspector General sat in a chair with Chi standing behind him.

Chi's eyes moved from one general to the other. He was impressed. Gen. Xi was a true Chinese hero, a living legend, who had earned more medals than anyone else. The Red Star, China's highest award, hung around his neck. Chi tried not to stare, forcing himself to look about the room. The walls were bare except for pictures of the president and Chairman Mao. The secretary busied herself with her computer, taking time to answer the battery of telephones.

Suddenly, Chi could feel it and he knew without looking that Gen. Xi was staring at him. Chi froze; then he turned his head slowly. Xi's dark eyes were lifeless—two dark pools of stagnant water. Chi remembered what the Inspector General had said: "The eyes of Gen. Xi will be on you."

The door of the chief executive's private office made a loud click and slowly swung open. The secretary announced that they might go in. The Inspector General, Xi, and Wu Ti rose to their feet in unison, marching off to the private office followed by Chi. The door seemed to have its own mind, magically closing behind them once they were in the room. Chief Executive Tung, although younger than the generals, did not get up. He just raised his eyes at the visitors. As they all bowed to the chief executive, he asked them to be seated. The Inspector General, Xi and Wu Ti sat in front of the massive desk, while Chi and the aides stayed at the back of the room.

"Well, let me hear this tale of the land grant, this deed,"the chief executive said.

"Rumors are everywhere," the Inspector General said. "My department has massed a great deal of information from our agents. I have been personally looking into this matter, half-believing, half-doubting, not sure. If it weren't for Sang Chi's discovery while in Hong Kong, I might have let the rumors be. But after my meeting with Chi last night, I did more research in the ancient books of the Ching Dynasty.

"I found an entry from Governor Ti Lu Chou. He wrote of the war with the English in great detail. He tells of the battles and of the peace talks with Sir James Lytle. It appears that the British field commander, Gen. H. R. Powell wasn't pleased with the talks and wanted to provoke another war. The price for Powell's peace was land, Hong Kong. Chou gave into the demands in order to prevent more bloodshed. He gave Powell a grant of land, in the name of the emperor, to the islands of Heung Kong, which is what the British called Hong Kong.

"Chou was saddened by this turn of events and ordered the writing about the land grant and peace talks to stop, but he did make another entry which said he would see Powell in his grave and return to China what was wrongfully taken. The English are acting as if they know of the land grant, but not where it is or who has it. We must find and destroy it. I assume that the land grant is still in China. If we do not find it before the British, it would mean—"

Before he could finish, Gen. Xi interrupted him.

"War."

"War is the last thing we need," the Inspector General said. "What I was about to say was that the existence of an authentic document would mean we would have to return to the negotiating table. We need the land grant and Hong Kong, not the blood of a million soldiers."

"War is the only way to make them understand. It is our destiny to rule the world," Xi shot back.

"Our destiny is to live in the world," said an angry Inspector General.

Chief Executive Tung held up his hand as if he were a cop directing traffic. Immediately, there was silence. Tung's eyes flashed with fury. His tongue slipped from his mouth ever so slightly to wet his dry lips. What he was hearing was causing his blood pressure to rise. Tung was trying to gain composure before he spoke. Closing his eyes, he seemed to be in a trance, speaking slowly and softly.

"On July first, I will assume my duties as the Chief Executive of Hong Kong. This is not an option. I do not intend to start my first official day in office with a war, nor do I intend to lose what belongs to us. Inspector General, what is your plan?"

"The best plan would be to prevent the land grant from leaving China. We will put every one of our agents on this immediately. We have sources everywhere. Chi here," the Inspector General said, pointing to Chi in the back of the room, "will be in charge of Hong Kong. He will run our operation there and, if by some chance, this land grant does get out of China, Chi will get it back at any cost."

Chi's knees began to buckle and only a deep breath kept him from falling. He couldn't believe his ears: His turn had finally come.

"Chi will have the manpower in Hong Kong to accomplish this. This land grant will be a hard secret to keep quiet, and it is obvious that the English and the Russians are all talking about it. The best course is to listen. Follow the sound and it will lead us where we want to go. This is the only way. There may be some loss of life, but it will not be a million soldiers."

"And what do you have to say about this?" Tung asked Gen. Xi.

Xi thought for a moment, not rushing to answer. He was no fool. As the head of all the Chinese armed forces, Xi was a powerful man. His was the largest standing army in the world, with more men under arms than the United States, Russia, and Great Britain combined. He ran a country, not just an army.

"I agree," said Xi, bowing his head toward Inspector General. "And I, too, will go to Hong Kong. I may be of service to Chi, assisting him in this endeavor by having a unit of the PLA Intelligence Corps do what it does best, supply reliable intelligence. We must all work together, but Mr. Chief Executive, it would be advisable to prepare for war just in case."

Chi felt the weight of China on his shoulders.

What was happening here? he wondered. They were talking as if it would be easy to find a piece of paper in a country the size of the People's Republic.

The chief executive was silent for a moment; then he asked each of them if they thought that the English would go to war over Hong Kong. There were a variety of comments and opinions, but no one had an answer, only guesses. The Inspector General hoped not and Gen. Xi hoped they would.

In the end, the chief executive gave the Inspector General permission to proceed with his plan, but he also granted Xi permission to go to Hong Kong. Then with the wave of a hand, he unceremoniously dismissed them.

Chi was stunned by what he had heard. He had never been in the presence of the chief executive before. Both excited and nervous, he couldn't wait to get out into the reception area to talk with Gen. Xi. He was happy to coordinate his work with Xi for China's glory. This time one of the aides opened the door and Xi led the small procession out into the reception room. The Inspector General walked much more slowly going out than he had going in. Chi again stayed tethered to his mentor.

The Inspector General whispered to Chi not to talk but to listen. Once they were outside the office, he said to Xi that they should meet later to formalize the plan. Xi agreed, saying he would have his aide call to set up a meeting. The two men again bowed and shook hands.

The Inspector General rode with Chi back to the office in silence. While Chi's mind raced with excitement, the Inspector General's raced with worry.

"Chi, you will have your hands full with Gen. Xi," the Inspector General said when they were back in his office. "He is ruthless. He wants war with the West. Xi's intelligence unit is nothing but a bunch of bandits. Remember what I'm about to tell you: Xi wants you to fail."

"With all due respect, sir, I don't think that Gen. Xi would disobey the chief executive. Working together was what he ordered—that is the only way to insure our success. Victory will be ours."

"Victory is like the wind, easy to feel, hard to hold. Xi will kill you if he gets the chance. Go back to Hong Kong. Be careful," the Inspector General said, suddenly feeling old.

Chi didn't doubt the Inspector General and, out of respect, he would obey, and stay away from Gen. Xi—for the moment. But he couldn't believe that the hero of the People's Liberation Army could have anything but patriotic feelings for his country.

"I will try to lead Gen. Xi on a false path. I can only hope we can find the land grant before it leaves China," the Inspector General said.

The Inspector General buzzed his secretary on the intercom, requesting that she bring her pad. He placed his hands behind his back in a parade rest position; then he began pacing back and forth as he dictated to her.

"Chi will have complete authority for the Hong Kong project, under my direction," he said. "All commands and orders coming from Chi shall be obeyed as if I were speaking."

The secretary dutifully wrote down his words and read them back.

"Circulate the memo to senior staff only. I want a staff meeting in one hour, my office, all must be present."

As his secretary reached the door, the Inspector General called her back.

"Mi Ler, if Gen. Xi calls, put him through immediately. We will be working with the army intelligence unit headed by Gen. Xi himself. I will coordinate the movements between the army and our field agents," the Inspector General said.

"Very well, sir."

After she left the office, Chi asked the Inspector General about the announcement of working with the army. "I thought you didn't want me to work with Gen. Xi."

"You won't be working with him, I will be. Besides, the announcement is for the benefit of Mi Ler. She is Xi's personal spy here at my office."

* * *

"Comrades," Gen. Xi said to his senior staff. "What we have hoped for has become a reality. Today we prepare for war with the English and maybe the Americans, too."

For years, his army had planned the invasion of Southeast Asia, Korea, and Hong Kong. Now they would have their chance—and Xi would get an opportunity to fulfill his destiny. When it was over, he would be in control of more territory than even the powerful emperors of the past. Xi was ready; he couldn't wait to give the orders. His staff knew what they had to do. They were ready, right down to the last detail.

"Start the countdown for a July 1st attack. Dismissed."

They all jumped to attention, with the senior officer giving the salute. Xi, pleased with himself, ordered Gen. Wu Ti to stay behind. Once they were alone, Xi confided to his longtime friend: "If we find the land grant documents, we turn them over to the English. Do you understand?"

Wu Ti understood perfectly.

CHAPTER 9

A small stone thrown in a pond
makes ripples on all sides.

— Old Chinese proverb

PRESIDENT Clark came from behind his desk to greet Bergen as he entered the Oval Office.

"How are you, Sam?" the president said, taking his national security advisor by the arm and leading him over to a couch.

"Want something to drink?" the president asked.

"No, sir," Bergen replied. "I'm anxious to get started with my report about the deed, Mr. President. I put Caruso on it and he found something very interesting."

The president's face showed some skepticism, but he leaned closer. Bergen had a habit of lowering his voice when he talked about something secret. The national security advisor gave the president all the information he had gathered.

When he was finished, the president picked up a phone.

"Betty, I want the vice president, the Joint Chiefs, and Admiral Charko here at eight tonight."

After hanging up, the president asked Bergen to give the matter some thought and attend the meeting with the Joint Chiefs.

"Of course, Mr. President," Bergen said. "I'll just gather up my papers and I'll be out of your way."'

"Leave 'em, Sam, if you don't mind," the president said.

The president was a quick study and he wanted to read and think about the problem himself. That nagging feeling was back.

His hand fell on his humidor and he removed a fine Cuban cigar. Rolling it with his fingers, he slowly sniffed the tobacco as he studied the reports.

His secretary knocked and entered the office. Spotting the cigar, she reminded him that the First Lady had forbidden smoking in the White House.

"I'm not going to smoke it, Betty," he said. "I'm just playing with it. It's my pacifier."

"Mr. President, I would like to go over tomorrow's social schedule. You're having a private dinner with the Reeds tomorrow night."

Deep in thought, the president didn't say anything for a moment.

"Mr. President?"

"I heard you. Harrison Reed and his daughter Astrid are here for dinner. Thank you and please see that I'm not disturbed, if that's possible."

* * *

At exactly twenty minutes to eight, the military contingent passed through the security check at the side entrance of the White House. There was always protocol with the military, regardless who entered through the door first, they would all stand aside until the highest ranking member passed through the security check first. That honor belonged to the Chairman of the Joint Chiefs. The chairman removed his hat, tucked it under his arm, and marched through the metal detector. From his hat, which was covered with gold braid on the visor and adorned with a brass eagle, to the brass buttons on his coat, to the medals on his chest, the chairman was a walking security device destroyer. The alarm screamed in protest. Two secret service agents politely requested the chairman to step aside while they ran a handheld metal detector over his body, looking for weapons.

Next, the chiefs of the Air Force, the Army, and the Navy, as well as the Commandant of the Marine Corps, went through the same drill. Each officer grew more annoyed than the previous one.

Last in the pecking order was Admiral E. J. Charko, who passed through without a sound. He was the only one in civilian clothes.

Charko was dressed in a dark blue suit, a white button down shirt, and a yellow-and-blue tie. The only thing military about his appearance was the mirror-like shine on his shoes. He spit shined them every night. The Admiral was also the only one of the men who had started his career as a raw recruit. He had been a deck jockey, swabbing them clean.

Charko's once-black hair was now gray, but it was still full. He was in excellent shape, looking even taller than his six-three height. There was still a hint of mischief and a zest for life in his eyes. He was doing a job that he loved.

When the former president had asked him to come out of retirement to run the Special Operations Division of the CIA, Charko had been promised a fourth star. The star meant nothing to him; he would have gladly given back his other three for the opportunity to serve. The Admiral had spent his whole life in the navy, joining at sixteen by lying about his age. He had retired at sixty.

Charko had been widowed for more than twenty years and he had never remarried. He lived alone in a small house near Annapolis that overlooked the Chesapeake River. His two sons were in the navy; both were stationed in San Diego.

During his short retirement, Charko had been miserable. Back at the helm for the past ten years, he had steered the agency's special operations through troubled waters, set new courses, and kept the politicians away. The previous president had learned the value of having good intelligence and more important, of having someone he could turn to, to get things done.

After the presidential election, the Admiral had called upon the new president to explain about his department. Although it was a part of the CIA, the Special Operations Division's chief reported directly to the president. The Admiral had assured Clark that the division was there to serve him.

"Mr. President," Admiral Charko had said. "I have my resignation here. All you have to do is accept it."

The president took the resignation and looked at it; then he noticed the Admiral's spit shined shoes.

"Admiral, your shoe tips are like mirrors."

"Well, sir, if you want the truth, and please don't repeat this, it gives me an advantage when standing next to the ladies," Charko had said.

The president laughed, throwing the Admiral's resignation back at him.

The secret service agents escorted the military chiefs through a winding hall to the elevator. When the elevator doors opened, there was another secret service agent there to greet them. He led them to the Oval Office. The president's secretary had gone home for the night, but a secret service agent was sitting at her desk. He rose as they entered, showing them into the office.

The vice president was wearing a jacket and tie, Bergen was in his shirt sleeves, the Secretary of Defense was looking very professorial, and the president was the most relaxed of the group. He was wearing a black sports shirt, open at the neck, and black slacks. All he needed was a white jacket and he would have been ready for the disco dance floor.

Bergen briefed them on what he had uncovered. His briefing was thorough, well organized, but he drew no conclusions. He wanted the others to draw their own about the existence of the land grant. The satellite pictures showed Chinese troop movements, and Bergen confirmed that Chinese submarines were cruising the Atlantic toward England. The chairman commented that the Chinese must believe that the land grant is real. The other chiefs nodded in agreement. The president asked the various chiefs what precautions they were taking. The navy reported that two of its attack subs were keeping the Chinese under surveillance; the Army had put a Delta force unit on standby; and the Air force had an extra wing in the air.

The meeting went on until two in the morning; then the room grew silent, not because of the hour, but because no one knew what to do.

"If we find this deed, what do we do?" the vice president asked.

"Good question," said the president. "Does anyone have an answer or suggestion?"

No one had an answer; all had different opinions. If they gave the land grant to the British, the Chinese could go to war with England. If they gave it to the Chinese, the British might go to war with China.

"We should do what is the least damaging to us and to the world," Clark said.

"And how do we do that, sir?" the Chairman of the Joint Chiefs asked.

"We must find the deed first," Bergen said.

"Mac Daniels," Admiral Charko said softly.

"For Christ's sake, Admiral," the president said. "Last year he almost started a war single-handedly and he caused a major incident in Colombia yesterday."

"Admiral, all he was supposed to do was take pictures of a drug operation," Bergen said. "Not blow up half of Colombia, killing a dozen people, and causing an air incident with the Colombian Air Force and a few of our Tomcats."

"That was my operation," the vice president said. "I requested your help. But the Colombians had their ambassador call Secretary Smith and lodge a formal protest. She has been on me all day."

That remark brought smiles on the faces of everyone but Gore.

"That's the wrong choice of words," the president said, smiling.

Admiral Charko's eyes locked on Bergen's, staring at him until Bergen was forced to look away. As the Admiral looked around the room, the chiefs found reasons to turn their heads.

"Sir," Charko said, "with all due respect, this war on drugs with our allies is bullshit, just that, plain old bullshit."

The president smiled. He appreciated the plain, good old boy talk—it sounded just like home.

"Mac had a job to do and he did it," Charko continued. "Hell, he could have brought back autographed pictures of the drug lords and they would have ended up framed and hung in a place of honor on some two-bit politician's wall in Colombia. What did you need pictures for, Mr. Vice President? When the Colombians reached the jungle site, they found the goddamn drug operation."

The Admiral was Clark's kind of guy, a man after his own heart. He laughed.

"Mac Daniels is the best we have, sir," Charko said. "You know it, so does the vice president and so does Mr. Bergen. Before we start a war over a rumor, we had better find out if the rumor is true. No matter which way we turn, it is like throwing a rock in a pond: the ripples go out in all directions. In this case, however, we are going to get tidal waves, not ripples. If there is some kind of deed, Mac will find it. If there is no deed, he'll stop the rumor, and more important, he will stop a war."

All the military men knew of Mac Daniels and their faces and nods showed they agreed that he was the man for the job.

After a moment, the president authorized the Admiral to put Daniels on the job, but asked to be kept informed. Then he thanked them all for attending the meeting and bade them good night. The Admiral stayed behind.

When the door to the Oval Office had closed, the president turned to Charko.

"What the hell is wrong, Admiral? You have been jumping around tonight like a man at an ant farm who just spilled honey on himself. What's up?"

"Mr. President, I need a favor," the Admiral said. "I know you're a friend of Harrison Reed. I wonder if you could call and ask him to put Daniels on the staff of World News to cover the Hong Kong story. That would be a great help."

"I'll do better than call Reed, I'm having dinner with him tomorrow night," he said.

"Where is your wonder boy now, Admiral?"

"He's on the Adams heading toward Puerto Rico. I'll get him here today."

"Goodnight, then," the president said, yawning.

"Mind if I have a few more minutes, sir?" the Admiral asked. "I have something to tell you, something very important."

The president looked glum. When the Admiral said "very important," it was a problem.

"There's more to this than Bergen knows, sir."

The president's political instincts took over: "Do I want to know?"

"Mr. President, what I am about to tell you is for your ears only," Charko said, his voice trailing off to a whisper.

Charko talked, the president listened, and when the Admiral left the White House, Betty Cook was back at her desk.

CHAPTER 10

A fool knows, a wise man asks.

— Old Chinese proverb

It was early afternoon when Gen. Zimkeroff and Petroff passed through customs like ordinary tourists. Once outside the restricted area, they were assaulted by a group of children trying to carry their luggage, hoping to earn a few extra coins. Petroff's snarl scared them away.

Exiting from the baggage area, they were surprised to see a uniformed chauffeur holding a sign that read *General Zimkeroff* neatly printed on a Sheraton Hotel placard. The chauffeur was a pro and immediately recognized Zimkeroff, calling out: "General, General!"

Zimkeroff shuddered. This was not what he had wanted. The chauffeur took their bags and led the two men to a white Rolls Royce in the no parking area. A chilled bottle of champagne was waiting for them inside. Petroff was pleased, but Zimkeroff did not want the attention. He had hoped to arrive in Hong Kong unnoticed.

The Sheraton, which was one of the finest hotels in the Far East, covered almost a square block, fronting on Salisbury Road, with its rear entrance on Middle Road. The side street was Nathan Road, separating the hotel from the world-famous Peninsula. Zimkeroff had provided false papers for Kertrinkoff and Bresneyev and booked rooms for them at the Ambassador, another first-class hotel, across the street from the Sheraton. Petroff, his bodyguard, stayed with the general, although he now had a counterfeit passport and a bogus name.

Zimkeroff, himself, traveled under his own passport and name because he was so well known that if he were caught using a spurious passport, he could have set off an international uproar. However, he was now sure that as soon as he had passed through customs, the Chinese, British, and the Russians knew he was in town. Zimkeroff sighed and sat back in the Rolls on the way to the hotel.

After checking in, he followed the bellboy to his spacious suite. Then he dismissed the boy with a generous tip. The suite had two bedrooms, an office, and a large living room. Taking the master bedroom, Zimkeroff gave Petroff the other. Petroff unpacked Zimkeroff's bags, putting everything away for the general. After he was done, he joined Zimkeroff, who was sitting in the living room.

"Look here," Zimkeroff said, pointing to a basket of fruit on the table. He tossed Petroff the card. It read: *Welcome to Hong Kong. If you need anything, please feel free to call.* The card was signed by the chief of protocol at the Russian consulate.

"So much for quietly slipping into Hong Kong," Zimkeroff said.

"What are you going to do?" Petroff asked.

"I will go to the consulate in the morning, as a courtesy. My story is simple. I am here as a civilian visitor to see the festivities for the turnover. When I get back from the consulate, we will meet Kertrinkoff and Bresneyev for lunch at the Sky Lounge upstairs. I think you should get the car now."

Petroff left the hotel through the rear door, walking up Middle Road, then west a few blocks to Kowloon Park Drive, where there was an indoor parking garage. On the fourth floor of the garage, he found a dark blue Chevy Suburban. He disengaged the alarm with his key and checked inside, noting a radio surveillance system, a global positioning system, several cell phones, a fax machine, and several weapons, well hidden in the passenger side door. Then he went back to the hotel to pick up Zimkeroff.

The two men drove in silence down to Salisbury Road, then toward the docks where the Star Line ferry picked up and discharged passengers from Hong Kong Island. Pulling off to the side of the road, Petroff waited while Zimkeroff placed a call on his cell phone.

"Harbor information. May I help you?" a woman's soft voice answered.

"What time does the ferry from the mainland arrive?" Zimkeroff said.

There was silence; then a man's voice came on the line.

"There is no ferry from the mainland. Is there anything else we can do?"

In a Cantonese dialect Zimkeroff said: "I am General Zimkeroff. You know who I am. I want to meet the Chief of Hong Kong Security."

"Where?"

"On the Star Line ferry," Zimkeroff said.

"When?"

"In one hour on the ferry leaving Kowloon for Hong Kong Island."

Zimkeroff flipped his phone off, nodded to Petroff, and left the car. Petroff purchased the ferry tickets for both of them.

As they approached the ferry entrance, Zimkeroff asked the sergeant major if he were hungry.

"A little, General."

"We have time," Zimkeroff said, pointing to the cafeteria at the Star House, next to the entrance for the ferry line. "This is one of the best places to get a quick meal, especially if you're hungry."

Making their purchases, they passed the time waiting for their meeting on the ferry. In the afternoon, the Star Line ferry ran between Hong Kong Island and the Kowloon Peninsula every fifteen minutes. In the morning and evening, it ran every five minutes. During the off hours and late at night, the ferry was full of tourists savoring the harbor view.

"Sergeant Major, the Chinese must be going insane because I called them on their secret line, asking to see their Chief of Security. For years we have known about their information line, but they never figured it out," Zimkeroff said.

"Well, General, maybe this time they will."

"Let's go," Zimkeroff said, standing up. " We don't want to keep their chief waiting."

They presented their tickets and Zimkeroff went on board first, taking a seat on a bow bench. Petroff sat two rows behind him. A few minutes from the dock, a distinguished-looking Chinese man sat down next to Zimkeroff.

In perfect Russian he said: "Good afternoon, General. It is a pleasure to see the former head of the KGB on one of our ferries, enjoying the harbor view. I won't ask how you got our number, but I will surely change it. What can I do for you?"

"It's not your ferry yet and, if you're not careful, it will belong to the British for another hundred and fifty years. I hear they have a land grant for Hong Kong," Zimkeroff said.

The man tried to ask some questions, but Zimkeroff cut him off.

"I will only talk with Sang Chi."

The man's eyes opened wide at the name Sang Chi. Zimkeroff caught the body language.

"Tell Chi I am here and, if he cares, I am at the Sheraton."

When the ferry docked the Chinese agent got off; Zimkeroff and Petroff stayed on for the ride back to Kowloon. The ferry rocked as it crossed the wake of another boat and the spray from the waves created a rainbow in the late afternoon sun.

"It's started," Zimkeroff said.

Petroff drove back to the hotel, thinking again about the bodies and the graves that would follow. This was a dangerous game, he thought, the most dangerous they had ever played.

Zimkeroff was passing through the lobby of the Sheraton, when he heard someone call his name. He turned toward the voice. It was Michael Montgomery.

"I am at a disadvantage. You seem to know me, but I don't know you," Zimkeroff said. "May I have your name?"

"A fool knows, a wise man asks. I'm Michael Montgomery from the British Embassy. I'm sorry I wasn't at the airport to meet you and your staff, General."

"There is no need to apologize, Mr. Montgomery," Zimkeroff said, extending his hand. "I am here as a private citizen, no longer with the army, and, unfortunately, I am my own staff. I'm here to enjoy the festivities."

Montgomery knew all about Petroff, Kertrinkoff, Bresneyev, and the false passports, but he didn't want to tip his hand until he had figured out what they were planning.

Zimkeroff, spotting Petroff from the corner of his eye, waved him over.

"Mr. Montgomery, this is my old comrade," he said, putting his arm around Petroff's shoulder. "Allow me to introduce you to Gen. Zed."

The two men shook hands.

"If there is anything we can do for you," Montgomery said, producing a newly printed business card.

"It was nice to meet you," Zimkeroff said. "Have a pleasant afternoon."

Outside the hotel, Montgomery climbed into Williams's car.

"Zimkeroff is up to something, introducing Sergeant Major Petroff to me as Gen. Zed. He must think we're stupid. Bloody fool. I had his suite bugged and two surveillance teams are ready to follow them. Another two teams are outside the Ambassador, ready to follow Kertrinkoff and Bresneyev. I'm not sure what is going on, but I intend to find out."

Once in the elevator, Zimkeroff looked at the card Montgomery had pressed into his hand. It read: Michael Montgomery, Cultural Affairs. Handing it to Petroff, Zimkeroff said, "Cultural Affairs, what bullshit. I bet the ink is not dry on that card. Montgomery SIS, would be more appropriate. You better debug the room."

"Yes sir."

* * *

The captain was on the bridge of the USS *Adams* as it ploughed its way through the waves. The sleek destroyer was making thirty knots, hurrying for a well-deserved week of R-and-R in Puerto Rico. The entire crew, including the captain, was counting the time until they hit the sandy beaches. The radioman entered the bridge and handed the captain a message.

"Where's Mr. Daniels?" the captain asked, after reading it.

"Sir, I believe he's in his cabin."

"The bridge is yours," the captain said, getting out of his command chair.

"Captain is off the bridge, the executive officer is on deck," a sailor bellowed.

The captain made his way down the steel hallways, dropping down two decks, until he arrived at Daniels's quarters. He knocked.

"Come on in, sir," Daniels said, opening the door. "I just had a shower and now I'm going to get some sleep before we hit Puerto Rico for some fun."

The captain shook his head.

"Sorry, but you've got a date with a jet," the captain said. "You must be an important person, Mr. Daniels. I received direct orders to turn the ship around and head toward the *Kennedy*. They were ordered to steam toward us. As soon as we get in range, a chopper will be over here to pick you up."

"Captain, are there any specific orders for me?" Daniels asked.

"No. Just get to the *Kennedy* as quickly as possible."

It wasn't long before Daniels was in the chopper heading toward the Kennedy. He wondered why the Admiral wanted him back stateside so soon. He knew that this must be Charko's doing; something big was up.

Over the headset he heard the carrier's flight controller talking with the chopper pilot. From the window, he saw the ship come into view. The giant aircraft carrier grew even larger as the chopper descended toward its decks. Daniels appreciated the skills needed to land a jet on the bouncing deck of a carrier. Those jet jockeys had nerves of steel, he thought.

The chopper landed with a thud on the aft deck.

A tall thin man wearing a flight suit was standing by and offered Daniels a cup of coffee.

"Welcome aboard, Mr. Daniels."

"You must be Lieutenant O'Connor," Daniels said, smiling.

"Lieutenant Ed O'Connor at your service. Welcome aboard the Kennedy."

"Glad to be here, thanks to you."

Before the two could talk, a seaman approached them and said that the carrier's captain was waiting. After two elevator rides and a few flights of stairs, Daniels was high above the water on the bridge deck of the ship.

Captain Packard's aide met Daniels in the passageway and escorted him to the bridge. The captain didn't look pleased to see him.

"Mr. Daniels," Packard said. "It seems that the United States Navy is at your disposal. I have been ordered to get you to Washington as fast as possible."

"When am I supposed to leave, sir?"

"How fast can you put on a flight suit?" the captain said.

Daniels was led to a ready room, where O'Connor gave him a flight suit. As Daniels dressed, O'Connor said: "A few hours, a couple of midair refuels, and you'll be home in D.C. for supper."

A few minutes later, Daniels was in the backseat of a Tomcat, pulling his harness tight. O'Connor pushed the throttles forward and the plane shook as the brakes strained to hold the aircraft in place. The deck crew gave the thumbs up sign, O'Connor saluted, and the catapult threw the plane into the air, pinning Daniels into his seat.

CHAPTER 11

An obedient child makes a parent's heart glow.
— Old Chinese proverb

IF Rome was built on seven hills, Atlanta, Georgia, was built on seven hundred. Unfortunately, other than its hilly terrain, Atlanta was far from being an Eternal City. Urban blight had taken hold of Atlanta, causing decay, and sending the middle class fleeing to the pleasant suburbs. A few visionaries, however, saw potential for the city—and a chance to make some money. One of those visionaries, an out-of-towner named Harrison Reed, had staked a claim in the heart of the city, purchasing the highest point in the business district to build his office complex. As the city began to rebuild and grow, so did his investment—tenfold.

Like the phoenix rising from the ashes, the World News Corporation building stood proudly overlooking downtown Atlanta. More important to Reed, all of Atlanta was looking up at its eighty stories of mirrored glass and steel. The reflection of the sun made the building look like a burning flare. Instead of a masterpiece, Reed had created an eyesore in the literal sense. The natives had fought the development and construction of the huge building in the heart of their city, but to no avail. The best lawyers the local groups could afford were no match for the batteries of high-priced legal talent Reed brought in to secure the building permits. Once that was accomplished, it had been widely rumored that Reed had bought and paid for a vote of approval.

Harrison Reed was the sole stockholder and chief executive officer of the World News Corporation, a company that provided information to hundreds of millions of people around the world through its films, radio, newspapers, magazines, Internet, television, cellular phones, and cable television. The crown jewel of the World News Corporation was its popular World News Cable television channel.

Reed had acquired untold wealth, making him one of the richest men in the United States, if not the world. With each success, his legend grew. He liked that. He also liked to have people think of him as the poor boy who had made good. If he had written his autobiography, Reed would have made himself a test tube orphan from the streets of Newark, New Jersey, struggling to find a meal each day. The truth was he hadn't been poor and certainly didn't have to fight his way to the top.

Born of wealthy British parents, Reed was distantly related to the Queen. After completing his studies at university, Reed went into the family business. His father was one of the major private bankers in the United Kingdom, the owner of Reed & Dunn, Ltd., bankers to royalty. As an executive with Reed & Dunn, Harrison Reed made many trips to the United States and he soon realized that the streets of America were paved with golden opportunities. Armed with a loan from his father's bank, Reed made some shrewd real estate investments. Gobbling up properties, his wealth began to grow, so that by the time he inherited his father's estate, he had become a major player in the United States.

One of his acquisitions was a newspaper that he bought for the real estate that came with the company. Instead of closing the paper, Reed decided to give publishing a chance. The media world became his darling, and he was soon acquiring television stations, cable channels, radio stations, magazines, and newspapers.

A major contributor to the Democratic party, Reed, from the bottom of his money-lined heart, believed in their ideals and, of course, in his opportunities. When the Democrats invited him to a fifty-thousand-dollar-a-plate dinner, Reed took ten seats. As a generous donor, Reed was soon attending private coffees with then Governor Clark, the Democratic nominee. The two had hit it off immediately. Invited to the White House on a regular basis, Reed and the president enjoyed each other's company, both being addicted to sports, golf, and good times. They were two good old boys, swapping jokes, competing vigorously on the golf course, and eyeing the pretty young women.

Reed's wife had died leaving him with a three-year-old daughter, Astrid, whom he loved dearly. A battery of nannies, nurses, butlers, cooks, and chauffeurs were never a substitute for Reed, who always had time for his little girl. When Astrid finished her master's degree at Harvard, she went to work for the company, learning every aspect of the business. By the time she was twenty-nine, Astrid was first executive vice president, reporting directly to her father. Reed hoped that one day he could step down from running the company, turning it over to her. She was well qualified, smart, and creative. She was also a real beauty. Fair skinned, not a blemish or freckle, Astrid was soft and smooth as silk. Her flaming red hair cascaded over her face, which made her deep emerald green eyes seem larger than they were. At five-foot-seven, with long legs, Astrid had a perfect shape. She worked hard at it every day in her private gym with her personal trainer. Although she was charming, Astrid was more than anything, her father's daughter.

Picking up the phone, Harrison Reed dialed his daughter's extension at company headquarters.

"Astrid," Reed said, "we're having dinner at the White House tonight and I don't want you to be late."

"Dad," she said in an exasperated voice. "I'll be ready."

Astrid had a small bedroom and bath as part of her office suite. Showering, she dressed in a short black dress, low cut in the front, revealing plenty of cleavage. About to put her favorite perfume, Joy, behind her ears, Astrid decided not to. Instead, she put a few drops on her breast. Looking at herself in the mirror, she was pleased with what she saw. One last touch, her mother's pearls. She clipped the single strand around her neck, threw a few items in her purse, and grabbed her overnight bag. Outside her office, she stopped at her personal secretary's desk, doing a fast spin.

Vivian, her secretary, said: "Very nice. I'll bet you're sitting next to the president for dinner and that man will not be able to keep his eyes off you."

Winking at Vivian, Astrid left, taking the private elevator to the roof where Reed was waiting for her in the helicopter. Then the chopper was off to the airport, where their private jet was waiting. In a few minutes they were comfortably seated in Reed's Gulfstream, flying at twenty thousand feet, headed for the capital.

On board, Reed was busy with paperwork, while Astrid was on the phone negotiating the final points of a contract for the first cable television channel in Hong Kong after the turnover to China. The Chinese Department of Information was looking favorably to giving the Reed organization its approval.

Lt. Ed O'Connor hit the mike button in his mask, giving his call sign to the air traffic controller at the Andrews Air Force Base. The tower radio cracked in his ear: "You're next in line to land. Hold steady at eleven thousand feet and fall in behind the Gulfstream flying at ten thousand."

O'Connor acknowledged the call, dropping his flaps a little, and pulling back on the throttle to slow the Tomcat. He had to hit the deck at two hundred knots, considerably faster than the Gulfstream in front of him.

"How come I'm behind a civilian jet, Andrews? Why's a civi landing at the air base anyway?" O'Connor asked the tower.

"It was by order of the boss, the president," the tower crackled back.

Daniels heard the chatter from his helmet earphones.

"I'm impressed, Ed," Daniels said. "Must be somebody important."

"Probably some party fat cat, Mac,"O'Connor said, as he pulled back on the throttle a little more, lowering to full flaps, and dropping the landing gear.

When the Gulfstream lowered its landing gear, Reed and Astrid instinctively buckled their seatbelts before the pilot confirmed they were on final approach to Andrews.The Navy Tomcat was now running at a right angle to the Gulfstream. From the cockpit Daniels could see the commercial jet cruising over the final airport marker, at the start of the runway. As the Gulfstream was about to hit the runway, O'Connor made a hard left turn, lining up with the runway. Daniels did a double take as he looked down; there on the tail of the private jet was the World News Corporation logo. From her window, Astrid had been looking up at the Tomcat. She didn't know it, but Daniels would soon play an important role in her life—again.

Reed's plane taxied to the parking area on the tarmac as the Tomcat hit the runway, smoke coming from the screaming tires.The Gulfstream was shutting down as the navy jet taxied to the parking area to tie down next to Reed's plane. Reed and Astrid were coming down the stairs as O'Connor pressed the lever raising the canopy. Reed stopped to admire the F-14 and, looking up, he saw Daniels.

"Mac, hey Mac. Astrid, it's Mac!"Reed yelled above the airport noise.

Daniels was surprised and pleased to see Reed and he waved. His eyes swept the ground, finding Astrid standing there. What a beautiful sight, he thought.

Climbing down after O'Connor, Daniels walked over to Reed who was standing by a presidential limousine.

"Harrison, how are you?"Daniels said, extending his hand.

Reed clasped Daniels's hand with both of his, giving him a hearty, hard handshake.

"Ed, this is Mr. World News himself, Harrison Reed,"Daniels said to O'Connor.Then he focused on Astrid.

"Hello, Astrid,"he said, holding out his hand.

Her hand felt like a cold, dead fish, he thought, and the message she sent with her green eyes wasn't a pleasant one. He dropped her hand and introduced her to O'Connor. O'Connor nodded and smiled. His eyes were magnetically drawn to her revealing cleavage. Astrid smiled, too. She was used to men gawking at her.

"Lieutenant, pleased to meet you. I do believe you were on my tail coming in,"she said, turning on her soft Southern drawl.

Not sure how to respond to her, O'Connor cleared his throat and said,"It is unusual to see a private jet here, Miss Reed."

"Please call me Astrid."

"What are you doing here at Andrews?"Reed asked Daniels."I didn't know that the navy ran a private taxi for adventurous cameramen."

"I'm sure he's here on an assignment, Dad" Astrid said. "You know how he's always running off. Well, we'll have to hurry."

Watching the limo's taillights fade into the night, O'Connor said to Daniels, "Did I sense a little hostility here? Don't tell me you let her get away."

"Ed," Daniels said, "that's another story. Thanks for the lift. I see my next ride is here. Take care." Shaking hands, they parted.

Daniels walked across the tarmac toward a black Ford. When he got closer, the driver's door opened and Ron Haig, the Admiral's right arm, stepped out. As chief of operations, Haig was a man who knew how to get things done. When Daniels had joined the agency, Ronald Haig was the person who had conducted his initial interview. Like Charko, Haig could see what a valuable asset Daniels would be to the Special Operations Division.

"What's so important that you came out to meet me yourself, Ron? Or are you moonlighting as a taxi driver?" Daniels said.

"The Admiral sent me. I was the only one left to pick you up. Hell, I would have let you take a cab. Anyway, get in I've got a lot to tell you," Haig said.

"Where to, Ron?"

"The White House."

As they drove out of the airport, Haig told Daniels about the security meeting that the president had called, the Bergen report, and the action that the armed forces were taking. Daniels listened in silence.

"If this deed exists, Ron, could the Chinese win a war in Asia?"

"Funny you ask that. Most people ask if China will go to war. You seem positive that war is inevitable. To answer your question, yes, they can win a war in Asia."

"What's the president's position?" Daniels asked.

"No one knows what the president is going to do, Mac, not even the president."

"Slow down, Ron, that's the Reeds in front of us," Daniels said spotting Reed's car pulling into the White House driveway. "I ran into them at the airport. It will be hard to explain what I'm doing here."

Haig slowed the Ford to a crawl, waiting until the Reeds were safely inside the White House before pulling the car under the East Wing portico.

They entered through a side door and went down the back stairs; then, they took the elevator to the sub-basement headquarters of the National Security Agency. Following Haig into the most inner rooms of the Security Council, Daniels saw Sam Bergen, the head of the agency, and his senior staff surrounded by mountains of papers, charts, graphs, and maps. Letting out a slight sigh, Daniels knew it was going to be a long night. The Admiral was nowhere to be seen.

* * *

It was a delightful dinner in the White House private dining room. Astrid was seated across from her father, between the Clarks, closer to the president than the First Lady. As her secretary Vivian had predicted, the president couldn't keep his eyes off her. After dinner the president led Reed into his private study, while the ladies moved to the library. Once alone, the president asked Reed, "Do you have them?"

"Have I ever let you down?" Reed said, reaching into his inside jacket pocket and pulling out several Cuban cigars. As not to comprise the president by giving him an expensive gift, Reed had removed the *Hecho en Cuba* labels. Handing them to the president, Reed said with a broad smile: "Enjoy them."

"This is the only reason to lift the embargo," Clark said. "But, hell, thanks to you, I can get all the cigars I want."

The two men lit up and the aroma of tobacco filled the study. As the conversation got around to world events, the president asked Reed if he knew anything about the so-called deed to Hong Kong.

"Yes, I know something about it," Reed said.

"I never knew it existed," the president said. "To be honest, I'm having the NSA look into the matter, but I thought you might know something about it. You seem to have information about everything else."

"I've always had an interest in the story, but I could never find the deed," Reed said.

"Harrison," the president asked, "what would you do if you found the deed?"

"Give it to the rightful owner," Reed said. "Do you believe the Chinese would go to war over Hong Kong?"

The president nodded.

The room fell silent, both men deep in thought.

"Time for a different subject," Reed said, breaking the silence. "On a personal note, this rumor about you and a White House intern. Of course this is off the record, way off the record. Did you sleep with her?"

"Harrison, I didn't sleep a wink with her."

"Now we've gotten that out of the way, was she any good?"

Both men laughed. Finishing their cigars, they rejoined the ladies in the library.

"Are you going to spend the night with us?" Mrs. Clark asked.

"I'm sorry," Reed said, "but some urgent business requires us to return to Atlanta tonight."

Astrid didn't say a word, protecting her father's lie. She was sure her father had a good reason for leaving. The president looked disappointed, calling for one of his staff to bring the limo around front. Reed walked to the entrance of the White House with Mrs. Clark. The president followed with Astrid on his arm.

"You sure smell good," the president whispered to her.

The aroma coming from between her breasts kept drawing the president's eyes to her cleavage.

"I'm sure gonna miss you," he said. "I really wish you would stay over tonight. I have a meeting, but we could get together for a late-night drink."

"My father would be suspicious. Perhaps another time," she whispered. "But I have a little present for you."

She opened her purse and took out a tin of Altoid mints.

"Here, Mr. President," she cooed. "Try these."

Once they were airborne, Reed told Astrid the story of the deed and what the president had said.

"What's the big deal?" Astrid asked. "We left the White House for that?"

"I have been working on this for some time," Reed said. "I want you to go to Hong Kong and help me find the deed, Astrid, you have the perfect cover. You are in the middle of negotiations for the cable system. Instead of doing it by phone, go in person. You can also use the pretext of covering the turnover for our newspapers and magazines. I'll get Mac Daniels to go with you as your photographer. Besides, finding the deed will give you a great story and some great pictures."

"Why are you so interested in this deed?" she asked, suspicious of her father's motives. "What's so important about it?"

"Trust me," Reed said.

"Sure," Astrid said. "Tell me."

Resigned, Reed began the story of Powell and the deed. He described the old general's return to England, his knighthood, and the honors bestowed upon him. Reed also included sketchy details of Powell's mysterious death. As her father rambled on and on, Astrid lost interest, failing to see the relevance of the deed to her father.

"Dad," she said, exasperation in her voice. "Am I missing something here?"

"Astrid, when Powell was widowed, his sister Elizabeth brought up his children. After he died, Elizabeth and her husband adopted the children and the children adopted a new name."

"What name?" Astrid asked, not caring very much.

"Reed," he said. "Gen. Powell was my great-great grandfather and we are his last direct descendents."

Astrid was stunned by the implications. Did her father own Hong Kong? She sat in silence, not knowing what to say. This was madness, she thought. What did he expect to accomplish?

"Trust me, do this for me," Reed said urgently.

"Aw, Dad," she said. "First, if there is a deed, which I doubt, don't you think someone would have found it by now? Second, if you do find it, what makes you think you'll be able to keep it? And third, and most important, I don't want to go to Hong Kong, least of all with Mac Daniels."

"I thought you liked him," Reed said.

She didn't reply, but made a face and shook her head.

Using everything in his arsenal, from logic to guilt, Reed persisted. He knew his daughter as well as she knew him, and knew that she would eventually give in to him.

"All right," she said, after he had worn her down. "I'll be on the plane for Hong Kong tomorrow, but one question—what about the Chinese?"

"I am very close to the right people. I'll take care of everything, just trust me. The deed will soon be in Hong Kong. Then, the rest of the puzzle will fall into place," he said, patting her on the hand. "Thanks, Astrid. You warm my heart, pumpkin."

Pumpkin? He hadn't called her that since she was six years old. He must really want that deed, she thought.

When the plane landed, instead of going home, Reed went to the office and Astrid to her apartment to prepare for her trip. At the office Reed made one call after another, cashing in all of the IOUs he had out there. He always had the best information money could buy, but now he had more. Up all night working the phones, Reed had his key people on the move. He felt it in his bones the prize was there for the taking.

It was nine in the morning when Daniels finally left the White House. The black Ford pulled up to the side entrance, where yesterday it let him off. Opening the door expecting Haig, he was surprised to find the Admiral driving the car himself.

"Christ, you look like shit, Mac. Get in," the Admiral said.

Daniels didn't argue with him, he felt like shit and was red-eyed from lack of sleep.

"You know, sir, thirty-six hours earlier I was running for my life through the jungle, blowing up a cocaine plant, engaging in air-to-air combat, in an old Cessna no less, and ditching my plane at sea. Now I'm on my way to the Far East to chase a deed that may or may not exist. And do you want to know the worst part about all this was? I had to spend the night with Sam Bergen, listening to his bullshit."

Charko just smiled as he drove Daniels to the downtown Hilton. The Admiral gave Daniels another quick briefing, his version of the facts, the ones that mattered. Then he handed Daniels a key to a room.

"Get some sleep," he ordered.

Still wearing the clothes he had been given on the USS *Adams*, Daniels dragged himself in slow motion across the lobby of the Hilton, making his way to the elevators, ignoring the stares of the other hotel guests. The cool air in his room provided him with temporary relief, giving him the strength to drag his worn, weary body over to the bed. But before he could even undress, the phone rang. He picked it up.

"It's Harrison Reed."

"How did you find me? I'm not even sure where I am. I'm dead tired."

"Sorry, Mac, but I have a job for you. I want you to cover the Hong Kong turnover for me," Reed said. "The company jet will pick you up at four. I'll see you later in Atlanta. You're leaving for Hong Kong tonight."

"Make it a six o'clock pickup, Harrison," Daniels said, hanging up.

The Admiral had told Daniels he would get a cover story. Now he had. Too tired to wonder how the Admiral did it, Daniels drifted off into a deep sleep.

CHAPTER 12

An unexpected offer deserves serious consideration.

— Old Chinese proverb

FOLLOWING the Inspector General through the halls, Chi stayed half a step behind as they worked their way toward his superior's office. With each step Chi was anxiously waiting to receive his orders, but the Inspector General was a man alone with his thoughts. Not sure where he belonged in the hunt for the deed, Chi wanted some direction from his boss.

After what seemed to be an eternity, the Inspector General spoke without stopping or looking at Chi.

"The first part of the operation is underway," he said.

Looking like a dog begging for a bone, Chi wanted to scream: what about me, when do I get started?

Entering his office, the Inspector General left Chi standing in the hall, alone. Chi stared at the door, feeling sorry for himself. He thought about slamming the door, but many years of training prevented the open show of emotion. He had to settle for a hard push. It wasn't fair, he thought, it wasn't fair. Time was running out.

* * *

A stack of documents was on his desk waiting for him. Chi flopped into his chair and began reading, but he did not comprehend what he read. He tried to dig in, but after an hour, he was not even halfway through the pile. He was glad to be interrupted by the phone.

"Sang Chi, here."

The excited voice on the other end was that of a field agent from Hong Kong. Chi listened intently, his eyes widening at the disclosures the field agent made. When he finished the call, Chi dropped the receiver into place and ran out the door. He dashed through the hallways at full speed, trying to stop at the Inspector General's office, but sliding past the door. He had to grab onto the door frame to catch himself. Rushing past the Inspector General's secretary, without waiting to be announced, he knocked on the door to the private office; then he let himself in. The Inspector General was displeased by Chi's behavior.

"You move like the rabbit who has seen the eagle," he said. "Does your haste make manners such a heavy load to carry? What is wrong?"

"The Hong Kong field office was contacted by Gen. Zimkeroff, who demanded a meeting with me about the land grant, the deed," Chi said.

"How did the notorious Zimkeroff contact the office?" the Inspector General asked, sitting back in his chair.

"He called on the secure line."

"I suppose the secure line is no longer secure," he said with a slight smile. "The Russians have the same agents on their payroll as we do. They often pass along the same information back and forth. It was a way to keep the peace, but I'm surprised Zimkeroff called himself. I wonder what he's up to? Why don't you fly down to Hong Kong right away? This unexpected offer deserves serious consideration. But be on guard. Remember, you are an information specialist, not a thug. Zimkeroff will kill you as easily as he breathes. Go now and be careful."

"Yes, sir. I'll leave right away. Thank you for having the confidence in me."

The ringing of the phone annoyed the Inspector General. He picked up the receiver and answered coldly. As he held the phone, his body rocked slowly, showing his impatience. His cheeks began to flush, his temper rising, he began to breathe heavily, and finally he slammed the phone down. Chi dared not speak.

"It seems Gen. Xi is making preparations to leave for Hong Kong tomorrow. This is all the more reason you should go now. Have Mi Ler get you a priority flight.

"The faster you get to Hong Kong, the faster we will know. In the game of life, things don't just happen. They're made to happen. Don't forget that. It may keep you alive."

Chi left the office and asked Mi Ler to make flight arrangements for him.

"Your tickets will be waiting at the airport," she told him.

Then she made another call.

Leaning back in his chair, Gen. Xi put his feet on the desk, showing off his highly polished boots. The telephone was cradled between his shoulder and his ear.

"Thank you," he said, hanging up the phone.

Alone with his trusted aide, Colonel Miu, he said: "That was Mi Ler, Chi is on his way to Hong Kong tonight. Change our plans. Instead of going tomorrow, let's go now. I want to be on the same plane with Chi.

Let's see who is meeting him at the airport. Besides, it will make the little bastard nervous with me on the plane. We have much to do."

Bowing his head, Miu left the room. Gen. Xi picked up the secure phone and placed calls to his generals. To each one he gave the same code words: "Move the queen."

He was days away from starting World War III, but it didn't bother him. He just smiled.

Gen. Xi had one more call to make—this one was for another plan, the special plan. The phone at the other end answered on the first ring.

"Move the king," Xi said.

* * *

Mac Daniels was sipping a Bloody Mary when he heard the phone. He let it ring a few times before he answered it.

"Afternoon, Admiral," he said.

"Up and at 'em, Mac. See you in the lobby in thirty minutes," the Admiral's baritone voice boomed over the line. "I'm taking you to the airport personally."

"Admiral, I'm hungry and I have to go to my apartment to get some clean clothes."

"Don't worry about food, Mac, and look in your closet. See you in thirty."

The phone went dead.

"Good-bye, Admiral, love working for you," he said into the dead line.

In the closet Daniels found his bags, already packed with fresh clothes. He was wondering how the Admiral had done that when there was a knock on his door.

"Who's there?" Daniels asked.

"Room service."

Daniels just shook his head.

* * *

"Hi, Mac," Reed greeted Daniels as he stepped on board the aircraft. "I expect some great shots from you and I want a great story from Astrid. History is about to be made and I want it to be recorded."

From the corner of his eye, Daniels saw Astrid sitting in one of the flight seats, staring straight ahead, not turning around to look at him or acknowledge his presence. The chill in the air was colder than an Arctic winter night. Daniels gave up any thoughts of a pleasant trip.

Their affair had ended the year before. Astrid had thought it was love, not understanding why he wouldn't marry her. Daniels couldn't make her understand that she couldn't just buy love like she bought everything else. He was fond of her, Daniels thought, and he could have grown to love her, but she was overly possessive and, for him, that made the relationship impossible. Astrid was smart, beautiful, and charming—easy to fall for, but he didn't love her. She had made much more of their relationship than Daniels had imagined. When he had moved on, she went through the emotions of the jilted lover—from hurt to angry to very angry. He had hoped that a year would have softened her, but she seemed as furious as ever.

Daniels assured Reed that the trip would produce good results.

"I know Astrid will get a great story," he said.

When she heard him mention her name, she shot him a look that would have melted titanium.

"Do I perceive a slight smile?" Daniels said with a grin.

Astrid turned away, not dignifying him with an answer. Then Reed gave them the fourth quarter, down by six points speech: "Mac, I can't make this trip with you two. You and Astrid will have to go it alone. I am depending on both of you. I want this done right and the two of you can do it for me."

Daniels asked Reed why he wasn't coming. Reed gave the usual executive answers—too busy, too many meetings, and just too much to do. Then Reed kissed his daughter good-bye and stepped off the plane as the ground crew slammed the door shut. Placing his bags in the onboard closet, he stopped by the bar and poured himself a Grey Goose vodka on the rocks. Then he went back to his seat across the aisle from Astrid. They didn't look at each other, which made him uncomfortable.

Daniels didn't know what to say, and he started to turn away when he noticed a button on her blouse was open, giving him a peek at her breast. The sight of her heaving breast made him remember the warm nights in Georgia, their bodies melting together, his tongue exploring the hills and valley of her body, her nipples growing hard in his mouth. He found himself staring at her. She noticed.

"Mac, you're still a piece of shit," she said, turning away from him to hide the tears.

CHAPTER 13

A plan without a leader is like a lion without teeth.
— Old Chinese proverb

MICHAEL Montgomery was surrounded by a mountain of paper-work—reports, leads, tips, and rumors. Every scrap of information his department could glean had ended up on his desk. His agents had followed up on all the leads, but to no avail. Frustrated, he jammed an old pipe into his mouth, wishing he hadn't given up smoking. The pipe went from one side of his mouth to the other in perpetual motion. He had to force himself to read on despite burning eyes and a sour stomach. Somewhere in the pile of paper was the answer. He hoped.

Standing up and stretching, he took a break. Out the window he saw Williams and Adams leaving work and, for a second, he was envious. His friends were going home to a normal life, complete with wives and children and a permanent address. Montgomery had so many passports, under so many different names, that half the time he didn't know who he was. He couldn't imagine what it would be like working at the same job, at the same place, every day.

He sat back down to his work, but before he could dig in, there was a knock at the door and someone entered the room.

Expecting more paperwork, he didn't bother looking up.

"Please put it down on the end of the table, thank you," he said.

"Sir," a woman's voice said. "I think you should look at this."

Montgomery glanced at the woman and saw that she held a list of names, one circled in red.

"Gen. Xi," he said, running a hand through his hair. "What the hell is he doing here?"

"I don't know, sir," the woman said. "But I thought you should be informed."

Montgomery took a closer look at the woman. She was about five-four with a tiny waist that made her ample breasts seem larger than they were. Her auburn hair contrasted with the biggest blue eyes he had ever seen. He wondered how he had missed her before.

As he was studying her, he noticed she was suppressing a laugh.

"What, may I ask, is so funny," he said in a professional tone.

"I am sorry, sir," she said.

But the more she tried to hold back the laugh, the more she couldn't. Finally, she gave in.

"Sir, your pipe is upside down, your glasses are half off your face, you have coffee spots on your shirt, and your hair, to say the least, is uncombed. You look funny. I'm sorry," she said, giggling.

"I'm sorry I look funny, too," Montgomery said, knowing she was right.

"I apologize, sir," she said.

"I don't recall your name," he said.

"Liz Browning," she said. "No poetry jokes, please."

"No jokes," he said. "And having Gen. Xi in town is no joke either."

He recalled the satellite pictures of the latest Chinese troop movements. Gen. Wu Ti was moving three divisions toward the New Territories and four divisions to the North Korean border. The aircraft carrier Mao Tse-tung was steaming south. Something big was on.

"Can you find out where Xi is staying?" he asked her.

"The Peninsula Hotel on Salisbury Street. We can take my car," she said.

He was taken by her efficiency and very impressed with her in other ways, too.

"You're very efficient. What department are you with?"

"I am in the intelligence service of the customs office. We have been checking on arrivals. When a big one like Gen. Xi lands, the alarm bells go off."

"Come with me. Let's find out what the general is up to."

* * *

The lobby of the Peninsula Hotel was a whirlwind of motion—people coming and going, bellboys scurrying and hurrying, and guests and sightseers gawking at the sumptuousness of the furnishings. The Peninsula was one of the most famous and luxurious hotels in the world, a place where even the staff was formally dressed and wore white gloves. The restaurants there were celebrated for their fine gourmet dining. Many local people went there for dinner and afternoon tea was something on every visitor's agenda.

Montgomery called Gen. Xi's room on a house phone, but he got no answer.

"Who's watching him?" he asked Browning.

"A team was sent over as soon as I had the report that he was here."

"Good," he said. "But where the hell is he now?"

"Over there," she said.

From the corner of his eye, Montgomery saw the general enter the dining room. He grabbed Browning by the arm, pulling her behind him. She almost had to run to keep up with him. Montgomery paid the maitre d' a big bribe for a table by the window, the one next to Xi's, and they entered the restaurant arm in arm. The headwaiter seated them with Montgomery's back to Xi, while Browning faced the general. Xi had an excellent view of the busty woman with the big blue eyes. He stared at her openly while sipping champagne.

They were enjoying their meal at the expense of Her Majesty's government when a waiter stopped by Xi's table and handed him an envelope. Opening it, Xi read it, and put it in his pocket. Then he took out a piece of paper, wrote a note, and folded the paper into the palm of his right hand. When Xi stood up, Browning nodded to Montgomery, but before he could move, Xi was standing at their table.

"Please forgive the interruption, but I have had the pleasure of admiring a beautiful woman tonight and I thought the least I could do was to share my champagne with you," Xi said.

"Please join us," Browning said.

Xi politely declined the invitation and introduced himself.

"I am Gen. Xi of the People's Liberation Army."

"Michael Montgomery of Her Majesty's Secret Intelligence Service," he said, shaking the general's hand.

Browning almost choked on her drink.

"My regards to your director. He is an old friend of mine," Xi said, bowing his head ever so slightly. Then he left the dining room.

"Michael Montgomery of Her Majesty's Secret Intelligence Service, indeed. A bit over-truthful, aren't we?" she said, still shocked by his candor.

"He knows who I am and I know who he is. Why should we pretend we are fooling each other?" Montgomery said, shrugging.

"Well, aren't we going to follow him?" she asked.

Montgomery shook his head.

"Let the two in the lobby follow him. This place is famous for its desserts and I want one. How about you, Liz?"

"No, thanks," she said, wondering how he could be so casual about Gen. Xi's sudden appearance.

He ordered dessert and she sat watching him with fascination as he finished it. Montgomery paid the bill and they left the dining room. Out in the lobby, Montgomery noticed Browning's two watch dogs were gone and he hoped they wouldn't spook Xi. In the elevator, Browning pressed the button for the valet parking area.

"Wrong floor," he said.

"My car is with the valet," she insisted.

"Not now," he said, giving her the note Xi had slipped to him when they had shaken hands. It read: *Your car is parked in the garage at space number twenty-one. See you there in thirty minutes.*

She folded the note before putting it in her pocketbook.

"What do you make of it?" she asked.

Shaking his head, Montgomery said he wasn't sure, but he thought it might get rough.

"Maybe you should take a cab home," he said. "I'll return your car tomorrow."

"Oh, no," she said. "I spotted him and I want to be in on this. Besides, how do I know you won't wreck my Jag? I'm still making payments on it."

"Tough as well as beautiful," he said. "Have you got a gun in your pocketbook?"

"No," she said, pulling up her skirt, revealing her very shapely legs. Strapped to her thigh was a holster. She was carrying a snub-nose Colt .38. Not a very accurate weapon at long distances, but at close range it could get the job done.

"You missed it because it's an outside holster and not between my legs," she said.

They found her car where the note had said it would be and sat inside. Montgomery scanned the perimeter, scouting for Xi or other trouble. The garage was deserted.

"Have any ideas?" he asked.

"Just one," she said, pulling his face into hers, kissing him.

His arms instinctively pulled her close. Montgomery forgot about Xi as he tasted her kisses on his lips. The mood was broken when Xi knocked on the window with his keys. Montgomery and Browning both jumped.

"Is this an act for my benefit or are you two enjoying each other's company? You British plan very well."

"Where to, general?" Montgomery asked.

"Drive to the Peak," Xi said. "It's a wonderful place for lovers, very private, and a good place for us to talk."

Montgomery got there fifteen minutes before Xi and parked the car facing the road, in case he had to make a quick exit. He left the motor running, telling Browning to stay put. Positioning himself where he had a clear view of the road, he reached under his jacket and pulled his 9 mm Beretta Model 90 FS from its holster. He loaded a round into the chamber and slipped off the safety. Xi's Rolls Royce pulled up and parked facing the mountain, which would make it difficult for him to escape. Poor planning, Montgomery thought. Xi stepped from the car and walked over to a bench.

"Join me," he said, sitting down. "And bring Miss Browning."

"No. She stays in the car," Montgomery said. "I have a feeling that this is just between the two of us."

Xi stood up and took off his jacket. It was his way of showing that he was not armed. Montgomery pulled back his jacket to show that he was.

"That's not necessary," Xi said. "This is a peace mission. I have your land grant papers, the deed to Hong Kong. Correction, I will have them soon."

From the Jaguar, Browning heard Xi. She went to join the men.

"What a magnificent view," Gen. Xi said. "How would you like to own as far as you can see?"

"What's on your mind, general?" Montgomery said, ignoring the question.

"You British are getting as bad as the Americans, always rushing around and never stopping to enjoy the scenery. What a shame. In a few days we will own this island, the waterway, and the view. You will leave with your tails between your legs like whipped dogs. But I can help you—for a price, that is."

"What are you talking about?" Montgomery asked.

"I have the land grant, what you call the deed, the deed to Hong Kong. Want it?" Xi said with a coy smile.

"I don't believe you," Montgomery said. "Even if you do, why tell us?"

Xi took out a cigar, lighting it, drawing in slowly, and blowing out a cloud of smoke. He smelled the cigar, clearly enjoying it.

"Do you know how much this cigar cost?" Xi asked. "Do you know what the champagne that I gave you at dinner tonight cost?"

Pointing to the Rolls Royce parked off in the distance, he asked: "Do you know what that car cost?"

He then answered his own questions. "Money! Lots of money. If China takes Hong Kong, I'll be back in Canton, retired to a pig farm. I have given my life to my country. I have been the leader of the Peoples Liberation Army. I am the chairman of the joint committee for all military affairs. I control the world's largest armed forces. In retirement I won't make enough money to live the life I deserve. I'll be expected to set an example for the people back home. Private or general we are all the same, but we are not. Well, I'm tired of the poor life. I want to enjoy myself. So here is what I want: I want to defect. The price for the deed is the right to live in England and have a lot of money in the bank."

He took another long draw on the cigar.

Montgomery asked him if there would be war if the British produced the deed. Xi told him that he had put a plan into effect to move troops into position to attack if the deed surfaced.

"But a plan without a leader," Xi said, "is like a lion without teeth. When there are no leaders the army can't move. Most of my senior staff officers, the entire general staff, are ready to defect with me."

Montgomery sat there in silence, needing time to think. He told Xi he would have to clear this with the director, but he was sure the general's request would be granted.

"I have dinner at the hotel every night, at the same table," Gen. Xi said.

He stood up and dropped the half-smoked cigar, grinding it out under the heel of his expensive handmade Italian shoes.

"Money up in smoke," Xi said. "The cigar cost seventy-five American dollars and the car is worth two hundred and sixty thousand."

"One question, general. How did you find the deed?" Browning asked.

"Spies. I have good spies," Xi said, walking toward his car. "Mr. Montgomery, come with me over to my car, alone." As they approached the Rolls Xi said, "Gen. Zimkeroff is in Hong Kong looking for the deed. He plans to sell it to us so he can finance a new Russian revolution. He is meeting with a Chinese agent soon. I'll keep you informed. Watch him, not me."

Xi nodded to his chauffeur who opened the rear door. Montgomery saw Browning's two men tied up on the floor.

Xi smiled broadly, showing his gold teeth.

"I will let them go unharmed," he said.

After Xi had driven away, Montgomery returned to the bench.

"Well, what did he say?" Browning asked.

Montgomery told her as he looked at his watch, quickly calculating the time difference between Hong Kong and London.

"We had better get back to the office for a secure phone to call the director," he said.

"It's the middle of the night there and it's so beautiful here, let's stay a minute," she said.

"You're right," he said, leaning into her, kissing her open mouth. He ran his hand up her dress softly stroking her legs. Moving his hand a little higher, he found her gun. As he pulled back, she laughed.

"Come to my place," she said.

CHAPTER 14

A stumble may prevent a fall.

— Old Chinese proverb

❦

THE hot June sun made the sea spray dance with color. But the beauty of the day was lost on Chi, who, with each passing minute, was growing more irritable. He paced the lower deck of the Star Line ferry like an expectant father, stopping only to look at his watch, and giving it an occasional tap to be sure it was still running. Where was Zimkeroff? he wondered. He had been waiting for the Russian general for more than an hour.

Suddenly, the wake of a passing tug rocked the ferry and Chi lost his footing. He stumbled—almost fell—when a strong hand caught him.

"You must be careful, Chi," a booming voice said in Cantonese.

Chi found himself staring into the chest of a man who was a foot taller than he was.

"You're late," Chi said. "I have been riding this damn ferry for more than an hour."

"I've been here," Zimkeroff said. "Although I must say, I was enjoying the ride more than you. I wanted to talk to you alone."

"I was here, where I was instructed to be, in plain sight. If you were on the ferry for the past hour, why didn't you contact me sooner?" Chi said, his anger barely controlled.

"You were supposed to come alone," Zimkeroff said.

"I am alone."

"You are now," Zimkeroff said. "Besides enjoying the ride, I was watching you from the first-class section, enjoying your lack of patience. Didn't the Inspector General teach you that all good things come to he who sits and waits? Your impatience caused you to compromise your men's positions. So now you are all alone. It's such a warm day; I believe your men have gone for a swim."

Petroff, who was stationed on the bridge, had identified and eliminated the Chinese agents in less than an hour.

85

In desperation, Chi opened his jacket so that the butt of the 9 mm Daewoo, which had been tucked into his waistband of his slacks, was visible.

Zimkeroff laughed at him.

"What are you going to do with that? Shoot me?"

"The thought had crossed my mind," Chi said.

Zimkeroff turned his back and walked away, showing his contempt for Chi. He entered the deserted first-class passenger area. Chi followed him. When he stepped inside, Petroff grabbed him by the neck with one hand and lifted him off his feet. Struggling and choking, Chi tried to loosen Petroff's vise-like grip, but he couldn't pry back a single finger of the claw that was squeezing the life out of him. Petroff extended his right arm fully, pressing Chi's head into the ceiling. With his free hand Petroff grabbed Chi's Daewoo and tossed it out the open porthole.

"Enough, Petroff, release him," Zimkeroff ordered as he went back on deck.

Like a robot, Petroff opened his hand and dropped Chi to the floor. For a few seconds he didn't move; then gasping for breath, he slowly rose to a sitting position. Petroff pointed to the general sitting on the deck. Chi, his head hanging in shame, sat next to Zimkeroff. The wind picked up, causing the spray to blow a gentle mist over the two men. They completed the trip in silence.

When the ferry landed on Hong Kong Island, Chi followed the Russians to a waiting car. He climbed into the back seat, while Zimkeroff and Petroff got in front. The driver took his time on the busy Connaught Road, creeping toward the Harbour Tunnel. Zimkeroff knew that the British were following him, but he didn't care. Chi started to speak, but Zimkeroff put his finger up to his lips to silence him.

The Russian driver pulled into a car wash. Several cars behind, the British tail parked near the front of the car wash waiting for Zimkeroff to emerge.

The driver of the British car told his microwave operator: "Looks like we're done for, the dish is useless with all this noise. We'll have to get him when he comes out."

After a few minutes, Zimkeroff's car exited the car wash. The micro dish operator, putting on the headset, smiled: "Got 'em. Let's go." They continued following the car, not knowing that it now contained three new passengers and a tape recorder playing Zimkeroff's voice.

Zimkeroff, Chi, and Petroff were in the Chevy Suburban heading toward a KGB warehouse near Queen's Pier, while the other car was speeding through the tunnel with the British close behind.

Inside the warehouse, Bresneyev, Kertinkoff, and a dozen former KGB agents were waiting for Zimkeroff. All the men came to attention when Zimkeroff entered into the room. Pointing to a chair, Zimkeroff ordered Chi to sit down. Then he pulled the canvas off a large board on the wall.

"The invasion of Hong Kong," the general said. "Order of battle, troop strengths, weapons distribution, air forces, artillery—the complete package. Your Gen. Xi is hoping that the land grant will fall into British hands, so he can start World War III. He's a lunatic, of course."

Chi's eyes practically jumped out of his head; his expression gave everything away.

Amateur, Zimkeroff thought.

Chi jumped from his chair, trying to interrupt Zimkeroff, but before he could reach the general, Petroff backhanded him across the face, sending him flying across the room. Chi could taste the blood as it trickled from his lips into his mouth. He lunged at Petroff with a flying drop kick. Petroff sidestepped Chi's airborne body, slamming his hand onto Chi's chest, and bringing his knee up into Chi's back. The pain shot through Chi's body as he fell to the floor. Petroff pressed his foot on Chi's throat and held the dazed Chinese agent to the floor. Chi wiggled like fish out of water, his legs kicking, his body convulsing. Petroff pressed harder. Chi was losing consciousness; his chest felt like it was going to burst. Zimkeroff signaled Petroff to let him up.

"You do not interrupt the general," Petroff said, kicking Chi in the ribs.

Chi tried to struggle to his feet, but the pain prevented him from moving. Zimkeroff nodded and two of his men picked up Chi, placing him back in the chair.

"I will deliver the land grant for a price or, if you wish, I will give it to the English, along with the invasion plans."

"Where is it?" Chi gasped. "The deed."

"My terms first. The price is not money."

"What then?" Chi asked.

"I will deliver the land grant for Hong Kong in exchange for BCV."

Chi's mind exploded with more pain than he was feeling in his body. He couldn't say BCV; he couldn't even think BCV. How did Zimkeroff even know about it, let alone demand it for the land grant papers? Zimkeroff was as mad as Gen. Xi, he thought.

"These demands need the approval of the highest levels. I must call the Inspector General immediately," Chi said.

"Do what you must, but do it soon," Gen. Zimkeroff said.

Chi was dragged to the car and taken back to the ferry where a half dozen wet Chinese agents were waiting for him. He managed to drive back to his office at Hong Kong International Airport. Once inside, Chi called the Inspector General, telling him of the events, but leaving out the fact that his armed escorts were caught and thrown off the ferry. He confessed that he received a quick but painful beating from the Russians; then he told the Inspector General of Zimkeroff's demand.

"How is this possible?" the Inspector General said. "How did the Russians know about BCV? This is a most serious problem. We still have to find the land grant and now we must catch a traitor. I will call you back."

Chief Executive Tung held a tall glass of Ng Ka P'ei, a Chinese wine that was as strong as whiskey. The dark circles under his eyes showed how tired he was. This should have been a time of joy, he thought, but even the repatriation of Hong Kong was somehow overshadowed by recent events. And when the Inspector General had called on his private line, demanding an interview, Tung knew something terrible had happened.

"Make yourself a drink and sit down, Lee," Tung said when the Inspector General arrived.

"Then tell me the bad news."

The chief executive was the only one who called the Inspector General by his given name and only when they were alone.

The Inspector General declined and told him Chi's story, finishing by saying: "The price of the land grant is BCV."

"How did this happen? How can anyone know about BCV?" Tung thundered.

Then, uncharacteristically, the chief executive threw his glass across the room where it exploded on the far wall like a grenade.

The Inspector General sat silently, knowing that a breach in security of this magnitude would affect the entire hierarchy of China. He knew about the BCV project, but he was never involved with it and at the moment, he was glad of that. But no one, from the lowliest guard to the president of the country, would be above suspicion. Someone would pay, he thought, someone always paid, for that was the way it was in China.

The Inspector General had a plan, but he would wait until the chief executive regained his composure. What he needed was time, not mistakes. Sometimes a little stumble prevents a fall, he thought.

CHAPTER 15

Beauty should blind the eye, not the mind.

— Old Chinese proverb

❦

IN the center of Beijing, across the street from the Chinese Overseas Hotel on Nan Hoygen Road, was a small store that sold tourist souvenirs: T-shirts, hats, fans, cards, toys, key chains, replicas of ancient artifacts, and other dust collectors. The House of Chan, as it was called, was the same kind of store that could be found in Times Square or at the wharf in San Francisco.

For the past five years the store had been owned and operated by a young couple, Anson Chan and his wife, Al Wan. Anson had been born in Beijing, where his mother had worked as a domestic at the French embassy and his father had been one of the embassy's grounds-keepers. His parents had managed to enroll him in an exclusive French school, where he had learned to read and write in French and English. Anson had met his wife Al Wan in the small town of Pao-ting, south of Beijing. He had literally bumped into her as she was coming out of a village store. Taken with her exotic beauty, he had stammered like a lovesick teenager, but all that had come out was a faint "lovely evening."

She had covered her mouth with her hands to hide her giggle. Al Wan, whose name translated to Lovely Evening, apologized for her laughter. It was love at first sight.

With the permission of her parents, Anson had courted Al Wan, and had eventually married her. Then he had returned to the capital with his bride. Because of his ability to speak foreign languages, the Communist Party allowed Anson Chan the privilege of operating the tourist shop.

The Chans were happy working together, enjoying what little China could offer those who were not of the elite governing class. They lived in a small apartment in the back of the store and that was an added incentive for the Chans: one rent for their business and their home.

Although the Chans made little money by Western standards, they were better off than most Chinese citizens, earning more in one month than they would have made in a small village for a whole year.

When Al Wan returned home to visit her parents she was inevitably questioned about grandchildren. The Chans were childless after five years of marriage, not because of any medical problem, but because they refused to bring children into a society where they would not be free. The bad part about working with tourists was that the Chans could not help but learn the truth about China. They had never told their parents about their reasons, knowing that the older generation would not understand. But he had a dream.

If Anson Chan had had a résumé, there would have been one word on it that would have made him proud. It was also the one word that could cost him his life—messenger. The store had offered him the perfect opportunity to pass along messages from the outside world to those who were trapped inside China. His wasn't a high-tech espionage operation, but rather a messenger service from family to family.

After all his hard work, Anson Chan was finally ready to escape with his wife to the free world. The yearning for freedom had grown within him, beginning with simple desire, changing to zeal, and then to a hunger that consumed his whole being. Now it was only a matter of hours until that burning lust for freedom would be cooled by the waters of Hong Kong.

It had started late one night. Anson had been closing the store when a customer had entered. Always anxious to make one more sale, he hadn't minded intrusion. Oddly enough, the customer had been an elderly Chinese man interested in purchasing a reproduction of an antique vase. The man had then asked Anson if he would take a message to Hong Kong for him. Feigning surprise and shock, Anson had told him that he didn't take messages and certainly wasn't going to Hong Kong. At first Anson had thought the old man was crazy; then he had become suspicious, suspecting a trap. Anson had denied wanting to leave the country, choking on his own words as they came out of his mouth.

The old man had stood his ground. He had picked up one of the vases and turned it in his hand.

"Inside one of these," he had said, tapping the vase, "will be a message. If you agree to deliver it, you will have permission to leave the country."

Anson had tried to usher him out of the store, but the mysterious old man had produced exit visas for Anson and his wife.

Thinking he had been set up, Anson had said: "How do you know I won't report this to the police?"

"You won't,"the old man had said."Because you want to go.You have all the qualifications for the job.You have been playing messenger for years.You and your wife can't wait to get out of the country."

He had held up the exit visas, waving them in front of Anson's face.

"What must I do?"Anson had blurted out, unable to stop himself.

"It is very simple," the old man had said, holding up the vase. "On Saturday, you will receive an early morning delivery, vases like this.You will know the one you must deliver."

"Where?"

"Two-oh-five Water Street, Hong Kong,"the old man had said, making the store owner memorize the address.

Anson had wrapped the vase and placed it in a red-and-yellow bag imprinted in English and Chinese with the *House of Chan*. He had handed the bag to the stranger, who had given Anson the two exit visas.

When the man had gone, Anson had doubled locked the door, pulled down the shades, and had leaned against the door. Staring at the exit visas, he had wondered if his dream had come true or if he were now on the arrest list of the Ministry of State Security.

* * *

For the next few days, Anson and Al Wan had carried on as if nothing had happened, but at night they were magically transformed into schoolchildren waiting impatiently for summer vacation.Their imaginations had run wild, wondering what their new life would be like in a free society. Al Wan had asked her neighbor and good friend, Ji Lee, to watch their store while they were gone. He had often helped out by running the shop when the Chans had gone to visit Al Wan's family in the country. Al Wan and Anson hoped Ji Lee would be able to keep the store once they had gone for good.

Al Wan had tried to pack their bags as she had in the past, but this was a permanent vacation from China. Anson's instruction had been clear, but she couldn't resist slipping a few photos into their suitcases, hoping he wouldn't be mad at her. Finding the photos, he had removed them, explaining that they might cause suspicion with the crossing guards.

"Why would someone leaving for one week take family pictures?"he had asked.

She had answered him with tears pooling in her dark, lustrous eyes.

Taking her in his arms, he had given her a reassuring hug.

"Ji Lee can send the family pictures and other mementoes when we are safely in Hong Kong."

Early Saturday morning, Ji Lee knocked on their door

"You and Al Wan must have a lot to do,"he said."I came over to help."

Anson returned to the apartment to finish dressing. Al Wan was wearing a Western-style dress and high-heel shoes that made her only two inches shorter than her husband. Anson looked at her with an affectionate smile, the smile of a man who loved his wife.

"Hurry up, Anson," she said. "You are slower than I am today."

Anson struggled with his tie. First it was too long; then it was too short. Al Wan shook her head watching the show, admiring her husband. He looked quite handsome in his dark blue suit, she thought.

Most deliveries in Beijing were made late at night or early in the morning, so as not to interfere with the pedestrian and bicycle traffic during the day. No one gave it a second thought when a green Toyota van pulled up to Chan's store. Two young men climbed out of the van carrying two boxes. Ji Lee unlocked the door for them.

The delivery men looked around the store.

"Are you Anson Chan?" the driver asked.

"He is getting dressed. May I help you?" Ji Lee asked in his high-pitched voice.

"Yeah," the other replied. "Sign here."

After the men had left, Ji Lee opened the boxes. He found twelve vases, the kind that the Chans sold in the store. The imitation antiques were hand-painted inside of the dark glass, allowing the design to show through. Each vase was eighteen inches high, with a small open mouth, and resembled a large pear. Standing on their little wooden platforms, the vases were pretty and very popular with tourists. They passed through customs all the time almost unnoticed.

The noise in the store brought Anson out from his apartment, his navy blue tie hanging from the collar of his white nylon shirt. As casually as possible, he picked out a brown vase in the corner of the box. It was clearly labeled "205," the address on Water Street where it was to be delivered.

"I'm going to take this one with me as a gift for one of my friends," he said, placing it on the counter by the cash register. The other vases in the box were open at the mouth, except for the one marked "205." He knew it was the right one because it was already filled with sand, corked, and ready for travel.

"Ji Lee, please put these vases on the shelf and the sand-filled one under the counter," Anson said, trying to sound unconcerned. When he returned to his apartment, he started to shake. He didn't know what was in the vase and he didn't want to know. He just wanted to get it to Hong Kong as quickly as possible. How was he going to make it through the day, he wondered.

* * *

The Galaxy Beauty Pageant contestants were the most beautiful women in the world. No talent was required, no high IQ was needed, and no hard questions were asked. The pageant was about pure beauty. All fifty contestants were stunningly beautiful, each one more gorgeous than the next. They were on a world tour, stopping in all the major cities, and making heads turn everywhere they went. This was their last day in Beijing before going on to their final stop, Hong Kong. The tour had been timed to capture the maximum publicity. After a week of festivities, the winner would be crowned in Hong Kong on the first day of China's control, July 1st.

Having some free time to do some shopping, four of the women from the beauty pageant had wandered away from the hotel and entered the House of Chan.

Ji Lee was speechless and gawked at the four tall Western women, who were all blondes. He could not help noticing how well endowed they were because his line of sight was at bust height.

"Ji Lee," snapped Al Wan, "you're staring."

Startled back to realty, his imagination now in check, Ji Lee asked if he could help them. He spoke some English, German, and French, enough to explain prices to the foreigners.

The women were used to being stared at, but sometimes it was annoying. The tallest of the four said in English: "At least he isn't drooling."

Ignoring Ji Lee, one of the women picked up a vase from the box that Ji Lee had not completely unpacked. Passing it around, the women inspected it carefully.

"Can you handle this?" Al Wan asked Ji Lee. "Beauty should blind the eye, not the mind. Pay attention to business."

He felt the jab in her words and bowed his head to her.

She left him to wait on the women and returned to the apartment.

The tallest woman noticed the sand-filled vase on the shelf and asked to see it. Eager to please, Ji Lee handed it to her. Conferring with her friends in French and English, she announced: they wanted five vases to take on the plane.

Ji Lee wrapped the one Anson had put aside and placed it in a House of Chan bag. Then he filled four other vases with sand, explaining in a mixture of languages that the sand would protect the vases and keep them from breaking during travel. Then he put each in its own bag. Handing over the five bags, he accepted payment and thanked the women profusely. Such a pleasant sight, he thought, as he watched them leave.

Ji Lee took another brown vase from the box, filled it with sand, and wrapped it carefully. Anson, he knew, would appreciate the gesture.

Anson came from the apartment dragging the luggage behind him, complaining that his wife had packed the kitchen sink. Al Wan pretended she hadn't heard the remark and gave Ji Lee his last minute instructions. When she had finished, the tears ran down her cheeks.

"Here," Ji Lee said, handing Anson the bag. "I wrapped your vase for travel. Who is it for?"

"A friend," Anson said, holding the bag tightly under his arm.

It was their passport to freedom.

CHAPTER 16

A fool's errand is just that.

— Old Chinese proverb

❧

NESTLED into the copilot's seat, Daniels was holding the Gulfstream steady over the Pacific, on a heading for Hong Kong. A skilled pilot, he loved to fly every chance he got.

"Correct to two-six-eight, Mac," the pilot said.

"Correcting to two-six-eight," Daniels repeated as Astrid Reed came into the cockpit. Looking around, she gave Daniels an icy stare.

"Where's the copilot?" she asked the pilot.

"He's taking a nap, Ms. Reed," the pilot replied.

She gave him a disgusted look, as if to say I'm not paying him to sleep.

"Captain, how long until we land?"

"About three hours, Ms. Reed."

Daniels looked straight ahead into a thousand miles of nothing, avoiding any eye contact with her.

She left the cockpit as quickly as she had entered.

Ignoring the comment, Daniels flipped on the intercom switch. "Steward, better wake up sleeping beauty," he said, referring to the copilot. Daniels waited for the copilot before leaving the cockpit.

"Thanks for the flying time, skipper," he said. "By the way, the bitch is a hot pepper."

Daniels found Astrid sitting in the owner's seat where he had seen Harrison Reed so many times before. The seat had a built-in set of phones, an Internet connection, and an intercom with the pilot. It also featured a climate control system, lights, and background music.

Not stopping at his seat, Daniels walked past her to the bar in the rear of the cabin. He poured himself a large vodka on the rocks and gulped it down, fortifying himself with liquid nourishment. He was tired of Astrid's behavior. This assignment was going to be hard enough without having to deal with her.

"Astrid," he said in a low voice.

She ignored him.

"Astrid, please," he said, trying to reason with her.

She stood up from the power chair and was about to retreat to her cabin, when Daniels came up behind her.

"Astrid," he said softly.

She turned to face him.

Without warning he pulled her close to him, kissing her. She pushed at him, but he held her, refusing to let her go. Her struggles soon began to subside and, after a few seconds, he let her go. Astrid pulled back, no expression on her face. Then she let him have a right hand across his face. It stung. His hand went to his cheek to rub it. She grabbed him by the shirt, staring into his dark eyes. Daniels was expecting another blast, but Astrid said nothing. She kissed him.

Soon they were in her private cabin undressing each other. No words were spoken; it was automatic. He knew her and she knew him. Their bodies entwined, their tongues and lips held together by uncontrolled passion. Daniels's hands ran down her back, then slowly up her legs, exploring her body, finding his way home. She was warm, wet, and waiting. Astrid rolled over on top of him, pressing her hips down hard, feeling him ready for her. Guiding herself down onto him, she began to shudder, pressing herself tightly against him, sliding back and forth, faster and faster, finally falling onto him in climatic exhaustion.

Daniels held her tightly, still pushing himself into her, until he felt himself explode inside her. He arched his body, then fell back onto the bed, and stopped moving. They lay there for a long time, motionless, without a word. Then Astrid rolled off of him and whispered: "Why?"

They fell asleep in each other's arms, her legs over his, her head buried in his chest, his arms holding her tight. Two hours later, the intercom shattered their peaceful world. The pilot asked them to return to their seats in preparation for landing.

"Let's get dressed," she said, knowing he hadn't answered her question, but there would be time enough.

Astrid took a passenger seat, giving the owner's seat to Daniels. The intercom crackled as the copilot announced that they would be landing in ten minutes.

"We're next in line, behind a charter seven-twenty-seven," came the copilot's voice over the speakers.

"That charter is the world beauty pageant that has been in the papers. Fifty of the prettiest women in the world are aboard," the pilot said over the intercom.

Daniels pressed the intercom button.

"So what?" he said. "The prettiest woman in the world is sitting right here next to me."

"Mac, you're so full of shit your eyes are brown," Astrid said. "But this time I won't argue with you."

Once they had landed, Daniels told Astrid he wanted to stay around and shoot the beauty pageant contestants.

"It's my job," he told her when she objected.

"You're not fooling anyone," she said, but she was smiling.

Daniels started shooting the girls as they disembarked from the plane. Each of the contestants gave wide smiles to the lone cameraman standing on the tarmac. Four of the prettiest contestants were carrying distinctive red-and-yellow bags marked *House of Chan*. Several rolls of film later, Daniels spotted what appeared to be one of the officials in charge of this flock of beauties.

"Excuse me," he said, flashing his press badge. "I'm Mac Daniels with the World News Corporation."

"How you doin'," the man said. "My name is Thomas Camarow, from Jersey City, New Jersey, USA."

Camarow was the chief promoter of the Galaxy Beauty Pageant. He was the brains behind it, having conceived the idea while he was on a golf course. The idea was simple: T and A, tits and ass, give men around the world what they wanted to see. Camarow's assessment of what men wanted was right on the mark and the pageant was a financial success. In every city they toured, the show was a sellout because it appealed to men who didn't want to sit around listening to some bimbo with big tits trying to explain why she was in favor of good family values—especially when everybody knew she had screwed half the judges to get where she was.

"Where are you stayin', Mac?" Camarow asked.

"At the Peninsula Hotel."

"Me, too. I've a floor reserved for me and my honeys," Camarow said, then sensing another opportunity he asked, "Would you like to do a photo shoot back at the hotel? You can cover the Grand Ball—everyone who's anyone in Hong Kong will be there. Maybe some candid shots for some of your magazines? Whata you say, Mac? Maybe some coverage on the *World News Tonight Show*."

"Hey, I'm just a freelancer, but I'll see what I can do. Astrid Reed flew in with me. Perhaps you'd like to meet her?"

"How about drinks tonight?" Camarow asked, salivating at the opportunity to meet the beautiful daughter of the media billionaire.

"I can't commit Miss Reed, but call me later," Daniels said, waving good-bye.

He made his way to the General Aviation receiving building where he found a pay phone. He dialed the number the Admiral had given him.

"Boucher residence."

"Is Mr. Harry Saltzman there?"

"One moment, please."

There was silence for a moment while he waited. Saltzman was in charge of public relations for the United States Mission. Because Hong

Kong was a colony and not a country, there was no ambassador, but a consul general, who was the diplomatic representative from the United States. Saltzman was actually the CIA station chief, running field operations in Hong Kong. A twenty-year veteran, he was responsible for supplying field agents with cover, weapons, money, and a safe house, if necessary. When there was a problem, when someone made a mess, a call to Harry was all it took. He arranged for a cleaner and saw to it that there were no incriminating details left behind to embarrass the United States. When an agent needed a cleaner, it meant there was a body to dispose of—no questions asked. Saltzman saw to it that the body was gone, as if it never existed.

"Saltzman, here."

"Harry," Daniels said. "I'm back."

"No, it can't be. What did I do to deserve this?" Saltzman said with an exaggerated groan.

He had worked with Daniels before and each time there had been a lot of cleaning to do.

"I begged for a new assignment when they told me you were coming. But what's the use. I'm paying for the sins of my past life. You better get over here."

"Where's here?"

"Consul General Boucher's house, 26 Garden Road, Hong Kong."

"Why not the mission?"

"No way. Boucher doesn't want you around there. This is a little more private. In fact, I have a surprise for you when you get here," Saltzman said and hung up.

Standing in line for a cab, Daniels noticed a man carrying the same bright red-and-yellow bags that he had seen some of the contestants carrying. As the man got into the cab, Daniels heard him tell the cab driver to go to 205 Water Street. He thought it was odd that a couple, who were obviously tourists, wanted to go to an industrial area on the river. But it was none of his business.

The Chans were on their way to freedom—nervously. Anson drummed his fingers on the bag containing the vase, while Al Wan marveled at the sights of Hong Kong. After they had cleared Hong Kong customs, Anson had finally told his wife he had some very important documents in the vase he was delivering for the Free China Society. He was so excited, he could hardly contain himself. Al Wan was frightened, believing that the mysterious Free China Society was a criminal organization filled with dangerous thugs. She was apprehensive and glad she did not know that the vase had anything in it.

"I never would have made it though the airport check, Anson," she had whispered to him. "My nerves would have given me away. What are you doing delivering secret messages, anyway? A fool's errand is just that, my love. Throw the vase away."

CHAPTER 17

Everyone dances with death.

— Old Chinese proverb

THE old Mercedes taxi had seen many miles, but the driver had a love affair with his car and kept it in mint condition. The leather seats were well worn with a comfortable feel like a good pair of gloves. The driver raced down the Lantau Expressway, cutting in and out of traffic. It wasn't until they managed to get onto Hong Kong Island that he was forced to slow down. Now Daniels knew why the seats were so well worn.

From the Star Line ferry landing it was only six hundred yards as the crow flew to the consul general's residence, but nothing on the island was in a straight line. He marveled at how the driver navigated the corkscrew roads, winding his way up Garden Road.

The consul general's residence, high up the steep incline of Garden Road, had a view of the South China Sea to the south and of Victoria Harbor to the north. The Victorian house, which had been built for the British royal governors more than a hundred years ago, was surrounded by an ivy-covered iron fence. From the second floor balcony, the American flag flapped in the summer breeze.

The taxi came to a stop as the marine guard approached. Daniels lowered the window and handed him his identity card. After a quick call to the house, the marine waved the taxi through the gate.

The taxi dropped Daniels off in front of the house, where to his surprise he found Harry Saltzman waiting for him. He was dressed in jodhpurs, knee-high leather boots, a khaki riding shirt, an ascot, and he was carrying a riding crop.

"Good to see you, Mac. Come in," Saltzman said.

"Christ, Harry, you've been here too long. Does the Admiral know you dress in a clown suit? Since when are you into riding?"

"Since the consul general's widowed sister arrived in Hong Kong two months ago."

Daniels smiled and followed Saltzman into the house. The main hall ran the entire length of the building, with first floor rooms to the left and right. Coming out of one of the rooms was Consul General Richard Boucher, his arms loaded with reading material. Casually dressed, he was heading for the back porch when he saw Daniels.

"Come here, Mac," Boucher said, motioning to him.

The two men talked for a moment while Saltzman stood at the other end of the hall.

After the consul general had gone, Saltzman didn't ask Daniels what had been said, but knowing the seriousness of the mission, he was sure that Boucher was wishing Mac good luck.

Saltzman opened the door to the consul general's office, leading Daniels in. The office was traditional, with a view of the front of the house and Victoria Harbor. Daniels was looking for a place to park his ass when Saltzman slid open a wall panel that led to a hidden stairway.

"The mystery deepens," Daniels said.

At the foot of the stairs was a steel door requiring a combination to be unlocked. Behind the door was a windowless room that was specially designed for safe private conversations. No listening device could penetrate the thick walls. The safe room, as Saltzman liked to call it, had been used for many private conversations—safe, even from Boucher's ears. There were many matters that the consul general was not made aware of and there were matters that he just didn't want to know about.

The room had a small table, several chairs, and a special radio linked to military satellites for direct safe calls to Washington. A couple of secure fax phones, a computer system, and a shredder completed the decor.

Glancing around the room, Daniels found what he had been looking for. He walked over to a steel filing cabinet, but instead of trying to pull open a drawer, he lifted the top off, revealing a small refrigerator, well-stocked with beer and soda. Taking out two cold Buds and a bag of pretzels, Daniels popped the tops and handed Saltzman a cold brew.

"How did you know?" Saltzman asked.

"I'm a psychic. Maybe I'll get one of those TV gigs when I retire," Daniels said. "Besides, the consul general told me it had just been stocked and that I had better leave him a few cold ones."

Putting his hand to his head as if he were deep in thought, Daniels said: "Yes, yes, I see it now. I'm getting a strong impulse. Next, the Admiral will want me to find the lost continent of Atlantis—then be back by Thursday."

"Not funny, Mac," Saltzman said. "We've got a lot of work to do and not much time to do it. Whatever you need of me or the staff, just name it and you got it."

"Before we get going, I want you to arrange to keep Astrid Reed busy. The Admiral got old man Reed to hire me, but I didn't bargain for his daughter to be on my back. I'll need room to operate. Could you line up some bullshit interviews for her?"

"Done," Saltzman said.

"Good. I'll tell Astrid to give you a call. Now that's out of the way, let's get down to business."

Saltzman was glad to see his old friend Mac Daniels, even if it meant that he would be working some serious overtime. He handed Daniels a large binder containing the summaries of all the reports he had been able to gather. Daniels looked them over quickly, noticing the fine details in the pages of information, history, and footnotes.

"Hell, this is as thick as a New York City phone book," Daniels said. "You expect me to read this? Who did this, as if I didn't know. I would say this is Haig's work."

"Bingo," Saltzman said. "And coming right from the fair city of Washington, D.C., I give you Ron Haig."

Saltzman hit the button to unlock the door. Ron Haig came strolling in as if on cue.

"Is this the surprise you had for me?"

"Nice to see you, too, Daniels," Haig said. "Give me a beer."

The Admiral had given Haig the point on the project, underlining its importance. Haig had left Washington to assume direct control of the operation. It wasn't often that he was in the field and his presence emphasized the importance of what was at stake. Haig had a genius for making sense of random bits of intelligence. No one was better.

From his briefcase, Haig pulled out two more binders, both bigger and thicker than the first. He dropped them on the table. Daniels groaned when he saw what Haig brought with him.

"Can we do this in ten minutes?" Daniels asked.

"If you want the ten-minute version, then your chances of living more than ten minutes are slim to none. If you spend the time and listen, you might make it," Haig said.

"I'll be running along," Saltzman said, looking at his watch. "I'll be back in a few hours. But before I go, I have some supplies for you."

Saltzman took two metal attaché cases stamped *Diplomatic Property of the United States of America* from under the table.

"Whatever you need should be here, Mac," Saltzman said. "A couple of Glock 19s with oversized clips, zoom silencers, plenty of 160-grain hollow points, a secure cell phone programed with all the right numbers, and an assortment of trinkets that any movie spy would be pleased to have. Is there anything else?"

Daniels reached for the cases and rummaged through them.

"Looks okay," he said. "But how about the new Mark 23 instead of these old Glocks?"

"Come, on, Mac," Haig said. "What do you need the H & K Mark 23 for? They cost more than two grand apiece and the way you use things...."

"I need them to stay alive," Daniels said. "I want a weapon with some punch. I don't want to be out there with the wrong tools. The Glock jams, as I well know, but the 23 has wide ejection ports so the shell casings don't get stuck. Get me a clean pair and screw the budget, and don't forget the Knight silencer."

Haig nodded his agreement. He knew Daniels was right.

"And remember, Harry," Daniels said, snapping the steel clasps on the case. "Keep Astrid busy. It's bad enough that we're in the same hotel. See what you can do."

Saltzman smiled.

"See what you can do," Haig said. "You screwed it up with her once. You might not get another chance."

Daniels was not offended. He knew his longtime friend cared about him.

"How do I get you, Ron?" Daniels asked.

"Cell phone. The Admiral is one, I'm two, and Harry is three," Haig said. "What are you going to do first?"

"You mean after I waste a million hours reading your paperwork?"

"Yeah."

"I plan to go back to the hotel and have dinner. Then, according to these reports, I have an Englishman to find," Daniels said. "An Englishman named Michael Montgomery."

* * *

The Chans's cab pulled up to the Water Street address. It was a large wooden building battered by the years of sea salt and rain. The wood had turned gray, a dull gray that had no life to it. The dry rot was evidence of neglect. The flat roof had a slight overhang and the windows were all on the second story to let in light, but to keep curious eyes out. The windows were covered with metal mesh to deter uninvited visitors. The warehouse backed onto the river and had a dock that ran the width of the building. The cleats used for boat moorings were insubstantial, not designed for large vessels. At the front of the building were big garage doors and a loading dock for trucks to discharge their contents. Next to the loading dock was the office. The door held a neatly stenciled sign that read in both English and Chinese: *Hong Kong Import Services.*

Al Wan froze a few feet from the entrance. She had a bad feeling about this place and she did not want to go in. Shadows danced on the side of the building, shadows caused by the setting sun, shadows that made grotesque figures on the gray wood. A sickness rose from the pit of her stomach. She saw death dancing on the side of the building.

"Don't go in there," she pleaded with her husband.

Anson Chan ignored her. He was only minutes away from freedom. Rapping hard on the office door, he waited. Above the stenciled sign was a small window covered with a blackout curtain. A hand grabbed the curtain, pulling it aside. A face in a ski mask appeared in the window momentarily; then disappeared. Anson heard the sound of the dead bolt snapping open. Al Wan jumped.

The door opened slowly, but not very far. Anson tried to push it open, but he couldn't. Poking his head inside, he was surprised to see that no one was there, just a wall—a wall that had been built on an angle to act as a permanent stop. The door could only be opened so that one person at a time could enter. Anson went in first, holding the bag that contained the brown vase. Al Wan passed their suitcases, one at a time, through the narrow opening. When it was her turn to go in, she closed her eyes.

They stood in a long narrow hallway, no more than three-feet wide, with no windows, and a door at the other end. That opened and the man with the ski mask appeared again. Stepping into the hall, he motioned for them to come ahead. Behind them, they heard the outer door lock.

"Let's leave now," Al Wan said. "Put the bag down and let's go."

"You sound like the Al Wan of China, not the Al Wan of Hong Kong. Come, let's deliver this as we agreed to. Then we will be free. Besides, my lovely wife, there seems to be no way out."

Cradling the bag in his arms like a baby, Anson puffed out his chest to reinforce his courage, and walked down the hallway toward the masked man. Al Wan watched him as he swaggered down the hall. He was a fool with that vase, she thought. He should have placed it inside the door and never entered the building. She had seen death dancing on the walls of the warehouse. Everyone dances with death, she knew, but she didn't want an invitation just yet. She felt her heart racing. The pounding was hard. It hurt.

Anson's heart was racing, too, but from excitement not fear. He was about to deliver something of such importance that he had been granted his freedom. This was the Free China Society and he was now part of it. For years he had had a dream, and now he was not only free but also on the front lines to liberate his beloved homeland. He wouldn't have been so confident if he had known more about the Society. The British viewed it as a criminal organization like the IRA and they wanted to shut it down. The Chinese demanded death for all members.

At the end of the passageway was a steel door that had a gun slit in it, but the Chans didn't know about such things. Had there been more light, they might have noticed the stains on the floor, but they wouldn't have known it was blood.

The steel door slowly pulled back allowing the Chans to enter into a gray sterile room. A small overhead light came on and a stairway fell down from the ceiling. Wordlessly the masked man motioned for the Chans to climb the stairs.

At the top of the stairs, three hooded men were sitting at a small table. The man in the center pointed to the two chairs that were in front of the table.

"Do you have it?" he asked.

Anson didn't answer, but took the vase out of the bag and handed it over. The hooded man held up the vase as if he were admiring it; then without a word he smashed it down on the table, shattering it into several pieces. Brushing the sand away, he looked up at the Chans.

"Where is it? Is this some kind of joke?"

"I don't know," Anson said, swallowing hard. "I don't know what was in the vase. I never asked. I wasn't told. I'm just a messenger."

The three men huddled together, their voices so low that the Chans couldn't hear what they were saying. The tears were now streaming down Al Wan's face. Between sobs, she asked him what was going on. He didn't have to tell her that something was very wrong. After what seemed like an eternity, the man in the middle stood up. His clenched fists were on the table, his arms shaking under the strain.

"Where are the papers, the land grant papers?"

Anson began to sweat as his mind raced through the events of the day. Tracing his steps from the cab to the airport, onto the plane, through customs, to where he now stood. He shook his head from side to side.

"I don't know what it is, but I think I know where it is," Al Wan sobbed. She told them about the blonde women who had purchased five similar vases.

"Yes, yes," Anson jumped in, "that's it. Now it makes sense. There must have been a mix up at the store. Our friend Ji Lee is watching the store. He sold the vase to one of the women in the beauty pageant. They were in the store just before we left for the airport. I remember seeing those pretty women at the airport carrying House of Chan bags."

The hooded man sat down hard in the chair, putting his hand on his forehead, his thumbs squeezing his temples. He pushed a button under the table and the stairs opened. Then he motioned for the Chans to leave.

Anson quickly led the way. At the foot of the stairs was another hooded man who led them back to the long hallway. Halfway to the outside door, Anson heard a thud. He whirled around to see his wife crumpled on the floor, the blood pooling around her. Before he could scream, he felt a searing pain in his chest; then feeling nothing, he joined his wife for eternity. Anson Chan and his wife had made it to Hong Kong and at last they were free.

In the upper room, the man who had done the talking was now alone. He had sent the others to find the blonde women with the vase.

It would take a little longer, but he would get it. Pulling off his hood, he ran his fingers through his graying hair. He had enough for one day.

Leaving the building through a rear door, he went to the dock, where a cabin cruiser was waiting for him. He pulled out a Cuban cigar and stepped onto the boat. A deck hand saluted him and asked: "A light, Gen. Xi?"

CHAPTER 18

When there is no wind, row.

— Old Chinese proverb

A S the black Ford pulled up to the front of the Peninsula Hotel, two uniformed bellboys ran to greet Daniels as he stepped from the car. Each reached for a silver case, trying to be helpful, but Daniels waved them off. He didn't want anybody touching them, but he gave the bellboys a couple of dollars anyway.

Inside the hotel, he flashed his passport and asked for the key to his room. The reception clerk politely handed him the key to a penthouse apartment suite where his luggage had been delivered. Not bad, he thought, Reed sure knew how to take care of his people.

Putting down the two silver cases, he inserted the key into the elevator to activate the control panel for the penthouse floor. The doors slid quietly together trapping him in the mirrored rocket as it lifted off for the top of the building. He thought about Astrid, wondering if she was going to be a royal pain in the ass. Perhaps he had made a mistake bedding her on the plane. Damn, he thought, I screwed this up. She was going to make more of this than it was meant to be, but he wasn't sure exactly what that was. Astrid would be around him all the time now, making his almost impossible job even more difficult to do.

Standing in front of the door to the suite, Daniels looked at the plastic key that resembled a credit card, trying to figure out which side of the magnetic strip went down. Swiping the plastic through the electronic lock, he tried the door, but it didn't open. Flipping the card around to realign the magnetic strip didn't work either. Cursing under his breath, he wished for an old fashioned key. One more swipe, he thought, and I'll go back to the desk or kick the damn door down. As he tried to swipe the card again, the door slowly opened and Astrid's head appeared. He was surprised, but knowing her he should have expected it.

"Hurry up and come in," she said. "Before I freeze to death."

Stepping into the suite, he saw that she was naked.

"Do you always come to the door like that?" he asked

"Nope," she purred, "only when I am waiting for you or when I'm about to hop in the tub."

Like a leashed dog, he followed her into the master bedroom. The one thing about Astrid, he thought, naked or dressed, she was sexy as hell. The cheeks of her backside were two-toned, smooth silky white and golden tan. Walking on her toes to keep her feet off the cold marble made her butt sway from side to side. She was in great shape, he observed, firm, seductive, and alluring. Suddenly, he wasn't that tired anymore.

The penthouse apartment had a living room, an office, a dining area, a large master bedroom, a guest bedroom, and three bathrooms. Astrid stayed on her toes until her feet felt the warmth of the soft rug in the master bedroom. Daniels followed her into the bedroom, threw his cases on the bed, and then went with her into the master bath. The two-person Jacuzzi was filled. Astrid slipped in and pressed the button on the top of the tub, bringing the water jets to life. The water became a mass of bubbles, exploding in every direction. Her half-submerged breasts bobbed in the wake of the bubbles. The steam from the water filled the air, fogging the mirrors. Astrid was relaxing, without a care in the world, when Daniels turned off the jets. He sat on the side of the tub.

"What are you doing in my suite?" he asked. Before she could answer, he said: "I have a lot of work to do, Astrid. My ass is dragging on the ground and I need some sleep."

"Silly boy," she gushed in her soft Southern drawl, "you're in my room. You didn't think Daddy was going to spend four thousand a night for you. Your room was on the second floor, but I got it canceled. If you're not happy here, I'm sure you can find a hotel somewhere in Hong Kong. Your luggage is in the other bedroom."

Daniels knew it was impossible to find a decent room anywhere in the city. The turnover was the biggest party in the Far East and there wasn't even a tent for rent. He was trapped.

"All right, Astrid, I'll take the other bedroom and camp out in there, but we have a lot of work to get done. You have stories to do, business to take care of, and I have a lot of photos to take. Let's give your Dad his money's worth."

Astrid didn't say anything, but with a lightening quick move, her hands shot out from the water, grabbing him, and pulling him into the tub.

* * *

The Inspector General was deep in thought when the ringing of his private line startled him. He picked up the receiver, listened, and made some notes on a pad. Then without a word, he hung up and quickly left his office. On the way out, he instructed his secretary to have his car brought around to the front of the building.

"Have a half dozen men go immediately to the House of Chan," he said, giving her the address.

In a matter of minutes the car pulled up to the Chan's store and the Inspector General knew he had the traitors who were going to try to sell the deed to Hong Kong. The driver was out of the car first, running toward the store. The Inspector General followed behind. The driver burst through the door. As the Inspector General entered the store, two more cars pulled up outside and six men jumped out.

Startled by the commotion, Ji Lee came rushing out of the back room and collided with the driver. Grabbing Ji Lee, the driver threw him against the wall. The Inspector General did not have to introduce himself or flash a badge; Ji Lee knew exactly who he was—the Committee for the Defense of the Revolution, the secret police, the Ministry of State Security. Beginning to shake and sweat, his legs barely able to hold him up, Ji Lee knew this was trouble, but he had no idea why.

From the center of the shop, the Inspector General surveyed the premises, ignoring the frightened shopkeeper. He nodded to his driver, who released his prisoner. Ji Lee was too scared to notice the blood running from his nose. Motioning with his finger, the Inspector General beckoned to Ji Lee.

"Are you Anson Chan?"

Looking at the floor, Ji Lee shook his head.

"Do you know where he is?"

Daring not to even raise his eyes Ji Lee shook his head yes.

"Can you speak?"

Ji Lee bobbed his head up and down.

"Where is he?" a frustrated Inspector General demanded.

Ji Lee answered in a whisper, his voiced cracking. He told the Inspector General the Chans were on vacation in Hong Kong, while he was watching the store.

"Very well. Sit down," the Inspector General said. "Search the place."

The men went to work searching the store. Ji Lee sat in a chair expecting at any moment to meet his ancestors. With every crash he heard, he jumped. For the half hour it took to search the store, Ji Lee didn't move. The Inspector General stood to the side by the counter, while his men carried out their orders, saying nothing. Noticing the sand-filled vases, he picked one up and examined it from every angle. He popped the cork on one of them and let some of the fine sand pour over his fingers. Finishing their search, his men admitted they had found nothing.

Too late, the Inspector General thought. The land grant had slipped through his fingers, just like the sand. The Inspector General could picture Gov. Patten presenting the deed to the United Nations. Then he had a more horrifying thought—Gen. Xi.

"Did Anson Chan mention anything about a land grant document?" he asked.

The confused look on Ji Lee's face answered the Inspector General's question.

"Ji Lee," he continued in a softer tone, hoping to calm the man's fears. "Please think. Try to answer my questions very carefully. Your country's future depends on it."

Ji Lee was puzzled. What could he possibly know that would be so important? He would not lie to the secret police, knowing what would happen to him if he did. He would just disappear. Ji Lee was not sure what he could do to help his country, but he would try.

"What did the Chans take with them to Hong Kong? Who had come to the store this morning? What did they buy?"

Ji Lee thought long and hard on these easy questions, but he had to have the right answers. Wrong answers in this game could cause him to lose his life.

"The Chans took some suitcases, but I don't know what was in them," Ji Lee said. "I am staying in the back apartment, where I have been many times. Nothing is missing that I can see."

The ringing of the cell phone interrupted Ji Lee, who immediately stopped speaking. The Inspector General turned away from Ji Lee, flipping open his phone. Airport security was confirming that the Chans had left on a flight for Hong Kong. They had all the necessary papers, nothing out of the ordinary. He slowly closed the phone turning back to Ji Lee.

"Go ahead," the Inspector general said.

"Anson had also taken one of the reproduction antique vases that had been delivered this morning. May I stand?" Ji Lee asked.

The Inspector General nodded.

Going behind the counter, Ji Lee took out the receipt for the vases that had been delivered that morning and handed it to the Inspector General.

The Inspector General gave the receipt to one of his men.

"Is that all?" he asked, as he tossed one of the vases to his driver.

"Yes," Ji Lee said, hoping that he had said the right thing.

"Was the vase that Chan took empty?" the Inspector General asked.

Thinking he had given the wrong answer, Ji Lee started to lose his composure.

"No. It was filled with sand, sir, just like the one you took, sir. Sand is a means of protecting the vase during shipment."

"But the vase wasn't shipped, the Chans took it with them," the Inspector General said.

Taking a piece of paper from the counter, the Inspector General placed it into an empty vase; then he poured the sand from another vase, covering the paper completely. Holding the vase up to the light he could not see anything.

The Inspector General knew the answer before he called, but he wanted to be sure. He called airport security to inquire if their X-ray machines could have penetrated the sand-filled vase to detect a piece of paper. What he heard confirmed his worst fears. The X-rays were useless in seeing through sand. The Chans had walked out of China with the deed to Hong Kong.

Ji Lee, in his most polite voice, spoke: "Sir, I also sold other vases this morning. Five to be exact. They were sold to four beautiful Western women, tourists."

"Describe them."

The stately girls had made a lasting impression on Ji Lee.

"All four were tall," he said, holding his hand above his head to indicate their height to be about six feet. Then he held his hands in a cupped fashion in front of his chest to indicate that they were all quite well endowed.

"They all had blonde hair and blue eyes," Ji Lee continued.

The Inspector General's eyes rolled up as if the answer was on the ceiling. He knew that the beauty pageant contestants had left China that day for Hong Kong. Did this bungling fool sell the vase to one of them, instead of the Chans taking it to Hong Kong? he wondered.

But there was still hope, he thought. Thankfully, Chi was in Hong Kong. The Inspector General had a few of his men planted in the Hong Kong customs office. It would be easy to find out where the Chans were and very easy to find the Galaxy pageant women.

"Your friends will not be returning to China," he said to Ji Lee. "I wish you good luck with your new store."

* * *

Stretched out on his sister's couch, Chi was relaxing after dinner when he was jarred by the sudden ringing of his cell phone. He answered it.

"Just listen," the Inspector General said.

He filled Chi in on what he had just learned. There were six persons who may be in possession of the land grant: the Chans and four women from the beauty pageant. The Inspector General gave Chi as much detail as he could over a non-secure line.

"Chi, a full report will be waiting for you in the usual place. You must do whatever is necessary. Do not fail! The deed must not reach the

British or anyone else. Spare no one, use everyone, and remember: When there is no wind, row."

The phone went dead.

CHAPTER 19

He who chases two rabbits catches none.

— Old Chinese proverb

ASTRID and Daniels were lying naked in bed. He was face down, while she was sleeping on her back, her head supported by several pillows. Daniels listened to her rhythmic breathing, trying to deny to himself that their relationship might work. Twice now he succumbed to her seduction. Twice he had made a mistake.

The ringing of the phone on the bedside table startled Daniels, but he managed to pick up the receiver before the second ring. Not wanting to wake Astrid, he answered in a soft whisper.

"Did I wake you?"

Daniels immediately recognized the deep baritone voice of Michael Montgomery. They had worked together in the past and the two men had developed a healthy respect for each other. But at times their friendly rivalry had caused friction. Daniels contended Montgomery was too conservative, while Montgomery accused Daniels of being a cowboy.

"It's almost midnight. What do you think?" Daniels said.

"I think we need to talk."

"Hold on," Daniels whispered. "I want to change phones. Astrid is sleeping and I don't want to wake her."

Once in his own bedroom, Daniels picked up the extension.

"Did I call at an inappropriate time?" Montgomery asked.

"You're bloody awful, Michael. And since when do you care? If you cared, you wouldn't have called at midnight."

"I knew you were in town and I do need to see you. We have precious little time left. Can we meet?"

"Sure. When?"

"Now," Montgomery answered. "I have a car downstairs waiting for you."

"I'll be down in front of the hotel in fifteen minutes."

Wiggling into a pair of old blue jeans and a T-shirt, Daniels finished dressing and slipped on his boots. As he was loading his pockets with his wallet, money, and keys, he heard Astrid's voice.

"Where are you going?" she asked from the doorway.

She was wearing only a T-shirt, making Daniels wish he was going back to bed with her and not meeting Montgomery in the middle of the night.

"I thought we would have a late dinner," she said. "I can order from room service."

No matter what Daniels said, he knew it wasn't going to work. How he wished now he had his own room. When he tried to explain, she would hear what she wanted to hear, be pissed at him, and he would be looking for a place to sleep.

"I'm sorry, Astrid. An old friend called and I agreed to meet him. It was late. I thought you were sleeping," he said, bracing himself for an emotional eruption. Her insatiable jealousy in the past had driven him crazy and had driven them apart.

"Okay, Mac. See you in the morning. Good night."

With that, she turned and walked away, leaving Daniels stunned. His eyes followed her until she shut the bedroom door.

* * *

Stepping out of the hotel's revolving doors into the cool evening air felt good. The aroma of the sea, just a block away, was refreshing after the air-conditioning in the suite. He was thinking about Astrid when the romance of the evening was spoiled by the sight of Winston Williams. The commissioner of foreign affairs was wearing a three-piece suit and holding open the door of a dark blue Austin sedan.

As he approached the car, Williams stepped forward to greet him, his hand extended.

"How did that S.O.B. Montgomery know that I would come out and play?" Daniels asked, shaking hands.

"You know I can't tell you Michael's secrets," Williams said, getting in the car.

Daniels had met Williams several years before while working with Montgomery.

"You know how important this is to us," Williams said. "We are all quite anxious to compare notes with you."

Daniels could see that Williams was quite worried and he understood why. The great powers were playing political football with Hong Kong in a game where the losers might end up starting a world war. It was a game with no winners. Regardless of what happened, the seven million people who had lived as British subjects were now in turmoil. Daniels may not have majored in political science at Princeton, but he understood that the turnover of Hong Kong to China was not what most of the residents wanted.

Williams peppered Daniels with questions—questions that Daniels managed to avoid answering. Talking about his assignment with anyone, let alone with someone who was not cleared by the agency, regardless of the position he held with the British government, was something he didn't do. Williams talked on for the entire trip to the government office building, as Daniels listened. Amateurs, he thought, would get us all killed.

Pulling his car into the underground parking lot, Williams led Daniels down a dark corridor. After he passed a swipe card through the electric reader, a small cover flipped open to reveal a keypad which required a personal code. Giving Williams privacy, Daniels looked away as Williams punched in his five digit number. The door opened into a small hall that had no exits other than the elevator. Williams had to repeat the same process using a swipe card and a personal code in order to call for the elevator. In the elevator, Williams repeated the security procedure and the elevator started to rise.

From his inner pocket Williams took an identity card and pinned it to his suit coat. Daniels was watching the demonstration, keeping his comments to himself. Williams, ever proud of British efficiency, told Daniels that the system was fail proof.

"If someone could gain entry, which they couldn't, they would be trapped in the hall. There is no way out, except by the elevator and without the swipe card and a code you're stuck," Williams said.

Daniels shook his head.

"Here, here, old man, you don't think you could get in, do you? Now really," Williams said.

"With a double-A battery and two wires, you can create a circuit that the lock would react to—opening the keypad."

"Granted, but what about the codes? Two false entries shut down the system and call security."

"I know, but once you punch in 8-2-5-4-8, the door will open," Daniels said.

"How did you know my personal code?" Williams said, aghast.

"Easy. It's your birthday, August twenty-fifth, nineteen forty eight. It's right there on your identity card. Bad choice of codes, Winston," he said.

Muttering to himself about changing his code, Williams led Daniels down the hall to the conference room. Sitting at the head of the table, his feet up on the fine dark wood, was an obviously exhausted Montgomery. The strain of the past few days showed on his face. Daniels couldn't remember seeing him look so disheveled: rolled up sleeves, no tie, a five o'clock shadow, and dark circles under his reddened eyes.

Along the wall across from the windows was a credenza used as a serving table. In the center there was a large platter of sandwiches and a plate of chocolate chip cookies. At the other end of the table, lined up in formation, were a variety of sodas, juices, and beers.

"Mind if I grab a sandwich? I'm starved," Daniels said.

"That's why they're here. Get me a beer, please," Montgomery said.

Daniels took several sandwiches, cookies, and a can of Diet Coke. He handed Montgomery a beer and sat down next to him, putting his feet up on the table.

"Nice boots," Montgomery said.

"Those are nice Guccis. I like those little tassels, so feminine," Daniels said.

Montgomery waited for Daniels to finish with the sandwiches before reaching inside his jacket pocket and coming out with two cigars. He handed one to Daniels, who sniffed it, then stuffed it in his pocket.

"Later," he said. "For now, it's these cookies."

Williams, who had followed Daniels into the room, was sitting across the table from Montgomery and him. He was anxious to get started with the meeting and his impatience showed. Finally, he spoke: "Mr. Daniels, are you ready to compare notes or are you going to eat cookies all night?"

The look on Montgomery's face showed he disapproved of Williams's remark.

"Hey, Michael these are really good. You'll have to give me the recipe," Daniels said, eating more cookies.

Realizing Daniels was having fun with Williams, Montgomery played along.

"A very good friend of mine made them, Mac. I'll ask her. By the way, is it true you are the best America has?"

"Best at what?" Daniels asked innocently.

"Not your sex life. Hell, you're an American."

"For this I left a naked lady to come here and be abused?"

"Your president called the prime minister and told him that his best field agent was being sent here to help. But let me remind you that the last time you offered your help, well, I'm sure you remember what happened."

"I rather not go there."

"Gentlemen, please. This is serious," Williams said. "I'm sorry if I was out of order before, but we should get down to business."

"Right," Daniels said. "But first would you do me a favor?"

"Of course, anything," Williams said.

"Would you be kind enough to leave the room," Daniels said.

Williams took the request as if his wife had asked for a divorce. He was genuinely upset that anyone would question his loyalty to the crown and country, but his protestations were useless.

"Please leave the room, Winston. No one doubts your patriotism or your ability to keep a secret, but it's my life on the line, not yours. You are a rank amateur whose mistakes could cost someone his life and it's not going to be mine," Daniels said.

Williams glanced over to Montgomery, looking for an ally. Montgomery had been silent, knowing that Daniels was right. With no reaction from his friend, a wounded Williams left the room.

Before he brought Daniels up to speed, Montgomery wanted to be sure that everyone understood the ground rules.

"Your president has assured the prime minister that the United States would be in full support of our efforts to find the land grant documents, this deed, so we may keep what is rightfully ours. You are here at the direct request of the British government and by presidential order to cooperate with SIS. I'm in charge of this operation and you are working for me. If you locate the deed, you are to turn it over to me immediately. Any questions?"

Daniels shook his head. He wasn't about to argue until he had heard what Montgomery had to say. There would be time to argue later. Whatever President Clark told the prime minister was of no concern to Daniels. He had specific orders from the Admiral, not the president. He worked for the Admiral, who was in charge of this operation, and Special Ops was certainly more involved than the British knew. The president, he knew, didn't want to know all the gory details, he just wanted results. The decision on the fate of the deed had not yet been decided.

Montgomery told Daniels about his meeting Gen. Xi at the Peninsula Hotel and later at the Peak, giving him all the details except for his trip to Liz Browning's home. He revealed his authorization to pay up to a billion dollars for the land grant documents, raising Daniels's eyebrows.

"If Xi has the documents, why not pay him and end all the bullshit? Seems simple enough," Daniels said.

"For one thing, we don't trust him. For another, he has not set up a time for the exchange. We have to keep looking until we have it or he comes through. Thanks to your satellites, we do know that there is a massive Chinese troop build up."

Daniels knew about the movements of the Chinese armies. He also knew much more than he told Montgomery. Two Chinese submarines had left port several days before armed with nuclear missiles. It looked as if they might be heading for the Atlantic. The British reaction, understandably, would be a preemptive strike, which would escalate into world war. The Navy had two Los Angeles-class attack submarines following the Chinese. If it became necessary, they would take them out before the subs were in launching range of Great Britain.

"The question," Montgomery said, "is whether Xi wants to sell the deed and defect or sell the deed and start a war. What's your take on this mess, Mac?"

"If Xi sold the deed and did defect, wouldn't someone else direct military operations? There must be back up plans."

"Xi runs the central committee for the entire military operation, the planning unit for the PLA. He has promised us two things: the secret plans for the attack and domination of Asia, which in itself is of great value. More important, he has also promised the defection of the entire general staff."

"Is the entire general staff here in Hong Kong?" Daniels asked.

"No. They're spread out all over the place to put the operation into effect if we try to double cross Xi. So, what shall we do?" Montgomery said.

"What are the Russians up to? Somehow I don't think Zimkeroff is here for the cultural aspects of the turnover," Daniels said.

"Zimkeroff is also trying to sell the land grant papers to the Chinese to finance a new Russian revolution. He's at the Sheraton with Petroff and a couple of his staff officers are up the block at the Ambassador," Montgomery said.

"Xi's at the Peninsula and Zimkeroff's at the Sheraton. Not too bad for good egalitarian Communists," Daniels said. "You stay with the Chinese and I'll pay a visit to the Russians. If they want money, I'm sure Uncle Sam has a few rubles to spread around."

Daniels had stopped talking to gather his thoughts when Liz Browning entered the room. She handed Montgomery an envelope and left without a word. Eyeing her, Daniels watched her as she left.

"I'll bet that's your friend the cookie maker. Nice cookies," Daniels said.

Montgomery opened the envelope, took out several black-and-white photos and a typed report. Glancing at the photographs of a dead Chinese man and woman, he handed them to Daniels, and began reading the report aloud:

"The two bodies were found floating in the lower harbor, both shot with .38-caliber bullets. The victims had Chinese passports, identifying them as Anson Chan and Al Wan Chan, who had arrived yesterday from Beijing. Robbery was not the motive. Both were in possession of money and jewelry."

Montgomery continued reading for several more minutes, handing each sheet to Daniels as he finished. In spite of their ghastly appearance, Daniels recognized the people in the picture as the couple who were in the taxi line ahead of him. A young couple, he remembered clearly, just tourists, lugging their baggage about. Then it came to him. There was something about the bag the man had been so carefully carrying.

"This mean anything to you, Mac?"

"Nope," he lied. "Why is this an issue for SIS? Murder is a police matter."

"Why do a couple of tourists from the mainland, who are not here more than an hour, get murdered and not robbed? Not even their passports were taken. No one made an attempt to make this appear as a robbery," Montgomery said. "That's strange enough to attract our attention."

By three in morning, both Daniels and Montgomery desperately needed some sleep. They decided to call it a night, agreeing to meet again later.

When Daniels had all of Montgomery's numbers, he asked him where he was staying.

"With the cookie maker."

Daniels gave him a smile.

"Thought so. I saw the look you gave me when I was checking her out. Nice cookies," Daniels said, grabbing a few more cookies as he was leaving.

When the elevator door opened Williams was waiting to drive Daniels back to his hotel. Daniels was going to apologize for asking him to leave the room, but he decided against it. There was no sense in opening the wound. The ride back was quick and silent.

This time he managed to unlock the door to the suite and quietly slipped into his bedroom. He needed some rest. He was going to be busy and his first stop was 205 Water Street. Sitting on the side of the bed, he managed to kick off his boots; then fully dressed, he stretched across the bed. It felt good as his body sunk into the mattress. He didn't want to move ever again.

He tried to put the day's events out of his mind, but that was impossible. Xi and Zimkeroff were like a merry-go-round in his head. Xi didn't have the deed, neither did Zimkeroff. Yet both of them were offering to sell it. Which one would get it, Xi or Zimkeroff? Which one could be dealt with? He who chases two rabbits catches none, he thought, remembering the old Chinese proverb. Turning over to get more comfortable, he felt something on the bed.

What now? he wondered.

He snapped on the light by the bed. Lying next to him was a thick envelope. He opened it up, finding the contact sheets from the shoot he had done at the airport. Too tired to care, he tossed the envelope on the floor and turned off the light.

CHAPTER 20

In the light of day one sees things clearly.

— Old Chinese proverb

❧

"I'LL be over to get you," Chi said into the dead phone line after the Inspector General had hung up. "See you soon."

He snapped his cell phone shut and told his sister he had to leave.

"Is something wrong?" Lu An asked.

"No," he lied. "In fact, that was a pleasant call, a good news call, from a friend of mine who just got in from China. To tell the truth, I'm anxious to see her. She just cleared customs and is waiting for me to pick her up at the airport."

"Don't tell me you finally have a girlfriend," Lu An said, with a smile.

"No," he protested. "She's just a friend. Now, I've got to be going."

He gave her a kiss on the cheek before he left.

As Chi drove away, he praised himself for the deception. He felt sure Lu An had believed him. He didn't mind lying to her when it was necessary for the greater good, the good of China. Brought up on lies, fed on lies, and believing lies to be the truth, Chi couldn't tell the difference. His mother's words came to him: a lie has many lives. But she was just a foolish old woman, he thought.

Quickly putting thoughts of his mother out of his mind, he knew he had to find the land grant documents without the help of the Russians. If he failed, Chi had been told privately by the Inspector General, the government would meet the Russian's price—the BCV. The thought of that made him shudder, but not because it was the newest weapon of mass destruction—he didn't care if they killed off the rest of the world. It just annoyed him that they would have China's most secret weapon. Shocked that the Supreme Leader had agreed to swap BCV for the deed, Chi thought money, a billion US dollars, was the way to get Zimkeroff's help without giving up the BCV. He couldn't understand how the Russians could be so sure they would have the land grant documents. Their confidence was maddening. What did they know?

Driving down Salisbury Road, Chi came to a traffic light at the corner of Nathan Road. To his right were the Sheraton and the Peninsula Hotels. Gen. Xi was in one of the rooms, he thought, ready to start World War III. With Xi on one side and Zimkeroff on the other, what a predicament to be in. He wondered which one was more dangerous. Answering his own question, Chi decided Zimkeroff was. What were the Russians going to do with BCV? It made no sense to him.

As he sat staring at the two hotels, the cars behind him began honking their horns, wanting him to move on. Amid the noise, the Inspector General's words came to him: "When there is no wind, row." It was time for him to row—to go on the offensive. Chi wasn't going to wait any longer. He was going to make something happen. Hitting the accelerator, he drove up to the Sheraton Hotel.

* * *

"Daddy, Daddy," Jessica Adams yelled, running toward her father. Bending down and taking her in his arms, Adams gave her a kiss and a hug.

"Aren't you up late, Jess?" he said, putting her down. Lu An saw the strain on her husband's face and the dark lines under his eyes. His lack of sleep showed.

Lu An took Jessica upstairs to put her to bed. When she came back down, she found Adams deep in thought, waiting for her.

She gave him a gentle hug; then she guided him into his favorite chair, an old oversized recliner, big enough for the two of them. He settled in and closed his eyes. When he opened them, Lu An was standing there with a large martini. He moved just enough to take it from her. Then she climbed into the chair and put her head on his chest. Feeling safe, she snuggled under his protective arm.

"Chi was here," she said. "And he's got a girlfriend."

"Why didn't he stay for a drink and spend the night?"

"He received a call from his girlfriend. She's just arrived from China. He was going to the airport to pick her up."

Odd, Adams thought, there were no late night flights from China. He was going to say something to Lu An, but she was half asleep and he was too tired to give it much thought.

* * *

Under the portico of the Sheraton Hotel, the night valet ran over to the car to open the door for Chi.

"Checking in, sir?"

Chi didn't answer. He would never think of staying in a place like this. Pushing his way through the revolving door, he stepped into the lobby. Ignoring its splendor, he found a house phone and dialed Zimkeroff's room.

"Yes."

Recognizing Petroff's voice, Chi decided not to apologize for the late night call. Identifying himself, he asked to speak with Zimkeroff.

"Yes, what is it?" Zimkeroff said, after a minute.

"General, I may not be able to deliver what you ordered, but I might have a substitute you may be able to use. May I come up to see you? I'm calling from the lobby phone."

"Call me back in ten minutes." Zimkeroff said, rolling his eyes toward the ceiling as he hung up the phone.

"At least the idiot had the sense to be vague on the phone," Zimkeroff said to Petroff. "You would think he would have enough sense to know the phone was tapped. I gave the moron my secure cell number, why didn't he use it?"

It was a question that Petroff wasn't about to answer.

"What does he want, General?"

"He wants to come up and see me."

"Not a good idea with the SIS all over the place."

"Sergeant Major, let's have some fun," Zimkeroff said, picking up a piece of hotel stationery and writing something down for Petroff to read.

* * *

Exactly ten minutes later the phone rang. This time Zimkeroff answered it himself.

"Go to bar and wait. I'll be down," Zimkeroff said.

Like an obedient servant Chi did as he was told, meandering through the lobby, trying to be inconspicuous as possible. That was a waste of time because as soon as he had dialed Zimkeroff's room, the lobby surveillance team was put on alert. His every step was being watched and recorded by the SIS agents in the lobby.

Chi stopped in front of the hotel's all-night bar, the Union Jack. A dozen flags were hung around the perimeter of the bar. Trying to act like a tourist, Chi took the time to read the card attached to a flag staff. It read: *The Union Jack is the name given to the national flag of the United Kingdom. It is formed by the union of the crosses of St. George, St. Andrew, and St. Patrick.*

The bar was a late night spot for lovers and cheaters, a discreet meeting place, and home of the famous high-priced Hong Kong working girls. The tables in the bar were made of old hatch covers; the walls were covered with nautical designs. Models of old British warships were on display in glass cases, shadowed by the portraits of famous admirals and generals, including one of Major General H. R. Powell.

Chi found a seat at the end of the teak bar. He took the second stool from the end, leaving a place for Zimkeroff. On the other side of him was another seat and next to that was a man who was deep in conversation with a very attractive lady. The bartender, dressed in a naval uniform, asked: "What are you drinking, mate?"

Surveying the amply stocked bar, Chi ordered a glass of Ng Ka P'ei wine.

The bartender shook his head. "Not here, mate, try again," he said.

"Do you have Mooi Kwai Lo?" Chi asked.

"Sorry, this is an English bar. If you want that Chinese stuff, you should go over to one of the joints across town. We don't carry Chinese wine like that, no demand for it. How about a Beefeater with a splash of tonic?"

"Why not?" Chi said, remembering that after July 1, he would be sure that this joint carried Chinese wines.

The bartender prepared his drink, serving it in a tall glass decorated with naval flags. Nursing his gin and turning around every few minutes to check the doorway made it obvious that he was waiting for someone. A few more couples entered the Union Jack, one took a table in the corner; the other sat at the other end of the bar. They were SIS agents choosing their positions carefully, watching the lobby, the elevator, and Chi. From the corner of his eye, Chi saw a tall Chinese woman wearing a low-cut dress stroll slowly into the bar. She was well built for a Chinese woman, Chi thought, too busty, probably implants. He disapproved. The slit up her dress revealed long shapely legs as she glided across the floor toward the bar. In the center of the room she stopped and glanced around at her targets. Her radar locked onto Chi.

Damn it, he thought. He didn't want to make a scene, but he didn't need the general finding him with a prostitute. The woman's breast brushed against him when she climbed onto the adjoining bar stool, the one Chi had saved for Zimkeroff. Chi could smell the overpowering aroma of her perfume, but he had no time for her.

"Sorry, that seat is taken," he said.

"Yes, I know. I have it. Thank you."

She signaled the bartender, who came right over to her.

"A White Russian," she said.

As the bartender was mixing her drink, she turned to Chi, rubbing her breasts against him. "Do you like White Russians?" she asked.

Chi got the message. Zimkeroff must have sent her.

"They're too rich for me, I can't get them down," Chi said, trying to be witty.

To anyone watching, this was nothing more than one of the girls working her customer. The role of the willing customer became easy for Chi to play. He was hooked. Her name was Anna and she was as charming as she was beautiful—the essence of Oriental erotic mysticism. At times, he was embarrassed that Anna had such an obvious effect on him. Chi changed his position on implants. They weren't so bad, after all. Several drinks and an hour later, Chi left the bar arm in arm with his new girl. The SIS couple was right behind.

Out in the lobby, another SIS couple was standing at the elevator when Chi arrived. The four SIS agents entered the elevator with Chi. One of the agents standing by the control panel turned to Chi and asked him his floor.

Not giving Chi a chance to answer Anna said: "Three, please."

Chi suppressed his surprise at her answer, knowing Zimkeroff was on another floor. He was in a state of controlled panic. Was there a misunderstanding? Had he actually picked up a hooker? Chi hoped he hadn't gotten the signals mixed up.

As the elevator door slid open, Anna took Chi by the arm and led him down the hall. A SIS couple also got off the elevator, going down the hall in the opposite direction. Standing in front of the room, Anna fumbled through her purse to find her key, finally handing it to Chi. He ran it through the electric lock reader. Opening the door to the darkened room, they stepped inside.

As Chi was riding up in the elevator, Zimkeroff was coming down in another. He had to make a show of missing Chi to throw the SIS agents off the trail. Stepping off the elevator, Zimkeroff marched across the lobby to the Union Jack. Standing there in the doorway, his huge body filling the opening, hands on hips, Zimkeroff surveyed the room. Not finding Chi, he asked the bartender if had seen a man fitting Chi's description. The bartender told him that he left with a hooker. Zimkeroff shook his head in disgust, said something, and left. As soon as Zimkeroff left the room, the SIS agent, who had been sitting at the bar, beckoned the bartender over.

"I heard most of the conversation you had with that man who just left, but he said something as he left what was it?"

"He called the Chinese bloke an arsehole."

Zimkeroff stomped across the lobby, seemingly furious with Chi's behavior. As he stepped into the elevator, he was followed by several men, all entering the elevator at the same time. The SIS agent was blocked from getting on. The door closed in his face.

Inside the elevator, Zimkeroff exchanged jackets with one of the men.

"Perfect timing. Did you see the expression on the British agent's face when he couldn't get in? I thought he was going to cry. I almost felt sorry for him," Zimkeroff said.

They all laughed.

"When you get off the elevator, don't walk, march down to my suite," Zimkeroff said to the man with whom he had exchanged jackets.

"Petroff has already removed some of the hallway light bulbs, so in the dark the SIS surveillance team will mistake you for me. Here's the key. Wait there for me."

The SIS agent in the lobby watched the outside indicator lights, waiting to see where the elevator stopped. On the radio to his team members, he counted off the floors.

"The elevator stopped at nine," he reported.

When the elevator came to Zimkeroff's floor, he radioed: "The bear is home. Be careful."

* * *

As Chi closed the door behind him, Anna turned on the lights. He was surprised by the size of the room and its luxurious appointments. Pulling the drapes closed, Anna turned on the soft table lamp, shut off the harsh overhead lights, and flipped on the CD player. Chi watched her as she glided about the room creating an atmosphere for romance. Soft music filled the room while she turned down the bed. Anna took Chi's hand and tried to pull him to the bed. Resisting her, he drew back his hand abruptly.

"Oh, baby," she cooed. "What's wrong? Don't be shy."

Very gently, she took his hand again, slowly and easily pulling him toward the bed. This time he gave way, following her to the bed.

"Come on, baby. Let's get undressed."

Chi could smell her intoxicating aroma. Staring at her breasts, he could see the outline of her nipples and his imagination took over.

"Come on," she said.

Reaching around her back, Anna unzipped her dress and let it fall slowly to the floor. She was naked underneath. Climbing into bed, Anna pulled the sheets between her legs up to her breast line. The sheet lay between her long shapely legs, symbolic of where he should be. Patting the bed, Anna mouthed the words "Come here," and ran her hands over her body, allowing them to come to rest between her legs. Her tongue moistened her lips; they seemed to glisten, inviting him to come closer.

"Aren't you going to get undressed?" she whispered sexily.

Anna had done her job—Chi had forgotten why he was there. It would have only taken him a few seconds to remember his "deed" mission, but that would have been if he hadn't been thinking with his other head that throbbed in his pants. Sitting on the edge of the bed to untie his shoes, he felt her hands running down his back; then slowly working their way around the front of him, unbuttoning his shirt. Feeling her breasts pressing against his back, he fumbled as he tried to unbutton his pants. Anna proved more adept than he was, managing to help him off with his pants.

She was now kneeling on the bed, her naked body exposed to him. She pressed her mouth against his stomach, her tongue flicking across his skin, her head moving down, her hands pulling him close. Anna tugged his boxer shorts until they fell to the floor; his erect manhood throbbed, ready to explode. She stopped for a moment, seeing a man in the doorway of the adjoining room.

Silently, Petroff stepped into the room and held a finger up to his mouth to indicate silence. Dropping his hands down to cover himself, Chi was embarrassed by his nudity. Petroff didn't seem to notice, motioning for Chi to go follow him. Trying to conceal his now limp member, Chi shuffled off into the adjoining room. Closing the door behind Chi, Petroff stayed with Anna.

In the next room, sitting on the edge of the bed, Zimkeroff threw Chi one of the hotel's plush terrycloth robes.

"Why the elaborate ploy?" Chi asked, tying the sash around his waist.

"Because you are an idiot. I am under surveillance by the British. Who did you think all those people in the bar and on the elevator were? My phone line is tapped. Fool, why didn't you use the number I gave you?"

"I did not think," Chi said, realizing he had screwed up.

"The next time you want to see me, call me on the secure number and I'll meet you. It's easier for me to lose these idiots out in the street than in here. Now what do you want?"

"To make a deal," Chi said.

"Good," Zimkeroff said. "You know the deed arrived here in Hong Kong."

Chi felt his heart skip a beat, wondering how Zimkeroff knew. He tried not to show any emotion, but Zimkeroff was quick to spot his reaction.

"You seemed surprised," Zimkeroff said. "Surprised that the deed is here or surprised that I know?"

Chi decided that it was no use to lie to Zimkeroff. He was an old fox, not easily fooled by a young rabbit.

"I'm surprised you know the land grant documents are here. How did you know so fast? I just found out myself." Chi said.

"It's a professional secret."

"I have permission to give you one vial of the BCV or one hundred million dollars. Why don't you take the money?"

"Money? What do I need money for? I have no family. We used to be a proud nation until the Americans took it away. Wait until you feel their economic hammer beating on you day and night. Wait until you have to change your way of life to please the Americans. We were once a great country, now we are third-rate. No, it's not money; it's a matter of honor. I want the BCV."

"Honor! All this for honor!" Chi said, getting angry. "There's more to this than honor, General. How much will it take, two, three hundred million? How much do you want for the deed?"

"Not even a billion dollars. I want the BCV, all twelve vials that you have coming to Hong Kong. Otherwise, you can kiss my ass and Hong Kong good-bye. If I sell the deed to the British, I'll have money and you will have war. The British will have this matter in the UN, before the World Court, and anyplace else they can gather popular support. Legally, Hong Kong belongs to them, don't forget that Chi. Of course, that crazy old bastard Gen. Xi believes he can win a war against the Americans. Wait until the cruise missiles start hitting your radar and the stealth bombers knock out your communications. Then, the long-range heavy bombers start taking apart your cities one by one, while your air force is powerless to stop them. You may have Hong Kong, but not much else. So stop fucking with me and give me what I want."

"Is this all for honor?"

"No, part for honor, part for revenge."

"You are going to use the BCV, aren't you?" Chi asked. "You're willing to kill millions of people for revenge."

"Xi's troops are ready to invade Korea, Viet Nam, and Hong Kong. Are you not ready to kill millions? Won't millions of Chinese die? And for what? I will use some of the BCV on the Americans, the rest of it, well, that's my business."

"When do I see the deed?" Chi asked.

"When do I get my BCV?"

Chi was silent, groping for an answer. The silence was broken by the moans coming from the next room.

"Petroff gives his all for his country," Zimkeroff said. "I'll show you the deed two days before the turnover, June 29th. However, once you see it, read it, and you are satisfied, I get my vials of BCV. Agreed?"

Chi nodded his consent.

Zimkeroff opened the door to the adjoining room. A naked Petroff was sitting on the bed smoking a cigarette. Anna was gone.

Putting out his cigarette, Petroff gathered up his clothes and marched back to the other room without a word. Passing Chi, he gave the Chinese agent a slap on the back of the head.

That humiliating slap made Chi vow he was going to win in the end. He had no intention of giving Zimkeroff anything. There were only two possibilities. Either he had to find the deed before Zimkeroff or give Zimkeroff the vials, but never let him leave with them.

Despite the Inspector General's warning, Chi knew that he had to tell Gen. Xi about what had happened. The Peninsula Hotel would be his first stop in the morning. He would report to Gen. Xi in the light of day when one saw things clearly.

CHAPTER 21

Keep your friends close, your enemies closer.

— Old Chinese proverb

✿

THE early light of dawn crept through the heavy blinds slowly making its way across the room toward Chi's bed. The sun was his alarm clock, but this morning he didn't want to rise. He was tired, having tossed and turned all night. Chi was haunted by Zimkeroff and no matter how he had tried to put him out of his mind, the Russian general was always there. Unless he found the land grant papers first, Zimkeroff would win. Now Chi also had to face Gen. Xi. He wished he could stay in bed and make the day go away. But knowing it was no use, he finally got up.

When Hong Kong International had been expanded, new terminals had been built in the southeast part of the airport and the facilities to the northwest were used for corporate headquarters, general maintenance, and cargo storage. No one had questioned the purchase of one of the largest hangars by Chinese Civil Air Administration, the owner and operator of the People's Republic of China Airline. The local newspapers ran the story on the financial pages, not considering it a real news item. The CAAC quickly turned the new facility into the center of southern Asian espionage for China, as well as Chi's Hong Kong home and office.

His apartment was small, but adequate for his needs. It had a bedroom, a bathroom, and a kitchen—perfect for a bachelor, perfect for a spy, perfect for someone to receive and send information back and forth to China with impunity. The apartment had two entrances. One door led from the bedroom to an outside stairway, which led down to the parking area. The other door led from the kitchen to Chi's office, an ultra modern communications center. The apartment and office were located on the second floor of the airplane hangar and, because it was owned by CAAC, it was considered foreign territory with diplomatic immunity.

127

The office was Chi's base of operations when he was in Hong Kong. It was equipped with all the latest communications devices, including microwave satellite transmission lines, high-speed secure fax lines, and several secure phone lines. The whole package was protected by an elaborate security system. From his office Chi kept the stream of information going back and forth to Beijing through the diplomatic cargo stored on the first floor. The hangar had also become a safe house for Chinese agents passing through Hong Kong.

The hangar was three-stories high, open from top to bottom, with the exception of the office-apartment on the second floor. The top of the hangar was ringed by a catwalk running the perimeter of the building. A set of tracks belonging to an overhead crane ran below the catwalk. At various parts of the catwalk there were stairs leading down to the second floor and one stairway led up to the roof. The end of the catwalk opened onto an operating platform where the crane operator worked. Opposite the platform on the second floor was the office. The area outside the second-floor office was a steel deck that had stairs leading up to the catwalk and another leading down to the first floor. The steel deck was twenty feet deep, running the entire width of the building. At the end of the deck, overlooking the hangar, was a steel pipe fence across the front; the rear of the deck led to the office, which was enclosed in a wall of bulletproof glass. The main floor was an open area that had been used for the maintenance of aircraft, but was now filled with boxes of cargo protected by diplomatic immunity, safe from the prying eyes of customs agents.

The office stretched across the width of the hangar. The side wall of the office was covered with television screens connected to video cameras that scanned the interior of the hangar and the outlying area. They all fed videotape recorders. The rear wall contained built-in fireproof filing cabinets with communications controls. In the center of the office was the large desk that was Chi's command center. From there he could operate cameras, security devices, computers, faxes, and phones. The only way into the office was through a vault-like steel door or from Chi's apartment. The door to Chi's apartment from the parking area looked as if were made of wood, but it too was solid steel.

Feeling safe in his glass-and-steel cocoon, Chi was nestled in his captain's chair overlooking a control panel that was similar to an airplane's. His fingers danced over the hodgepodge of lights and switches as he checked the security and panned all eighteen cameras. He activated the motion sensors, but he picked up no movement. Then he switched on the satellite uplink and waited for the buzz that indicated the satellite was online. He pressed the button to transfer to a secure line before dialing the Inspector General. After several rings, the Inspector General answered.

Apologizing for the early morning call, Chi told him of his meeting with the Russian general.

"Then there is no hope in getting Zimkeroff to take the money?" the Inspector General said. It was more a statement than a question.

Chi was silent.

"Be careful when you meet with Gen. Xi this morning. Don't let him know about the BCV," he ordered.

"Yes, sir. I had no intention of letting him know."

"Good. The Supreme Leader, our president, has authorized the use of the BCV for the swap. It will be sent to you today by courier. Wa Chung shall be arriving shortly and he will brief you on the plan."

"Wa Chung?"

"Yes, is there a problem with him?"

"No, sir, it is just that I—"

"It's for your own good. You use your head, Wa Chung uses his brawn. You have not qualified in the use of handguns. Wa Chung is an expert and has used a weapon more than once. No more talk. Remember, between Zimkeroff and Xi you will be tested to your limits."

"Yes, Inspector General."

"Some advice from an old man: Keep your friends close, your enemies closer."

"Which one is which?" Chi asked.

He heard the phone line go dead. Chi pressed the switches transferring the lines back and disconnecting the satellite uplink.

Even though it was still early, he decided he would leave for the Peninsula Hotel. The sooner he confronted Gen. Xi, the sooner the plan would get under way.

The doorman bowed as Chi entered the pinnacle of elegance, the grand lobby of the Peninsula Hotel. Scanning the massive space for house phones, he couldn't help to be impressed by what he saw. Finding the phones by the elevators, Chi asked the operator for Gen. Xi.

A colonel in dress uniform met Chi and escorted him to Xi's suite on the private fortieth floor. After waiting for a few minutes, Gen. Xi, in military dress uniform, his chest adorned with metals, greeted Chi with a crushing handshake.

Before Chi could say anything, Xi took him by the arm and pulled him into the dining room where breakfast was being served. Standing around the table were three colonels and a general, all waiting for Xi to be seated. Xi introduced Chi to the officers and indicated for him to sit.

"What brings you here so early?" Gen. Xi asked. "The more normal procedure would have been for the Inspector General to arrange a meeting. But no matter. We are all working together."

"This is important," Chi said. He was uncomfortable speaking in front of the others.

Sensing his reluctance, Gen. Xi tried to put the young man at ease.

"Please feel free to speak"he said."You are among friends.This is my most trusted staff."

Chi told them about his meeting with Zimkeroff in every detail except the part about the BCV. Gen. Xi nodded, taking it all in. He reported the deed was now in Hong Kong, and told the general about the Chans, the four beauty contestants, and the vase. Xi listened as if he were surprised at this intelligence. He asked questions to which he already knew the answers.

"It is important we find the deed first and get it directly back to China,"Chi said, finishing his story.

"The deed might be right here in the hotel, as we speak,"Gen. Xi said.

"Here? Now?"

"The women from the beauty contest are staying here in the hotel. They have their own floor. Between contestants and chaperones, there must be more than one hundred of them.You look for the Chans and I will have my men search the rooms of the various contestants to find the vase."

"Where would I begin to look for the Chans?"Chi asked.

"The Free China Society,"Gen. Xi answered."I'll get you the address of their headquarters. They were probably behind the Chans involvement and it would be natural for them to go there. I will have someone check with our contacts at customs to see where they are staying. As soon as I get that information, I will pass it on to you. It will be easier for you to move around Hong Kong than for me, but it will be easy for us to cover the hotel."

Pleased that Xi was being cooperative and forgetting the Inspector General's advice, Chi agreed to the general's plan.

After breakfast, Gen. Xi led Chi from the suite, asking him:"Do you have a gun?"

Chi didn't want to tell him that his Daewoo was at the bottom of Victoria Harbor, thanks to the Russians, so he said: "I haven't had a chance to pick one up."

"One moment,"Gen. Xi said.

He disappeared into a room and returned with a .38-caliber Smith and Wesson, the same gun that had been used to kill the Chans.

"Here,"he said, throwing it to Chi.

"Thank you, General,"Chi said, feeling very good about the meeting and thinking for the first time that the Inspector General might have been wrong about Xi.

Back into his study Xi called his chief of staff, Col. Miu.

"Send two of our best men to the warehouse to provide a welcome for Chi. He must find the Chans—and join them,"Gen. Xi said, laughing.

*   *   *

Col. Leslie Adams was plowing through the surveillance reports on Gen. Zimkeroff when he saw at the top of the page in bold type: *Sang Chi.* That got his immediate interest. The report traced Chi's movements the previous night at the Sheraton Hotel, detailing the calls to Zimkeroff, the meeting with the hooker, and Zimkeroff's encounter with the bartender at the Union Jack. Adams flipped through the dozen photographs and skimmed the transcripts of conversations. Scratching his head, he wondered what Chi would be doing with Zimkeroff. He put the report aside; he would come back to it later. Going through the rest of the stack on his desk, he was interrupted by Liz Browning.

"I thought you should see the morning surveillance report on Gen. Xi right away," she said. "Xi had an early morning visitor, the same man who was trying to see Zimkeroff's last night, Sang Chi."

Adams felt a lump in his throat as he reached for the report. Quickly glancing through it, he saw Sang Chi's photograph and a transcript of his phone conversation. This was more than a coincidence, he thought. Only Williams knew that Chi was his wife's brother. He would have to report this to Montgomery. It would be the end of his career.

* * *

When Montgomery put the phone down, the look on his face told Williams something important was up.

"Winston," he said. "Gen. Xi wants to meet me. He's ready to make the deal."

"May I go with you to meet him?" Williams asked.

"No," Montgomery replied. "I don't want to spook him. He knows Browning. I'll go with her. Besides she's a lot prettier than you."

After Montgomery had left, Adams came into the conference room.

"Where's Michael? I need to talk with him."

"Gone to see Gen. Xi. Something is about to break. They are meeting for lunch at one of the floating restaurants," Williams said. "He took Liz Browning with him."

"Why didn't you go, Winny?"

"She's prettier than I."

Adams hesitated, but decided to tell Williams about Chi.

"Come on, Les. He didn't actually meet with Zimkeroff; he just had a jolly good time with an expensive prostitute. And Gen. Xi is a national hero. Perhaps Chi was just paying his respects. I don't think Michael need be bothered with this."

Adams appreciated the kind words, but he knew in his heart that Williams was wrong. He had to report this to Montgomery at once. What nagged at him was whether to tell Lu An. Maybe it was nothing, just maybe. . . .

CHAPTER 22

Better to bend than to break.

— Old Chinese proverb

✧❀✧

A LTHOUGH he was still exhausted, Daniels was up early trying to enjoy the breakfast that room service had delivered. Running the facts over in his mind, he unconsciously stirred his coffee with a fork. The little black whirlpools he made were about as clear as this case was to him. Everything was on a need to know basis, but his gut told him the Admiral left out something important. Still, Daniels trusted the Admiral. Slowly pouring the cream into the cup, he hoped that Saltzman had called Astrid to invite her to the consulate or to lunch with Boucher to keep her busy and away from him.

He had to admit that being with her could be a lot of fun, but he had to fight the thought that maybe she had changed and she, no they, deserved a chance for happiness. Hell, unless he found the land grant, they might be dead anyway.

"A spoon works better, Mac," Astrid said, standing by the table.

He looked up, startled.

"Hey, cowboy, did I see you jump? Are you losing it? I never could get within ten feet of you before without your radar going off."

"I may be getting older, but like wine, I'm getting better," he retorted.

She extended her hand straight out, her palm facing the floor and rocked it back and forth.

"Well, what are you doing today, Astrid?"

"Well, waz up?" she said, making fun of his New Jersey accent.

Switching to her imitation English accent, she said: "I've an appointment with Mr. Saltzman and a lunch with the consul general at his residence. And you, my fine Chablis?"

"Just going to shoot a few locals."

"Why don't I cancel my appointment with Boucher and let's sneak off and have lunch. We can go to the Victoria Club up on the Peak."

"Your father isn't paying me to have lunch with his daughter."

"Neither is he paying you to screw her," she said.

"Nolo contende," he pleaded. "I would love to have lunch with you, especially at the Peak. It's one of our favorite spots, great food, great view, great times, but I do have a few things to do. What time is your appointment with Saltzman?"

"When I get there," she said.

"Join me for some breakfast," he suggested.

Daniels was sitting at the table in just a pair of boxer shorts; she was wearing a large T-shirt. Leaning over the table, Astrid dipped a silver spoon in a dish of raspberry jam, bringing the spoon up to her mouth as if she were going to eat it. Suddenly, she shot the jam at Daniels, hitting him in the chest.

"What the f—"

Before he could finish the sentence, she followed up with another salvo of the sticky red jam that landed in a giant blob over his heart. She threw her long leg over him, straddling him, and began rubbing the jam over his chest. Pulling down the top of her T-shirt, she pressed her breasts against his chest continuing the massage. She pushed her mouth tightly around his mouth, their tongues feverishly exploring each other. Reaching around her, feeling naked ass, he pulled her close. Her hips pressed down hard, slowly pumping him. As Daniels started to lick the jam off her, she thrust her nipple into his mouth. It grew hard as he sucked. Raising herself off his lap, she reached down to free his hardened shaft from his shorts. Slowly stroking him, she guided Daniels into her. Lifting herself up and down, back and forth, picking up speed with each thrust, her tongue invaded his mouth. Daniels felt her warmth as she pressed down hard on him, her body shuddering. It took only a moment before both their bodies began to explode. She let out a moan.

"Mac, Mac," she groaned, as she climaxed.

She lay against him for a moment, her face pressed into the nape of his neck. Neither moved nor spoke. When Astrid felt him fall out of her, she slowly climbed off his lap.

"Thanks for breakfast," she said, walking to her room.

Daniels suddenly realized that this was crazy and it had to stop. But Astrid was hard to resist. She was beautiful, intelligent, sexy, and everything a man could want. If and when he got out of this Hong Kong mess, he would be assigned to another part of the world for who knew how long? There was no way he could make a stable life for them. The thought of resigning from the agency and taking up Reed's job offer was, at times like this, tempting. Damn, he thought, she was good at seducing him and he was powerless to stop her. Maybe it was better to bend than to break.

After a quick shave, Daniels showered, scrubbing the jam off his chest. Drying his hair, he ran his fingers through it combing it straight back. Wrapping the towel around his waist, he crossed the bedroom to the walk-in closet where his few belongings hung. Grabbing underwear, blue jeans, and a black T-shirt, he quickly dressed. From one of the locked diplomatic cases he took out a shoulder holster and a 9 mm Glock 19. Strapping on the shoulder holster, he adjusted it so the butt of the pistol hung low under his armpit. Pressing the release button, he removed the clip from the pistol butt. He checked the ammunition and pushed the clip back into the pistol grip, drew back the slide, released it, and chambered one deadly round. He flipped on the safety and holstered the pistol. He was ready.

Standing in the hall, he could hear the shower running in Astrid's bathroom. Not wanting to leave without saying good-bye, he decided to leave her a voice mail message. He picked up the phone and started to dial when he saw the envelope lying on the floor where he had left it the previous night. Opening the envelope, Daniels pulled out the contact sheets. The top one showed an attractive blonde holding the red-and-yellow House of Chan bag under her arm. She was now on his list of people to visit. But first he would try 205 Water Street.

* * *

The old Austin taxi rattled and chugged its way down Salisbury Road, leaving a trail of smoke. The driver tried to convince Daniels to stop at every tourist shop they passed, guaranteeing him a great deal. But Daniels wasn't buying. Once through the tunnel the driver turned west onto Gloucester Road, driving into the Wanchai district of Hong Kong, famous for its night life and strip clubs. By then the driver had given up trying to persuade Daniels to stop, resigning himself to taking this cheap tourist to 226 Water Street. The old Austin bounced to a stop at the traffic light at the corner of Luard Road. From the corner of his eye, Daniels spotted something that made him look out the window. Following Daniels's gaze, the driver saw what had caught his passenger's eye. It was the sign for the Hi-Jinks Club, featuring an American named Happy Holiday, better known to Daniels as Kelly Brook. The driver wanted to take him there at once, but Daniels fell back on the well-worn leather seat and shook his head.

Getting out at 226 Water Street, Daniels was two blocks away from where he wanted to go. He didn't know what was waiting for him there, he just hoped to ask a few questions and get out. Walking down the street on the opposite side of the warehouse, Daniels checked the buildings. Water Street was the main road that ran along the Victoria Harbor. Walking two blocks past 205, Daniels crossed the street, repeating his route.

The traffic was considerable, but the trailer jockeys were adept at maneuvering their mechanical horses through the maze of cars, bikes, and people milling around the waterfront district. Goods were transferred from the boats to the warehouses where the trucks picked up the materials to make their deliveries. The trucks were queued up and down the street. Daniels walked past 205 Water Street again. Its outward appearance was no different from any of the other warehouses on the block. All of them had vehicle entrances off the street and an office to one side. But there were no trucks waiting to get into 205.

Daniels glanced at the sign on the office door: *Hong Kong Import Services*. Then he noticed that the driveway was exceptionally clean. It wasn't spotted with puddles of oil from the leaky crankcases of the trucks. He went to the building next to 205 and walked up the driveway toward several of the truck drivers who were talking while waiting for their turn to make a pick up. His arrival caused them to stop speaking and they watched him as he approached.

"Good day, mates," he said in his best Australian accent.

For business and for pleasure, Hong Kong was a favorite stop for Australians and he figured they would ignore him. They did.

He continued through the warehouse to the other side where he stepped through the door onto the dock. A small barge was moored there. Its cargo was being unloaded by several longshoremen who were too busy working to pay any attention to him. Looking toward 205, he could see that the dock was clean and free of lines. Daniels had a bad feeling about that place, but it was time for him to pay a visit. As he turned to leave, the dock foreman saw Daniels and yelled at him. Rather than cause a scene, he politely explained he was looking for the distribution manager because he hadn't received his shipment.

"I'm expectin' my delivery, mate. It's overdue. It was a shipment of supplies for the Hi-Jinks Club. No one here knows what happened to our stuff," he said, resuming the Aussie accent.

"Hi-Jinks, Hi-Jinks?" the foreman said, taking out a list from his pocket. "There's nothing here for Hi-Jinks Club."

"Whatcha mean, mate?" Daniels said. "Isn't this the Hong Kong Import Services?"

The foreman, relieved that he wasn't missing a shipment, explained to Daniels he was in the wrong building.

"Sorry 'bout that," Daniels said, turning to go.

"You're wasting your time going over there," the foreman said.

"Why's that?"

"Because as long as I've been working here, and that's more than five years, I have never seen a barge tie up to make a drop. Every so often a cabin cruiser pulls in, but that's about it. In fact, the other day there was a small cruiser tied up back there for about an hour. Sorry about your supplies,"the foreman said.

"What about truck deliveries?"Daniels asked.

"Never seen a truck there, either, just a few cars."

"What about the other day when the boat was there?"Daniels asked.

"Yep, there were a few cars then."

"Anybody there today?"Daniels asked.

"Seems like it."

Thinking that if the place was occupied, he had to be on his guard, Daniels retraced his steps and walked slowly to the deserted-looking warehouse.

Pressing the bell, Daniels waited, but there was no answer. Persistent, he began knocking on the weathered door. Figuring that he was being watched, Daniels put on his best salesman's face. He pretended not to notice a hand pulling away the curtain at the second-floor window; he kept smiling. The door did not open, but a voice came over the speaker:"Private property. Go away."

Flashing his best grin, Daniels said into the speaker:"I'm interested in renting space."

"No space available. Go away."

"I am a friend of Mr. Chan. He told me you had space,"Daniels said.

The speaker went dead.

Daniels was trying to decide what to do when the decision was made for him. He heard a click of the lock and the door opened slightly. With his left hand he pushed, surprised it didn't open farther. Turning his body sideways, he edged his left shoulder in first as he entered. He pulled out the Glock, flipped off the safety, and pressed the gun tight along the thigh of his right leg. Then he eased the rest of his body inside. The door shut behind him, automatically locking.

Daniels spotted the door at the end of the dim corridor, the door with a gun slit in it. That was trouble, he knew. There was nowhere to hide. He started running toward the door as fast as he could. The closer he got, the better chance he would have.

Standing behind the door, the gunman waited a few seconds before dropping the gun slit open. The metal cover fell back with a clung. He pressed his face toward the slit and he was startled to see that the man running toward him was so close. Before the gunman pushed the barrel of his gun out, Daniels squeezed off six shots at the slit. He didn't expect to hit the man. He just wanted to divert his attention for a moment. It worked. Instinctively the gunman dropped to the floor.

Then, without looking, the gunman stuck the barrel of his gun through the slit, firing rapidly emptying the clip. Pulling the gun back, he lifted up the metal cover and listened. Hearing nothing, he opened the slit and looked through. He saw nothing. Then he opened the slit fully, scanning the long narrow hall. Still nothing. Where was the body? he wondered. Jamming down the metal cover, he locked it into place.

Daniels was above the door, his body pressed against the ceiling. The narrow hallway made it easy for him to hold himself up with his legs pushing on one wall, his hands on the other. He clung there like a spider, defying gravity, until the gunman came out. He heard the click of a dead bolt and the door slowly opened. The gunman stuck his head out; then he stepped out into the hallway. He couldn't figure out what had happened to the intruder. Daniels dropped down behind the gunman, who quickly turned, but it was too late. Grabbing the man by the shirt and pulling him close, Daniels shoved his Glock into the man's gut and pulled the trigger. He got off two shots so quickly that it sounded like one explosion. The blast from the Glock picked the gunman off the ground and he fell lifeless to the floor. Stepping into the room, Daniels shut the steel door, leaving the body on the other side.

Finding himself in a small office, Daniels went through desk drawers, but they were all empty. The same was true for the filing cabinets. There was nothing else in the room. He tried the side door. It wasn't locked, it was nailed shut.

Where was the intercom that he had spoken through? he wondered. There had to be another room somewhere. Then he noticed a cord dangling from an overhead light. Odd, he thought, why one light bulb when the room was bathed in fluorescent light? He pulled the cord and a set of stairs fell from the ceiling.

"*Gankuai,*" a voice yelled down in Chinese.

While he wasn't fluent in Chinese, he understood they wanted to hurry up.

"*Pa jen du sha senti dao hod, Chi wamen masan hui loi teri,*" the voice continued.

Daniels picked a few of the words out, the rest was easy to complete: "*Drop, body, river, Chi here, soon.*"

Taking the stairs two at a time, Daniels popped up like a cork through the hole in the floor, surprising two men sitting by a table. As they reached for their weapons, Daniels rolled onto the floor, firing two shots; both found their targets.

Searching the upper office, Daniels discovered the controls for the intercom and not much else. On the desk were pieces of broken glass and a mound of sand. Picking up the sand, he let it fall through his fingers. It was a very fine sand. The broken glass was colored, some type of pottery glass, painted on the inside. On the floor was a red-and-yellow shopping bag from the House of Chan.

What had happened here? he wondered, playing with the sand. In the other corner of the room was another set of ceiling stairs that opened down to the floor below. He pushed them down and found they led to the warehouse. Lying on his stomach, he put his head over the side. Except for two late-model Mercedes Benzes parked inside, there was nothing else.

Daniels dropped into the warehouse and opened the door of one of the cars. He pressed the latch to release the glove box and took out the registration papers. The car was registered to Peoples Republic of China, an embassy car. He chose the Mercedes 600, deciding that he had always wanted to drive a twelve-cylinder luxury model. He started it up. Over the sun visor was a radio control button that opened the garage doors.

It was time to leave. The doors creaked open and Daniels drove out in style. He had much to do.

CHAPTER 23

Never count on chance. It has a bad memory.

— Old Chinese proverb

❦

"WHERE are you, Mac?" Harry Saltzman asked over the cell phone.

"Cruising down Connaught Road Central in a dream machine. I'm on my way back to the hotel. I have a lead I want to follow up."

"If by chance that dream machine is a black Mercedes 600, I suggest you park it right now and take a cab over to the government office building. According to our sources, someone fitting your description made a mess at a Water Street warehouse. Looks like the suspect is driving a stolen car."

"Is your source a dock foreman?"

"Good guess."

"Are the police looking for the Benz yet, Harry?"

"Not that we know of. We didn't call the police, but as soon as the trio you left behind doesn't report in, it's a safe bet that the car will be reported stolen."

"I guess I have to return the loaner, Harry. What a shame, I really am enjoying driving this car. Why the government building?"

"Montgomery is on his way to meet with Gen. Xi. Something is brewing, so check it out. Go pay him a courtesy call and see what's going on. Then call me."

"Will do, but first I want to return the car to the Chinese. Call you later."

Guiding the Mercedes effortlessly, listening to the twelve cylinders purring every time he pressed the gas petal, Daniels turned off onto Murray Road, which led to the Bank of China building. The bank was twelve stories of glass and mirrors occupying an entire block. Stopping in the parking lot, Daniels took a long look at the shimmering tower, which represented China's commitment to the economic future of Hong Kong. He smiled.

* * *

Montgomery downshifted and the engine roared, sending torque to the rear wheels, forcing the Jaguar to spin around the hairpin turn onto Garden Road. Coming out of the turn, he pressed down on the accelerator, sending the tachometer climbing to the red line. Then he shifted up and the car lurched forward to the top of Mt. Kellett, one of the high points on Hong Kong Island. Reaching the summit, he braked hard, and skidded to a stop.

The ride had been exhilarating for Montgomery, but not for Liz Browning. Her knuckles had been white all the way. From the lookout they could see the Aberdeen Harbor in the distance. It was home to fifteen thousand vessels and more than thirty thousand people—boat people, who lived, worked, and died on their boats. In the midst of this floating city were several floating restaurants.

"It's quite beautiful," Liz said, looking out at the variety of boats and floating restaurants "Let's be sure we keep it," Montgomery said. "We've got to get that deed from Gen. Xi. He's a sly son-of-a-bitch, though, picking a place like this. He knows there was no way for us to get to him without a boat. No way to set him up. That damn restaurant is in the middle of the harbor."

Their destination was the Jumbo Restaurant, a popular floating tourist trap, and a favorite of the many visitors to Hong Kong. Originally an old ferry, the restaurant had been converted into a multilevel floating palace of Oriental cuisine. It bobbed gently in the leeward harbor between Apleichau Island and Hong Kong Island. The only way to get to the Jumbo was by private boat, water taxi, or the shuttle that ran back and forth between Aberdeen and the restaurant.

Montgomery maneuvered the sleek car down the corkscrew road to the village, then over to the waterfront service road where he pulled into the parking lot for the Jumbo Restaurant. They waited patiently in line, slowly making their way to the reservation booth. The clerk, dressed in a naval uniform, asked if they had reservations.

"Yes. Montgomery."

"I'm sorry, there are no reservations for Montgomery," the clerk said, looking at his list.

"We are Gen. Xi's guests, please check carefully," Browning said.

At the mention of Gen. Xi, the clerk snapped to attention.

"Yes, I see your name listed next to the General's. Please go over to his boat," he said pointing to the sleek cabin cruiser docked next to the shuttle. "The General is waiting for you."

Walking to the cruiser, they passed the line of tourists waiting for their water taxis.

"Gen. Xi certainly does things first class," Browning said.

After a five-minute trip, they reached the restaurant. On the main deck, they were greeted by the host who was dressed in a blue nautical blazer with gold braid. He looked like a cartoon admiral on a cereal box. Recognizing the cruiser, the host didn't ask about reservations. He just snapped his fingers, summoning a waiter.

"Take Mr. Montgomery and his guest to Gen. Xi's private dining room," he said.

At the bow of the ferry was the old wheelhouse, which had been converted into a private dining room. It was the highest point on the ship, offering the utmost in privacy and an unobstructed view in all directions.

The waiter knocked on the wheelhouse door. It was opened by Col. Miu. He stepped aside allowing Montgomery and Browning into the dining room.

"Thank you for coming," Gen. Xi said.

"It is not often that a lowly customs clerk has the privilege of dining with someone as famous as the Chairman of the Central Military Commission," Liz said.

Gen. Xi bowed to Browning. He was wearing slacks and a sport shirt that looked as if it was leftover from the Sixties. Montgomery had never seen Xi dressed in anything but his military uniform.

"I wouldn't have recognized you, General. You're out of uniform," Montgomery said.

"Perhaps this will be my new uniform. Please be seated," Xi said.

The chairs had been crafted from old sea kegs and stuffed with pillows. Liz was amazed how comfortable they were.

Looking around the room Montgomery appreciated the meeting place. Xi was no fool. The restaurant was secure from interference, free of taps, and safe from prying eyes. He was sure that the reservations clerk at the dock, the host, and the waiters on board were Xi's men. No one was getting on or off the old tub without being seen, or for that matter, without Xi's permission.

Montgomery, knowing better than to push the conversation, ordered, ate, and engaged in small talk. After dessert and several cups of tea, Xi got down to business.

"Do you have my money?" he asked Montgomery.

"Of course," Montgomery said, not hesitating. "Do you have the land grant documents?"

"When I get the money, you get the land grant."

"When do we do the transfer, General?"

"June 29th at my hotel suite," Xi said. "The money must be deposited into these accounts. Upon verification, I'll hand over the land grant documents to you."

Gen. Xi gave Montgomery a slip of paper that contained the numbers of several accounts at different Swiss banks.

Montgomery folded the paper and handed it back to Xi.

"But you will need this," Xi said, surprised.

"Not until I see the land grant documents," Montgomery said. "I'm not giving you a billion US dollars for some piece of paper you got out of a fortune cookie."

Col. Miu sat up in his chair. Gen. Xi was not to be spoken to like that.

Xi leaned closer to Montgomery, staring at him, trying to read him. He was here to deal, not to be put off by the logistics of the transfer.

"What's the problem, Mr. Montgomery?"

"The money will not be transferred until the land grant documents are turned over first," Montgomery said.

"I see," Xi said, "it is a question of trust."

"To be honest, General, it is more a question of mistrust."

Xi broke into a toothy smile.

"Mr. Montgomery, it is very simple. You come to my hotel suite. I'll show you the papers. You call your office. They wire the money. We all stay in my suite until I confirm the money is in my account. The papers will never leave your sight. When I know I have the money, you walk out with the land grant. I'll go to the airport with my staff and fly to London or wherever we feel like going, since we will all be carrying British passports as Her Majesty's newest subjects. As I said, it is very simple; all you need to supply us with is money and passports."

Montgomery thought for a moment. Then seeing no alternative, he said: "Move the transfer date up one day to the 28th and agree that I may bring along someone to authenticate the documents."

Without hesitation, Xi agreed to his request with the proviso they come unarmed.

"There is no need for anyone to get killed," Gen. Xi said. "If I don't get the money, the deed will be destroyed."

Montgomery agreed.

"After all," Xi said, "you really have no choice. Pay me and get the land grant documents. Don't pay me and lose Hong Kong."

"Or we can find the deed ourselves," Montgomery said.

"Never count on chance, Mr. Montgomery, it has a bad memory."

Montgomery was about to respond when Xi's cell phone rang. He excused himself and stepped away from the table to take the call. He stood on the deck for privacy, his back to the wheelhouse.

"Someone shot the three men you sent to the warehouse to kill Chi," one of his aides reported. "As far as we know, Chi is still alive."

"How is this possible?" Gen. Xi demanded. "That idiot Chi couldn't have done it. Who did?"

The voice on the other end didn't answer his question, but told the general about the stolen car registered to the embassy. That set Xi off again.

Inside the wheelhouse, everyone at the table could hear Xi sputtering with rage, but they all pretended to be deaf. When the general returned, Liz Browning asked him if everything was all right.

"I am sorry to say I have received some distressing news, but it was personal. Something that I will have to tend to at a later time."

"Is our deal still on, General?" Montgomery asked.

"You bring the money. I'll bring the deed. However, there is a matter in which I could use the help of the Secret Intelligence Service."

"Anything for Her Majesty's newest subjects," Montgomery said.

"Do you know Col. Leslie Adams?"

A bit taken back by the question, Montgomery assured him that he not only knew Adams but also was his best friend.

"Adams's brother-in-law, Sang Chi, is a spy for our government. He is trying to intercept the documents," Xi said.

Montgomery tried not to let the shock register on his face.

"As far as I know, Adams is not on our payroll," Xi continued, knowing he had hit a nerve. "Chi was responsible for the murder of two Chinese tourists named Chan. They were bringing the land grant here from the mainland. Fortunately, he didn't get the documents."

"What if Chi does get the deed?" Montgomery asked.

"There will be no deal," Xi replied. "The Chans took the precaution of hiding the deed. Chi killed them when they failed to produce it. If Chi finds out that I have it, well, use your imagination. Your help would be appreciated."

"Do you have a photo of Chi? I'll have him picked up."

"I will have a photo of Chi sent to you at your office."

Gen. Xi handed Montgomery the folded paper with the list of bank account numbers. This time Montgomery took it and, without looking at it, passed it to Browning.

The meeting was over.

Montgomery sat holding his head in his hand as the cruiser sped them back to the shore. Approaching the parked Jaguar, he handed the keys to Browning. He didn't feel like driving. Getting into the car, she hit the unlock button and waited for him to get in. But he was standing by the car, looking out over the water, trying to digest what he had just learned. It didn't go down easy. This would be hard on Adams, he thought. The SIS would take a dim view of a British officer having a spy for an in-law. This was going to kill Adams's career. Worse, it could destroy his marriage.

Standing on the deck of the wheelhouse, Xi watched his cruiser return from the short trip to Hong Kong Island. He was pleased with the meeting. He heard Miu's footsteps approaching from behind.

"All in order, Colonel?"

"Yes, sir. I paid for the meal in US dollars and left a very generous tip as you had instructed. Are you ready to leave, sir?"

As the cruiser came alongside the ferry, the deck hands threw lines around cleats to temporarily tie it down. Gen. Xi ventured down the gangway to a small floating dock; then he stepped into the cockpit of the sleek sports cruiser. Climbing to the flying bridge, he took a seat in front of the helm. Miu was right behind him, waiting for permission to sit. Without a word Xi pointed to the seat next to him.

Xi ordered the helmsmen to go. The twin engines slowly pushed the cruiser away from the restaurant. Clear of the dock, the helmsmen pushed the throttles forward and the props cut into the sea, forcing the bow to rise out of the water when the cruiser picked up speed. The white foam from the props mixed with the deep blue of the harbor, pouring forth from the stern, and spreading out in a wide arc. Other boats bounced in their wake. There was a chorus of curses and raised fists as Xi's cruiser barreled through the harbor. But Xi didn't care. He was returning to the Kowloon public pier, which was a short walk through the waterfront park to the Peninsula Hotel.

"Sir, a question."

"Yes, Colonel."

"Why did you give Chi up to the British?"

"Since we weren't able to kill him, maybe the British will. I gave them that little pain in the ass because he could easily ruin our plans. Let the Brits take care of eliminating Chi. Besides, it gives us more credibility."

Miu understood. If the SIS caught Chi with the gun used to kill the Chans, he would be finished.

"Did you see the look on Montgomery's face when I called his bluff?" Xi asked. "As the Americans say, 'he blinked.'"

* * *

Later that day, Chi drove slowly down Water Street looking for number 205. The traffic was heavier than usual and the street was crowded with people. The flashing lights from the police cars hovering around the warehouse had slowed traffic to a standstill. Chi was wise enough not to barge into a police investigation and drove on. He would never know that Daniels had just saved his life.

CHAPTER 24

After counsel, fools counsel.

— Old Chinese proverb

IN the elevator of the government building, Montgomery pulled Liz close to him and kissed her. He ran his hands up and down her back, finally coming to rest on the cheeks of her ass. He was enjoying the sensations when the elevator doors opened, breaking the spell. They stepped into the hallway to be confronted by Mac Daniels, who had been sitting on a bench waiting for them. Liz blushed. It was not lost on Daniels.

"Like a bad penny, he always turns up," Montgomery said, introducing Liz to Daniels. "But a good-looking penny," Liz said, looking the American agent in the eye.

"You have no taste, Miss Browning," Montgomery muttered, making a face.

Opening the door to the conference room that served as his office, Montgomery frowned at the long table covered with stacks of reports.

"What's wrong? You look like you lost your best friend, Michael," Daniels said.

"I just may have," Montgomery said. "I just may have."

Browning was impressed with Daniels's perception and thought that this would be a good time for her to exit. Announcing she was going to her office, she turned to leave.

"Please tell Col. Adams to come right over," Montgomery said.

"Want to tell me about it?" Daniels asked.

"I will in due time, Mac, but first I have to tell you about my meeting with Gen. Xi. I think we have our deed."

Daniels listened intently making mental notes; then he asked questions. After the briefing Montgomery asked: "Well, Mac, what do you think? Are we going to keep our Crown Colony?"

"I hope so, Michael, I hope so."

145

"In this business nothing is as easy as it seems. Did you turn up anything?"

Before Daniels could speak, Adams and Browning came into the room.

"You wanted to see me, Michael?" Adams asked.

"Yes. Please sit down. Don't go, Liz, I want you here too, please."

"Perhaps Mr. Daniels would like to come over to my office to use the phone," Liz said tactfully.

"Want me out of here?" Daniels asked, blunt as usual. "I've been thrown out of better places."

"No, Mac, you better stay. We're on the same side."

"I know why I'm here," Adams said. "In fact, I was going to come to you. It's Sang Chi, isn't it?"

The name Chi caught Daniels's attention. He had heard it at the warehouse.

"Here, Michael," Browning said, handing him two large envelopes, one plain, the other clearly marked with the seal of the Chinese embassy. "These just arrived."

Opening the envelope from the embassy first, Montgomery took out an eight-by-ten photograph and a black-and-white head shot of Chi.

"The general works fast," Montgomery said, handing the photo to Adams.

"I know," Adams said. "He's working for the Ministry of State Security, isn't he?"

"He's one of China's top agents in Southeast Asia," Montgomery said.

Adams's face lost all color, as if Montgomery's words were a kick in the stomach.

The room was dead silent, so silent that the ticking of the mantel clock could clearly be heard. They all sat there looking at Adams, then at each other, waiting for him or someone to say something. Pouring a glass of water, Browning handed it to Adams. His hands shook, spilling some.

"My wife, my wife," Adams said, his voice filled with pain. "She's not involved. I never knew. I never even suspected anything until this morning."

Adams believed in his heart that Lu An knew nothing, but Chi was her brother. No matter how tight-lipped he had tried to be, in truth, he did confide in her, trusting her with his life.

"It's not about you or Lu An," Montgomery said. "Everyone in this room knows you had no knowledge of Chi's activities. No one ever doubted your loyalty, but we have a problem."

No shit, Daniels thought. This was a death sentence in the spy business. No matter how much you believed in your friends, you couldn't work in this racket when your wife's brother was the enemy. Men always told their wives things they shouldn't. That was common, every night pillow talk. Hell, the British had had their share of spy scandals, he thought, usually involving some bimbo sleeping with the right person.

"Where did you get this info, Michael?" Daniels asked.

"Gen. Xi told me at lunch," he answered. "He wanted us to know what was going on. If Chi found the deed, he would destroy it. Chi's forces are out looking for it now. Xi tells me that he runs a major ring throughout Asia, one with plenty of resources. He wants us to pick up Chi to eliminate any problems for him."

"Michael, Chi was at Xi's hotel suite early this morning. Last night he called on Gen. Zimkeroff," Adams said, handing him the reports he had read that morning. "When I came down this morning to see you, to report this, you had just left for your meeting. I felt you should know and I wanted to tell you myself. A full written report was prepared for you. It's in the file. Winston was here and I told him about Chi, but he too didn't think much of it."

"Mac, some of this adds up," Montgomery said to the only person in the room who would really understand. "Chi paid a visit to Gen. Xi and told him that he's looking for the deed or maybe he knows where it is. He wants Xi's cooperation. Xi knows Chi reports directly to the ministry. Xi doesn't want to raise suspicions, being close to a deal with us, so he feigns cooperation. Then he gives up Chi to us. We arrest the bastard and hold him while Xi delivers the deed and is gone. Makes sense.

"Liz, please get copies of this photo made and pass them on to the special squads. I want Chi picked up and I want him alive."

"Do you want my resignation?" Adams asked.

"No. Just promise me you will say nothing to Lu An. I'm not even thinking that she knew anything, Les. I just don't want her involved. She's not in this business and I don't know how she will react," Montgomery said.

Adams let out a long sign of relief.

"If you see or hear from Chi, stay out of it," he continued. "Call me immediately and that's an order."

Montgomery waited for his words to sink in; then he told Liz to take Adams to her office. He wanted to talk to Daniels alone.

"Well?" Montgomery said when Liz and Adams had left the room.

"About Chi or Adams?"

"Both."

"Your reading of Chi could be right, but why did he call on Zimkeroff? As to your friend Adams, you may not have done him any favors. I guess he's clean and his wife may be, too. There's no way his wife could have gone on all these years undetected with you being so close to them. You know Adams is going to try to prove his loyalty, and if he's not careful, he'll end up dead. But Adams is none of my business, Chi is."

Montgomery didn't answer. He opened the plain envelope and took out the pictures of the three men who were shot at Water Street. Handing them to Daniels, Montgomery read the report.

"What the bloody hell is going on?" he said, slapping the report. "The Chinese embassy reports two Mercedes Benz 600s stolen from its compound. One of the cars is found inside the Bank of China. Someone drove it through the front windows and into the main lobby. They left a note reading: *For deposit only: Hong Kong Import Services, 205 Water Street.* The police respond to 205 Water Street, where they find the other car and these three shot dead. Do you believe in coincidences, Mac?"

"Not if I want to stay alive. Why?"

"The young Chinese couple floating in the river, the Chans, they were taken to 205 Water Street. We found the cab driver who took them there. The lab boys have matched some of the blood stains found at the site to the Chans. They were shot at Water Street, then dumped into the harbor. These three men were also killed there. Well, any ideas?"

"Let me think about it." Daniels said.

He wasn't about to tell Montgomery about the three dead men at Water Street or about the Mercedes. Going over the facts in his mind, he was getting a clearer picture of Gen. Xi. The three goons at the warehouse were waiting for Chi when Daniels stumbled into their trap. Someone wanted Chi out of the way and that someone was Xi. The Chans were probably bringing the deed into Hong Kong, but somehow they didn't have it with them. Gen. Xi killed them for their failure. Chi got word that the papers were in Honk Kong and told Xi about it at the morning meeting. In order to prevent Chi from finding the deed, Xi tried to have Chi killed. When that failed, he handed him over to Montgomery. If Xi really had the deed there would be no need to worry about Chi, so Xi must have bullshited Montgomery, who fell for it. Gen. Xi didn't have the deed. He was bluffing.

Recalling the photos of the beauty pageant contestants, Daniels had an idea where the deed might be. It was almost humorous, he thought. By mistake, one of the women from the contest had managed to pick up the deed and was probably strolling around Hong Kong with it. He hoped that Gen. Xi hadn't figured it out or there would be a lot of dead bodies, beautiful dead bodies.

"Well, Mac, what's your advice?"

"Michael, the only advice I have for you is watch out for the love bug. There's no real good vaccine. Other than that, I can't help you. You have been with SIS a long time, go with your instincts. Remember after counsel, fools counsel."

"Thanks, I'll try to remember that."

Tapping his fingers like a drummer, Montgomery thought for a while, apparently unable to decide the next course of action. Reaching over, Daniels grabbed Montgomery's hand.

"That won't help," he said. "You don't have any rhythm. Just do what you have to do. Screw the bastards. Xi gave you the Chinese plan of attack, why pay the ransom? Don't turn over Hong Kong. Screw 'em."

"Because," Montgomery said, "the deed is the proof we need to establish our claim. Without the deed, it wouldn't be cricket."

"Cricket?" Daniels said, shaking his head in wonderment. "Screw cricket, Michael, this is hardball. Look, if you want to play cricket that's up to you. I have got some matters to attend to. See you later."

There was something nagging Daniels, but the answer wasn't at the government offices with a bunch of cricket players. He had to call the Admiral.

"Mac, please keep me informed and stay out of trouble," Montgomery said, waving as Daniels left.

The door had hardly closed when Montgomery got on the phone.

"Put Mac Daniels under immediate surveillance, twenty-four hours a day."

"No problem," the chief of surveillance said. "One American cowboy should be easy."

Montgomery spread out the latest pictures and the Water Street report, looking for a connection as Browning came in.

"What are you thinking?" she asked.

"Somehow my gut tells me this is Daniels's handy work," he said, tapping the photographs. "There will be a lot more bodies showing up, I'm afraid. That's why I put a tail on him."

"Is he that bad?"

"Worse, he's that good."

CHAPTER 25

Hoping does not always make it so.

— Old Chinese proverb

BY the time Daniels reached the lobby, the surveillance team was set up outside waiting for him. Stepping out onto the sidewalk, he stopped and looked up and down the street. He didn't have any place in particular to go. He just wanted to get far away from the cricket crap.

As if he were out for a Sunday stroll, Daniels started to walk in the opposite direction of the traffic. He didn't have to think about it—it was instinctive. That way no one in a car could follow him.

The facts of the case were spinning in his mind; something was nagging him. Reaching for his satellite-linked cell phone, he decided to call the Admiral. As he was about to punch in the key codes, he realized he was at the intersection of Garden Road, not far from the consul general's residence. Why not call from there? he thought.

Though his cell phone was secure, he was outside, which meant that anyone with a cheap micro dish could pick up his voice. With a good dish, they could also hear what was being said over the receiver. It was ironic that his very expensive phone was safe from all types of electronic intercepts—except a cheap micro dish that anyone could buy.

Now that he had a destination, Daniels quickened his pace. That made the surveillance team behind him crazy. Following someone on foot was much more difficult than in a car because there was no place to hide on the open sidewalk. Daniels noticed a couple of men walking up the hill on the other side of Upper Garden Road. In the art of surveillance there was one major rule: never be seen. Although he paid them no attention, Daniels had seen the two men; they had broken rule number one: once you're seen, you're remembered; seen again, and you're busted.

At the front gate of the residence, Daniels was stopped by the Marine guard, who, after calling the residence, cleared him to enter. Ron Haig answered the door.

"I thought you would be on your way back to D.C., Ron," Daniels said.

"Me, too, but the Admiral told me to stick around for a while, just in case."

"In case of what? I screw up or get killed?"

"Something like that. By the way, if you need me, I'm an official guest here at the residence. You need to see Mr. Boucher?"

"No. I need a phone and need to get rid of this," he said, tapping the outside of his jacket where his gun was hidden. "It's dirty."

"Already?" Haig said in amazement. "Come on, follow me."

Leading the way to Boucher's vacant office, Haig opened the wall panel that led to the stairway to the safe room.

"I need to talk to the Admiral," Daniels said, producing the Glock.

He handed the gun to Haig. "Harry's got to get rid of this."

"Does Harry know?" Haig asked.

"One of his men spotted me. He knows what went down. I didn't need him to clean up this time. Now, dial the Admiral."

"You're going to wake the boss," Haig said, looking at his watch to compute the time difference between Hong Kong and Washington.

"Chickenshit," Daniels said.

Haig dialed the Admiral's private number, while Daniels opened the false filing cabinet and grabbed a cold Bud. The Admiral answered the phone on the first ring, sounding completely awake. Haig, apologizing for the late night call, explained that Daniels needed to talk to him.

"Mind, sir, if I put you on the speaker for Ron's benefit?" Daniels asked.

"Go ahead," the Admiral said.

For the next ten minutes, Daniels filled the Admiral in on Montgomery, Adams, Chi, Gen. Xi, and what had happened at the warehouse.

"In my opinion, sir, Gen. Xi doesn't have the deed," Daniels said. "If he did, he would have completed the sale. Xi wants Chi out of the way to prevent him from finding the deed. Xi's plans for an invasion make no sense. In fact, it's a crock of crap and Montgomery bought it. I have a hunch we will find the deed with one of the Galaxy contestants."

"Go to it," the Admiral said.

"What about Chi?"

"Forget about him for now. What bothers me is the goddamn Russians. Watch those sons-of-bitches. You never know what they'll do. They're the wild card here. Our intelligence tells us they're trying to peddle the deed. But to whom? Mac, press the Russians. I want that deed."

"Sir, what may I do to help?" Haig asked.

"Just stand by, Ron. Stand by," the Admiral said and hung up.

"Well, shall we call it a day, Ron?" Daniels asked.

"Not quite yet," Haig said.

He opened the drawer of a filing cabinet and lifted out a thin leather-covered case.

"Here," he said, presenting the case to Daniels. "Harry wanted me to give this to you."

Daniels took the case and pressed the release catch. The snap sprung open, revealing a Heckler and Koch Mark 23 pistol.

"I loaded it for you," Haig said.

Daniels took the weapon out of the box and hefted it in his hand, feeling its weight.

"It's loaded," Daniels said. "But the clip is not full."

Daniels pressed the release button and the magazine dropped down out of the grip into his left hand. With great dexterity, he flicked out each round. There were only six.

"Never half load a weapon, Ron. Someone could get hurt. Namely me."

Haig handed him a box of .45-caliber bullets.

"Don't lose that gun, Mac. It costs more than two grand. And try to keep it clean—for at least a day."

Daniels didn't answer. When he finished loading the magazine, he pressed the clip back into the grip and drew back the slide. When it was fully drawn back, it locked in the open position. Holding the pistol straight out, Daniels's thumb pressed the decocking lever on the firing grip. Suddenly the slide sprang forward, driving a lethal round into the firing chamber. The clunk of the slide falling back into place jolted Haig. Daniels gave him a sly smile. With his thumb on the hammer, Daniels squeezed the trigger allowing it to gently fall into place. Pressing the magazine release again, Daniels pushed one more round back into the clip.

"Now it's loaded, Ron, and ready for action. Twelve rounds in the clip and one in the chamber. Here, catch."

Haig reached for the weapon as it spun through the air. He grabbed it with both hands as not to drop it.

"Are you crazy, throwing a loaded gun? It could have gone off," Haig said.

"It's safe," Daniels said. "The weapon can't be fired until it's cocked."

A look of relief came over Haig's face. Feeling strangely more comfortable with the automatic pistol in his hand, Haig bounced it up and down in his hand.

"This is pretty light," he said.

"Yeah. It's only two-and-a-half pounds, including the magazine," Daniels said. "You know that automatic you're playing with can penetrate a car's engine block? It's accurate, fast, and it doesn't jam. The Special Forces have just ordered a batch of them. Where's the sound suppressor?"

Feeling a bit cocky, Haig tossed the weapon back to Daniels. As if he were catching a ball, Daniels snatched the pistol out of the air. Haig handed him another box that looked like a large cigar tube.

Opening the box, Daniels took out a five-inch long metal tube, the sound suppressor, made by Knight Armament. He screwed the suppressor onto the tip of the Mark 23 barrel. Holding the weapon at arm's length, Daniels took aim at the light switch. Both his eyes were wide open and stared down the barrel. The Mark 23 was more than eleven-inches long with the sound suppressor.

A shiver ran up Haig's back. He noticed Daniels's arm was frozen; his breathing had seemed to stop. The gun looked sinister. This was for real, Haig thought, this was for real.

Daniels lowered his arm, unscrewed the suppressor, slipped the weapon into his holster, and the suppressor into his pocket with a box of bullets.

"Come on, Ron, let's go," he said.

* * *

Daniels and Haig stood on the porch waiting for the car to take Daniels to the hotel. A Ford Explorer pulled up and a young Marine driver ran around to open the rear passenger door for Daniels. As the Explorer pulled through the gate, Daniels saw two men—one was hailing a cab and the other on a cell phone. They both looked at the Explorer as it went by. Making a note of the two, Daniels slouched in the back of the car for the rest of the ride. The two men were only a few car lengths behind Daniels's car when the Explorer finally pulled up to the hotel.

Stopping at the front desk to check for messages, Daniels found none, so he took the elevator up to the suite. It was empty; not even a note from Astrid. Dialing the bell captain, he inquired if Miss Reed left the hotel.

"Yes, Mr. Daniels, Miss Reed left in the hotel Rolls Royce around noon. Would you like the phone number for the Rolls?"

"Please."

Given the number, he dialed it and the chauffeur answered immediately. He asked for Astrid.

"Miss Reed is unavailable. May I take a message?" the chauffeur asked.

"This is Mac Daniels. When is she due back at the hotel?"

"I'm sorry, sir, I don't know. She is in a meeting with the American Consul."

Harry Saltzman had come through, Daniels thought. The chauffeur asked if he wanted Miss Reed to call when she returned to the car. Daniels told him that it was not necessary and hung up.

Flopping down on a posh leather office chair, he pulled himself up to the ornate desk, and took out the contact sheets of the beauty contestants. Using an eight-X loupe, he bent over the desk and examined each sheet. He studied each picture, committing to memory the faces and figures of those he had caught with the House of Chan bags. He wondered which one had the deed. Grabbing his camera, Daniels left the suite.

Halfway across the lobby, Daniels noticed the same two men he spotted on Garden Road. Then he saw the two men who were outside the residence when he had left. Shaking his head in disgust, he was surprised Montgomery had placed such an amateurish tail on him. It was almost an insult, two teams of two, but for now he didn't care. If he had to lose those morons, it would be easy.

In one corner of the lobby was a large display of photographs of the various beauty pageant contestants, their names, and their countries. Studying each photo until he found the ones he had an interest in, Daniels jotted down their names. He was going to try to get into the ballroom to meet the women, when he heard his name being called.

"Mac! Mac!"

Turning to the sound of the voice, he saw Tom Camarow coming over to him, a tall redheaded beauty in tow.

"Mac, this is Tara, our Irish representative."

"Mr. Daniels, I'm so pleased to meet you," the redhead gushed.

"The pleasure is mine, Tara, and my name is Mac."

"Maybe the pleasure is mine, Mac," she said, extending her hand.

Daniels took her tiny hand in his massive paw and he was surprised by her hearty shake. The woman had quite a grip. He stopped shaking, but she managed to continue to hold his hand, while her green eyes explored his face, then his body. The tip of her tongue darted out, wetting her red-coated lips. Daniels slowly but forcefully withdrew his hand, keeping his eyes locked onto hers.

"See, Tara" Camarow said. "I told you we were friends. Mac, do me a favor. Shoot some photos of this gorgeous creature for your papers and magazines."

Turning aside, he gave Daniels a wink.

Daniels thought this was the new version of the old producer's couch, but this could be of use to him.

"Sure, Tom, I would be pleased to photograph her," he said. "Any friend of yours is a friend of mine. But let me talk to you alone for a minute."

He pulled Camarow aside.

"I'll help you in your lame effort to get laid, but I have a favor to request in return," Daniels said.

Camarow would have said yes to anything.

"I want some interviews," Daniels said, handing him the list of the names. "Can you arrange for me to meet with them in their rooms this evening?"

"No problem, pal," Camarow said. "I'll set it up for you, whenever you want. Looking at the list, I see you like blondes. You have good taste. They're all very pretty and some of them are pretty wild.

"Say, why don't you come into the Grand Ballroom where the rehearsals are going on. Meet some of the girls now."

Bingo, thought Daniels, following Camarow, who introduced him to the contestants and officials. As he met each of the women he had photographed with the House of Chan bags, he made arrangements to interview them later that evening. Every time Daniels asked for and received a room number, Camarow smiled knowingly. Enough, thought Daniels, trying to ditch the promoter, who seemed to be tethered to his elbow. In desperation, he decided to take some pictures to keep up the appearance of his cover and to get rid of his new best friend. With his eye glued to the viewing lens, Daniels snapped away, pretending to be absorbed by his job and ignoring Camarow who had moved on to other prey.

He was about to leave the ballroom when he saw Tara coming through the crowd toward him. He tried to slip away from her, but she was locked onto him, closing in for the kill. Cutting him off as he headed for the door, she gently grabbed Daniels by the camera strap.

"How about a feature shoot?" she asked him. "Perhaps we could arrange a more convenient time and place—like my room at midnight?"

"Midnight?"

"That's when the big hand is on top of the little hand. You know, the big one on the little one, a time when most people are sleeping. That way we won't be disturbed."

She was leaning against the door in one of the standard sexy poses, so he raised the camera and twisted the lens into focus. That's when he saw Gen. Zimkeroff standing in the hall behind her. Daniels zoomed in on the general and snapped the picture; then he brought the camera into focus on Tara and snapped again. Thanking her, he said he would call her later. As he finally managed to get away from her, Daniels heard her soft voice.

"Remember, one on top of the other."

"Hands, that is," Daniels said.

Gen. Zimkeroff was standing in the hall immediately outside the door of the Grand Ballroom. Next to him was his permanent shadow, Sergeant Major Petroff, his ever vigilant watch dog.

The Admiral's words echoed in Daniels's mind: press the Russians. Maybe it was time, he thought.

Showing no sign that he had recognized the general, Daniels walked out of the ballroom. But the two had met before when Daniels had been in Moscow on assignment. Perhaps Zimkeroff didn't remember him, Daniels thought. Although their last meeting had been short, Daniels knew he had made a hit with Zimkeroff when they had been involved in a car accident early one morning—an accident Daniels had caused on purpose.

That Sunday morning Zimkeroff should have been at his villa outside of Moscow, having a day off, but unexpectedly he had decided to return to his office. His presence would have caused a major disaster, compromising the whole American operation in Moscow. Another agent had managed to infiltrate Zimkeroff's private office when Daniels had gotten the call to stop the general's return. Acting like a lost tourist, he had run a stop sign, causing his car to broadside Zimkeroff's vehicle. Daniels had done his job only too well. Zimkeroff hadn't gotten to the office that morning; he hadn't gotten anywhere.

The accident was more dangerous than Daniels had planned. He had hit Zimkeroff's car so hard that he had knocked it into the oncoming traffic. Petroff, who had been driving, jumped out of the wreckage, bleeding from the side of his head. After he had checked on Zimkeroff, the sergeant major had pulled the dazed Daniels out of his car, lifted him off the ground with one hand, and pushed his pistol into his gut with the other. Daniels had thought that Petroff was going to kill him. Fortunately, Zimkeroff had called him off in time.

Walking past Zimkeroff, Daniels hoped the general had forgotten the incident, but he heard a thunderous voice.

"Mr. Daniels, I hope your driving has improved," Zimkeroff boomed.

Stopping in his tracks, Daniels remembered that hoping does not always make it so.

CHAPTER 26

Wish not, for you may get your wish.

— Old Chinese proverb

❦

AT three in the morning, when most people were asleep, there were always a few who had to work. The Admiral didn't have to work. He wanted to. His life was his job. Still in the office, he had no reason to go home—his executive suite was his home. A widower, still grieving for his wife, he had found that his zest for living had deserted him. He was married to his job, in a literal sense. He lived at the office where he had a little bedroom and bath.

Hanging up the phone, the Admiral stared into space, as if he were waiting for some angelic messenger to tell him what to do. The plan they had conceived was working nicely; the few hitches could be overcome. It was time, he thought, to push the second phase. That was the hard part.

The Admiral lifted the handset of a red phone, the hotline, that was free from all types of intercepts. Nevertheless, he put the receiver onto a voice scrambling device. Still not satisfied with the double security he had in place, the Admiral transmitted his message in code. If anyone could penetrate the secure line, they would hear a series of beeps—an electronic scrambled egg. Then assuming they had the appropriate unscrambling device, they would need a code book.

Before dialing, he put the message into code; then he pressed a button on the scrambler. It got its electronic beaters going. He heard a ringing sound; then silence, until the green light came on the scrambler, indicating the connection was secure. The Admiral began reading what appeared to be a series of meaningless numbers and names: "Eight, two, five, four, eight, plus nine, one, seven, four, three, equals eleven, two, six, eight, three, and four, one, five, eight, five, Kay, Lee, Anthony, Roger three, five, two, five, seven, four."

There was silence on the line; then, after a few minutes, the lights on the scrambler began flashing. The Admiral listened carefully, his ear

157

close to the speaker. He could hear the metallic voice of the scrambler reeling off a string of numbers and names. He wrote them down.

The Admiral turned off the scrambler and deciphered the message. He shook his head in disbelief as he read. It was three-thirty and he had one more call to make.

"Yes," a familiar, but groggy voice answered.

"Good morning, Mr. President. I need to see you," the Admiral said.

"Now?"

"Yes, sir. Now is fine. I'll be right over."

* * *

Pacing the floor like an expectant father and glancing at his watch every few minutes, Chi was waiting for a package of tiny vials—the BCV that could change the balance of world power. The deadly bio-chemical virus was so top secret that its development was under the direct supervision of the Supreme Leader himself, Jiang Zemin. No one but a select few, not even the Inspector General, had access to the BCV or any involvement with it. But somehow Gen. Zimkeroff knew all about China's most closely guarded secret. The Supreme Leader, however, had agreed to Zimkeroff's demands. He was willing to trade the BCV for the deed to Hong Kong. As the go-between for such a momentous transaction, Chi could see himself standing in the Great Hall as the Supreme Leader pinned the Star of China on him. That brought a smile to his face, a smile that widened when he thought about how he had outfoxed Gen. Xi, who didn't even know about the deal.

To divert himself, Chi activated all the surveillance cameras. The eighteen black reflective screens turned into a hodgepodge of lights and pictures: north side, south side, east side, west side, roof, driveway; first floor, three views; second floor, four views; perimeter views looking in and interior views looking out.

Using the joystick, he could pick any screen and focus on any object, enlarging it up to two hundred times. He could read a newspaper at the front of the building as if it were in his hands at the kitchen table. Playing with the cameras until his attention wandered, Chi turned on his computer. He went online to the CAAC site to check the incoming flights from China. Scrolling through the list, Chi found what he was looking for: the words "landing, landing" were flashing on the screen.

The wait was almost over, Chi thought. The excitement made his heart race. The diplomatic courier should be arriving at the hangar in a few minutes. The ringing of the phone interrupted his wait.

"*Ni hao, duile,*" he said.

"*Ni hao.* Has it arrived yet?"

Chi immediately recognized the Inspector General's voice.

"No, but the plane has landed. It will be here soon."

"Be careful. This will not be easy."

"I'm not afraid of the Russians," Chi said.

"There is more to worry about than just the Russians. Never forget the Americans. Look at the videotape first before doing anything else; then decide if there is another way to do this."

Feeling more confident than ever, Chi said: "Sir, the Americans are weak. They have no stomach for this. They will not get in our way. President Clark worries so much about trading with our country that he will not interfere. I can handle anyone the Americans send. In fact, I wish they would send someone. We will ship them home in body bags, along with Zimkeroff and that animal Petroff."

"Wish not, my young friend, for you may get your wish."

Chi was silent, not sure what the Inspector General meant.

"You are to call me after viewing the tape," the Inspector General said.

"Yes, sir," Chi said without hesitation.

The motion detectors signaled the approach of a car on the outer roadway. Manipulating the joystick, Chi brought the driver into view. As he expected, it was his courier. The rented Ford Taurus rolled to a slow stop at the front gate and the driver reached for the call button. Not waiting for the driver, Chi pressed the switch causing the gate to roll back on its wheels. The driver, surprised, jerked back his arm.

Pulling the car through the gate, the courier drove up the front door and got out of the car. Chi turned the joystick and a camera zoomed in on the young man's face until it filled the entire screen. The courier was no more than twenty years old, Chi thought, so young for this delivery. Panning back, he saw the package the courier was carrying. He zoomed in on the sealed diplomatic pouch, clearly reading the Chinese markings: *Privileged diplomatic material. Property of the People's Republic of China.* The courier reached for the buzzer and was about to press it when he heard Chi's metallic voice on the intercom.

"What do you want?"

"Delivery for Sang Chi from Office of Science Administration."

That was the right answer—the only answer. Without comment, Chi pressed a button and the bolt shot back into its sheath. Another button opened the door. The driver stepped into the cavernous hangar and wandered through the maze of boxes and crates, finally finding his way to the staircase. All the time Chi was following him with the cameras, watching his every step, and enjoying the omnipotent feeling of playing an all-seeing god—a god with the power of life and death. With the push of a button, Chi could detonate any one of the special crates packed with explosives. He could set off a small charge or, if needed, he could destroy the entire hangar.

The courier's footsteps on the metal stairs were the only sound in the enormous building. When he finally reached Chi, the young man bowed his head and handed over the diplomatic pouch. Reaching to accept it, Chi nodded his approval. Without a word, the courier bowed again and left. Within an hour he would be back on the plane for China.

The pouch was light. Chi was surprised something so small could kill so many; that China finally had the power to deal with the Americans. Dead Americans, he thought, what a pleasant thought. Wanting to feel secure while he watched the video, Chi armed the electric fence and the explosives in the crates. There would be no unwanted visitors. When he was done, he checked the wall of monitors, made sure the current was running through the fence, and saw to it that the motion detectors were functioning properly.

Then he opened the leather pouch. Inside was a sealed box printed with the words: *Keep Cool.* Heeding the Inspector General's warning, he did not open the box, but placed it in the refrigerator. The only other object in the box was a videocassette. He pushed it into the VCR and pressed play.

A tiny white spot appeared at the center of the black screen; then the screen was covered with black-and-white lines as the VCR tracked the tape. Suddenly appearing on the screen was what Chi had been waiting for. He sat back in his chair and smiled.

Anyone else would have been sick.

* * *

Home to visiting kings and queens, the Peninsula was one of the finest hotels in the world, boasting that it has the most pampered guests anywhere. Now it could boast it was also home to the most beautiful women in the world, the Galaxy Beauty Pageant contestants. The excitement of the pageant was highly contagious. The hotel staff and the guests were being consumed by the festivities. The usually starchy afternoon tea, attended by women in white dresses and white gloves and men in jackets and ties, had been transformed into a dazzling event featuring beautiful women wearing a rainbow of bright colors. Mozart had given way to the Back Street Boys as the background music. The lobby tables, once covered with the *International Times* and *Barrons*, were now littered with *Vogue* and *Cosmopolitan*. Older men were thrilled to have their pictures taken with the beauty queens, knowing that back home they would be envied. The wives of these ancient Lotharios enjoyed watching their husbands making fools of themselves. But no one seemed to mind; it was all in good fun.

The Grand Ballroom was decorated with bunting and balloons. The flags of the various countries represented were carefully hung from the ceiling in alphabetical order, so as not to offend anyone's sensibilities. Beneath her country's flag, each contestant held court in a booth styled to be reminiscent of her homeland. The ballroom filled rapidly once the doors were open to the public. The judges engaged the contestants in general conversations and observed them in their interaction with the other people in the ballroom. As a result of the festive atmosphere, the bar was doing a brisk business, which pleased Tom Camarow. It was his bar; his little profit center.

All the beauty contestants were housed on the twenty-ninth floor. At the request of the show's promoters, the hotel management had arranged to have the elevators' floor buttons keyed. That meant the passenger had to insert his room key into the elevator panel. All reporters, television crews, and photographers had to be cleared by the show's officials to gain entry to the floor. The fire exits at each end of the floor allowed someone to leave, but access from the stairway was denied. The promoters had tried to enforce a no men after midnight rule, usually to no avail. It didn't take a genius to figure out how to beat the system. All an after hours visitor had to do was call up from the lobby and get into one of the waiting elevators while the person on the floor pressed the call button. The elevator car panels may have had the floor button locked out, but the call buttons on the floor worked as usual. Although the contestants were highly competitive, they kept their mouths closed, never reporting after hours guests.

* * *

Frank Shen sat on a metal chair at the end of the hall. He had taken his shoes off and was wiggling his toes. It felt good. When Shen had joined the Hong Kong Police Department in 1966, he had walked a beat. Sometimes, he thought that his feet still hurt all these years later. A hardworking constable, Shen had risen in the ranks, achieving the position of chief of detectives for the burglary unit, a post he had held until he retired. Now he was just a security guard.

After his wife had died, his two married children had moved to England. They did not want to be part of the new Hong Kong under Chinese control. Promising them he would only stay until the turnover, Shen had assured them he would then join them in England. He missed his family, but in truth, the thought of relocating scared him. He had been born in Hong Kong and had spent his whole life there. It was the only home he had ever known; the only place he wanted to be. Besides, his children didn't understand. Love didn't stop with death. Every day on the way to work, he stopped at his wife's grave to speak with her, to tell her what was happening, to get her advice, and to remind her that he loved her.

Pushing thoughts of his wife from his mind, Frank Shen put his shoes back on and went to work. As a security guard for AA Security Services, his job was simple: Guard the women's floor at the hotel. That was easy living—getting paid to make rounds through the halls.

Between rounds, he had a chance to relax and read a book. But now it was time to take a walk.

* * *

Room 2917 was directly across from the elevator. It was a location that many older guests disliked because it was too noisy. But for the young, sleep was not as important as having fun. The proximity to the elevator made it a great room because it was easy to sneak in and out, as the current occupant, Inga Holm of Sweden, could attest.

At that moment, room 2917 had a visitor—a visitor Inga hadn't invited. In fact, she didn't know anyone was there at all. The intruder had picked her room for two reasons. First, it was right across from the elevator. Second, Inga Holm was a strikingly beautiful blonde who had a House of Chan bag. The intruder had other rooms to visit, but this was the place to start.

The open curtain allowed the afternoon light to enter the large room, highlighting the two king-size beds. One was covered with suitcases and six pairs of shoes. On the other, were sweat socks, jeans, and a backpack. The corner desk was littered with an assortment of post cards, key chains, hats, T-shirts, guide books, and other tourist souvenirs. The dresser drawers were half opened, packed with underwear and bras, while the armoire was overflowing with bathing suits, blouses, and a variety of very expensive clothes.

Neatness was not one of Inga's strengths as the pile of clothes and dirty laundry on the floor confirmed. The bathroom was a jumble of makeup, cosmetics, hair dryers, curlers, brushes, and piles of dirty towels on the floor. In the hall off the entrance was a large dressing room with a walk-in closet filled with dresses, gowns, and outfits for all occasions. On the floor of the closet were a dozen pair of shoes, sneakers, flip flops, and slippers.

The intruder emptied the clothes from the armoire, looked through Inga's jewelry and money before searching the suitcases on the bed. In the last suitcase the intruder found a House of Chan bag containing a vase. Holding the vase to the light, the intruder turned it around slowly, admiring it. How ingenious it was to store an ancient deed in a sand-filled vase. Extracting the cork, the intruder poured the fine white sand into the suitcase. The vase was empty.

"Damn it," the intruder muttered.

The intruder dropped the vase back into the suitcase, thinking that the pig who occupied this room would think the cork had fallen out. Or maybe she wouldn't notice at all.

* * *

Walking down the hall, Shen tried the doors of each of the rooms, the odd-numbered rooms going up the hall, the even-numbered ones coming down the hall. When he got to 2917, he noticed the door wasn't closed all the way.

"Anyone home?" he asked in his best English.

No answer.

"Security," he said, pushing the door open a few inches.

Quiet.

Opening the door all the way, he walked into the entrance hall. Stepping a little farther into the room, he was shocked by what he saw. The place was such a mess, he was convinced that someone had tossed it. As he was checking the bathroom, which was filled with a forest of pantyhose suspended from the shower rod and the several damp bras hanging out to dry on the towel racks, the intruder quietly stepped from the hall closet and slipped out the open door. Shen hadn't heard or seen anything, but he had a feeling, an instinct, that raised the hair on the back of his neck.

Stepping into the hall, Shen saw a pretty young woman by the elevator. He asked her if she had seen anyone come out of the room.

"No," she said, stepping into the elevator.

He shrugged; then he pressed the button on his two-way radio to report in to the main office.

"H.Q., this is Shen at the Peninsula. Come in please."

"Go ahead, Frank."

He reported the incident and suggested that the police be called. The dispatcher told him to wait a moment while he called the supervisor.

"Frank, what the hell is going on?" the supervisor asked, annoyed.

Shen told the supervisor what he had found.

"Frank, you're letting your imagination run wild. Some teenage beany brain, who's living in the lap of luxury, keeps her room like a shit house and you think there's a break in. You were in the burglary unit too long. Forget about it. Go read your book. And, Frank, no police."

Shen was a lot of things, but he wasn't stupid. He knew there had been an unlawful entry and he would do something about it. Picking up the house phone, he called the front desk. The desk manager answered.

After identifying himself, Shen asked who was in room 2917.

"Miss Inga Holm," the manager said.

"Can you find her and send her up to her room? Thank you," he said, hanging up.

He had been told not to call the police, but no one told him he couldn't do a little old-fashioned investigating of his own.

CHAPTER 27

Only a fool rushes to fight with a tiger. A wise man waits.

— Old Chinese proverb

A<small>T</small> the sound of his name, Daniels stopped short and turned around.

"What is the CIA's number one field agent doing at a beauty contest?" Gen. Zimkeroff asked.

"I'm not a field agent with the CIA. I'm a photographer for World News Corporation," Daniels said, trying the denial route.

"How foolish of me. I forgot. You are the number one photographer of the Special Operations Division of the CIA run by Admiral E. J. Charko. Now, Commander Daniels, what are you doing at a beauty contest?"

"Trying to get laid," Daniels said. "What's the head of the KGB doing here?"

"The *ex*-head of the KGB is also trying to get laid," Zimkeroff said with a hollow laugh.

"Well, General it was nice running into you again," Daniels said as he turned to leave.

"Wait!" Zimkeroff bellowed.

Daniels stopped his retreat.

"You said something that triggered an unpleasant memory—running into me again," Zimkeroff said. "You didn't have to ruin my brand-new car, Mr. Daniels, the last time you ran into me in Moscow. I'm sure you could have found an easier way to prevent me from getting to my office so I wouldn't catch your partner as he broke in. At first, I thought the accident was truly an accident, but you were too calm, too cool. Most tourists would have insisted on calling their embassy. But not you. You just wanted to keep me there as long as you could. Well, you did a good job, so I now give you my hearty congratulations. Sorry they're a little bit late.

"The truth is, your man didn't find anything, but I found your bugging devices, which, by the way, are still there. I had my fun giving you false information all these years."

"Well, General, you got me. But as long as we're playing Truth or Dare, I have to confess that the bugs planted in your office were meant to be found. My job was to make you suspicious so you would debug the office."

Zimkeroff stared at him.

"I see by the look on your face that you don't understand, General. The real purpose for the break in was to copy the code book you had in the wall safe behind that picture of Stalin with that shit-eating grin. We thought that if you found the bugs, you wouldn't notice the code book had been compromised. Oh, by the way, the list of your agents in the States was a lucky find for us. We had a ball, too, feeding them false information all these years."

Zimkeroff's face turned red, but he quickly controlled his anger. He did not want to show the American he had the upper hand.

"Mr. Daniels—"Gen. Zimkeroff began.

It was Daniels turn to gloat. Deciding to press the bastards, and add salt to Zimkeroff's wounded ego, Daniels raised his camera and snapped the general's picture. Petroff tried to grab the camera, but Daniels quickly pushed the camera into the bridge of Petroff's nose with enough force to break the cartilage. Blood flowed from both of Petroff's nostrils. It ran down to his lips, coloring them a dark red. Petroff's eyes watered, he saw stars, and he reached for his nose. Daniels's right hand grabbed Petroff's crotch and squeezed hard. The sergeant major's knees buckled, and he folded like an old bridge chair. Turning away from Petroff, Daniels stepped closer to Zimkeroff until they were only inches apart.

"Go ahead, General, take your best shot,"Daniels said."The next time I shoot you it won't be with a camera."

"You're dead, Daniels,"Zimkeroff whispered menacingly.

"Not yet, General, not yet,"Daniels said and walked away.

As Zimkeroff bent down to help Petroff to his feet, he saw a flash go off.

"Great shot, General. True Russian compassion,"Daniels said.

"I'll kill him,"Petroff gasped.

"No, you won't,"Zimkeroff said."I'll kill him myself."

In the lobby, Daniels found Camarow leashed to a tall blonde. So much for redheads, he thought. Camarow led the woman to the elevator banks. Daniels followed close behind.

"Hi, Mac,"Camarow said."Meet Inga Holm, our Miss Sweden. Isn't she beautiful?"

"Absolutely,"Daniels said.

Inga was without a doubt a beauty, a typical Scandinavian type, blonde, fair, blue eyed, and tall. More important, Daniels immediately recognized her as one of the contestants he had photographed with a House of Chan bag. He wanted a chance to speak with her.

"Inga's room has been broken into," Camarow said. "Why don't you come along?"

When the elevator doors opened on the twenty-ninth floor, Frank Shen was waiting for them.

"Lead the way," Camarow said.

Shen gave Daniels the once over.

"Hey, don't I know you?" the security guard asked.

"No, I don't think we've met. I'm Mac Daniels with the World News Corporation."

Actually, they had met several years before when Shen had been investigating an attempted break-in at the American Consulate. Daniels had been posing as a cultural attaché at the time. He hoped the security guard didn't remember.

Shen looked at him curiously, but being an old pro, he said no more—for the time being. Opening the door to Inga's room, Shen stepped aside as she walked in, followed by Daniels snapping pictures and Camarow bringing up the rear. Looking around, saying nothing, Inga just nodded her head like one of those dogs that sits on the dashboard of a car.

"What's missing, Inga?" Camarow asked finally.

"I don't know," she said in heavily accented English. "Everything seems to be here. Ya, it looks like the way I left it."

"Check your suitcases," Camarow said. "See if everything is there."

Inga carefully opened each bag until she found the one that contained the vase.

"Oh, look," she said. "There's sand all over the place."

Daniels looked over her shoulder and saw the soft sand smoothly pooled in her suitcase. He instantly remembered a similar pile of sand he found at the warehouse—sand and broken glass. Another vase? he wondered.

"Please go over the room carefully," Frank Shen said to her. "And Mr. Daniels, may I see you for a second?"

Daniels did not reply; he just followed Shen out to the hallway.

"Why the charade? You are with the State Department," Shen said, suddenly remembering where he had seen Daniels before.

"No longer," Daniels said. "I'm now a freelance photographer working for the World News Corporation."

"Sure," Shen said, "and I'm the Emperor of China."

"You're a tough cop, Frank, you got me. I'm with the F.B.I., on special assignment," Daniels lied. "I could use your help."

That was more digestible to Shen. Daniels looked like a cop and no cop ever really retired.

"What do you make of the sand?" Daniels asked.

"Packing sand used in the shipment of glass," Shen said, confirming Daniel's analysis. "It must have spilled from the vase in her suitcase."

"You could be a great help," Daniels said.

"Whatever I can do," Shen said.

"Keep an eye on these women," he said, producing a list of the women who had the House of Chen bags.

"All right," Shen said. "You know when I went into Miss Holm's room before, I had the feeling that someone was in there with me. The strangest feeling. When I went out into the hall there was a beautiful woman waiting for the elevator."

"Can you describe her?"

"Sure, I can," Shen said and he did.

Too many coincidences, Daniels thought, something he didn't believe in.

* * *

Astrid was talking on the phone in the sitting room when Daniels returned to the suite. He kissed her on the top of her head; she pursed her lips and blew him a kiss. From the bar freezer Daniels took out a bottle of Grey Goose vodka and poured some into a pitcher filled with ice. Then he poured vermouth into a glass, swirled it around, and threw it into the sink. Filling the glass with vodka, he added a lemon twist.

"Here you are," he said to Astrid. "A Daniels very, very dry vodka Martini, my special in and out."

"In and out, just like you, Mac," she said, laughing.

"The vermouth, wise guy, the vermouth."

He made himself a drink and sat next to her on the couch.

"How was your interview with Harry Saltzman at the consulate?"

Astrid didn't answer him; she had questions of her own. He told her what he could about the day's events.

"I got some great shots at the rehearsal earlier today," he said. "I even got a touching shot of Gen. Zimkeroff rendering first aid to his orderly."

"Alexis?" she asked.

"You know him?" he asked.

"Not in the biblical sense, darling, but we are having dinner with him tonight."

"What?"

She handed him an invitation to the Galaxy Grand Ball. It listed the VIPs in attendance; at the end of the alphabetical listing was Alexis Zimkeroff.

"How about being my date tonight for dinner and dancing?" Astrid asked.

Before he could answer, the phone in her bedroom rang.

His eyes followed her out of the room. It was the best offer he had all day. Picking up the invitation again, he glanced at the names, recognizing many of them.

Cocktails were at seven and dinner at eight. Perfect, he thought. His mind raced through a series of options, evaluating the pros and cons of each move. Unfortunately, there was no time for dinner with Astrid.

"Are you going to drink that or play with it?" she asked, her voice breaking the silence.

"Drink it," he said, finishing it with a gulp. "Honey, I can't make it tonight, I didn't know you were invited. I'm sorry. I really am."

He meant it, she knew. She sat on his lap and he pulled her close. With her head on his chest, they sat there just holding each other, wishing everything else would go away. She never wanted to leave him. She loved him.

Daniels slowly rubbed her back, thinking that it was time to pay Gen. Zimkeroff a visit. He shook his head at his own foolishness. Only a fool rushes to fight with a tiger. A wise man waits. He looked at Astrid cuddled in his arms. What a fool am I, he thought, what a fool am I.

CHAPTER 28

Sometimes it's chance that takes you.

— Old Chinese proverb

FLASHING lights in a variety of colors made Luard Road look like Christmas in June. Every night it pulsed with a nonstop neon glow. Sitting prominently on the corner of Luard and Gloucester Roads, in the Wanchai section of Hong Kong, was the Hi-Jinks Club, the number one hot spot on the island. Like most of the strip clubs, the Hi-Jinks had an abundance of exotic Chinese girls, some topless and some wearing glittering pasties and tassels hanging from their nipples. Most of them wore thongs, showing off their less-than-round rear ends. A large square bar, featuring topless barmaids, occupied the center of the room. The customers liked to watch them as they shook and gyrated while mixing drinks. Surrounding the bar was a sea of tables, served by near naked cocktail waitresses, who were happy to oblige a customer with a table dance.

At the end of the room was heaven, figuratively speaking, an elevated stage which was the focus of the spotlights. There, bathed in smoke and surrounded by mirrors, was the goddess of erotica, an American woman who gave the customers plenty to look at. The stage belonged to Happy Holiday—the goddess men dreamed of.

Standing six-feet tall in flats and growing six more inches in the platform heels she wore, Happy Holiday stood out no matter where she danced. Her hair was golden blonde, naturally blonde, soft, silky, and piled on top of her head to accent her deep blue eyes. Her face was tanned, which highlighted her chiseled features. Breasts as tan as her face, defied gravity. Happy's long shapely legs never seemed to end.

As a teenager she was called Legs, and when she started to dance professionally back in the States, she was known as Legs Diamond. Happy's act was tame by American standards, but in Hong Kong she put on the hottest show in Wanchai. She was the reason that the Chinese, Japanese, and Korean men put behind them their thousand years of war and hatred, standing on line, shoulder to shoulder, just to get into the Hi-Jinks Club. They wanted to see her, to touch her, and if they were fortunate enough, to have their picture taken with her—a picture that would sit on the altar of their imaginations for years to come.

As the star of the Hi-Jinks Club, Happy Holiday was paid more than five-thousand US dollars a week. She cleared another five thousand a week in tips from the generous men she smiled at. Happy was happy making more money than she had ever dreamed of.

Her life hadn't always been this fun. Born in a little town in upstate New York, she had lost her parents at an early age. Then her older brother had died. She had danced in strip clubs on the circuit: New York City, Washington, D.C., Atlanta, and Miami. For years she had fought off unwelcome advances and had resisted the idiots who were her bosses. That put her on the stage instead of in the audience where the table dancers made the big tips. Most people thought that the performers on the stage were the stars, but in reality they were paid only a few hundred dollars to keep the audience occupied, while the real stars and big earners worked the crowd.

By the time she was thirty, she had had enough. Over the hill for an exotic dancer in the United States, and tired of the bull she had had to take for not being sexually cooperative, she had decided to head west— way west, ending up in Hong Kong.

Not only did Happy make a lot of money at the Hi-Jinks Club, she was truly appreciated by the owners. Being in the business for many years, Happy had learned the number one rule of club life: mind your own business. The backrooms of many clubs were occupied with other things—drugs, gambling, and escort services. She wanted no part of those enterprises and stayed away.

One of Hi-Jinks Club's specialties was its very discreet escort service. High-priced call girls showed men around town during the day and ended up in their rooms at night. All fees were paid to the club. The escorts never received any money, not even a tip, from their customers. Without money changing hands, the police could never prove anything.

Happy Holiday ignored the backroom shenanigans, minding her own business, never dating the owners, and never telling anyone her real name. She was Happy Holiday, making a lot of money, and hoping to return to the United States one day to enjoy her life. She dreamed of owning a beach house on the coast of New Jersey.

* * *

Kwangtung is the most southern province in China. It is separated from Hong Kong by the Shumchun River. Canton, the capital of the province, is located on the northern edge of the Pearl River about a hundred miles from Hong Kong, a two-hour trip by train. Canton is often considered the birthplace of the Chinese Revolution and the founding city of the Chinese People's Republic. The Chinese still came to Canton, the city of liberation, but for other reasons now. They tried to cross the Shumchun River to freedom, to Hong Kong. Many never made it across; their bodies were never found.

On April 27, 1911, Dr. Sun Yat-sen, who would go on to found the Chinese Republic, was handed a terrible defeat there. The resulting bloodbath in Canton led many people to believe that their hopes and dreams of freedom were shattered forever. Thousands fled south to Hong Kong. One of those who made it was Yi Leng and his family.

Yi Leng had no money or skills when he arrived in Hong Kong. He was a leader of the failed revolution, a wanted man, worth a lot more dead than alive. He vowed never again to suffer from the tyranny of a dictator. But when there was no food to eat, he knew, lofty ideals lasted little longer than hay in a windstorm. Desperate to support his family, Yi Leng at first stole little things. Seeing an opportunity, he sold drugs; then he opened gambling parlors. Several generations later, the Lengs ran the largest crime organization in Hong Kong. Its poisonous tentacles reached far into Southeast Asia, Japan, Korea, and the Pacific rim.

Eighty-year-old Johnny Leng, barely five-two, and commonly called the Little Guy, was the great-grandson of Yi Leng. He was the head of the Leng criminal enterprise and he controlled it like a multinational corporation. His lieutenants were responsible for various divisions, reporting to him, and were held accountable for the profitability and growth of their turf. The gross revenues of the Lengs's empire were larger than most Third World countries.

Johnny's grandson, Jeffery Leng, had been instrumental in setting up the structure of the empire, something that greatly pleased his grandfather. After spending several years in the United States, Jeffery had adopted Western ways while doing his undergraduate and graduate studies at Harvard University.

If there was such a thing as the chief financial officer of a criminal empire, Jeffery held that position. Using what he learned at Harvard and making the best of his worldwide contacts, Jeffery Leng invested their illegal profits in legitimate business ventures, adding to the wealth and power of the Leng family. If the drug business made a billion, Jeff turned it into two billion. Jeffery Leng was ready to take the empire to new heights when the time came for him to take over. Both Lengs were pleased. They had a perfect division of labor, bonded by love. If someone wanted to see Jeffery Leng, he went to a modern high-rise office near the Mandarin Hotel, a block from the Star Line ferry, and a dozen or so blocks away from the Hi-Jinks Club. If someone wanted to see Johnny Leng, he went to his office at the Hi-Jinks Club. Johnny Leng owned it.

* * *

When her dance routine ended to the loud cheers and thunderous applause, Happy made her way backstage. One of her attendants handed her a robe and she walked down the hall to her private dressing room, one of the perks of being a star. The club had been unusually crowded that night, probably because of the great number of tourists in town for the turnover, she thought, wondering if the Chinese government would let the club stay in business. The boss, as she referred to Johnny Leng, showed no concern. For him, it was business as usual.

Naked, except for a garter, she lit a cigarette. Extending her long leg, she pulled out the wad of bills stuffing her garter. Then she made neat piles, dividing the bills by country: American, British, Japanese, Korean, Hong Kong, Russian, and Chinese. On the top of the Hong Kong pile was a crisp new thousand-dollar bill. On it, written in perfect script, was: Thanks, J. L. She smiled. Every time Jeff was in the club, he had one of his aides slip her money, always with a "thanks" written on it. He told her she was the reason for the club's success. Happy appreciated his kind words, but that was all.

Counting her money and placing it in the small safe in her dressing room, she finished her cigarette and climbed into the shower. Her batteries recharged, she slithered into a low cut, red silk dress that miraculously held her in. Clinging to her body, the dress fit as if it were painted on. The sides were cut high almost to her waist, revealing plenty of leg. With each step, she flashed a glimpse of her ass cheek. Looking in the mirror, she nodded her approval, and said: "Kelly Brook, you're looking good."

Between sets, she would mix with the customers. That was fun for her because she was a natural at working the crowd. They lined up to buy her drinks or, better yet, to have a picture taken with her. She never refused. The bartenders poured her ginger ale, charging the customer for the most expensive champagne. No one seemed to care; she was there, that was all that mattered. The cheering for Kelly stopped the show. Discordant voices called her name as she moved about the club. Because she was a head taller than most of the men in the room, their eyes were focused on her bustline. When she bent over to give a man a hug, inevitably smothering his head in between her breasts, everyone laughed—earning her an extra hundred dollars.

* * *

In his office, a large room with linen wall coverings, Johnny Leng sat behind a massive teak desk, working the phones. His grandson had tried in vain to move him to the high-rise office tower, but Johnny was content and comfortable in his back room office at the club. At one end of the desk was a computer terminal that was never turned on. It was connected to an ultra thin monitor covered with Post-it Notes. The keyboard was used to hold telephone notepad messages, which fit neatly between the rows of keys. At the other end of the desk were several telephones ringing constantly. It was not unusual for one receiver to be on his right ear, one on his left, while the speaker phone was on at the same time. Other than a few papers, which were of no importance, his desk was clear.

Along one wall of the office was a soft leather couch, flanked by teak end tables, holding massive Waterford lamps that cast a glow on the gold-framed photographs of his grandson, Jeff. In front of his desk were two large leather armchairs where his visitors waited for Johnny Leng to speak. The entertainment center at the other end of the office housed a large-screen television connected to the club's closed circuit video system. That gave him a private view of the club, the stage, and, the old man's favorite channel, the dressing rooms of the dancers.

Johnny Leng's visitors crossed the threshold of his office and waded through an ocean of light blue carpet to have an audience with the purveyor of vice. Whatever doubts they may have had about the reach of the Little Man were quickly dispelled by the photographs on the wall. Scores of rich, famous, and powerful people had sent him pictures, signed: *To my friend, Johnny.*

Jeffery Leng was seated across from his grandfather, sipping Perrier Jouet champagne. Holding a cell phone to his ear, he looked like the billionaire he was. The dark-blue silk suit was custom tailored and had cost three thousand dollars. His Gucci shoes were specially designed for him at a thousand dollars a pair. Crisp white cuffs extended exactly one quarter inch from his jacket sleeve, displaying diamond studs that cost ten thousand dollars. The overhead lights reflected a kaleidoscope of colors from his thirty-thousand-dollar diamond encrusted Rolex.

Unlike his grandson, Johnny Leng looked more like a homeless person than the multi-billionaire he was. He didn't care about fashionable Western dress, leaving that to Jeff, his heir, and the last of the Leng line. After Jeffery's parents had been killed in a car accident, Johnny had taken charge of his eight-year-old grandson. The hurt and pain of losing his son had been made bearable by his promise to himself to raise his heir.

Every night Jeff made the ritual stop by the club to visit his grandfather and to report on the day's activities. He gave his grandfather the highlights of his business deals and he was there to answer the question Johnny would ask all the time: "How's business?"

Finishing his call, Jeff crossed his legs and watched his grandfather work the phones. The old man was amazing, he thought, like a conductor directing a band. He moved from phone to phone, playing them like instruments. Jeff knew better than to interrupt his grandfather, but he was anxious to tell him about a very interesting offer he had received that day.

Turning toward the giant television screen tuned to the club's video system, he watched one of the strippers perform. The patrons were not paying attention to the act. All eyes were on the tall blonde moving through the crowd. Amazing, he thought, as he focused in on her. She was sipping ginger ale from a champagne glass. The men were pressing up to her, trying to get close. One customer held up a camera. Jeff was able to read his lips. "Picture, please, picture," the man was saying. She was incredible, he thought. He couldn't help smiling.

Jeff watched as Happy grabbed the small man while his friend snapped photographs. Then she said something and quickly pulled his head into her breast. The men surrounding her laughed and applauded. Recovering from the shock, the customer slipped Happy a handful of bills.

Turning away, she bumped into another patron spilling his drink. Jeff saw it splash all over her dress. Never losing her infectious smile, she used the man's tie to dry her dress; then, with a comic twist, she patted her breast—smiling, all the time, smiling. The man gave her some money and she made her way to her dressing room. Jeff thought that the man would probably frame his tie and hang it in his office. He would have a story to tell.

Happy's dressing room was next to Johnny's office and Jeff heard the door close. He found himself staring at the wall, thinking that his grandfather must have a hidden camera or a peephole so he could watch her in her dressing room. But he had never asked, not wanting to embarrass the elder Leng. Finally, his grandfather spoke: "How's business?"

In her dressing room, Happy rummaged through her closet for another dress to wear. That's when she heard the Lengs talking. She didn't want to listen; she didn't want to hear. She knew what the Lengs did and she didn't want to be involved, but it was fate. It was chance that had taken her to her dressing room that night in time to hear the words that would change her life.

CHAPTER 29

An old rabbit always watches the fox.

— Old Chinese proverb

C HI kept clearing his throat as the elevator took him up to Gen. Zimkeroff's floor. The briefcase he held had a strange, hypnotic effect on him. No matter how hard he tried to avoid looking at it, his eyes were drawn to the case. Chi was about to embark on the most important task he had ever undertaken—he was going to show Gen. Zimkeroff one of China's most closely guarded secrets, a biochemical virus, the BCV. This was the first step in securing Hong Kong for his country. Clearing his throat, taking a deep breath, Chi knocked on the door of Zimkeroff's suite. Maj. Joseph Bresneyev answered.

Chi recognized Bresneyev from the warehouse where Petroff had given him a beating that still hurt. He followed the major down the hall and into a sitting room.

"Sit there," Bresneyev said, pointing to the couch.

In a few minutes, Zimkeroff came into the room wearing his dress uniform. Chi didn't want to be impressed, but he was. He jumped to his feet, came to attention, and bowed his head. Chi was a good foot shorter than the hulking general and he felt overpowered.

"Drink?" Zimkeroff asked.

"No, thank you, General," Chi said.

"Where is it?" Zimkeroff demanded.

Reaching into his briefcase, Chi pulled out a videotape.

"Right here," he said, waiving the tape.

"Col. Kertrinkoff, Maj. Bresneyev, come here," Zimkeroff said in a booming voice that echoed through the suite.

Immediately, Kertrinkoff and Bresneyev entered the room both in dress uniform. They stood at attention until the general sat down.

"Gentlemen," said Zimkeroff, pointing to two chairs. "Please be seated."

"Go ahead, Chi," the general said, snapping his fingers.

Chi placed the videotape into the VCR and pressed the play button.

The black screen came to life, filled up with Chinese writing, then faded to a modern laboratory. The voice-over was in Chinese. The camera panned the laboratory, which was filled with high-tech equipment. A man wearing what looked like a space suit was moving around the lab. The camera followed the technician as he went to a freezer and took out a container of what looked like ice cubes. He held the container so the camera could zoom in; then he shook the container. The ice-like substance rattled around. Placing the container back into the freezer, the technician opened a cooler and picked up a beaker containing what Zimkeroff thought was water. Again the technician held up the beaker for a close-up.

As the camera moved in, he started swirling the liquid in the beaker. Returning the beaker to the cooler, the technician crossed the lab to a desk where he picked up an empty sealed flask. He held the flask in front of a black background and the camera zoomed in so close that the small print on the flask could be read: *Made in USA.*

"What does all this mean, General?" Kertrinkoff asked, obviously puzzled.

"It's quite simple," Zimkeroff said. "The lab technician is demonstrating the BCV in its three forms: solid, liquid, and gas. In the gas form, it is colorless and has only a slight odor. As a liquid, it looks like water, and as a solid, it has the characteristics of ice. The beauty of BCV is its ease of use. It is simple to transport and a little bit goes a very long way."

All eyes returned to the screen. The technician took the ice form of the BCV from the freezer and carefully chipped off a thin sliver. He placed it in a flask and sealed the flask with a rubber stopper. The camera zoomed in on the flask, while the narrator spoke in a soft voice as if he were witnessing a miracle. The man in the space suit held the flask over a flame. The ice quickly turned to liquid. A few more seconds and it turned to a gas. Removing the flask from the flame and placing it in cold water, the gas condensed and liquefied. Placing the liquid in the freezer, the technician leaned back to let the camera record it solidifying.

"Chi," Zimkeroff bellowed. "I understand its chemical reaction, but I want a further explanation of the virus part."

Chi stopped the tape, barely able to contain his glee at having the general admit he didn't understand something.

"General, I'm not a scientist, just a messenger, but I'll try to explain," Chi said. "The virus is dormant when it is solid or liquid, but when it is ingested as a gas, it is activated and lethal. The natural state for the virus is sub-microscopic airborne gaseous particles that have a life of their own. They multiply."

"How do you control it?" Zimkeroff asked.

"The life cycle of the virus is about six hours. After that, it will dissipate. It will also become inactive when the temperature reaches forty degrees Celsius."

"Does it work?" Bresneyev asked.

"Watch this," Chi said, pointing to the screen, as if to say "here comes the good part." He fast forwarded through various scientific explanations and demonstrations until he came to the section he wanted.

On the screen was a large room, a type of auditorium. The cameraman was in the center, rotating the camera in a circle trying to show the size of the room. As he passed each corner, the cameraman stopped, zooming into a man tied to a chair. Then the camera pulled back. Apparently, he was exiting the room. Appearing on the television screen, filling the entire picture, was a gloved hand holding a tiny glass vial no bigger than half a toothpick.

"It's the BCV in the gaseous state," Chi said.

The camera followed the technician as he placed the vial on a table in the center of the room. Suspended over the vial was a small watchmaker's hammer, rigged to a triggering device. On a signal from someone off-screen, the hammer hit the vial cracking it in two. The screen divided into four different shots and a stopwatch was superimposed at the bottom. The narrator's voice was silent, only the ticking of the stopwatch could be heard. Three, four, five, seconds went by. No change. At six seconds, all four men began to cough. At nine seconds, the vomiting began. At thirteen seconds, their eyes were watering and their noses were bleeding. There was more coughing, violent convulsive coughing. At twenty-five seconds, their chests were heaving and their ears were bleeding. Thirty seconds after the vial had been broken, all four men in the vast room were dead.

The screen went black for a second, then a large bowl filled with some type of punch appeared. A man with an eye dropper carefully squeezed one drop of liquid into the bowl. A dozen men wearing prison garb marched into the room, followed by two uniformed soldiers. Chi explained that the men were political prisoners about to be released. All of the men except the guards took some punch. They were all dead in twenty-four seconds.

"A liter in a reservoir would kill millions of..." Chi paused for effect. "Americans."

"Which is the preferred method of use: gas or liquid?" Col. Kertrinkoff asked.

"Gas is very effective, covering large areas because of its ability to multiply, but in the air it's only lethal for about six hours. The liquid is lethal from ten to twenty hours, depending what it is mixed in. In water, it is potent for twenty hours; in milk about fifteen hours; in beer or wine about ten hours. But you need a larger quantity of liquid BCV because it doesn't multiply."

"I'll deliver the deed when you are ready to hand over the BCV," Zimkeroff said.

"I'm ready now," Chi said. "You will get the BCV when I get the deed. When?"

"Two days before the turnover. Where?"

"My place at the airport. CAAC hangar on the perimeter road."

"Agreed."

Chi stood up to retrieve the tape from the VCR. Zimkeroff snapped his fingers with such force it sounded like a firecracker. Chi spun around.

"Leave it. Petroff has not seen it," Zimkeroff said.

"When we exchange, I want the tape back," Chi said.

The general agreed.

"Major, show Mr. Sang Chi out," Zimkeroff said.

His groin packed with ice and still in pain, Petroff lay on his bed. He turned his head to see Zimkeroff standing in the doorway.

"Sir," he said, trying to rise.

"No, no," Zimkeroff told him, waiving him back down with his hand. Pulling up a chair next to Petroff's bed, Zimkeroff was anxious to tell his sergeant major what he had seen.

"When you get a chance watch the tape, Yuri," Zimkeroff said.

"Yes, sir," came the reply in a weak voice.

"I'm going with the colonel and the major to the Galaxy Grand Ball tonight. I'm sorry you are out of commission."

"When we get the BCV, I'd like permission to use it on the American, Daniels," Petroff said.

"Perhaps," Zimkeroff said. "Although I would like to kill him myself. But don't worry about the BCV. You will get your chance to use it."

* * *

As soon as he was back at his office at the CAAC hangar, Chi called the Inspector General. He was excited about the evening's events and feeling so smug that he could hardly contain himself. The secure phone rang several times before it was answered.

Chi gave him all the details about his meeting with Gen. Zimkeroff. He went on for ten minutes without a word from his boss.

"Making the trade at the hangar is a wise move. Wa Chung will be able to protect you there. Do not forget, we want both the deed and the BCV back," the Inspector General said.

Chi didn't want Wa Chung around, but he had lost that argument the last time. The next time it would be different.

"Once I have the deed, I'm going to give the BCV to Zimkeroff right up his red Russian ass. I'm really going to give it to him and that son-of-a-bitch Petroff. It will be the last thing those Russian bastards ever get," Chi said, his cockiness overruling his head.

"Don't underestimate the Russians," the Inspector General said, his voice becoming stern before the line went dead.

Sitting back in his chair, his feet on the desk, Chi laughed, pleased with himself, thinking that the Inspector General worried too much. I'll bring the deed back to China, save Hong Kong, prevent crazy Gen. Xi from starting a war, eliminate the Russians, and protect the BCV, he thought. He could picture the Supreme Leader pinning the Star of China on him and shaking his hand in the Great Hall. Maybe, he thought, the Supreme Leader would promote him. After all, he reasoned, the Inspector General was old and would retire soon. Sang Chi, Inspector General. That had a nice ring to it.

The Inspector General reviewed his notes and shook his head. In spite of Chi's unbridled optimism, this was far from over. He remembered something he learned a long time ago—an old rabbit always watches the fox.

CHAPTER 30

Time is a formidable foe. It never relents.

— Old Chinese proverb

⚜

THE last staff meeting of the day was always the worst, Liz Browning thought, especially when things were going badly. As each department head completed his report, Montgomery's voice seemed to grow more agitated and his pacing became more relentless. Although he claimed to have quit smoking, he was lighting one cigarette with the stub of another. Disgusted with the day's results, yet trying to be civilized to his staff, he dismissed them for the night.

Montgomery didn't hear any "good nights," but if he had listened carefully, he might have heard a couple of "up yours" and even a fuck you or two. Alone in the room with Browning and Williams, he picked up his pacing, holding a pile of reports high over his head and shaking them.

"I want results and I'm given pounds of worthless paper filled with theories and conjecture," he said, throwing the papers in the air. The room was quiet except for the sound of the paper fluttering down on the table.

"Mr. Montgomery."

Browning's soft voice stopped the raging bull in his tracks. He glared at her.

"I hope you don't think I'm going to clean up this mess you made," she said.

For the first time all day, Montgomery smiled.

"You're wearing out my carpet, Michael. It comes out of my budget," Williams said, feeling the tension subside.

"The night's young, let's get back to work," Browning said. "Michael, anything from Jeffery Leng?"

"Leng! My God, Michael," Williams said, shocked. "He's the grandson of Johnny Leng. Bad people. What on God's good earth are you doing with him?"

"To answer Liz's question first: No, I haven't heard from him. As to your question, Winston, I'm trying to keep Hong Kong as part of Her Majesty's good green earth. These are desperate times, Winston, calling for desperate measures. I made the Lengs an offer they couldn't refuse. We need them, they need us, and we need the deed to Hong Kong. Does anybody have any other suggestions?"

Williams felt helpless. He didn't know how to help, he didn't know what to do, and in some way he felt responsible. Each strike of the clock meant it was that much closer to the turnover.

The ringing of a cell phone brought them back to reality. All three of them reached for their own.

"Mine," Montgomery said.

"No contact with Chi, nothing," Montgomery said, after hanging up. "Not a single lead. I authorized surveillance at the Chinese embassy and I've put a watch on Adams's home, just in case he shows up there. Don't jump to any conclusions. I believe Les and Lu An are innocent."

In his heart, Montgomery was betting on Gen. Xi. In his head, he knew he had better keep looking for the deed. So far, all the information provided by Xi had been accurate, right down to the details of the troop movements and, of course, the truth about Chi. His cell phone rang again.

It was one of the men who were following Daniels, reporting that he was still in his hotel suite.

"Any further instruction, sir?"

"Stay with him. He can cause more trouble than anyone I know. I'll be at the hotel for dinner. I'll see you then."

"Dinner at the Peninsula without me?" Liz asked.

"Didn't he tell you?" Williams asked. "The governor was invited to the Galaxy Grand Ball tonight. But due to scheduling problems, he couldn't attend, so he gave me his invitations. If Michael forgot to mention that I am inviting you to join us, then he is a lug head."

"I would be honored to accept your invitation. I'll try to get a date."

"Lug head is available," Montgomery said.

* * *

High above the Peninsula lobby, where the rich and famous were gathering for the evening's events, Gen. Xi and six of his top officers were gathering for other purposes. The chief of staff, Col. Miu, reported on Chi's movements, including the fact that a special courier from China had dropped off a package to him. Gen. Xi asked if anybody knew anything about the delivery. No one did.

"Check with Mi Ler, the Inspector General's secretary, and find out what was sent," Gen. Xi told the colonel.

"Sir, I already spoke to Mi Ler. She has no idea what was sent. She is checking and will report to me as soon as she has any information," the chief of staff said.

"Excellent, continue."

"Chi met with Gen. Zimkeroff this afternoon, after he had received the diplomatic pouch. They met at Zimkeroff's hotel, the Sheraton."

"The British are inept," Xi said. "Chi is coming and going as he pleases. Why haven't the British picked him up yet? Weren't they watching Zimkeroff when Chi met with him?"

"Sir," the colonel replied, "Chi has more than one man's luck. How did he avoid the trap we set for him at Water Street?"

"Better yet, colonel, who killed our men at the warehouse? I don't think it was Chi. He hasn't the ability."

"What does Zimkeroff want for the deed?" Miu asked.

"Actually, it doesn't matter what he wants because we will have the deed," Xi said.

Miu handed Xi an envelope. Looking through the contents, Xi threw down pictures of the Galaxy World beauty contestants.

"Are we ready?" Gen. Xi asked.

They were.

"Excellent, now gather round the coffee table," Xi said, laying out the pictures of the beauty contestants into two piles. One stack he placed back into the envelope; the other he spread out.

The men's eyes were glued to the photographs of the blonde beauty contestants, but when Gen. Xi cleared his throat, they snapped to attention.

"Each one of these women came to Hong Kong with a House of Chan bag containing a vase," the general said. "One of the vases has the deed to Hong Kong in it. Tonight, when these women are attending the Grand Ball, each of you will take a man and search their rooms. You will take all the vases you find and bring them to me."

It sounded as if he were ordering an attack on an enemy position.

"I will not be denied my victory. Each officer is responsible for the success of this mission. This time there is no room for error. Col. Miu has arranged for the elevators to be shut down. The fire doors are locked. You will have as much time as you need. No one will enter the floor until you are finished. You will take no prisoners."

"Sir, you mean—" one of his men said.

"I know what I mean. Do you know what taking no prisoners means? It means that if anyone comes into a room being searched they will be shot. I don't care if you kill every bitch in the show or anyone else. I want the deed to Hong Kong."

There was absolute silence in the room. Gen. Xi looked at each one of his officers, staring at them one by one.

There was a knock on the door. An orderly came into the living room and handed Gen. Xi a box. It contained six Walther P-5 9 mm semi-automatic pistols with silencers attached. Each man took one, along with a magazine holding ten rounds of ammunition.

Gen. Xi went to his bedroom to place a call.

"I'm pleased to tell you that all is going well," he said on the phone. "At eight tonight I'm going down to the Galaxy Grand Ball. At eight-thirty, my officers will be on their way to get the vase and the deed. When I get it, I'll call you."

* * *

Astrid tried to quietly open the door to Daniels's room. She wanted to surprise him, but the door was locked.

"Mac, Mac, are you up? Open up, it's me," she said softly against the door.

"Who's 'me'? I'm sleeping."

"Come on, Mac, open up. How come you locked the door?"

"Be right there, sweetie. Sorry, didn't know it was locked."

Daniels quickly put away his diplomatic case containing surveillance equipment and an assortment of weapons he didn't want her to see. Wearing only a pair of boxer shorts, he opened the door for her.

She was wearing a black evening gown that was extremely low cut to accentuate her voluptuous breasts. The split up the front of her dress exposed her long tanned legs as she floated into the room. Her red hair was piled high on her head making her look even taller than five-feet-seven. The black dress and red hair made her emerald green eyes shine. She wore a single piece of jewelry, a turquoise-and-silver necklace her father had purchased for her mother many years before.

Daniels stood there speechless as she turned around showing off her outfit.

"Well, how do I look?" she purred.

He ran his eyes up and down, taking her all in, absorbing her looks, studying every detail, impressing it into his memory, in the area of the brain that is marked do not erase.

"Beautiful is not the word to describe you," Daniels said. "I'm not sure what to say about such a wonderful sight. God, you're gorgeous. Perhaps I should just thank you for allowing me the privilege of looking at you."

"Mac Daniels, I do believe you're a romantic," she cooed in her soft drawl. "And I thank you. It's a privilege I would gladly share only with you."

Reaching out, he ran his fingers gently down her smooth face. His touch was warm, soft, and somehow erotic. Their eyes locked. She felt a glow spread over her body; neither one of them could speak. His index finger moved gently over her lips. She closed her eyes, her mouth opening slightly, letting her tongue touch his finger. Her heart was pounding and she wondered if he could feel it.

Letting out a breath he didn't know he was holding, Daniels pulled her close. Their lips met gently. Pulling back, he cupped her face in his hands, just looking at her. Then his hand moved down from her face and he brushed her necklace. The cold stones had no warmth and that brought him back to Earth.

Intellectually he knew this was not the time to fall in love. It wouldn't work, at least not now. Feeling his hand on her necklace broke the trance for her, too.

"Oh, Mac, darling, I don't want to go to the Grand Ball without you. If you like, we could stay right here and, if you're lucky, I'll give you something else to look at."

Oh, Lord, tempt me not, he thought.

"Sweetie, you are the belle of the ball. You have to show up," he said, summoning up every bit of his intellectual strength. "You're sitting with the consul general, his wife, and Harry Saltzman. You can't disappoint the consul general. Hell, after seeing you, he'll really have something to talk about. I have something to do, believe me, believe me."

Astrid knew more than he realized she did. She accepted his excuse and didn't press the issue. This was going to be a busy night for him, she thought.

"When you're done with your business," she said, "I'll be right here to do our business."

She left him when she heard the doorbell ring. He let out a sigh of frustration. At least her attitude had changed, he thought. She didn't go crazy when she didn't get what she wanted. Maybe she really had changed.

"You are an idiot. Why didn't you go with her?" he said looking in the mirror. The face in the mirror spoke back: "Because you have a job to do."

* * *

For the Galaxy Beauty Pageant the Grand Ball was one of the most important events of the Hong Kong leg of the tour. Dinner, dancing, a chance to see the world beauties up close, and to socialize with them, appealed to those who had the money to pay—money that went directly into Tom Camarow's pockets.

He was a genius at promotion, making a profit on every stop of the tour. And Hong Kong would be no exception. The whole world would be watching the turnover and his show was right there in the middle. What was more poetic than having the reigning world beauty queen there to help symbolize peace and beauty with a new Hong Kong—especially if the new Miss Galaxy was Chinese? Camarow had it all figured out.

For the evening's entertainment, Camarow had arranged for one contestant to be at each table, giving the guests a chance to meet and talk to the young women. The idea had sold well; the room was packed. He had even made the seating of the contestants a spectacle in itself. After the guests had been seated, he had each beauty contestant pick a number from a glass bowl—a number corresponding to a table and a seat. The person at the table and seat would come up to escort the woman back to the table. It made the evening fun for everyone and Camarow a few hundred thousand dollars more.

Sitting at his table with his senior staff officers, Gen. Xi was enjoying the evening, not because of his surroundings, but because his men were on the way to finding the deed. Relaxing for the first time since he had arrived in Hong Kong, he let himself have some fun.

Miss Italy reached into a large glass bowl and pulled out a card. She handed it to Camarow, who read it over the loud speaker: "Table eight, seat four."

Table eight was Gen. Xi's table and seat four belonged to Col. Miu. The colonel jumped up and marched up to the podium. He extended his arm for Miss Italy and escorted her back to the table. Xi may have lost the first chance, but rank had its privileges, and he quickly moved the officers around so that Miss Italy was sitting next to him. This was a sign of good luck, he thought. As she came closer to the table he saw she was even prettier in person than she was in her photographs.

"Michael, you look smashing in a tux," Liz Browning said.

"Funny, I don't feel smashing," Montgomery said, as they made their way toward the table. Scanning the room, Montgomery saw Zimkeroff and Xi, which gave him a degree of comfort knowing that they were in the same place. But he was tired and frustrated with the slow progress of his staff. It showed.

"Easy, Michael, easy," Liz said. "Let's try to enjoy the night."

"Who is that beautiful woman?" Ashley Williams asked.

All heads turned toward the entrance as Astrid Reed entered on the arm of the American Consul General. Astrid caused quite a stir. No one could miss her. Every eye, male and female, followed the red-haired beauty as she glided across the ballroom. Montgomery looked, but what bothered him was the absence of Daniels. He forced himself not to worry. Mac wasn't going anyplace tonight without one of Montgomery's surveillance teams following him. There were six teams in the lobby and garage, all for Daniels. There was no way that he was getting out of the hotel alone.

Gen. Xi glanced at his watch. It was eight-thirty. His thin lips turned upward into a devious smile. Col. Miu saw Xi looking at his watch and he knew why the general was smiling. It had begun. None of the hotel elevators would stop on the Galaxy floor. The switches and keys just didn't work, disabled by Xi's men. As an extra precaution, Miu had paid the hotel maintenance staff a small fortune to be sure that the elevators weren't fixed until he gave the order. Miu was the planner, the architect of the invasion of the Galaxy dormitory. Each detail had been meticulously laid out, each man had a specific assignment, and each man was ready to kill if necessary.

Taking a break, Frank Shen had gone down to the lobby to pick up a container of tea. He was anxious to get back to his post because he didn't like leaving the floor unattended. Using his passkey to unlock the elevator panel, he tried to activate the floor button, but it didn't work. He tried another elevator and another, but they were all having the same problem. Getting an uneasy feeling, he went to the front desk to complain. The desk clerk, taken aback at the suggestion that all the elevators were out of order, indigently told Shen that he hadn't received any complaints, but he would look into it.

"Of course this is the first complaint. All the women are at the Grand Ball. It's a private floor," Shen said.

Then he grabbed the house phone and called the maintenance office. He was told they were working on the problem. Shen knew it would be of no use to use the stairs because the fire doors were locked from the inside. He didn't like the situation, but he reasoned that if he couldn't get up there, no one else could either. To be sure, he sat where he could watch the elevators anyway. His gut started to gnaw at him. He had been a cop too long. The hair on the back of his neck told him this was no coincidence.

* * *

From where he sat, Harry Saltzman could see Xi, Zimkeroff, and Montgomery. Odd, he thought, Xi and Zimkeroff seemed to be having a good time. What did they know that Montgomery, who was twisting and turning in his seat, didn't? Harry Saltzman knew that more than a piece of real estate was at stake. What he wasn't sure of was who else knew what was really going on. The deed had to be found and found quickly. And it was up to Mac Daniels to find it. Daniels, he knew, had three things going against him: Xi, Zimkeroff, and time. Of the three, time was the most formidable foe. It never relented.

CHAPTER 31

Being brave is sometimes being stupid.

— Old Chinese proverb

JEFFERY Leng laughed watching his grandfather juggle four phones at once. One was cradled between his left shoulder and left ear, the speaker phone was on, and he held one receiver in each hand going back and forth to his right ear. How did he do it? Jeff wondered. He was amazed, as he was having trouble following any one of the conversations himself.

Looking down at his Rolex, he saw it was almost nine. He placed an overdue call to Michael Montgomery at the government office building. Not getting an answer and not wanting to leave a message on voice mail, he decided he would call again later. Slipping his cell phone into his pocket, he saw that his grandfather was off the phones, sitting at his desk with his hands folded. Jeff knew he was in for it now.

"It is my fault," his grandfather said. "I sent you to the best American schools. I should have sent you to the best Chinese schools where at least you would have learned manners. Is this the way you treat an old man by talking on the phone while I, who have little time left on this Earth, must sit and wait for you?"

"A thousand apologizes, Grandfather, but I'm sure the gods will extend your time as compensation for my ill manners," Jeff said. This was his grandfather's ritual whenever Johnny Leng managed to hang up before Jeff. Now it was time for the usual first question.

"Well, how's business?"

"Just great, Grandfather. Have you eaten your supper? Do you have time for a meal?"

"Eat? I have too much to do. There is no time to eat. Well, tell me. Let's hear it."

"Hear about what?" Jeff asked.

"The visit, the visit from the American."

"How did you know about that, Grandfather?"

"Never mind how I know. If I didn't know, how could I ask the question? What did they want, as if I didn't know."

"Like the rest of them, they want and need our help. But the Americans are different. They bring intrigue and betrayal into the mix. For the Russians, the Chinese, the British, it's all about money. The Americans are different."

Jeff told his grandfather what the American wanted and what they would receive in return. As his grandfather sat back looking off into space, a chill came over Jeff. He saw his grandfather's hand tremble slightly. Funny, he thought, I never noticed that before.

"Grandfather, I offered the American the same deal I made with the rest. No matter how this turns out, we should get the credit regardless of who wins," Jeff said.

Johnny Leng shook his head.

"No. We should stay out of this."

"I'm not sure I understand, Grandfather. The American brings us opportunity and new businesses for us to expand into."

"My grandson, I disagree with you. Let's put this off until the morning. Perhaps we should call the council into session," Johnny Leng said.

Knowing it would be useless, Jeff did not argue with his grandfather. He would let it go for now. As an afterthought, Jeff handed his grandfather several photographs given to him by the American. His grandfather looked through them, stopping at one staring at it. Then he dropped the other pictures on the desk, unable to put down the one in his hand.

"Jeff," he said. "Do you know what many Chinese believe about photographs, that they capture the soul of man? That is why many elderly people refuse to have their pictures taken."

Jeff smiled at that quaint belief. "Well, Grandfather, this is the one the American wants dead."

"He is trouble; he is death. I see it in his eyes," Johnny Lang said, his voice rising. "Those dark eyes are looking into my soul. This man is my destroyer."

"Don't worry, Grandfather," Jeff said, still smiling.

With a shaking hand, Johnny threw the picture, a black-and-white head shot of a man, on the desk.

"Jeff, be careful—this is the face of death," he said.

Johnny Leng was scared and for the first time his fear was showing. Jeff had never seen his grandfather this way. Not sure how to handle it, he decided to say nothing for the time being. The old Chinese were very superstitious, he thought, and his grandfather was no exception. He picked up the picture, but he saw nothing unusual about it.

"Who is that demon?" Johnny Leng asked his grandson.

"Mackenzie Daniels," Jeff said, reading the name at the bottom of the picture.

"Tell Charlie I want to see him. He will do the job for me." Charlie was one of Johnny Leng's hit men.

"Grandfather, do you think we should wait to hear from the American?"

"No. I want this Daniels dead. Tomorrow at the latest. Or it will be my death you will mourn. Do not argue. Do what I want."

"I will send Charlie over right away."

"Be careful, Jeff, be careful."

"I will be careful, Grandfather. I will heed your warnings."

Without further discussion Jeff rose, gave a polite bow, and left.

Standing in front of her closet, Kelly turned pale when she heard the Lengs talking. She wondered if it could be true. She wasn't sure, but had to find out. Kicking off her shoes and dropping her stained dress to the floor, she grabbed a blue one-piece jump suit. Climbing into it, she was ready to intercept Jeff. She listened until she heard the door to Johnny Leng's office shut; then she took a deep breath and stepped out into the hallway.

"Hi, there," she said, giving him a friendly kiss on the cheek. "Thanks for the tip."

Touching his cheek, he said, "Thanks for the tip."

Putting his left arm around her shoulder, he motioned toward the door that led to the public area of the club.

"Going my way?" she asked.

"Anywhere you go, I'll follow," he said.

When they got to the door, Jeff reached to open it, and Kelly saw he was holding photos. She could clearly see the top one.

"Is your grandfather looking at dirty pictures?"

"No," Jeff said, laughing. "Well, if he is, I hope he shares them with me."

Jeff held the photos for her to see. Glancing at the photos quickly as if she didn't care, she said: "Tell him if he has any of my pictures, he has to pay me."

Jeff was still laughing as Kelly disappeared into the crowd to chants, cheers, and applause. What he didn't see was that she was white as a sheet.

* * *

The suite was so quiet that for the first time Daniels noticed the ticking of the wall clock in his room. Each tick reminded him that the official turnover was that much closer. He was going to visit Zimkeroff's suite, knowing the general was at the Grand Ball. The only question was Petroff. If the sergeant major was well enough, he would be at Zimkeroff's side. If he was in the suite, he would be too weak to offer much resistance.

Daniels planned to break into the room, plant a few listening devices, and leave. There was no need for a backup. It was what he called a one-two-three job, a piece of cake. Surveying his meager wardrobe, he decided that the appropriate attire for an evening break in would be basic black. Astrid would be proud of him, he thought, as he squeezed into a black T-shirt. It clung to his body, showing off his well-defined physique. He opted for his black jeans, but abandoned his boots in favor of a pair of black sneakers. From the supplies that Saltzman had given him, Daniels took the black underarm shoulder holster and adjusted it to accommodate the Mark 23. Its barrel was almost an inch-and-half longer than the Glock's. He slipped it on like a sleeveless jacket and tightened the buckle. It felt right. He screwed the Knight sound suppressor onto the threaded barrel tip and it was ready.

He put on a lightweight black windbreaker to cover his armament and stuffed an extra clip in each zippered pocket. Then he checked architectural plans of the Sheraton Hotel that Saltzman had given him. Daniels knew everything he could about Gen. Zimkeroff's suite. Such detailed information could save his life. He packed his black camera bag with everything he would need. As the clock struck nine, he left the suite.

Daniels took the stairs two at a time as he flew up the emergency stairwell to the roof on the east end of the hotel. Over the exit door was a small uncovered light bulb casting a dim glow, barely illuminating the door release marked with the words: Alarm will sound if opened.

Disregarding the warning, he pushed open the door, and quickly stepped outside. The alarm began to wail, but as soon as he shut the door, it fell silent. At the edge of the roof, he put on the night vision scope that made him look like a modern Cyclops.

Across Nathan Road was the Sheraton Hotel. He scanned the rooftop. The pool deck was supposed to be closed after eight-thirty, but sometimes a few stragglers or wayward lovers took advantage of the romantic setting. He saw no one. So far, his luck was holding.

In the corner of the pool deck closest to Nathan Road was the rooftop emergency exit. Over the entrance sat the tower holding the satellite dish. An easy shot, he thought.

Daniels loaded the crossbow with a grappling dart attached to a plastic-coated wire cable. Propping his arms on the edge of the roof, he took careful aim and squeezed the trigger. The arched bow sprang back to its original shape, hurling the dart towing the cable silently across the street and through the cross beams of the satellite tower. The dart fell harmlessly to the rooftop with a metallic clink. On impact the dart sprung open, forming a "T." Daniels wound down on the cable retractor until the steel tips of the "T" were wedged between the cross frames of the satellite tower. He fastened a metal eye hook into the brick facing on the side of the building. Then he attached the cable reel to the eye hook. From his bag he took out a silicon-coated strap with wrist loops on each side. Slipping the camera case over his head, Daniels sat on the roof ledge, his feet dangling over the side. Those words of wisdom passed through his mind: Don't look down. Where was he supposed to look when he was forty stories above the street? he wondered. He placed the strap over the cable, slipped his hands through loops, and pushed off from the hotel.

The night was still, but at that height any breeze felt like a strong wind. His windbreaker was bellowing as he quietly slid across the street. Clearing the Sheraton's roof by several feet, he let go of the strap just before the tower, and fell lightly to the deck. Lying still for a few seconds, he wondered if anyone had heard him. There was no sound, no movement.

Feeling confident his entry onto the roof was secure, he slowly rose to his feet and immediately climbed the tower to rearrange the grappling dart. Daniels worked the dart higher up the tower to create a downward angle for his return trip to the Peninsula. Even with the slight angle, he was concerned that he might not slide back across the street and find himself stuck high above Nathan Road.

Sliding toward the exit door, he pushed his night vision scope off his eyes and onto the top of his head. If the stairway was well lit, the scope light enhancement would have a blinding effect on him. Opening the door, a wall of light sprang out at him, illuminating the deck area. Too much light, he thought, stepping inside. It was better to keep everything in the dark. With the butt of his pistol, he smashed the flood lights. Blending into the blackness, he pulled on his night vision scope again. Two floors below was Zimkeroff.

Running down the stairs, Daniels covered the two flights in a matter of seconds.

The emergency door had no handle; he couldn't get in.

"Shit," he said.

Worse, the door was made of metal and it was fireproof. If he used explosives, the world would know it. The air vent, he thought. Daniels ran back up the stairs.

The main air duct for the hotel's heating and air-conditioning system ran through the adjoining wall from the basement to the roof. Off the main duct was a series of feeder ducts that ran perpendicular to the main one.

From his bag Daniels took a small power screwdriver. He pressed the tip against screw heads, quickly freeing the vent. Climbing halfway through the vent, Daniels looked straight down to the basement, four hundred feet away. He dropped back onto the stairway landing, taking a nylon line and a tin of paste wax from his bag. Securing one end of the line to an overhead cross beam, he let the line fall freely down the duct. He lined the vent with the paste wax. Then he pulled himself up into the opening, sat on the edge, and lifted the vent into place. The paste wax would hold it there without the necessity of screws.

Daniels grabbed the line and started to lower himself down. He tried to stay in the center of the duct and not to hit the aluminum sides. The noise would carry throughout the hotel. He stopped his descent when he reached the thirty-seventh floor. Hanging there in the darkness, one slip away from death, he reached for the feeder duct. The aluminum felt cold to his touch. Letting go of the line, he pulled himself into the feeder duct. On his hands and knees, he moved along the system until he came to a smaller duct that delivered the air flow to Zimkeroff's suite. He inched along on his stomach, his elbows pulling, his knees pushing.

Finally, he came to the exit vent over the Zimkeroff's sitting room. Through his night vision scope, the room glowed eerily. Gently forcing the vent screen off, Daniels lowered himself into the sitting room. Drawing his Mark 23 from the holster and slipping off the safety, he moved toward the door to the hallway. He heard nothing on the other side, so he opened the door. The hallway was empty. He saw two doors. Bedrooms, he thought, one for the general and the other for Petroff.

Moving with cat-like steps, he crossed the hall to the bedroom doors. Pressing his ear to the master bedroom door, he listened. It was quiet. Opening it, he surveyed the room, but he saw nothing out of the ordinary. He went through the closet, feeling the pockets of the clothes hanging there; then he went through the drawers of the dresser and desk. Nothing, not even a matchbook cover. The room was too clean.

When he had finished, he moved silently toward the second bedroom. As he approached, he could hear the sound of a television set playing. Petroff didn't go to the Grand Ball, he thought, suppressing a smile. Going through the rest of the suite, he found nothing. Returning to the sitting room, he saw a few half-empty glasses and cigarette butts stubbed out in an ashtray. The meeting room, he thought, the place to plant a few listening devices. Taking three bugs from his bag, he decided to place one in the desk chair. He used his pocket knife to pry out a few tacks. Then he placed the bug into the stuffing of the chair and replaced the tacks.

On the far wall was a bookcase, the spot for the second bug. The third, he decided, would be in the entertainment center that housed the television, stereo, and VCR. As he leaned over the VCR that sat on top of the television set, he noticed that there was a tape still inserted in the player. He hit the eject button. The VCR spit forth a tape with Chinese writing on it. This was no commercial tape, he thought. It might be interesting.

He turned off the night vision scope and turned on the television set. Muting the sound, he pushed the tape into the gaping mouth of the VCR and pressed the play button.

The scenes were confusing at first, but as it played on it became apparent to him what he was watching. Was Zimkeroff trying to procure some type of new chemical weapon from the Chinese? Was he going to trade the deed for this new weapon of mass destruction? That had to be it, he decided. He had another piece of the puzzle, but this piece had to get to the Admiral.

Daniels needed the tape and he had to have it duped without Zimkeroff finding out it was missing. He stuck the tape in his bag, abandoning his plans to bug the rest of the place. No time to crawl through the ducts, he thought, pushing the air vent screen back into place. His luck still holding, he stepped out into the empty hallway. After looking both ways, he ran down to the end of the hall to the emergency exit door. The door shut behind him with a thud.

Racing up the stairs, Daniels was on the rooftop in a matter of seconds. Opening the door slightly, he heard something. He was not quite sure what it was, but having no time to waste he pressed himself against the side of the building and worked his way back toward the tower. Before climbing the tower, Daniels took out his cell phone and made a call. Haig answered.

"Get over here fast," Daniels whispered. "This is no drill. Bring a blank VCR videotape and a duplicating machine. Hurry up." Not waiting for an answer, Daniels snapped the phone shut.

"Be there in ten minutes," Haig said into the dead phone.

Throwing the slide strap over the cable, Daniels pushed off from the tower, and slid toward the Peninsula Hotel. Passing over the pool deck, he saw the reason for the noise he had heard. A couple on a lounge chair six feet below him were making love. Fortunately, the woman had her eyes closed as he passed silently overhead. Not bad, he thought, looking down.

Because the Peninsula was the taller of the two hotels, the return trip was more difficult. After a short, quiet ride, he slammed into the side of the Peninsula and hung forty stories above the street. The eye hook was about a foot below the rooftop ledge. He used the cable for leverage and pushed up. Just as he was reaching for the ledge, the eye hook fell from the wall and he fell. Catching the edge of the roof with his right hand, his left tangled in the cable attached to the reel, he hung by one hand, four hundred feet in the air. Gravity was pulling him down and the cable tension was pulling him away from the side of the hotel. He could hear the eye hook bounce off the building, pinging as it fell through the still night.

He felt himself start to slip. His fingers dug into the concrete facing. Needing two hands to pull himself up, he tried bringing the left hand around, but the cable was still taut and it cut into his skin. He ground his teeth as he tried with all his might to free his left hand. The cable bit deeper, drawing blood, but his fingers were only inches away from the roof.

A little more, he thought, a little more. He pulled hard again. It felt as if the cable was cutting his arm off, but he made one last effort. Just a hair more, he thought. When his fingers finally touched the top of the roof, he let out a hoarse "yes."

He pulled himself up until one arm was on the roof and the other was hanging in thin air, still attached to the cable. He lay there, not moving. He breathed deeply, waiting for his racing heart to slow down. Moving his feet onto the roof, he reached for the tension release knob with his free hand. The cable loosened around his left arm and the blood surged through his fingers. He felt them coming back to life.

Sliding onto the roof, he loosened the tension on the dart and it folded up into its original shape. Then he pressed the retract button and the reel began to wind in the cable until the grappling dart was dangling from the front of the bow. Throwing the bow and dart back into his bag, he sat there noticing for the first time a trickle of blood running down his arm. Letting out a long sigh, he thought of the couple at the Sheraton making love. Thoughts of Astrid passed before his eyes.

"Christ," he muttered. "Am I an idiot or what?"

There has to be a better way to make a living than this, he thought. Being brave is sometimes being stupid.

CHAPTER 32

Victory is not always a straight road.
Sometimes it must curve.

— Old Chinese proverb

ALTHOUGH Miss Italy was as charming as she was beautiful, the evening wore on slowly for Gen. Xi. The rest of his party was captivated by the vivacious dark-eyed beauty who had kept them laughing and their temperatures rising all night long. When Donna Marie laughed, her whole body, especially her breasts, shook like Jell-O on springs. That even wrung a smile from the stoic Xi.

After the table had been cleaned, a waiter took orders for coffee, tea, or cappuccino. All ordered, except Xi, who could no longer stand the suspense and wanted to get back to his suite. He knew that the vase containing the deed for Hong Kong, his ticket to a life of luxury, was waiting for him.

Pushing back from the table and standing up, Xi nodded to Miu, who popped up obediently from his chair. As the rest of the officers began to rise, Gen. Xi held up his hand.

"Stay, gentlemen, enjoy the rest of the evening. Col. Miu, shall we?" Xi said.

Italy's offering to the world of beauty had never dealt with a Chinese general. She protested that he couldn't leave and grabbed Xi's arm. Miu's mouth dropped open, the table fell silent, and all eyes were on her. Feeling uncomfortable with their stares, she let go. No one had ever grabbed the general's arm like that before. Xi's eyes narrowed, his gaze bored into her, and his thin lips seemed to disappear. Donna Marie looked up at Xi.

"Santa Maria," she said softly, as if she were praying.

Nothing else was said. Xi left the table with Miu following close behind. Their departure did not go unnoticed by Zimkeroff or Montgomery.

195

* * *

Opening the exit door slowly, Daniels peeked down the hallway. Satisfied, he hurried to the suite. He was pleased to find that Astrid was still at the Grand Ball because he needed a little more time without her looking over his shoulder. In his room, he slipped the tape into the VCR and he hit the play button. His eyes widened as he watched. He didn't understand what the narrator was saying, but he understood what he saw. Where the hell was Haig? he wondered.

He knew he had to get the tape to the Admiral; this couldn't wait. It was vital to the national security of the United States. Looking at the clock on the mantel, Daniels knew time was running out—for him, for Hong Kong, and for the rest of the world. The tape had to be returned before Gen. Zimkeroff got back to his room. His thoughts were interrupted by the ringing of the doorbell. Hitting the VCR stop button, Daniels ran to the front door of the suite. He looked through the peep hole and seeing it was Haig, he opened the door. Without any words, he motioned Haig in. He looked up and down the hall as he shut the door.

A member of the British surveillance team stationed in the lobby made his way through the crowd in the Grand Ballroom until he reached Montgomery's table. Then he bent over and whispered something to Montgomery—something that caused the SIS man to raise his eyebrows. His body language gave away his surprise. As silently as he had appeared, the man left. Montgomery sat back from the table, drumming his fingers and contemplating his next move.

Leaning toward him, Liz Browning asked: "Is every thing all right, Michael?"

Tilting his head so his mouth would be close to her ear, he said: "Ron Haig has just come into the hotel with a package. He's up in Daniels's suite now." He could smell her perfume. She smelled delicious, he thought.

From his table Gen. Zimkeroff watched, taking it all in.

"Michael, what does this mean?" she asked him.

"With Daniels, only God knows," Montgomery whispered, still buried in her ear. "Only God knows."

Feeling the eyes of Williams and Adams on him, Montgomery sat up straight, pulling his chair into the table.

"Haig is in the hotel. For a man who doesn't do field work, he's out late," he said to the rest of his dinner companions.

"Isn't he Admiral Charko's right-hand man?" Williams asked.

"Yes, he's the Admiral's alter ego," Montgomery said. "He's the man who puts it all together; the one who makes sense out of the endless information. And he's the one who keeps the likes of our friend, Mac Daniels, informed. Well, at least with our men in the lobby, we know where Daniels and company are. He isn't going anywhere without us right behind him. Come on, let's enjoy the rest of the evening. We're at a party."

Somehow, no one believed Montgomery about enjoying the rest of the evening. He hadn't smiled all night.

"A toast," Liz said, picking up her glass. "To our Three Musketeers, ladies—Michael, Leslie, and Winston. And to the women who stand by them."

To a chorus of "Hear! Hear!" they all took a drink. As he swallowed his champagne, Montgomery glanced at his watch. The party was almost over. Perhaps he would pay Daniels a visit for a nightcap, he thought.

*　*　*

"What's going on, Mac," Haig said, following Daniels to his room.

Daniels flipped him the tape.

"Copy it quick," Daniels said. "I've got to get it back."

"What is it?" Haig asked, looking at the tape.

"The blueprint of a new weapon of mass destruction. It's unbelievable, Ron. You must get it to the Admiral at any cost. Now dupe it quickly," he said.

Following Daniels's orders, Haig began making the copy. The high-speed tape duplicating device whirled as the recording process began. Daniels looked at his watch. The dinner must be almost over, he thought. He was not sure he could get into Gen. Zimkeroff's suite undetected again.

"How long?" he asked Haig.

"I'm not sure, about five minutes more," Haig said.

"Damn."

"Mac, the machine won't go any faster."

"It's no use. The dinner will be over. Unless Zimkeroff hangs around the ballroom, we have two choices. One is to wait until late night when everyone should be sleeping; then try to replace the tape. But that runs the risk that someone would try to play it before the night was over—a very real possibility. Or we—"

"What's this we shit, Mac? I don't like the sound of your voice," Haig said. Strictly an inside man, Daniels had dragged him into compromising positions before—situations which he found very uncomfortable. He truly liked Daniels, they were the best of friends, but Haig wasn't a field agent. He would have rather been back in Washington, where he had the world at his fingertips playing with his super computers.

"We can pull the switch, Ron. Come on, it's a piece of cake," Daniels said, ignoring Haig's comments.

"I'm a lover, not a fighter. You're going to get me killed," he said, handing Daniels the original tape back.

"Come on, we go in the front door, you do your bit, and I'll pull an old-fashioned switch. Besides, it's too small," Daniels said, putting the tape inside his windbreaker. "Let's go."

* * *

Battles are sometimes won by chance. Moving a force left instead of right or being at the right place at the right time, had changed the course of history. The key to this approach, as Zimkeroff had told Petroff many times, was to go with your gut. Miss South Africa's beauty and charm were not enough to overcome Zimkeroff's gut feeling it was time to leave. Maj. Bresneyev and Capt. Kertrinkoff followed their general out of the hotel, whispering about the heavenly bodies that kept their attention at the Galaxy Grand Ball.

Out on the veranda, Zimkeroff stopped and took a deep breath.

"Smell the sea," he said. "In a few days, gentlemen, in a few days, it will be over."

"Yes, sir," both men said, almost simultaneously.

Clasping his hands behind his back as if he were reviewing the troops, Zimkeroff led the march out of the protected portico toward Salisbury Road. They turned left toward the Sheraton.

"It's going to be a good day tomorrow," the general said. "I will have the deed very soon, maybe even tonight. Then we will trade with Chi. Yes, I believe tomorrow will be a good day for us and a bad day, or per-haps the last day, for Chi."

As they got closer to the Sheraton, he said: "That tape is very inter-esting. Let's drag Petroff out of bed and watch it again. Yes, it is very interesting."

* * *

Daniels had Haig by the arm leading him out the door, forcing him to run, in order to keep up with Daniels's quick pace. Only when they were in the elevator did Daniels let go of him.

"Listen, here's the plan. It's real simple," he said.

"Nothing is real simple with you, Mac," Haig said, shaking his head.

"What about London, Ron?"

"What about it? I got shot instead of you," Haig complained.

"It was only a scratch," Daniels reminded him.

"A scratch to you, a shot to me," Haig said sourly.

"There are several British agents in the lobby following me. They should be sitting around on their fat asses just beginning to relax. When the door of the elevator opens, I want you to run as fast as you can toward the side door, out and across Nathan Road, and into the Sheraton. Don't stop running until we are at the elevators. Don't look at anyone, just run."

Haig didn't have a chance to answer. The elevator doors opened in the lobby and they ran as if the starter's gun had been fired. The two British agents who were sitting didn't have a chance. Hampered by the crowd of guests exiting from the Grand Ball, the agents were unable to pursue the dashing duo.

Daniels and Haig were safely across the street in the lobby of the Sheraton by the time the two British agents managed to reach the side entrance of the Peninsula Hotel. Looking up and down the street, they didn't see either man. One agent swung his clinched fist in the air and the other yelled: "I'll check the Salisbury taxi stand. You check the Sheraton."

Both men took off running; both knowing that Montgomery would be furious with them. This was a major screw up.

Inside the Sheraton, Daniels and Haig were lucky there was an elevator waiting for them. They entered unseen by the British.

The agent who had checked the taxi stand found his cohort wandering around the Sheraton lobby. Breathlessly he said: "No luck at the taxi stand. No one saw them. They must be here."

"Or in one of the parked cars, now long gone," the other man said.

"Bloody awful!" the first agent said.

"We've been snookered," the other said. "When Montgomery finds out we lost them, we'll be counting penguins in the South Pole."

As the elevator sped them up to Zimkeroff's floor, Daniels and Haig caught their breaths. Shaking his head, Haig didn't believe he was mixed up with Daniels again. Looking at Daniels standing there, as relaxed as if he were at a church picnic, Haig envied his friend. Didn't anything bother him? he wondered. The butterflies flew about his stomach and his legs felt like rubber about to buckle under his body weight. He thought he was going to be sick. Turning to Daniels, he said: "What's too small?"

"Your dick is too small to be a lover."

"Up yours, Mac. I have a good mind to turn around and leave you here."

"Too late."

As the elevator doors slid silently open, Daniels stepped off first, followed closely by Haig. Looking down the hall he saw Gen. Zimkeroff closing the door to his suite. Running the distance in a few seconds Daniels rang the doorbell. Before the ringing had stopped, Haig was standing right behind him.

In the lobby, the two British agents were beside themselves. They had no idea where Daniels had gone. Finally, in desperation, one of them took out his cell phone and pressed a preset number for Montgomery.

In the hall between the ballroom and the lobby, Montgomery and Browning were talking with Astrid, Harry Saltzman, and Mr. and

Mrs. Boucher, when his phone rang. Politely excusing himself, he answered.

"Sir," the apprehensive voice began, "we lost Daniels."

"Where are you?" he asked in a tone so cold that the agent on the other end froze.

"Lobby of the Sheraton, sir," he said.

"Stay there. I'll be right over."

Looking at Montgomery, Saltzman noticed the clinched fist and the squinting eyes behind the glasses. Montgomery's face said it all—trouble, as in Daniels. Browning and Astrid were in animated conversation, neither one noticing that Montgomery's fuse was about to ignite.

"Are you all right, Michael?" Saltzman asked.

"Yes, thank you."

"We are on the same side," he said. "The look on your face tells me trouble. I'm willing to bet a month's pay that Daniels has something to do with it."

"I had Daniels under surveillance as a protective measure. But he and Haig have disappeared."

"Haig! Ron Haig was with Daniels?" a stunned Saltzman said. "Let me help."

Their conversation was interrupted by Astrid.

"The counsel general and his wife are joining me in my suite for a nightcap. Michael, would you, Liz, and Harry join us?"

"Wonderful idea, Astrid," Saltzman said quickly. "Michael and I will pick up a few cigars. Then, we will be right up."

Outside of the hotel Montgomery said: "Daniels is probably at Zimkeroff's hotel suite at the Sheraton."

"Oh, no," Saltzman said. "There's a lot of bad blood between those two and before there is any more blood, we had better get over there."

Opening the door of the suite, Gen. Zimkeroff was shocked to see Daniels and Haig standing there. Before he could protest, Daniels stepped inside followed by Haig. From down the hall, Bresneyev and Kertrinkoff saw them enter the suite, but they were not sure what to do. Neither one was armed. Daniels walked past Zimkeroff toward the sitting room. Haig, stopping in front of the glowering general, whose face was as red as his uniform, introduced himself to Zimkeroff. He extended his hand. Zimkeroff slapped it away. The slap stung the back of Haig's hand. Instinctively, he rubbed it.

"How dare you break in here, Daniels. What do you want?" Zimkeroff bellowed.

Daniels turned, forcing a grieved look on his face, said in an offended tone: "That's no way to talk, General. Come on in here."

Motioning to the sitting room, Daniels opened the door and went in. Zimkeroff ran after him, followed by Bresneyev and Kertrinkoff with Haig bringing up the rear.

"Well, what do you want?" Zimkeroff yelled.

The commotion brought Petroff from his room. Wearing just a robe, he hobbled toward the sitting room. Haig was standing in the doorway when Petroff knocked him down bursting into the room. The sergeant major placed himself between Zimkeroff and Daniels, acting as a human shield. Zimkeroff tapped his guard dog on the shoulder and Petroff slowly moved aside. Daniels turned to see Haig picking himself up from the floor. There was a slight trickle of blood coming form the corner of his right nostril.

"You okay, Ron?" Daniels asked.

"Yeah," he replied.

Standing up, Haig reached for a handkerchief. Then, trying to be diplomatic, he said: "General, please, I'm from the—"

"If you don't get the hell out of here, I'll call the police," Zimkeroff said, cutting him off.

Picking up the phone, Daniels held the receiver out toward Zimkeroff.

"Here, call them," he said.

Zimkeroff stood there, the veins on his head showing. Giving the general his trademark smirk, Daniels unceremoniously dropped the receiver back into its cradle.

"How about we have a little talk?" Daniels said, as he walked toward the television and turned it on. "Or maybe we can watch the news? We can find out how the turnover is going. Or is it going? Did you find the deed to Hong Kong yet, General?"

The mention of the deed got Zimkeroff's attention and that seemed to calm him down. His face became almost a normal color again.

Hearing his cue, Haig went into his act.

"General," he said, "I want to talk to you about this deed."

Haig was very deliberate using the words "this deed." Reaching into his pocket, he took out some papers. All eyes were focused on Haig. Out of the limelight for a second, Daniels took the videotape from his windbreaker. He was about to push it into the VCR when Petroff spotted him and grabbed his arm, causing Daniels to drop the tape.

"Hey, Yuri," Daniels said. "Take it easy. I was just checking out what you were watching."

Now all eyes were on Daniels as he bent down to pick up the tape and tossed it to Zimkeroff.

"It looks like your man here is watching Chinese porn."

Petroff took a swing at Daniels, throwing a right roundhouse. Blocking the punch with his left arm, Daniels's right hand flew into his jacket, pulled out his Mark 23, and jammed it into Petroff's face. He pushed the gun hard under Petroff's chin, forcing the sergeant major's head back violently.

"Go on, breathe too hard and you're dead," Daniels said. With that, he gave Petroff a hard shove knocking him into the couch. Turning toward Zimkeroff, he asked: "What's on that tape, General?"

Daniels shoved Zimkeroff back hard into Bresneyev and Kertrinkoff, forcing the three of them to fall onto the club chair. Daniels followed up, pressing his knee on Zimkeroff's chest, holding the gun barrel inches away from the general's face.

"Say something, General, I can't hear you."

Zimkeroff tried to speak, but he suddenly found the cold barrel of the Mark 23 in his mouth.

"Come on, General, blink. I dare you to blink. Blink! One bullet and I get all three of you. Come, General, do something. Why don't you grab my hand? That's it, grab my hand. Hell, the safety is off. It's a hair trigger."

Zimkeroff's eyes opened wide. Seeing the safety was off, he wasn't going to blink.

Petroff started to get up. "Move, asshole, and they're dead," Daniels snarled. Petroff dropped back into his chair.

"Why is your bald-headed gorilla bent out of shape? Is there something on that tape you don't want me to see?"

Slowly, very slowly, Zimkeroff shook his head, still forcing his eyes to remain wide open. Daniels pulled the gun away, slowly retreating toward Haig, who stood there with his mouth open. He had never seen Daniels like this before. He thought Daniels was really going to kill them all. He couldn't speak.

Zimkeroff's ability to remain calm was impressive.

"Put that gun away, Daniels, before someone gets hurt," he said as if nothing had happened.

Throwing the tape at Daniels, he continued: "Here, you want to take this porn movie with you? Take the fucking thing. Just get out of here."

"No, thanks," Daniels said, throwing it back casually.

His hands shaking, Haig stuffed the papers back into his pocket. Still unable to speak, he motioned toward the door. Daniels nodded in agreement. Backing away, he passed Petroff on the couch and hit him with a backhand across the face. Petroff's nose began to bleed.

"That's for my friend, Ron," Daniels said, as he holstered his weapon. They ran for the front door of the suite, reaching it just as the doorbell sounded. Daniels shrugged and opened the door. Standing there was an enraged Michael Montgomery and very upset Harry Saltzman.

"Well, fancy seeing you here. Come on in boys, the party is in the sitting room. We were just leaving," he said.

As Montgomery and Saltzman stepped into the suite, Daniels and Haig left.

* * *

Opening the door to his suite, Gen. Xi slowly walked down the long darkened hall toward the sitting room with Col. Miu still in tow. Several of his officers were milling about as he entered. All the men jumped to attention.

"As you were," Xi ordered.

The junior officers returned to their seats. One senior officer was still standing and he bowed his head toward the desk. There, on the general's desk were nine vases, lined up in rows three by three—all in perfect alignment, a mini military formation. Slowly circling his desk like a vulture homing in on its prey, Xi rubbed his hands together in satisfaction. Col. Miu and the rest of the men waited for their leader to speak.

"Nine," Gen. Xi said. "I thought there were only four women who had vases?"

"Sir, I had the men search the rooms of all the women who had blonde hair. I hope you are not upset with my actions, sir," the senior officer said.

"Men," Gen. Xi snapped in the military tradition. "Thank you. Your efforts will be rewarded beyond your expectations. Please go into the living room. There is food and drink there. Wait for further orders. Col. Miu, stay here with me."

"Sir," Miu said. That the general requested his presence was an honor Miu cherished. With the senior officer in the lead, the men trooped out of the sitting room with Miu bringing up the rear. As the last man exited, he locked the door behind them.

This was the moment they had been waiting for. One of the vases held the deed to Hong Kong. Now, after one hundred and fifty years, Hong Kong was going back to China—this time at a cost, a cost more dear than anyone would know. Sitting behind his desk, looking over the field of vases, Xi held up his hands like a surgeon ready to be gloved. Finally, he picked up one of them and held it to the light. Satisfied he couldn't see through the sand, he turned it over, and studied the bottom. Then he placed it back on the table without opening it.

"Shall we start, Colonel?" Xi said. It was more of a statement than a question.

"Yes, sir. It seems we have had a few delays in our pursuit of victory, but it has arrived at last. The straight line may be the shortest way between two points, but not always the easiest."

"Col. Miu, victory is not always a straight road. Sometimes it must curve."

CHAPTER 33

What has to be sometimes is not.

— Old Chinese proverb

RETURNING to the Peninsula, this time by the front door, Daniels and Haig walked through the lobby past the two sullen British agents to The Beefeater, the hotel watering hole designed to resemble an old English pub.

"You need a drink, Ron," Daniels said.

Haig was barely able to speak. He nodded.

The bartender was wearing an old apron with *Murphy* embossed over the heart. He stroked his moustache and asked: "What will ye have of me?"

"You sure talk funny, Murph. Where are you from?" Daniels asked.

Looking left and right to see if the boss was close, Murphy whispered: "New Jersey."

"Me, too. Princeton."

"Rich kid. I'm a Hudson County boy."

"How did you end up here?" Daniels asked.

"Three ex-wives. Hell, this is the life. All I can drink, golf all day, and if I get lucky, a little action. What about you?"

"I'm covering the turnover for World News Corporation. How about a vodka on the rocks."

"What's your poison?" Daniels asked Haig.

"Same," he stammered. "Make that a double."

Taking a bottle of vodka from the freezer, Murphy poured the thick clear liquid over ice. Haig downed the drink in one gulp.

"Another," he said.

Murphy poured another two inches. When Haig picked it up, Daniels grabbed his arm. "Take it easy, Ron. Have one with us, Murph."

Ignoring the advice, Haig gulped the drink. Still pale, his hands shaking, he thought he was going to throw up.

"I'm not like you, Mac," Haig said. "That was too close for me. When you jammed the gun into Zimkeroff's mouth, I thought you were going to shoot him."

"So did I," Daniels said.

"Then you threw the tape at him and he threw it back. Christ, I didn't know what to do," Haig said, shaking his head in disbelief.

"Zimkeroff had no choice. He had to act like it was nothing. That son-of-a-bitch knew I wouldn't take a porn film. He called my bluff and I gladly gave in."

"Mac, you're fast on your feet. I think we got away with it," Haig said.

"I know we got a way with it. If we hadn't, there would be some dead bodies over there."

"Let's get back to your room. I better take care of the tape," Haig said.

* * *

Picking up the vase closest to him and cradling it in his hands, Gen. Xi gently twisted the cork until it came out with a slight pop. Turning the vase over, he let the sand pour through his fingers into the wastebasket beside his desk. Returning the empty vase to its place in formation, Xi picked a second vase. He repeated the procedure until there were only three full vases left.

Xi was losing his patience. There was no longer any reverence for the vases or for what they might contain. Giving in to his temper, Xi ripped out a cork and dumped out the sand. Just to be sure, he looked inside. Nothing. Disgusted, he dropped the vase into the wastepaper basket. Two vases left.

"Which one?" he asked Col. Miu.

Without hesitation, Miu reached for a brown vase and presented it to his general.

"This is the one. Eight is the lucky number, sir," Miu said.

Nodding in agreement, Xi pulled the cork and turned it over. Just sand. Both men stared at the last vase.

"Wouldn't you know it? It's in the last one, general," Miu said.

Xi stood up holding the vase. Then he slammed the vase down, breaking it into several pieces. Pushing the sand away, he found nothing.

"Impossible," Xi growled. "It has to be there."

* * *

As Daniels opened the door to the suite, he could hear voices and laughter coming from the living room.

"Sounds like a party," Daniels said.

With Haig trailing behind him, Daniels led the way down the long hall toward the living room. He wondered what was going on. Astrid saw them first as they stood by the living room entrance.

"Mac, glad you're home early. Join us for a nightcap, darling?" she said, introducing herself to Haig.

Daniels followed close behind Astrid as she introduced Haig to Mr. and Mrs. Boucher and Liz Browning. Haig, who had been using the consul general's office, pretended he didn't know Boucher. Fortunately, Boucher was astute enough to play along.

"What are you drinking, Ron?" Astrid asked.

Haig had reached his limit already and he knew any more liquor would knock him flat. He asked for a cup of coffee while Daniels poured himself a vodka. He played with his drink, swirling the vodka around the glass and letting it rise to the rim before allowing it to settle back down. His mind was elsewhere. He was thinking of an excuse to get Haig out of there before Montgomery arrived. Time was still the enemy and every second counted. The tape had to be digitally re-recorded so it could be electronically transmitted to Washington for further study. There was no time to send the hard copy.

Astrid returned with Haig's coffee and said to Daniels: "I just noticed the message light flashing, Mac. When I checked the voice mail there was a message from a security guard named Shen. He said it was important. Is everything all right?"

"Thanks, Astrid. Everything is fine. Please excuse us. Ron, we have a call to make."

"What's this all about, Mac?" Haig asked when they were halfway down the hall.

"I don't know, Ron, but it's an excuse to get you out of here. Take the tape before Montgomery gets here."

Inside Daniels's room, Haig stuck the videotape in the small of his back and covered it with his jacket. As he was picking up the phone to call Shen, Daniels heard the doorbell.

"Shit, it's Montgomery,' he said. "Come on, let's face the music. No matter what happens, just leave."

He opened the door and faced Montgomery, who was not looking happy. Standing behind the SIS agent was Harry Saltzman.

"What in God's name are you up to?" Montgomery said, putting his index finger in Daniels's face.

"Didn't your mother tell you it's not polite to point," Daniels said in a cold monotone, pushing Montgomery's finger away.

Turning away from Montgomery, he started to walk toward the living room. But Montgomery grabbed him by the arm, spinning him around.

"Daniels," Montgomery said. "I'm talking to you."

Montgomery was glaring at Daniels, his nose flaring with every breath, and his fists were clinched tightly. He didn't notice Haig quietly leaving the suite. Paying no attention to Montgomery, Daniels turned away again.

"Daniels," Montgomery said, going after him. "Are you trying to start a major incident? You can't go around breaking into hotel rooms and beating up innocent people. Where do you think you are, back in the States?"

Daniels stopped short and spun on his heel. He had had it with the remark about the States. They were about to go at it when Astrid heard the commotion and came down the hall. The sound of her southern drawl seemed to act like a dose of Valium, causing the two men to back down.

"Michael, Harry, we are waiting for you two. What's all the ruckus? Now you all come on with me. Stop standing here in the hallway like grandma's old coat rack," she said taking Montgomery by the arm and leading him away. Saltzman stayed behind with Daniels.

"You made quite a mess at Zimkeroff's place. Montgomery is really pissed," Saltzman whispered.

"What do you mean mess? There was no blood, no bodies to clean up. You got off easy. I don't care about Montgomery being pissed. I'm sure what I did was not cricket."

"You know what I mean," Saltzman said.

"Listen carefully, Harry. I don't have a lot of time. Ron has a tape that you have to see. You'll need a translator. It's unbelievable. The Russians are in this for a weapon of mass destruction. Christ, Harry, it's scary."

When Daniels used words like scary and unbelievable, Saltzman got worried. He didn't think those words were in Mac's vocabulary.

"As soon as I'm out of here, I'll take care of it. Here comes Astrid," he said.

"By the way, thanks for babysitting her today," Daniels said.

"I didn't see Astrid today," Saltzman said.

Daniels was surprised, but Astrid was too close to continue the conversation.

With her hands on her hips, she said: "Harry Saltzman, are you or are you not, my beau for the evening? You're keeping a lady waiting. Now come on."

"Guilty as charged," Saltzman said, clearing his throat.

"Harry, be a darling. I'll join you and the others, but I need a minute alone with Mac here. I want to soothe his ruffled feathers and I don't want this hothead doing anything foolish."

When Saltzman was gone, Astrid said: "You owe me a big one. I saw Mr. Haig sneaking out and I saved your butt by charming Mr. Montgomery before he realized that one of the dynamic duo was missing. Are you running out on me again for that detective? I thought we were going to have some time together?"

"We will, Astrid. I'm sorry, but there is something that I have to finish," he said softly, leaning close to her. "Forgive me. I would love a rain check. I mean that, Astrid."

"My whole life is a rain check for you," Astrid said without emotion. "But be careful. The ticket may be getting soggy."

He kissed her and pulled her close. She threw her arms around him, holding him tight in a long passionate embrace. Finally, they released each other, Astrid forced a smile, and went to join her guests. Daniels left not seeing her wipe the tears from her eyes.

* * *

Pacing the floor and seething, Gen. Zimkeroff couldn't figure out what Daniels's stunt had been all about. It made no sense to him. There was nothing in the suite to see, he thought, except the videotape and it wasn't possible that Daniels had seen what was on it. But his gut told him something was wrong; it didn't feel right. He was annoyed at himself for not figuring it out. What was Haig doing with Daniels? he wondered. That was an odd match—oil and water—that made no sense either. Why did Haig admit they knew about the deed? Were the Americans looking for the deed, too? He had no time to waste, he thought. He had to move quickly to make the trade with Chi.

Zimkeroff stopped pacing long enough to pour himself a drink, trying to calm himself down. He should have had the deed by now, he thought. What had gone wrong?

His cell phone rang and the general listened without saying a word. When he hung up, he threw the phone on the floor and crushed it with his massive boot.

In the hall by the elevators, Daniels picked up the house phone. He dialed Frank Shen's extension. A woman's voice answered: "Galaxy floor."

"Frank Shen, please."

Daniels heard her calling for Shen, reminding him of his dormitory life back at Princeton. Waiting for Shen to pick up, Daniels found himself thinking about Astrid. She had looked gorgeous tonight, he thought. But—there was always a but. This time the but was the deed to Hong Kong. No, he thought. This time it was a weapon of mass destruction and the American way of life. The very essence of our existence was at stake. This was something he had to do. Shen came on the line.

"Frank Shen here."

"Frank, it's Mac Daniels. What's up?"

"We have a problem. I think you better get up here."

"Be right up."

* * *

Gen. Xi separated the photographs of the beauty contestants into three piles. One held the pictures of those women who had had House of Chan bags; a second pile contained the blondes; and the third pile consisted of the rest of the women. Burying his face in his hands for a moment, he searched the recesses of his mind for answers. He knew from the reports he had received from China that the deed was in one of the vases. He had had the rooms of every blonde and everyone who had had a House of Chan bag searched. His men had turned up nine vases—nine empty vases.

"Where is the deed?" Gen. Xi said aloud.

Col. Miu could not answer; Xi did not expect him to. Running his hands over the pictures as if he were feeling them for an answer, Xi studied each one carefully.

"Colonel, is it possible that one of these women found the deed?" Xi asked. "Then, not knowing what it was, threw it away? Let me see the captain that led the search party."

Unlocking the door, Miu ordered the captain into the room. From the tone of Miu's voice, the captain knew this was not going to be good news. Beginning to perspire as he entered the room, he came to attention in front of the general's desk. He saw the empty vases. Whatever was supposed to be in them, wasn't, he knew. Before Miu could give him orders, the captain said: "Permission to speak, sir?"

"Go ahead," Gen. Xi said, his voice showing the frustration he felt.

"Sir, when we were searching the rooms we found one of the vases empty. The sand was poured out and it was lying in a suitcase. We left it," the captain said.

"Ah, she must have found it," Xi said. "Let us hope she kept it or at least can tell us where it is."

"What, sir?" the captain asked.

"Papers," Xi said. "Old documents. Col. Miu knows what to look for. Which room had the empty vase?"

"The one directly across from the elevator, 2917."

"Colonel, take the captain and investigate," Xi said.

"Yes, sir," Col. Miu said, bowing his head.

When they had gone, the general looked at the empty vases and shook his head. He had thought the deed had to be there, but then, what has to be sometimes is not.

CHAPTER 34

When two foxes chase a rabbit one goes hungry.

— Old Chinese proverb

❦

"WHAT'S wrong, Frank?" Daniels asked, stepping off the elevator on the Galaxy floor.

"Some of the girls had their rooms tossed. Doesn't make much sense. I told them to let me know what was missing."

"When did this happen?" Daniels asked.

"Sometime between eight and eight-thirty when everyone was at the Grand Ball," Shen said. "I had gone down to the lobby to pick up a cup of tea. But I couldn't get back onto the floor because the elevators were out. Since all the women were at the dinner, I didn't give it too much thought. I just sat in a chair waiting until they were working again. I kept my eyes on the indicator panel. No car stopped on the floor. When I got back up here, I did a quick look see and everything seemed to be in order. If anyone had been here, they were long gone. Then the ladies returned from dinner and some of them began to complain about their rooms being messed up. That's when we discovered the break ins."

"Did you call the police?" Daniels asked.

"Sure I did, but the guys down at the burglary unit knew it was me calling. They told me to write it up and send it in. I doubt there are any fingerprints. I don't know, what do you think?"

"Does anyone know what's missing yet?"

"No."

"Come on, Frank, let's find out what is going on here. Who's first?"

"Ashley Aston, Miss United States," Shen said as he led the way down the hall toward her room. This was one of the women Daniels wanted to interview; one of the women he had photographed getting off the plane with a House of Chan bag. This was not a coincidence, he thought, there was a connection.

Daniels introduced himself to the tall, willowy blonde, holding her hand much longer than necessary. Her eyes were red from crying, her face streaked with eyeliner, and she was truly shaken.

"Take a deep breath, nice and easy. You're all right and that's all that is important," he said, feeling sorry for her.

Stepping aside, she allowed Daniels to enter her room. Surveying the damage, he understood why she was so upset. Piled on the bed, in a mountainous heap, were the dresser drawers, the contents, the clothes from the closet, her bathroom toiletries and, topping off the summit, were her empty suitcases.

"Who could have done this to my room?" she asked, waving her arms at the pile.

"Somebody who wanted something pretty badly," Daniels said.

"I feel so violated," she moaned, holding back the tears. "I could have been here. Then what?"

Daniels ignored her question, knowing that the answer would only upset her more.

"Is your jewelry missing?" he asked her.

"It's all there," she said, shaking her head and pointing to the mess on the bed.

"Do you know what's missing?" Daniels asked.

"No."

"I've been working burglary most of my police life, Miss Aston, and you probably won't know what is missing until you need it," Shen said. "Put away your clothes. Perhaps as you do, it will come to you."

If Daniels had to bet, he was sure he knew what was missing.

"Miss Aston," he started to ask, but she cut him off.

"Call me Ashley."

"Ashley, when you arrived in Hong Kong, you were carrying a House of Chan bag. You had a vase in the bag. May I see the vase, please?"

"Sure, but how did you know?"

"It's not important. Please, the vase."

"It's on the top shelf of the closet. I'll get it for you."

Daniels followed her over to the closet.

"Funny, it's not here," she said. "They must have thrown it on the bed."

"Now you know what they stole," Shen said, helping her rummage through the pile. She shook her head in disgust.

Daniels thought it was time to leave, so he and Shen left a frightened Miss USA to sort out her things.

"Don't tell me," Daniels said out in the hall. "The rooms hit were the same ones on the list I gave you earlier."

"Those and more," Shen said. "How did you know?"

"Because Aston, Holm, Miss Norway, and Miss England, all came off the plane with House of Chan bags. See you later."

"Where you going?" Shen asked as Daniels abruptly walked away from him.

"To pay a visit to our Swedish girlfriend, Miss Holm," he answered.

Shen took off after Daniels. His sixth sense, his cop sense, told him there was more to this. He had caught up to him just as Daniels began knocking on Inga Holm's door.

"Ya, who is there?"

"May we please see you?" Daniels asked, identifying himself.

There was no immediate response. Then they heard some noise from behind the closed door. It sounded like the scurrying of feet.

"Ya, jus da minute," Inga said in her sultry voice.

Daniels tapped his foot, while Shen shifted weight from one foot to another. Their body language betrayed their impatience. After what seemed an eternity, the door slowly opened and Inga's head appeared.

"Come in, come in," she said.

She was wrapped in a towel and apparently nothing else. Shen was flustered and slightly embarrassed. Daniels wasn't fazed and Inga didn't seem to care either. She was irritated at being disturbed.

"What do you want? It's late. I was sleeping. Is something wrong?"

"No. Nothing is wrong. Where's your vase?"

"You get me out of bed to ask where my vase is?" she asked, clearly annoyed.

Daniels didn't answer her. He just stared. The weight of the stare began to bother her and she said: "What do you want with a cheap reproduction of a Ching Dynasty vase?"

"I want to see it."

"Now? Is it necessary?" she asked.

"Yes, it is," Daniels said. His tone indicated it was an order not a request. "The vase is still in my suitcase. It's on the floor there."

Throwing the suitcase on the bed, Daniels opened it. The vase was still there surrounded by sand.

"Thank you, Miss Holm. Sorry we had to disturb you. Let's go, Frank."

As they left the room, Daniels said: "You can come out of the closet now, Camarow."

Pulling the door to the room shut, he turned to see Shen standing in front of him, arms crossed in front of his chest.

"This is my beat, Daniels, please explain what the hell is going on," Shen said.

"Four women got off the China flight the other day carrying House of Chan bags. They must have been shopping before they caught the plane, and not having the time to pack their purchases, they carried the bags on and off the plane. I happened to have been at the airport when they arrived and I took pictures. The four with the bags were all blondes, all very pretty, an unforgettable foursome. One of them picked up a vase that was meant for someone else. When the vase didn't show up in Hong Kong, they discovered the screw up. They were given a description of the women who had made purchases. Blondes, tall blondes. All the women who had their rooms tossed were tall blondes. And I'll bet you all the vases are gone."

"Two questions," Shen said. "One, who is *they*. And two, why didn't they take Miss Holm's vase?"

"One, I don't know who they are, but I have a good idea. And two, because someone was already in her room this afternoon. The vase was empty. The cork didn't fall out, it was pulled out. Whatever was supposed to be in the vase wasn't. They didn't have the time to go through the vases tonight, so they just took them. Whatever they were looking for, they thought was in one of the vases."

"And what was that?"

"Not sure," Daniels said.

"What's in the goddamn vase!" Shen demanded.

For a second, Daniels said nothing.

"If you're not going to tell me, how the fuck do you expect me to help?" Shen said, exasperated beyond all measure.

"Frank, one of the vases is real, not some cheap reproduction," Daniels said, making it up as he went along. "It is priceless. Taken from a museum."

"Really?"

"Please see if any other vases are missing," Daniels said.

Shen dutifully went in search of stolen vases leaving Daniels alone in the hall gathering his thoughts. As Daniels stood there, he heard the door to Inga Holm's room open. Stepping back against the wall, he watched with amusement as Tom Camarow, his shoes in hand, tiptoed toward the elevator.

"Evening, Tom. Out for a late night stroll?"

A red-faced Camarow said: "You were going to help me with Tara, but she told me not to come by because she had other plans—you."

"Tom, she invited me up, but I didn't tell her I was coming. Besides, you don't owe me any explanations. It's just a bit silly for a grown man to be hiding in a closet, especially wearing high heel shoes. Didn't your feet hurt in those shoes?"

Not about to attempt an explanation, Camarow tried changing the subject.

"Well, Tara is waiting for you. Don't piss that redhead off. She has some temper. She's expecting you, so you had better put your face in or she might make a scene when she sees you again."

Christ, Daniels thought, that's all I need, a goddamn scene in front of Astrid.

Frank Shen slipped up noiselessly behind Daniels and Camarow.

"You're right. All the vases are missing," the security guard said.

There was only one place they could be, Daniels thought, and he was sure he knew where that was.

"Hey," Shen said, in surprise, realizing that Camarow was still there. "It's after twelve-thirty. You shouldn't be here. It's time to lock the floor down. Good night, Mr. Camarow."

Stepping into the elevator, his shoes still in his hands, Camarow gave a big toothy smile as the doors slid shut.

"He's not a bad guy once you get to know him," Daniels said. "Girls and golf, what a life."

"What's next?" Shen asked.

"I need to see Tara for a minute," Daniels said. "Come with me."

Walking down the hall to the end room, Daniels was relieved. He didn't think Tara would make a scene if Shen were with him. He knocked on the door and it swung open by itself.

"Tara?" he called.

"Maybe she went to bed early," Shen whispered.

Ignoring Shen, Daniels went farther into the darkened room. The only light came from the soft glow of the television set. Lying in bed, apparently asleep, Tara was on her side, her back to the door. Moving closer, Daniels saw that there was a sheet covering the lower part of her body, but her bare back was exposed. She wasn't moving at all.

"Tara?" he said softly, but there was no response.

He walked over to her side of the bed. She was topless and her eyes were wide open. When he touched her, he knew for sure that she was dead.

"Frank, close the door," he said. "She's dead."

Following his orders and closing the door, Shen turned on the lights. Then he took out a handkerchief and used it to pick up the phone.

"Call the police," Shen said.

The operator had been trained not to simply call the police, but to find out what the problem was and to see if the staff could assist instead. After all, this was the magnificent and efficient Peninsula Hotel.

"What's wrong?" the operator asked.

"Just call the police," Shen said, his voice agitated. "I have a dead woman up here."

He heard her gasp; then he hung up.

Daniels didn't want to wait for the police. He pulled back the sheet, exposing Tara's naked body. He was looking for what might have killed her. Her flaming red hair hung over her white shoulders, her lifeless green eyes stared blankly off into space, her lips were painted red like her hair, and her skin was cool to the touch. Her body showed no signs of trauma, no stab wounds, bullet holes, or blood.

Taking her hands into his, Daniels carefully examined her finger-nails, but he found no sign of flesh under the nails; no signs of a struggle. There wasn't any indication of rape, no bruising in the genital area, no spots or stains on the bed. Dropping the sheet back over her body, he tried to figure out what she had been doing before she died. Taking Shen's handkerchief, he picked up a half-full glass on the bedside table.

"Wine," he said aloud, after sniffing it.

The glass was clean—too clean. It was probably devoid of finger-prints.

Daniels pulled out the desk chair to the end of the bed and stood on it. He looked down on the body, rubbing his chin. Shen looked up at him, ready to call the asylum. Jumping off the chair, Daniels lay down on the bed next to her, on his back. He locked his hands behind his head. Shen had been a cop a long time, but this was new to him. Before he could speak, Daniels was up.

"She died of a drug overdose," he said. "She was lying on her side talking to a man or a woman, who was on the bed next to her. He or she slipped her the drugs, mixed with the wine, and killed her. If the medical examiner isn't careful, he will miss the trace of the opiates because of the wine. This is murder."

"How did you know all this?" Shen asked.

"There is no sign of any violence and she is in a relaxed position as if she were talking to someone. Her body is not at the edge of the bed, but over toward the middle, leaving room for someone to lie down next to her. The pillows are puffed up to take away the head indentation, but the wrinkles, when observed from above, show the outline of another person. The wine glass is the one the killer drank out of. The killer took Tara's glass, leaving the clean glass behind. Look at her lips. There's no way she could have had a drink and not have left lipstick on the rim. Be sure the police run a DNA test on the wine. I'm sure there is some saliva in it."

"Amazing," Shen said.

Daniels started going through the drawers in the dresser, opening each one carefully. Tara's clothes were put away very neatly. Her underwear was rolled military style and her T-shirts were pressed: she was the epitome of neatness. No one had gone through her room looking for anything. Finding her suitcase under her bed, he pulled it out and opened it. Empty. He pushed it back and said: "Don't forget to tell the police what you've discovered, Frank. I wasn't here."

Stepping out into the dimly lit and deserted hall, Daniels knew that in a few minutes the police would be there and the place would be crawling with life—for the wrong reasons. Tara's death didn't make sense to him. There seemed to be no reason for it, at least no reason connected to the deed. She wasn't blonde, there was no vase, and her room hadn't been searched. But she was dead anyway.

He heard the elevator doors open and wondered who it was. The police couldn't be here that fast, he thought. Maybe it was the hotel security staff. His instincts told him to wait and he pressed himself into a doorway. Three men crossed the short distance to Inga Holm's room. They let themselves in. Something was wrong, he thought, very wrong. He could feel it in his gut. Pressing his ear against the door, he could hear a man talking, Inga Holm's voice, a loud slap, and a cry of pain. He couldn't make out what they were saying, but whatever it was, it wasn't good for Inga. Knocking on the door, he said: "Room service."

A heavily accented voice yelled: "Go away."

"Hey, come on, I got an order here I have to deliver. If you don't want it, it's okay with me. But sign the check that shows I delivered it. This comes out of my pay. Please."

Daniels could hear the muffled voices, then the distinctive sound of the dead bolt, and the door swung open. Backing up across the hall to give himself a running start, Daniels waited for just the right moment. Then he threw himself into the door with all his weight. The door flew back hitting the man on the other side with such force that it knocked him cold, relocated his nose, and covered his face in blood. The two other men were taken by surprise. Before they could reach for their weapons, Daniels was flying through the air, hitting them with a cross check, sending the two of them back over a table and onto the floor. He rolled, rising to his feet. Of the two men he hit, the shorter one was getting up and pulling out his gun from under his jacket. A swift scissor kick by Daniels sent him back down, out cold. The taller of the two, who got most of the impact from Daniels's aerial acrobatics, groaned and started to sit up. Grabbing him by the lapels and pulling him to his feet, Daniels tossed him face down on the bed. With his knee pushing hard into the man's back, he pressed the barrel of his Mark 23 into the man's head, forcing it into the mattress. A muffled voice cried: "Don't shoot, don't shoot."

Daniels took his knee off the man's back, keeping the gun barrel painfully pressed into the man's head. Reaching into the man's jacket with his free hand, he pulled out a Daewoo DP51 fast fire, a small 9 mm automatic used by Chinese Army officers. Looking at the pistol, Daniels sneered: "I should have guessed."

Dropping the Daewoo into his pocket, Daniels looked around the room to make sure the other two were still out. With the gun barrel away from his head, the man on the bed slowly turned toward Daniels. For the first time Daniels got a good look at him. He immediately recognized Col. Miu.

"Don't move another inch and spread your arms across the bed."

Miu did as he was told. Picking up a pillow, Daniels dropped it over Miu's face. Miu, thinking he was going to use the pillow to muffle the sound of the gunshot, started begging again.

"Don't shoot, don't shoot," he pleaded.

Daniels had no intention of shooting the colonel. He just wanted the pillow over Miu's face to prevent the man from seeing, making it more difficult for him.

"Shut up, Col. Miu!" Daniels yelled.

Hearing his name shocked and stunned Miu into silence.

Inga Holm sat cowering in a chair, her knees pulled up to her breast, and her arms and hands tucked in. The tears rolled down from her blue eyes, leaving a trail across her cheeks that mixed with the blood running from her nose. Her face was red where she had been slapped.

"Are you all right?" Daniels asked.

When she didn't answer, Daniels walked over and patted her arm.

"You're going to be fine," he said in a soothing voice. "No one will hurt you."

She wiped the tears from her eyes and took a deep breath, trying to get hold of herself.

"What happened?" he asked.

"They, they," she said, pointing to Miu, "came in here. I was just about to go to sleep, when that bastard had his hand over my mouth. I couldn't scream. He told me to be quiet or he would kill me. He had a gun. He asked me questions about the vase, that goddamn vase. He wanted to know if I had opened it or if I had another one. I was so scared, I couldn't talk. Then that son-of-a-bitch slapped me."

She was angry now. She stood up and clinched her fists. Staring down at Miu, her blue eyes were no longer soft, but now glowed with the heat of anger.

"Then you came through the door. What's going on here? People break in, threatening to kill me. I want to get out of here."

The man at the foot of the bed was beginning to stir. Daniels reached down and picked another Daewoo off the floor. The body by the door was still lifeless. Taking no chances, he searched the body and found a third automatic pistol. Lifting the pillow off Miu's face, he pressed the pistol hard under Miu's chin.

"Get up real slow, against the wall. Move too fast and you're dead."

Pushing himself off the bed away from Daniels and pressing his back against the wall, Miu moved slowly not wanting to give Daniels an excuse to shoot him. Stretching his arms high above his head, he spoke: "I'm a diplomat. Diplomatic immunity. I'm going to reach into my coat and take out my wallet to show you my identification."

Very slowly he dropped his left hand and turned his body so Daniels could see him reaching for his wallet. With two fingers he pulled it out of his pocket. Holding the wallet with two fingers, Miu let it fall open, revealing an embassy card identifying him as Col. Lo Miu, military attaché to the embassy of the People's Republic of China.

This sucks, Daniels thought, the bastard was safe from criminal prosecution. Miu must have seen Daniels's disgusted look, because he smiled, lowered his arms, and said: "I will leave now."

As Miu turned, Daniels cracked him across the face with the barrel of his pistol.

"You didn't say 'May I.'"

The blow knocked the colonel to the floor and his face instantly became a pool of blood.

"Let's see what the diplomat has in his pockets," Daniels said searching Miu. He found nothing of interest except a room key, which he slipped into his pocket.

"What will happen to them?" Inga asked, now ready for a fight.

"Col. Miu is safe from any type of criminal prosecution, but I think he has learned a lesson in manners."

As the two other men were coming to, Daniels asked Miu if they too had diplomatic status. Miu, holding his face, shook his head, "no."

"Good," Daniels said. "Now get up."

Miu worked his way to his feet still holding his hand to his face. It was beginning to swell and turn black and blue. Daniels kicked the one by the foot of the bed with his toe and the man groaned. He opened his eyes to see the barrel of the Mark 23 pointing down at him. Turning over on all fours, he slowly got up. The man hit with the door was still not fully conscious.

"Pick him up," Daniels ordered.

The two men gathered up their fallen comrade and dragged him out of the room.

"Down the hall," Daniels barked. "March!"

He followed the trio down the hall to Tara's room where Shen was waiting for the police.

"Hold 'em and watch 'em, Frank," he said. "Especially Col. Miu here. He's a big-time diplomat. The police may have a few questions for them, but I doubt they will be talkative. Miu won't talk, claiming his diplomatic immunity. The other two goons will be back in China before the ink is dry on their bail papers."

"Where are you going now?" Shen asked as Daniels turned to leave. "The police may want to talk to you. How can they find you?"

Daniels didn't answer him. He wanted nothing to do with the police. He had nothing to say to them, but he did have something to say to Gen. Xi. He was going to pay the general a visit before someone else got hurt. It was obvious now that Xi had the vases, the empty vases. The deed was still missing, which was why Xi had sent Miu to hassle Inga Holm.

Zimkeroff didn't have the deed either. This party was far from over, he thought, because when two foxes chase one rabbit, one goes hungry, and gets mad—very mad.

CHAPTER 35

The kitten learns from the cat.

— Old Chinese proverb

T HE elevator whisked Daniels to the top floor of the Peninsula Hotel, the location of the famed Peninsula penthouse apartments. Although the twelve duplex units were on the same floor as Astrid's suite, the area could only be accessed by special elevators.

Stepping off the elevator and sinking into the plush blue carpet, he knew he was in the arena of the rich and powerful. He walked down a hallway that was adorned with art works and passed under the crystal chandeliers that bathed him in a soft yellow glow. Stopping at Suite A, he listened at the door. He didn't hear anything. Not that it mattered, he thought, he was going to see Gen. Xi no matter what. Sliding the magnetic key through the electronic lock, he got a flashing green light indicating the door was open. He gently turned the handle and pushed the door halfway open. He saw no one, but he heard the sounds of a television coming from one of the rooms on the lower floor of the duplex. He quietly stepped in. This apartment made Astrid's suite look small, he thought. The upper level, the sleeping area, was dark. Off the entrance was a short hall with doors on each side. At the end of the hall was a staircase that led to the lower level. Deciding to take a look around before venturing down to the next level, Daniels placed his ear to the first door on the right. No sound. Opening it, he stepped into a small sitting room, which was part of a bedroom suite. The sitting room was appointed like an office. Turning on the desk lamp, he went through the drawers. Nothing.

He entered the bedroom and quickly went through the drawers of the dresser, but again he found nothing. The closet revealed a Chinese army officer's uniform hanging neatly on a wooden hanger. The insignia on the epaulets indicated it belonged to a colonel, probably Miu's, he thought.

Leaving Miu's suite, he crossed the hallway to the first room on the left, again listening at the door, and again hearing nothing. He opened the door and discovered another bedroom suite, smaller than Miu's. This time he turned on the overhead lights, feeling comfortable that the room's occupant was with Miu being held by Shen for the police. The search of this room revealed nothing except the uniform of a non-commissioned officer, with the gold braid of a general's aide dangling from the right shoulder. As Daniels moved down the hall toward the master bedroom suite, the noise from below grew louder. Several voices were talking over the sound of the television. He would have to deal with them later. He was just grateful that the television kept them entertained while he finished searching their rooms.

Daniels entered the master suite and quickly went through the rooms—an office, a sitting room, a bedroom, and a large bathroom. It was an apartment within an apartment. Going through the desk drawers in the office, he found nothing but hotel stationery and a few tourist brochures. On the desk by the phone was a note pad. The top page was blank, but to play it safe, he pulled off several pages for the lab. They had the ability to read the imprint of what was written on the prior pages.

The sitting room had a few chairs pulled around a television, a recliner, and a bar. The closet in the bedroom held civilian clothes and the regal uniform of a general. So this is how the comrade general lives, he thought, not too shabby. On the end table next to the bed he found a cell phone—possible treasure. Assuming the general was like most people, himself included, he would have programmed his phone with frequently called numbers, and of course, the phone retained the last number dialed. Debating whether or not to take it, Daniels pressed the send button. The display showed a number. It appeared to be local, but he wasn't sure until the voice answering said: "Good evening, the Sheraton Hotel. How may I help you?" Flipping the cell phone shut, he slipped it into his pocket.

As he was about to leave Gen. Xi's bedroom, he took a last look around. The luxurious room inspired him with an idea that he considered close to genius. A smile spread across his face. This, he thought, was for the beauty pageant contestants who had had their rooms tossed.

Taking Xi's uniform from the closet and rolling it into a ball, he used the sleeves and legs to tie it into knots. He threw it onto the bed. Then he emptied the rest of the closet, including the shoes, on the balled up uniform. Dumping the contents of the drawers onto the ever growing pile, he then placed the emptied drawers on the bed. From the bathroom he took all the shaving cream, shampoo, anything that wasn't screwed down, and poured the contents on the towering pile. Stepping back to admire his work of art, he realized something was missing.

"Ah," he said in a soft whisper. "The final piece."

On the coffee table was a large bouquet of flowers. He took the flowers from the vase and he laid them neatly on top of the pile he had built.

"See if you can find your pajamas tonight, General," he said as he shut the light.

The staircase at the end of the hall was open to the floor below. He lay down on his stomach and lowered himself so that only his head was over the steps. The open staircase made it easy for him to view the rooms below, but made it difficult for Daniels to descend without being noticed. The staircase emptied into a large living room, off of which were two more rooms: the dining room on one side and a closed door on the other. The living room was large and decorated with couches, large chairs, tables, and an entertainment center that housed the widescreen television. Fortunately, the entertainment center was at the opposite end of the living room, farthest from the staircase.

Daniels could see one man glued to the set, watching some skin flick, while another was fast asleep in one of the luxurious chairs, his feet propped up on an equally luxurious ottoman. In the dining room, two more men were eating. Both had their backs to the staircase. Lady luck was smiling on him, he thought.

Pulling his Mark 23 from its holster, Daniels screwed on the Knight sound suppressor, thumbed off the safety, and started down the stairs. Coming up behind the man watching television, Daniels gave him a quick chop of the gun barrel hard across the back of the neck. The man slumped over. He would have fallen out of the chair, but for the quick save by Daniels, who pulled him back, making it appear that he was sleeping.

The two men in the dining room were talking and stuffing their faces at the end of each sentence. They didn't see or hear Daniels until he was a few feet away from them and he said in a low soft voice: "Quiet, don't want to wake the sleeping babies." Both men turned toward the voice and found themselves staring down the business end of a Mark 23.

Bringing his finger up to his lips, Daniels gave the universal sign for silence, which the men readily understood. Putting down their chopsticks without further orders from Daniels, they placed their hands high in the air. Daniels was pleased with their actions.

"Very good," he said. "I'm glad I don't have to shoot you."

A voice from behind Daniels said: "And I hope I don't have to shoot you, either, Mr. Daniels. Put your gun down. I've been expecting you."

Daniels couldn't get a read on the voice. He wanted to turn away from the gun hand, making himself a narrower target, but he wondered which way. The two men at the dinner table lowered their hands and got up. Daniels knew he couldn't get off more than two shots, so he decided to toss his gun. Picturing the layout of the room, he knew the couch was to his left. That's where he wanted to land the weapon. Leaving the safety off, he threw the Mark 23, hoping the impact would set off the hair trigger, discharging the weapon. It landed without going off.

He turned to his left, putting himself closer to the couch, and hoped he would have the opportunity to get his pistol. Raising his hands, he slowly turned around and came face to face with Gen. Xi. The general was holding a large brandy snifter in one hand, a cigar in the other—and nothing else. Daniels lowered hands.

"Were you going to shoot me with that, General?" he asked, pointing to the brandy snifter.

Xi smiled, showing off the gold tooth in the front of his mouth.

"No, I will drink this," he said, lifting up the glass. "This is very old, very good, and very expensive. They say this was Napoleon's drink. Come into my study, Mr. Daniels."

Without waiting for an answer, Gen. Xi turned toward the study with Daniels following close behind.

Inside the study, without asking, Xi pulled the cork from of the smoked glass bottle of Courvoisier, pouring Daniels a large cognac in a crystal snifter. Daniels held the drink up to the light, admiring the dark amber color. He swirled the cognac in the glass, letting the aroma waft up to his nostrils; then he took a long sip. While playing with the cognac, Daniels thought Xi had a lot of balls to pull a stunt like that. He must be one hell of a poker player, a man not afraid to pull the ultimate bluff.

"Excellent," Daniels said. "Nineteen-sixty-five was a good year."

"You know your cognac. Sit down."

Taking a seat in front of the general's desk, Daniels eyed the mound of sand and the pile of vases. "General, you like playing with sand?"

"I was just looking for gold, but I had no luck. Then you stopped by and maybe my luck is changing."

"You didn't invite me here just to get me drunk, did you?"

"You didn't break in here just to look around, did you?"

"I didn't break in. I had a key, General."

"You mean the key you took from Col. Miu?"

"A mere technicality," Daniels said, finishing his drink and putting the empty glass on the desk. He ran his fingers through the sand, picking some up and letting it cascade through his fingers.

"How about a refill, General?" he asked. "I think we need to talk."

Gen. Xi poured a healthy amount in Daniels's glass and both men raised their glasses. Watching Xi carefully, Daniels was looking for some sign, expecting Xi to give himself away. Xi put his feet up on the desk, took a long draw on his cigar, and blew out a thin continuous stream of smoke. Breaking the silence, Daniels went right for the jugular: "Was it necessary for your goons to kill that young woman tonight?"

Gen. Xi sat up and his feet hit the floor. Daniels knew from his body language that Xi did not know about the murder.

"I don't know what you are talking about. As I understand it, you showed up just after Miu got to the first room. I am under the impression that you stopped the interrogation before anyone was hurt—except my men, that is. You did a lot of damage to my staff."

"I hope your men don't try to save face," he said.

"Save face," Xi repeated, laughing. "That's what you Americans call a pun, right?"

Suddenly, Xi lost the laughter as if it were turned off by a switch. He said in a serious tone: "Why are you here? What do you want?"

"The same reason that you're here," Daniels answered.

"The deed to Hong Kong," Xi said, deciding to play his ace.

Daniels nodded.

"Two questions, Mr. Daniels," Xi said. "What do you really know about the deed and what's your interest—your real interest in it."

"Fair questions, General, and good questions. Do I get two questions also?"

"Yes, you have my word on it."

Daniels told him what he knew of the deed.

"Is it real or a myth, General?" Daniels asked when he was done. "If it's real, then the British don't have to turn Hong Kong over to China. If it's a myth, then all this is for nothing. As to my interest, I don't give a damn about the deed, but my orders are to find it and I will. After that, it's up to the president. Maybe he'll give it to the Brits; maybe he'll give it to your government. I don't know, but I'm sure there will be a price to pay either way. The president has something up his sleeve."

"It's not your president's sleeve I would look up, but up Admiral Charko's sleeve. That's what has me worried. You have a good understanding about the deed, almost perfect, but not quite. Let me fill you in on the missing pieces."

Gen. Xi explained the history of the land grant, the extortion by Major General Powell, and the setting aside of the treaty of Nanking to force the deed from the Chinese at the threat of war.

"The deed was given without consideration. It was stolen by force of arms. Hong Kong does not belong to the British, but to the Chinese," Xi said, finishing.

"Now answer my first question, General. What's your interest in the deed? Are you here to see that it gets returned to China?"

"No, no. I'm here to see that it never goes back to China. You might say I'm here on my own mission."

"Second question, what are you going to do with the deed if you find it?"

"That's a third question, Mr. Daniels, but I'm happy to tell you because you're going to help me find it. I intend to sell the deed to the British and retire to England on a country estate."

"But there is a problem," Daniels said. "You don't have the deed and Montgomery or I could find it first—or perhaps your friend Sang Chi. If he finds it, you're screwed."

The smile disappeared from Xi's face. Daniels knew he had hit a raw nerve.

"I'm too old a cat to be screwed by a young kitten," Xi said, controlling his anger. "Remember, it's the kitten that learns from the cat. Chi is working for the Chinese internal security, under a relic of a leader. If it were not for some intruder, Chi would be dead and one less thing for me to be concerned about."

"You mean the warehouse on Water Street?"

"I should have known it was you. How did you do it?" Xi said, slapping his knee.

"That's your third question, General."

Both men smiled. Daniels told him what had happened.

"They were very good men," Xi said.

"My turn, General. What about the Chinese couple? The Chans."

"They had been set up to think that they were working for the Free China Society, a society dedicated to the overthrow of the Chinese government. Unfortunately for them, the society does not exist. It was made up by internal security to keep check on the would-be rebels. People need hope, Mr. Daniels, and as long as they have hope, they are manageable. The Chans were supposed to bring the deed to Hong Kong in a brown, sand-filled vase. But some clerk at their store sold the vase to one of the blonde women in the beauty contest. During the Grand Ball this evening, my men slipped onto the women's floor to search the rooms of all the tall blonde women to retrieve what we thought were four vases. To my surprise, they found nine," he said pointing to the vases on his desk.

"But the vase with the deed is still missing. When you caught Col. Miu, he was questioning the women about the vases."

"What happens if the deed is returned to China?"

"Politically, it will disappear. China will have sovereignty over Hong Kong, the way it should be. Practically, the liberals in government will argue we can gain more by economic competition than by military might. The economy of Hong Kong will add greatly to China's.

"As for me, and this is my only concern now, I am one who believes in a very strong military. But if I stay in China, I will be retired to some farm to spend my remaining years. There will be no need for me. To some, I'm an old useless general, Mr. Daniels. I have given my whole life to my country and I want more than a few yen and a few pigs. The more the people see of the West, the more they want. Like me. I intend to spend my retirement in England. I've worked out a deal with Montgomery for myself and a few of my senior officers and aides."

"And if I find the deed first, then what?" Daniels asked.

"That raises many possibilities, Mr. Daniels. I'm not concerned about Montgomery. It's you I'm worried about—you and Charko. For the sake of your question, I don't think Montgomery will ever find the deed. He's not looking in the right places. But if he does find it first, I believe he will pay me to prevent war. Not as much as I would have gotten if I had sold the deed to him, but something substantial. You see, I told him of the invasions plans for Southeast Asia. I actually gave him most of the central committee's plans—or at least enough for him to verify the troop movements. The British are a very practical people. It's cheaper to pay me for the information, keep the peace, and, of course, Hong Kong.

"So if Montgomery finds the deed, I still win. Now, if you find the deed, your president will convene a meeting with Secretary of State Smith and your National Security Advisor Sam Bergen, and they will tell him if he gives the deed to the British, it will make crazy Gen. Xi stronger, leading to war. Smith will argue that the stronger China's economy, the greater the chance for democracy. You will be instructed to turn the deed over to me because the prime minister has already told your president of my deal with them. So, if you find it, I still win."

Xi waited a few long seconds for the impact of his words to sink in. Then leaning close to Daniels, he said: "I assure you, I will lead the invasion of Taiwan. You see, Mr. Daniels, my government wants what belongs to it. For now it's Hong Kong, but if we can't have it, we have an excuse to take Taiwan."

Daniels didn't blink at the threat, not believing Xi, thinking it was another bluff.

"You know, General, personally I think you're nuts and if I had my gun I would shoot you. We always put down mad dogs."

"I don't like being referred to as a mad dog, Mr. Daniels, and I have my gun. I tell you this, I'm not mad and, contrary to what you are thinking, this is not a bluff."

"General, if you're playing with a full deck, why start a war you can't win?"

"This is a war we can win. You will not use nuclear force to stop us. Your president would not dare. The consequences are too great. The nuclear submarines cruising the Taiwan Strait are useless because the water is too shallow for them to run undetected. We know where they are. I have three divisions ready to move and short-range missiles that will knock out all the defensive positions on the island. Once we are there, your rapid deployment forces will have no place to launch a counter invasion. You will find the invasion of the island a lot more difficult than the Gulf War. But there is no need for all this saber rattling, that's why we are having this little talk. I want you to get the deed for me. I still win."

Daniels wanted to reach across the desk and bury the bastard's face in the pile of sand.

"Listen, you pompous little prick, I don't take orders from you."

"Do you know why the Russians are here?" Xi asked quickly, not allowing Daniels to get worked up. "They are trying to find the deed, too. They made a deal with Chi."

"Doesn't that screw up your plans, General? Hell, what if I give the deed to the Russians, who sell it to your man Chi. The deed goes back to China, no war, everyone is happy, and you're on your pig farm where you belong."

"It's a possible scenario, except you Americans dislike the Russians even more than you dislike us. I can't see you giving an ultraconservative like Zimkeroff a chance to make a deal with us."

Xi was right, Daniels thought. There was no way they could let the Russians get the deed. It all made sense now, the Russians were trading the deed for the biological weapon he saw on the videotape. A weapon of mass destruction in the hands of Zimkeroff would be a major world problem.

"Where is Chi now?" Daniels asked.

"He should be on a plane back to China or in a British jail. Unfortunately, Montgomery can't seem to find him although he has been at his office at the old CAAC hangar on the perimeter road at the airport. My sources back home tell me he's waiting for Gen. Zimkeroff to deliver the deed. Whatever Zimkeroff wants in exchange for the deed is probably there. A courier made a delivery to him. Get me my deed, Mr. Daniels. It's the answer to everyone's problems."

Gen. Xi called to his aides, who came quickly into the study. He instructed them to show Daniels out.

"I can show myself out," Daniels said.

One of the men grabbed his arm. Daniels snapped his arm back, twisting the man around and shoving him into the other aide. They both fell backwards. The sound of the commotion brought two more men running into the room, one holding Daniels's gun and saying something in Chinese. Jumping up from his desk, Gen. Xi ordered his men to stand down.

"Thanks, General. Do you think I can have my gun back now?"

"You're a funny man. Remember, you shoot mad dogs. I don't think that would be a good idea."

"Come on, General, can't you take a joke? If I don't return that Mark 23, it comes out of my pay and it costs more than two grand."

"Capitalist," Gen. Xi said with a laugh.

"Don't lose your sense of humor, General. I only hope you still have it when you go to bed."

Just before Daniels reached the front door of the apartment, one of the aides who had been following him handed him back his gun, butt first. A surprised Daniels took his Mark 23 and from the feel of it, he knew that they had taken out the bullets. Making no comment, he unscrewed the sound suppressor and holstered the weapon.

Daniels had his hand on the doorknob when a bruised and bloody Col. Miu came in, followed by a uniformed policeman and Michael Montgomery. Montgomery shot Daniels a dirty look.

"Good to see you again, Michael," Daniels said, smiling. "And Col Miu, you'd better put some ice on that."

CHAPTER 36

A man must do what must be done.

— Old Chinese proverb

NOT wanting to wake Astrid, Daniels dragged his weary body to his room with the evening's events spinning in his head. All he wanted was sleep and time to recharge his batteries. The bathroom nightlight cast a subdued glow over the room. There was just enough illumination to see that the bed had been turned down. Kicking off his shoes as he crossed the room, he dropped his jeans to the floor, and threw his jacket onto the chair. He tossed the Mark 23 onto a pillow and kicked the holster under the bed. Finally, he thought, sleep. Falling across the bed, he pulled the sheet up, felt for the gun, and slid it under the pillow. He practiced yoga breathing before falling into a deep sleep.

The creaking of the door woke him after what seemed only a few minutes. Not moving, he listened to someone trying to sneak across the bedroom. Making no quick movements, he forced rhythmic breathing, slow and deep. He let his right hand slide under the pillow until he felt the butt of his weapon. His fingers crawled over the stock, his thumb found the safety, and pushed it off. As the footsteps grew louder, he thought the person should be just about by the side of the bed. He was ready to fire when he heard Astrid say: "Wake up sleepy head. It's morning."

Rolling over, he opened his eyes, and found himself staring into a pair of lace panties.

"I must have died and gone to heaven," he said groggily.

She bent over and her robe opened. His eyes focused on her breasts.

"Well, good morning to you and to you," he said, nodding toward the firm pair that caught his attention.

He pulled her down on the bed and kissed her.

"And good morning to you, too," he said.

"Come on now, Mac. Get up."

"I am," he said with a sly smile.

"A cold shower will settle things back down," she said.

Daniels made a face.

In her best Tweety Bird voice, she said: "Da poor wittle guy. He's all up with no pwace to go."

Daniels grabbed her robe and pulled her down on top of him. Her breasts were pressing on his chest. She smelled good, he thought. Her very essence was seductive. Whispering in her ear, he said: "You feel good. Stay, Astrid, don't go."

"Darlin'," she purred, in her Southern drawl, "there is some good news and some bad news."

"What's the bad news?" he asked, not sure if she was serious.

"Well," she said, pulling herself up from his grasp and letting her breasts rub across his face, "Harry Saltzman is out in the living room waiting for you."

"And what's the good news?" he said, letting out a groan.

She walked away from the bed, her behind swinging provocatively. Without looking back, she said: "There's always later."

*   *   *

Harry Saltzman stood by the picture window looking out at the harbor. It was a view that he had seen many times over the years, a view he usually enjoyed. But not today. He didn't see the beauty of the harbor, just millions of dead bodies. Saltzman saw the last horseman of the apocalypse galloping toward him. It was so real; he stepped back from the window.

The horror Saltzman had witnessed on the Chinese videotape had kept him up all night and now he was having a nightmare just looking out the window. The sound of Astrid's footsteps, snapped him from his reverie.

"He'll be right out," Astrid said. "Help yourself to coffee."

"Christ, Harry. You look like shit," Daniels said, entering the room. "Didn't you sleep last night? Astrid, what did you do to him?"

"Not a thing," she said. "I haven't had time. And I don't have time now."

As soon as Astrid was out of the room, Saltzman took from his pocket several pieces of paper which were neatly folded. The folds looked liked Haig's work, Daniels thought.

"What is it, Harry?" he asked

"It's the tape," Saltzman said in a barely audible whisper. "It's the goddamn tape. You can't believe what the Chinese have."

"I saw part of it, Harry. Looks like they have some kind of poison gas. We've dealt with that kind of shit before."

"No, Mac, not like this. This is a doomsday device," Saltzman said, handing the folded papers to Daniels.

Daniels read the English translation of what was on the tape and when he got to the projections and analysis provided by Haig, it was his turn to lose his color.

"Is this possible?" he asked, pushing the papers back to Saltzman. "This is crazy."

Saltzman nodded.

"A biochemical virus. Christ, Harry they managed to make a living virus. A fucking strain that could wipe humanity off the face of the earth. Unbelievable."

"Mac, here," Saltzman said, handing him another slip of paper. "It's from the Admiral."

Daniels took the slip of paper in his hand, not immediately opening it. He knew what it would say. He had received this type of order before.

"Mac, you have to get us a sample of this."

"Would you trade the deed for it, Harry?" Daniels asked.

"Mac, we would trade you for it. We need it; we must have it. We have to know what it can do in order to build a defense for it. Do whatever it takes. Get it for us."

Opening the note, Daniels read the three words on it out loud, "At any cost." He knew what this meant. He was to do whatever he had to do—no rules, no questions asked. He just had to do it and he would—or he would die trying. Crumpling the paper into a ball, he tossed it into a wastebasket. Holding his mug like a hand warmer, he told Saltzman about his encounter with Gen. Xi, leaving out no details.

"Chi must have the bio-weapon, Harry," Daniels said. "Gen. Xi said something arrived for him yesterday. Now we know what it was."

"That confirms our Chinese source," Saltzman said. "We have information that Chi is going to trade the biochemical weapon to the Russians for the deed."

"Not unless I can get the deed first and I have a good idea where it is. Chi's at the old CAAC hangar."

"And if you can't get the deed? Then what?"

"Then we'll all be dead. But I'll get the weapon for you, Harry, I promise."

Ashen-faced, Saltzman stood up to leave.

"One more thing, Mac. Montgomery called the consul general, complaining about you. He was madder than hell at your late night antics. He wants you out of the country. You better make peace. Fill him in."

"Do I tell him everything?" Daniels asked walking Saltzman to the door.

"Whatever you want. Remember, it's your call. Do what you have to do—at any cost."

* * *

Astrid came out of her bedroom, intercepting Daniels as he headed to his room. She had a phone message in her hand. Daniels quickly glanced at it. It was from Kelly Brook. Trying not to show his surprise, he slipped the note into his pocket. Reaching out for Astrid and pulling her close, he embraced her silently.

Astrid knew he was leaving again and she knew she had to let him go if she were ever going to keep him. She had known the truth about Daniels for a month. In a moment of candor, her father had told her about Mac's real profession and she felt embarrassed that she had been such a bitch in the past. But she was determined to make it up to him. She wasn't going to lose him again. Looking at his face, she could see that he was worried.

"Darling," her soft voice made the words sing. "What's wrong? Is there something I can do to help?"

"I have to go. I have to find someone. It's very important, Astrid," he said, thinking about Chi.

She knew it was coming and she swore she wasn't going to be jealous of this woman, Kelly Brook.

"I understand. When will you be back?"

"Dinner time. The two of us at Hugo's, seven sharp."

Her face showed she was pleased with Daniels's suggestion of Hugo's Restaurant located at the Hyatt Regency. It was one of the finest restaurants in the Far East and one of Astrid's favorite places. She liked to sing with the strolling musicians.

"You have a date," she said smiling. "Meet you here at six-thirty. See you later, darling."

Giving him a kiss and a pat on the butt, she walked off to her room.

Daniels stood outside his room watching her as she went down the hall, not believing this was the same woman whose jealous rage would have broken everything in the place. She had really changed. But his pleasant thoughts were interrupted by the reality that this might be his last day on Earth.

Stepping into his room, he slipped the note from Kelly out of his pocket. Astrid's fine handwriting read: *"Please call A.S.A.P. Very important. 4-788877."*

He hadn't seen Kelly in years and he wondered how she knew he was in town. What could possibly be important? He thought it was strange, but he would definitely call her. He owed her that.

Dick Brook, Kelly's older brother, had been Daniels's roommate at Princeton. When Kelly had come to visit them at school, she had been just a starry-eyed teenager who had had a crush on Daniels. Kelly had never missed a home football game. She had been a one-person rooting section for the two running backs, her brother and Mac. Much to her chagrin, however, Daniels had regarded her as a little sister, often introducing her that way to his campus buddies.

After graduation, the inseparable pair had gone their separate ways, Daniels to the navy, and Dick to the air force, where he had become a jet jockey, flying the F-15 Eagle. Dick had been a top pilot who had loved to fly. No one had seemed to be as relaxed as he when cruising at fifty thousand feet, going three times the speed of sound. Over the years the two of them had corresponded. Dick Brook had often described a pilot's life as hours of boredom, punctuated by moments of terror. It had been one of those moments of terror that had taken his life. Not wanting to eject with the possibility that his plane would crash into a populated area, he had tried to land. His bravery had been rewarded with a posthumous Medal of Honor. Kelly had received the tribute from the President of the United States, but Daniels had been on assignment in the Gulf and had been unable to attend either the presentation or his friend's interment in Arlington National Cemetery.

Kelly's life had gone to hell with Dick's death. Not ready to face the world alone, she had been in and out of jobs until she had found exotic dancing. Daniels had continued to write to her, but by the time he had returned to the States, he had lost track of her—until one night, when their paths had crossed again in one of Washington, D.C.'s clubs.

He had been going to meet a few friends, have a drink, and call it a night. Sitting by the side of the bar away from the melee, he had spotted Kelly. She had finished dancing for a few of the customers and she had been walking topless toward her dressing room. Daniels couldn't believe his eyes. The kid was now a grown woman, an attractive well-grown woman. Overcoming the initial shock, he had called to her. The sound of her real name had caused her to stop. Their eyes had met and, like Eve expelled from the Garden of Eden, her nakedness now shamed her. Her face had flushed and she had tried to cover her breasts with her hands.

He had grabbed her by the arms to prevent her from walking away from him. She had tried to free herself. One of the club's muscle-bound bouncers had seen what was going on and had rushed over to intercede, but he had made the mistake of pushing Daniels. The bouncer went down with Daniels's foot pressed on his throat. He had flopped on the floor like a fish out of water. Kelly had screamed.

In a soft voice Daniels had said: "Come on, Kelly. Let's get out of here."

"Let me get dressed. I'll meet you in the parking lot."

"Good," he had said, lifting his foot off the throat of the bouncer, who had turned blue. Without a second look, Daniels had walked out into the night to meet Kelly.

They had spent hours in an all-night coffee shop, catching up on old times. She was on her way to Florida to spend the winter months dancing in the Fort Lauderdale clubs. Although he had not been pleased that she was a stripper working the club circuit, Daniels hadn't tried to preach to her. He had known better. He had just been glad to see her and had suggested that she use the spare bedroom at his Georgetown townhouse while she was in Washington. She had accepted his invitation and had moved in.

Daniels had been glad to have his little sister back again, but for Kelly, it had been different. She had become a lovesick teenager once more. Yet in the two weeks she had stayed there, she had gotten no closer to his bedroom door than she had when he had been at Princeton. Finally, she had realized that she was always going to be his kid sister and nothing more. She had made other plans.

A call from the Admiral had sent Daniels to France for an overnight meeting. When he had returned, Kelly was gone. She had left him a note promising to write and thanking him for the love and support. She had signed it: Sis.

Every once in a while there had been a letter, a Christmas card, but they had tapered off and she was gone again. Now, out of nowhere, she was back. Picking up the phone, Daniels dialed her number, letting it ring until he heard her voice on the answering machine. He left a message.

"Mac, I'm going out for a while," Astrid said, opening the door and peeking in. "Just want to say good-bye. See you later, love."

"Where are you going?" he asked, noticing her backpack.

"Oh, I have few things I want to do. I'm going to run an errand or two. See you later. Bye."

He retrieved his holster from under the bed and picked up the Mark 23, which was lying beneath his pillow. After he had dressed, he looked at himself in the mirror and saw a typical American tourist—except for the shoulder holster. The windbreaker would cover the weapon, but he would always know it was there. Before this gun became standard issue for special forces, it had to pass stringent testing. The Mark 23 had to fire two thousand rounds without stoppage and be accurate at seventy-five feet, so that all the rounds were within a two-and-one-half inch circle. His life depended on his ability to fire off thirteen rounds without a jam; then reload and be ready to fire again. Now for the finishing touch, he thought, putting on a dark blue New York Yankees baseball cap. Ready, he thought. He patted his holster. A man must be ready to do what must be done—at any cost.

CHAPTER 37

When a loved one dies, death takes a piece of everyone.
— Old Chinese proverb

❧❧

WALKING down the hallway toward the elevators, Daniels was thinking about Kelly, not paying attention to the two matronly ladies he passed on the way.

"Please hold it. Thank you," one of the ladies called to him.

He held the doors open for the two women and tipped his baseball cap when they reached him.

"There are still some gentlemen left in this part of the world," the larger of the two ladies said on their way down.

In the lobby, he heard his name being called. It was Kelly and she was running toward him. Her long legs were unhampered by yellow short shorts and her Hi-Jinks Club T-shirt did little to stop her oversize breasts from bouncing around enthusiastically. She gave the hotel patrons quite a show.

She jumped into his arms as he lifted her off her feet. She threw her legs around him and he held her tight, spinning her around. All eyes in the lobby were glued on them. Most of the male guests gave smiling approvals while the women gave mixed reviews. Daniels's two elevator companions, observing the show by the side door, gave disapproving looks, followed by a "hmm."

"Kelly, you look great," he said, hugging her. "But what in God's name are you doing here?"

"You look pretty good yourself," she said. "But you're in great danger, Mac. I'm trying to save your life."

"What?"

"Come on," she said, "we have to find a place to talk."

Pulling him by the arm, she led him toward the side door.

"I called you earlier this morning from the lobby and Astrid answered. She said you were in a meeting and she would give you the message. I gave her my number, but to be honest, knowing how she is, I wasn't sure you would have gotten my message. I didn't want to cause you any aggravation, so I decided to camp here for a while. When I saw Astrid leaving the hotel, I decided to wait a little longer in case you were coming down behind her. When you didn't show up, I tried to call you again. I got the voice mail, but I didn't leave a message. You must have been in the elevator. I was coming back to my spot when I saw that stupid Yankee hat."

Reaching over, she grabbed his cap.

"Gimme that," she said playfully, putting it on. "There. Now let's get out of here."

They left the hotel by the side entrance, exiting onto Middle Road.

"This way," she said, leading Daniels up the street toward her car, a beaten-up Ford Taurus. The black Ford was in desperate need of a bath and some polish. The bumpers and fenders were dinged and the car's windows were tinted black, affording them some privacy.

"Fancy car, Kelly. Where did you get this old heap?" he asked her, giving the car a once over. "And why the blackout windows?"

"This is not an old heap, Mac. There is a lot of good life left in my car. Don't let the looks fool you. Anyway, I bought it from my boss at a great price," she said throwing him the keys. "Here, you drive. You always liked to drive."

"Where to, Kell?" he asked, getting into the car and turning on the engine.

"How about the park?" she said.

"Kowloon Park coming up," he said easing up on the clutch and pulling out onto Middle Road. Maneuvering the Tarus through the stubborn city traffic, Daniels crept along until he came to Hankow Road, where he turned right. Hankow Road dead ended on Haiphong Road, a one-way street going counterclockwise around the park.

Kowloon Park was a favorite of the locals. It featured meandering paths lined with benches, little ponds, and streams containing the obligatory ducks and swans. It was rare to see a tourist at the park, as it offered nothing more than a serene place to enjoy a stroll or a lunch.

"Kelly, I'm so glad to see you," Daniels said after he had parked. "You look great, kid. The Far East agrees with you. But I have a bone to pick with you. Why did you dump me in D.C.? Why did you leave without so much as a good-bye? What happened?"

"I was your little sister, Mac. I loved you for it, but I wanted to be more. After you left for France, I decided it was time for me to leave. I danced the circuit, made a little money, and thought about going back to Washington. But when I read about you and Astrid Reed in the social pages.... Hell, Mac, you didn't need me hanging around and getting in the way."

"Oh, Kelly," he said, "you were never in the way. Astrid and I, well that's a story for another day. You're always welcome to come back with me."

"It's better this way. Trust me on this. The kitchen is only big enough for one woman," she said, with sadness in her voice.

"So what did you do then?" he asked.

"After a few years I was considered old for the business. My dancing days were numbered, so I came here to make a few bucks. Believe it or not, I'm a star here, Mac."

"I believe you would be a star anywhere. I saw the poster of you when I drove past the club, Miss Happy Holiday," he said using her stage name. "I recognized the face, but not the name. I was sure about the body, though."

She was topless in the picture. Dancing naked was one thing; Daniels seeing her was another. She blushed. He saw her embarrassment and changed the subject.

"Come home," he said.

"I will, but to my own home. I've been saving my money. I've done very well here and at the end of the year I plan to quit. I want to buy a place on the New Jersey shore. Remember when you and Dick took me to your parents' home on Long Beach Island? Well, that's where I'm going. I'm buying a house there and I'm going to watch the sunrise over the Atlantic."

"That sounds like a plan, a great plan. I'll be your first house guest, I promise. Now what's this about you saving my life?"

"Well," she started, "the club where I dance is owned by Johnny Leng."

"*The* Johnny Leng?" he asked.

"You know him?"

"That explains why this car has its windows darkened. If this car could talk, Johnny would get a hundred years in a British prison."

"Since I am his star attraction, I am privileged to have a private dressing room, which is next to Johnny's office. The old pervert has a hole in the wall that he uses to peek through. The other night a customer spilled a drink on my dress and when I went to change, I could hear Johnny's grandson Jeff talking about some type of land grant, a deed of some type. Jeff told his grandfather that some American who had visited with him had a great plan where they all would make out well. I tried not to pay attention, but the old man kept yelling about some destroyer who was going to kill him. I thought I heard Jeff say 'Daniels' but I wasn't sure. From what I could hear, it sounded like the old man wanted someone to kill this person before he got killed."

Daniels was listening intently and wishing she would get to the point.

"Go on," he said.

"Jeff showed me a photo of you."

She had his attention now. "Yes, you. It was a head and shoulder shot. It looked like a photo from work. You even had a tie on. Across the bottom of the picture, in magic marker were the words *Peninsula Hotel* and it had the initials *WNC* printed on the picture in the corner."

He knew where the picture had come from, but it didn't make any sense. Then again, what did these days? he thought. Kelly had no idea what she had stumbled on—another player in the race for the deed and one who wanted him dead. Deep in thought, Daniels was trying to plan his next move when he was interrupted by Kelly.

"Mac, are you happy being married to Astrid?"

In the midst of a life and death struggle, it finally dawned on Daniels that she still had a schoolgirl crush on him, except that now that she was a woman, it was called love.

"You silly kid. I never married Astrid."

With those magic words, Kelly's appearance changed; a veil was lifted. Her face lit up and she was aglow. She may have assumed too much, but that was her prerogative, she thought. It was time to tell him how she felt.

As she was about to declare her love, the passenger side window shattered. A bullet found its way into the side of Kelly's head. Her twisted and contorted body fell across the front seat, dead. At the sound of the shattering glass, Daniels's Mark 23 was in his hand and his instincts took over.

While Daniels and Kelly had been talking, a black Chevy Suburban had pulled up next to the Ford. Inside the Chevy were two Chinese men, both looking very professional. The driver pulled out from under his jacket a Ruger SP-101, a .22-caliber pistol, good at close range. This was close enough, only about four feet separated the two vehicles. Lowering his window just a few inches and waiting for the word, the shooter screwed on the sound suppressor. He could barely see the face of his target from behind the darkened glass, but the head with the baseball cap made a great silhouette. Too easy, he thought. His smile revealed a mouth full of stained yellow teeth.

The passenger was on his cell phone confirming that the Ford belonged to Happy Holiday. The voice on the other end told him what he needed to know: Daniels had on a baseball cap when he had stepped out of the elevator at the hotel. Betty Carper, the woman who had ridden down on the elevator with him, had given a detailed description of Daniels. The passenger nodded. The driver raised the pistol to the open window, aimed, and squeezed off one shot.

The passenger exited the Chevy Suburban, walking around to the rear of both vehicles. Stopping at the driver's side door of the Ford, he said: "Get out of the car, Happy. You bad girl, you're with a bad man."

Correcting himself with a laugh, he said: "A dead bad man. If you don't get your white ass out here, I'll drag it out. Maybe I fucky you."

He was laughing loudly now, having a good time with his own humor. He jerked the door opened, but the driver's side was empty—except for Kelly's body lying across the seat. A look of horror came over the man's face as he leaned into the car. Up from the back seat, Daniels whipped the barrel of the Mark 23 across the man's neck, knocking him out.

Easing himself out the rear door of the Ford, Daniels worked his way to the Suburban. He stayed low to avoid the driver spotting him in the side mirror. Yanking open the door, Daniels, in one fluid motion, pulled the shooter to the ground.

"Crawl, you fucking snake, crawl," Daniels growled.

The man tried to get on his hands and knees, but Daniels pushed him down.

"Not like a dog, like a snake, you piece of shit."

Daniels stopped the crawling man with his foot and searched him. He found the Ruger, which he threw on the floor of the Ford.

"Get in the back, you piece of shit," his voice seething with anger.

Daniels then pulled the semiconscious man from the front seat, searched him, and found only a cell phone, which he dropped into his pocket. As the man regained his senses, Daniels ordered him into the back seat with the shooter. Shutting the rear door of the Ford, he climbed into the front of the car facing the back. The two Chinese men, considering the position they were in, looked calm. They were professional, Daniels thought. He wasn't sure he was going to get anything out of them, but he would try.

"Who sent you?" he asked.

Neither man said a thing; both stared straight ahead in silence.

"I am going to ask you this just once more and I'm going to make it easy for you, just a yes or no. Did Johnny Leng send you?"

At the name Leng, both men reacted. The driver of the Suburban, the shooter, sat back smiling, showing his stained teeth. In excellent English, he answered: "Go fuck yourself. Johnny will get you. Are you really going to shoot an unarmed man? Go ahead—if you got the balls."

Daniels glanced at the lifeless body of Kelly, then back to the smiling shooter.

"All right," he said, squeezing the trigger. The Mark 23 recoiled, a puff of smoke, a flash. Daniels squeezed the trigger again, again, and again, so fast that it seemed liked one continuous shot. The sound suppressor did the job. There was no noise, just a wiz as the first bullet went through the shooter's heart, throwing him back against the seat. Blood splattered over the rear window. Each of the rounds found its mark, each one punching the shooter against the rear seat and spreading more of his blood and tissue over the interior of the car. After the last shot, the body seemed to be suspended in air, hanging there before finally falling forward.

Daniels turned to the passenger, the second man and said: "Do you want me to shoot you, too?"

Holding up his hands, waiving them frantically, the passenger said: "No! No! Johnny tell Charley to kill you. He give Charley job. Pay much money. He says you are very dangerous. You a cowboy, you destroyer."

"Why did he want me dead?"

"I do not know. Never ask why. Charley get job. I go with Charley."

"Tell Johnny the destroyer is coming for him."

The man shook his head. "You tell him. Not me. He's at Hi-Jinks Club tonight. He's there every night. If I tell Johnny I talk to you, Charley not kill you, Johnny will kill me, wife, children, all family. Maybe it's good for family if you kill me now."

Daniels understood. "Get out of here," he said.

Slowly opening the door of the Ford, the man stepped out of the car and walked toward the exit of the parking lot. Looking back from the exit just once, he broke into a run, never stopping. He would gather up his family, cross the border into China, and get lost forever.

Picking up the cell phone he had taken, Daniels pressed the send button. After several rings, a male voice answered in Chinese: "*Duile.*"

"Johnny Leng," Daniels said.

"Who is this speaking, please," Jeff Leng said in English.

"Your worst nightmare, Johnny, your soul taker, your destroyer. It's the cowboy. I'm going to kill you."

He hung up and tossed the phone into the Ford. Then he used his own cell to call Harry Saltzman.

While he waited for the connection, he stared at Kelly's body, his eyes filling with tears.

"Send the cleaner," he said, telling Saltzman where he was. No more was said; no more needed to be said.

By the time a white van marked in Chinese and English *Frank's Painting Service* pulled along side of the Taurus, Daniels had regained his composure. A tall man in painter's overalls got out the driver side and Saltzman exited the passenger's side.

"Are you okay, Mac?" Saltzman asked, pretending not to notice Daniels's reddened eyes.

Daniels didn't reply; he just nodded his head.

"Who's the woman? What happened?"

"She's Kelly Brook, my sister," Daniels said simply.

"I'm sorry. What can we do?"

"See that she gets buried at Love Ladies on Long Beach Island. Saint Lucy's Church by the ocean," Daniels said.

Saltzman started to say something, but Daniels held up his hand. "I'm all right, Harry. I have a job to do. I'll do what must be done."

The man in the white overalls taped a heavy piece of plastic over the broken window, sprayed the window with black paint, and hitched a tow bar to the Ford. Before they left, Daniels told Saltzman to check the number on the passenger's cell phone and get back to him.

Watching the Ford disappear as the van pulled out of the parking lot, he took a moment to practice his breathing exercises, trying to get himself centered. It's true, he thought, death takes a piece of you when a loved one dies.

Opening the door of the Chevy Suburban, Daniels climbed in. His job, as he saw it, was to find Chi, get the biochemical weapon, retrieve the deed, and kill Johnny Leng.

CHAPTER 38

Revenge is a dish best served cold.

— Old Chinese proverb

❧

"*DA sveedanya*," Gen. Zimkeroff said, shutting the door to his suite. Turning the safety lock, he heard the dead bolt fall into place with a reassuring clunk. For extra protection, he slipped the useless safety chain into its holder. He wasn't usually a cautious man. More typically, he was aggressive, willing to take the chance and to push his luck—but not now.

He reached for the expensive leather briefcase sitting next to the door, grabbing it first by the handles; he then slipped it under his massive arms and strode off down the hall, his footsteps echoing on the marble floor. He stepped inside his room and kicked the door shut. The sound of the door closing brought Petroff running from his room.

"Is everything all right, General?" the sergeant major called from the hallway.

"Yes. Go away. When I want you, I will call." Zimkeroff's voice sounded like thunder. Petroff returned to his room to wait until the general wanted him.

Zimkeroff placed the leather briefcase on the coffee table. He rubbed his hands together, feeling his heart begin to race. This was the moment he had been waiting for all his life. Without hesitation, he opened the case—and there it was: the vase containing the land grant, the deed to Hong Kong. He picked up the dark-brown glass vase and admired the hand-painted picture of a woman surrounded by butterflies on one side and the portrait of a man with flowers on the other. The two figures, he knew, had something to do with life and birth, but he really didn't care. For him the vase meant untold wealth and the death of millions of Americans. The taste of revenge was sweet on his tongue.

Placing the vase on the table, he worked the wide cork from side to side, pulling it until it gave way with a pop, followed by a puff of smoke.

Zimkeroff pulled back in surprise, waiting perhaps for a genie to appear. Picking up a wastepaper basket from the side of the desk, he poured the sand out slowly. When the cascading sand slowed to a trickle, he looked at the mouth of the vase and found a rolled piece of parchment clogging the opening. Gently, ever so gently, he brought his thick thumb and forefinger together like a tweezer and slowly pulled the parchment out of the vase. He was surprised that it was not as brittle as he would have thought. But then he remembered that bodies found in the Egyptian desert, buried in the dry sand, were well preserved after thousands of years.

As he pressed the unfurled parchment against the desk, the Chinese characters blended together into a magnificent scrolling script. Even though Zimkeroff couldn't read it, he saw a beauty about the ancient document. Toward the center of the document, neatly printed in bold strokes, was the word *Powell*. This was it, he thought, the deed to Hong Kong.

Rubbing his fingers over the document, he could feel the power and wealth being absorbed into his body. Rolling the parchment and slipping it back into the vase, Zimkeroff poured the sand back in. Putting the vase back into the expensive leather case, he pressed the gold snaps into place.

"Sergeant Major," he roared.

Answering his call, Petroff came running into Zimkeroff's room.

"Yes, General."

"Are we ready to pay a visit to Chi?"

"Yes, General, we are ready. With your permission I would like to show you what I have done."

Not waiting for Zimkeroff's answer, Petroff left the room, returning moments later with a black leather case similar to the one Zimkeroff had on the desk. Holding it up, Petroff offered it for Zimkeroff's inspection. It was empty.

Zimkeroff told Petroff to turn it upside down, which he did. At this, Zimkeroff gave his laughing approval.

"Very good. Where is it?" the general asked.

Petroff reached into the empty case and pulled out a Benelli M1 Super 90, a 12-gauge semi-automatic shotgun. Applauding Petroff's trick, Zimkeroff said: "Sergeant Major, I hereby promote you to Major Magician. Excellent, excellent, but what did you do to that beautiful shotgun, Yuri?"

Holding the weapon up for close inspection, Petroff explained that he had cut the twenty-one-inch barrel down to ten inches; then he had reduced the stock by twelve inches, shrinking the original forty-inch Italian shotgun to a mere seventeen inches. Handing the miniaturized version of the Benelli to Zimkeroff, Petroff said: "How does it feel?"

"It weighs a little more than an automatic pistol. Very good," Zimkeroff said, hefting the weapon.

He handed it back to Petroff, who could not contain his delight at the praise he had received from the general.

Petroff pushed five 12-gauge shells into the magazine; then he pulled back the bolt and released it. The action caused a shell to be pushed into firing position.

"Almost ready, General," Petroff said.

From his pocket, Petroff took another 12-gauge shell and pushed it into the magazine chamber.

"It's a large ball shot, General, the kind that tears a man in half," Petroff said.

"Well done," Zimkeroff said as he watched as Petroff place the shot-gun back into the case, where it promptly disappeared.

"Where is it?" Zimkeroff asked.

"Under the false bottom," Petroff said, showing him. "I think this will do."

"Yes, it will do," Zimkeroff said, smiling his approval. "Are the men ready?"

"They are waiting, General."

"Call them and let's go."

While Petroff went to make the call, Zimkeroff looked out the window of the Sheraton, thinking that this was his time—a time of wealth and power. He dialed his own cell phone and said: "We are ready to go. Everything is as planned."

Petroff followed the general to the garage where two vans were idling. Zimkeroff went to the rear van first. Sliding the door open, he asked: "Ready?"

Like a well-trained chorus, eight of his best men said that they were.

Satisfied, he moved to the lead vehicle where Petroff was holding the door open. Col. Kertrinkoff and Maj. Bresneyev were waiting patiently for him. The convoy was ready to roll.

* * *

Chi was pacing the bedroom floor, his nerves beginning to get the best of him, when the phone rang. Diving across the bed, he managed to grab it before the second ring. The tension in his voice was evident as he rattled out in Chinese: "*Ni hao, tongzhi Chi.*"

"Chi, I have it. I'm on my way," Zimkeroff roared into the phone. "I'll be there soon."

Petroff's eyes were in constant motion, checking the traffic all around them. He kept to the right lane whenever possible, keeping the general out of the line of fire from cars passing on his left. The sergeant major had hoped to beat the traffic, but they weren't going to be that lucky. It seemed to take forever to get to the expressway leading to the airport.

Beads of perspiration were forming on Petroff's forehead and in the pit of his stomach the first butterfly was taking wing. Reviewing the plan in his mind, going over each step, he was ready to do his job. Petroff didn't fear dying. He was in the business of death and killing was what he was trained to do—dying was what all men had to do. Yet somehow this was different; it didn't seem the same. Soldiers should die in combat, he thought, not in some old airplane hangar by a biological virus or whatever it was. This would be the moment of truth, when they exchanged the deed for the BCV, the ultimate weapon of mass destruction. That was when he would make his play.

Agreeing with Zimkeroff that Chi wasn't going to let them out of there alive, Petroff had to make the first move. Trusting Zimkeroff, he had complete faith in the plan and he would obey without question, but the rules of engagement for this operation were different. They violated Zimkeroff's first two rules: know when to fight and know where to fight.

No one really knew the interior layout of the hangar. They were going in blind, but at least Zimkeroff had managed to obtain a plan of the surrounding area. Petroff's other concern was for the men in the second van. They might not be in a position to use the firepower they had. The only thing for sure was that wherever Zimkeroff was, Petroff would be next to him with the shotgun close at hand.

He glanced furtively at Zimkeroff. Look at him, Petroff thought, sitting ramrod straight like he had a broom stick up his ass. If Zimkeroff had any fear, he didn't show it. In the annals of tank warfare, Petroff believed that no one, not even Patton or Rommel, could compare to Zimkeroff. Over the years and through many battles, they had been in tough positions before, but Zimkeroff had always gotten them out safely. The resourcefulness of this great man always amazed Petroff. It was no wonder, he thought, that we followed him to hell and thanked him for the trip. Zimkeroff had cast iron balls. It was amazing they didn't clang when he walked.

Looking at the briefcase on Zimkeroff's lap, Petroff wondered how the general had gotten the deed. When the phone had rung that morning, Zimkeroff had jumped on it like a cat on a mouse. After spending a few minutes on the phone on what appeared to be a pleasant call, Zimkeroff had ordered Petroff to stay in his room until called for. The order hadn't bothered Petroff; he readily obeyed. From his room Petroff later heard the doorbell and, although he was tempted to answer it, he decided to stay put as ordered. He could hear Zimkeroff marching past, almost at a run, to answer the door himself. When it was over, somehow Zimkeroff had the deed. Sometime, when it suited Zimkeroff, the general would tell him who had delivered the land grant, but for now it didn't matter.

Zimkeroff twisted in his seat and asked Maj. Bresneyev if the buyers were ready to close the deal.

"Yes, sir," the major said, handing him a list of buyers and the prices that were negotiated for the sale of the weapon.

"Impressive, Major," Zimkeroff said.

He began to read the names softly to himself, his lips barely moving as he recited the buyers: "North Korea, Iran, Iraq, Syria, Libya, and Cuba. Congratulations, Major, I'm impressed. Four billion US dollars exceeds my expectations."

Zimkeroff pondered the buyers of the BCV. The countries on the list were all pariahs in the international community. Each one had the ability to support terrorism, to disrupt their part of the world, to tip the balance of power and, most important, they all hated the United States. Providing these rogue nations with this weapon would change the face of the world. This would be Zimkeroff's shining moment. By doing nothing, at no risk, with no Russian involvement, except Russian satisfaction, he would bring down the United States. He wondered how many millions of Americans would die. Estimates he had seen indicated at least fifty million. Such a massive death toll in so short a time would be devastating—the final Russian revenge. Honor satisfied, he thought about the more tangible satisfaction he would feel being incredibly rich. The world would be his. He would take good care of his men, especially Petroff, he swore.

* * *

From his window in the Peninsula Hotel, Gen. Xi could see the British flag flying from the old train station clock tower. Across the harbor on Hong Kong Island, Xi imagined what Gov. Patten must be going through closing down the residence and packing up the trappings of more than one hundred and fifty years of British rule.

Xi was supposed to hoist the Chinese flag, a task he had hoped he would never have to perform. What would really happen to Hong Kong? he wondered. Politicians lie, they would say what they had to, when it suited them, and make promises they couldn't keep, blaming each other for the trouble they caused. Everything was a lie. All the promises made to the people were just that—empty promises. He wanted to find peace in the West and live out his days in luxury. His dreams were a phone call away. Nothing was going to stop him, but there was little he could do now. Like the wind teasing the British flag, taunting it, pushing it one way then another, the plan was set in motion, and all he could do was wait.

Col. Miu sat nervously on the couch not knowing what to say. The waiting in silence was nerve-wracking. Finally, the phone rang.

"General Xi's room, Colonel Miu speaking. May I help you?" he said in perfect English. Then he handed the phone to Xi, who grabbed it from him, placed the receiver to his ear, and listened. Never having said a word, the general hung up the phone. Miu rose to his feet, sucked his stomach in, puffed up his chest, threw back his shoulders, and snapped a salute.

"Congratulations, sir, you did it," Miu said, reading the triumphant expression on the general's face.

Falling back into a large armchair, the pillows engulfing his body, Xi waived Miu down. Not wanting to be premature with the celebration, Xi tried to rein in his emotions. He couldn't help it. The more he tried to suppress it, the more he wanted to laugh.

"Yes, we did it. The deed will be delivered to the hotel and I will go get it," Xi said, his satisfaction apparent.

It was time to call Montgomery and set into motion the final stage of the plan.

*   *   *

In the crowded conference room, Montgomery's phone could hardly be heard over the din of voices. But he could feel it vibrating in his jacket pocket.

"Mr. Montgomery, I have the deed. Do you have the money?" Xi said.

There was complete silence on the phone. A stunned Montgomery was lost for words. "Mr. Montgomery are you there? Hello. Hello," Xi said.

"I'll need proof that the document is real, General. I'll want to have it authenticated before I release a billion US dollars to you. What do you have in mind? Is the plan still the same?"

"There is no reason to change it. I will call you when I am ready. You will send Commissioner Williams, who can read and write Chinese, over to my hotel suite. I'll give him the proof he needs. You may even send someone from the museum. They will call you and you will wire the money. When my bank notifies me the money is received, Mr. Williams may leave with the deed and I shall leave with my new passports. It's all very simple, Mr. Montgomery. Remember, please no guns, no tricks. One match and the old parchment will quickly burn. By the way, do you know who Powell was? His name is on the deed as the grantee."

"He has it. Gen. Xi has the deed," Montgomery announced.

The room broke into a loud cheer. Williams turned from the crowd and placed a hand over his eyes to hide the tears. Montgomery was about to call the prime minister, but Liz Browning had other ideas. She threw her arms around Montgomery and pressed her mouth against his. He held her tight and kissed her back. The cheers for the deed soon became an applause for the loving couple.

* * *

Like storm clouds rolling across the summer sky, Daniels's mood was darkening as he guided the black Suburban through city traffic toward the tunnel. The picture of Kelly lying across the seat was etched into his mind forever. He had two missions driving him: One was to get the biochemical weapon and the other was to get the Lengs, all of them. They were going to pay for Kelly. As he was planning his revenge, the ringing of the cell phone interrupted him.

"Mac, you okay? Can you finish this?" Admiral Charko asked.

"Don't you ever sleep, Admiral?"

"Don't you ever answer my questions?" Charko asked.

"I'm all right, Admiral, just pissed about Kelly. But I know what I have to do and I'll do it."

"Mac, you have to get the bio-weapon. It's imperative. Millions of lives are at stake. There can be no mistakes. I also want the deed. That's the priority and that's an order. Leave the Lengs to the local authorities. Don't get involved."

"I am involved, Admiral. You'll get the bio-weapon and that's a promise. The deed, well, that's another story. But I'll get the Lengs."

"Drop the vendetta. That's an order."

"Come again, Admiral. You're breaking up . I can't hear you," Daniels lied.

"Stop screwing around, Mac, this is a satellite-linked phone. There is no static interference. You heard me—leave the Lengs alone and do your job."

"Can't hear you, sir," replied Daniels pressing the end call button.

Pulling up in front of the government office building, Daniels found a New York parking spot—a space four inches smaller than the Suburban he was driving. Throwing the truck into reverse and cutting the wheel hard, he managed to get the back end of the truck into the space, leaving the front end sticking out in the street.

Still in an ugly mood, he turned the dashboard switch from its all-wheel drive to its four-wheel drive. The truck inched backward until its rear bumper was pressing against the front of the car behind it, causing its alarm to go off. He pressed on the accelerator and the big Suburban's wheels dug in, pushing the car back until it hit another car and set its alarm off, too. Oh, what the hell, he thought, dropping the truck into drive, Daniels hit the car in front, pushing it forward and setting off its alarm. Satisfied with his parking, he shut the truck off, and walked into the office building amidst the cacophony of horns and sirens.

Knowing that it would be about as pleasant as Saturday afternoon root canal, Daniels didn't want to waste time with the British. Walking by the large directory on the wall without glancing at it, he came to the security desk ensconced behind thick bulletproof glass. Stationed behind the desk was a large man wearing the uniform of the Royal Scots Guards. His red moustache was bushy and his arms were covered with chevrons indicating the rank of master sergeant. Hanging from his hip was his pistol.

As Daniels approached the desk, the barrel-chested sergeant stood up to his full six feet and leaned toward the grill in the window. Daniels took out his identity card and held it against the glass so that the guard could read it. He asked to speak with Michael Montgomery. The guard picked up the phone and got the name Daniels out; then he stopped talking. Hanging up, the guard pressed the buzzer releasing the lock on the door.

The click of the retreating bolt was the signal for Daniels to push open the door. As he passed through the metal detector, it whistled loudly as Daniels's gun set it off. The guard jumped to his feet and grabbed Daniels's arm, pulling him back as he started to pull his weapon out of its holster. Daniels caught the man's wrist, turning him around, and giving him a swift kick in the ass. The guard fell forward onto his face, embarrassed more than hurt. He turned over quickly reaching for his gun, only to find the holster empty.

Looking up, he found himself staring down the barrel of his own pistol aimed directly at his head. Daniels pressed the release button on the grip and the magazine fell out into his left hand. With his thumb, he ejected the bullets from the clip, letting the deadly pellets bounce off the tile floor. Pulling back the slide, he ejected the shell in the chamber. Then he pressed the spring release causing the guide pin to fall from the weapon and the slide came away from the trigger housing. In a matter of seconds the gun was in pieces and Daniels was throwing the pieces at the guard one at a time.

His face as red as his beret, the guard was coiled and ready to lunge at Daniels.

"Don't do it. I'm tired, hungry, and I've had a bad day," Daniels said to the guard.

He opened his jacket to reveal the Mark 23 with the sound suppressor attached. Daniels could see the guard's jaw tightening and the veins swelling in his neck.

"Don't try it, Sergeant," Daniels said. His tone anchored the guard to the floor.

"I'm going to see Montgomery; then I'm leaving here. No trouble, no one gets hurt. Don't screw it up."

The guard wasn't sure what to make of this, but he stayed on the floor.

Liz Browning opened the door to let Daniels into the conference room. Knowing that the Royal Scots Guard would soon be coming after him, Daniels moved quickly toward the head of the long teak conference table where Montgomery was seated. He wanted to put as much distance between the door and himself as possible. All eyes followed him as he moved about the room, passing Adams, who was seated to the left of Montgomery. Winston Williams sat to the right.

As Montgomery started to speak, they heard a loud stampeding noise coming from the hall.

"Here they come," Daniels said like an announcer. "My lords, ladies, and gentlemen, the Royal Scots Guards."

On cue the beefy sergeant came bursting through the door, followed by several more Scots Guards, their weapons drawn. At the sight of the guns, everyone in the room dropped to the floor except for Montgomery, Adams, and Daniels.

"If you move, it will be your last one," shouted the sergeant, his English laced with a thick Scottish brogue. "Get him men."

Holding up his hand like a traffic cop, Daniels yelled: "Hold it."

His words stopped them in their tracks.

"Michael?" Daniels said.

"I'll take care of it, Sergeant," Montgomery said, dismissing the guards.

"Yes, sir," replied the sergeant. "But we have a nice cell for this man. Just big enough for the two of us, where we'd teach you some manners."

Montgomery and Daniels waited until the last of the Royal Scots Guards were out of the room before either spoke.

"What juvenile activity have you been engaged in now?" he asked Daniels.

Daniels shrugged.

Montgomery's staff took their seats at the conference table, surrounded by mounds of papers and bottles of champagne.

"Having a party?" Daniels asked, spotting the empty champagne bottles.

"No," was Montgomery's emphatic reply. He waited as if he were counting to ten; then he said: "It's an early celebration."

"Of what?"

"Gen. Xi called. He has the deed and we are going to pick it up this afternoon," Montgomery said.

That was wrong, Daniels thought, Xi didn't have the deed. He had been there last night and he had seen the empty vases. There was no way Xi could have gotten back onto the Galaxy floor with all the police there.

"Mike, we have to talk."

Montgomery hated being called Mike, but correcting Daniels would only worsen matters. "Let's talk, Mackenzie. What's on your mind?"

"I would like a little privacy. Alone, Mike, now."

Recognizing the tone in Daniels's voice was as serious as it got, he led him to a small room off the conference area. The room was lined with an acoustical fabric, making it look like a giant egg carton. Shutting the door behind him, Daniels surveyed the surroundings.

"I guess it's safe to talk in here," he said sarcastically.

"Eminently," Montgomery said. "But before we talk, I have something to say to you. Breaking into Gen. Zimkeroff's and Gen. Xi's rooms was not exactly cricket. What were you hoping to gain? All you did was embarrass yourself and your country."

Daniels exploded, not giving Montgomery a chance to finish.

"I told you before, I don't play cricket. Where I come from, we play hardball—in the street. I have no time for playing by the rules and neither do you. In the next few hours the deed will be in Sang Chi's hands and you lose," he said jamming his index finger into Montgomery's chest. "If you want to see your flag flapping here in the morning, you'd better get into the game."

"Lovely speech, a jolly good pep talk, but it's too late. In a few hours Williams will meet with Gen. Xi; then we'll wire the money. You don't think we are going to wire a billion US dollars without the deed, do you? Why would Gen. Xi tell us he had the deed if he didn't? What would he gain by doing that? As soon as we have the deed, we're putting Gen. Xi and his men on a plane for England. So save your dramatics."

"You're wrong. You're dead wrong," protested Daniels. "There are two reasons why Xi would tell you he has the deed. Either to keep you here having your early celebration and not on the street where you belong. Or—"

"Or what," demanded Montgomery.

"Or he doesn't have the deed yet, but expects it to be delivered. Yes, that's it. He's still waiting for it to be delivered. That's why he told you to come over later, not now. If he had the deed, you would have it by now. Yes, I get it now. That sly old bastard," Daniels said, his voice trailing off.

"Rubbish! Enough of this. Whether he has it now or he will have it in a few hours, the point is, we will get it. The deed to Hong Kong will keep the colony where it belongs, with us."

"Gen. Xi is playing with you, Mike, trust me on that. The plans for the invasion of Southeast Asia are bullshit. The deed is on its way to Sang Chi. When Chi gets it, he will be on a plane to China and your friend Xi will be really pissed."

Daniels didn't tell Montgomery that Zimkeroff would then have the most dangerous weapon of mass destruction since the hydrogen bomb. But everything was coming together for him. Xi wanted Chi out of the way, but maybe he had ordered Chi to bring him the deed after the swap with Zimkeroff. Xi gets the deed, kills Chi, and turns it over to

Montgomery. It was a long shot, but better than playing cricket with Montgomery. If he were right, then the place to be was the airport.

"I have to disagree with you. Our intelligence tells us that the information provided by Gen. Xi was accurate. We have no reason to disbelieve him and we are prepared to give him political asylum," Montgomery said, looking at Daniels as if the American was nuts.

"I'm going to the airport to find Sang Chi. I'll get the deed," Daniels said.

"Chi has a diplomatic passport. He is an agent for the Chinese government. Stay away from him," Montgomery said, alarmed.

"Look, all I'm going to do is be sure Chi doesn't have the deed. If I'm wrong, there's no harm done," Daniels said.

"No harm done? You leave a trail of bodies behind you like markers and you'll muck this up. No, you stay here. That's an order. You are under my command and you'll stay here or I'll have you locked up. Do you understand?"

Without another word, Daniels hit Montgomery with a punch to the jaw, knocking him out cold.

"I understand you're out of the game," Daniels said to the unconscious body as he took off Montgomery's belt to tie his feet. Then he used the Englishman's silk tie to bind his hands. Daniels knew this would not hold him for long, but he had to get out of the building.

Backing out of the soundproof safe room, he said to the unconscious Montgomery: "Finish reading that report and I'll get the rest of the information out of my car."

He turned to face the room full of people, all of whom were watching him intently, and said: "Michael does not want to be disturbed. I have to get something from the car. Be right back."

Trying to be as casual as he could, he grabbed a chocolate chip cookie as he left the room. Walking very quickly, almost at a jog, he went down to the end of hall where the sergeant was still trying to put his gun back together. The guard glowered at him as he went past.

Outside, the din of horns and sirens had subsided, Daniels jumped into the truck and started it. Throwing it into reverse, he slammed the Suburban against the car in the rear; then he went forward, hitting the car in front. He left the area with a renewed chorus of discordant sounds in his ears.

Finally, he began to smile, knowing the well-mannered Brits would sit there all day waiting for Montgomery to open the door. The look on their faces would be priceless.

As he drove through the Wanchai district, he stopped at a traffic light and saw a poster advertising the Hi-Jinks Club. There was Kelly's picture and her death came back to him like a fist in the stomach. Not now, he told himself, there will be time for this later. Revenge, he remembered, is a dish best served cold.

CHAPTER 39

The worst of enemies may be the best of friends.

— Old Chinese proverb

CHI sat nervously at the master control panel, intently studying the video monitors as if he were watching the final match of the World Cup. His eyes went relentlessly from screen to screen, looking for movement. The Russians were coming and he was on his way to close one of the most important transactions in Chinese history. The weight of the deal rested on his shoulders, Chi thought. He could not, no, he must not fail. Everyone was counting on him. Once he had the deed, he swore the Russians would not leave the hangar alive. They had to die and the BCV had to be returned to China. Nothing less was acceptable. The Inspector General had trusted him, the Supreme Leader had approved the venture himself, and Chi would not let them down.

Thinking about the biochemical weapon, Chi unconsciously looked over at the door of the refrigerator where the deadly virus lay dormant. Harmless they said, as long as it was sealed or, if opened, kept cool. Deciding it was better to be safe, even though the vials were not open, Chi kept the deadly solution refrigerated.

It would all be over soon, he thought, once the exchange was made the Russians would leave his office and then he would have his revenge. In his mind Chi played out the role, rehearsing his act for their departure. He didn't want to make them suspicious; it was important that they left his office feeling no animosity. They had to get to the lower level alone because Chi couldn't afford to be their hostage. No one was going to make it out of the warehouse alive. The trap was set. Wa Chung and his men would be waiting on the lower level ready to kill the Russians and anyone else who happened to be with them.

Chi scanned the lower level of the hangar. He was impressed by the labyrinth Wa Chung had created out of boxes and crates. All was in place, this was going to work, Chi thought as he let out a sigh of relief. There was no way anyone could get through the maze unscathed. At

253

each turn there was some dangerous pitfall awaiting the unsuspecting Russians.

His eyes told him all was well, that the plan was foolproof, but his nerves told him another story. Not wanting to admit it, Chi was scared—scared of Zimkeroff, scared of Petroff, scared of dying. Never before had he been in this type of situation. He had never fired a gun in anger, let alone been in a gun battle. He questioned his own courage, wondering what he would do when the time came. Trying to calm his nerves, he pressed the intercom button, calling for Wa Chung.

Climbing the stairs two steps at a time, Wa Chung demonstrated great agility for such a big man. As broad as he was tall, his massive fifty-inch chest looked so much bigger because of his small waist. A neckless man with biceps as large as most men's thighs, Wa Chung could have been an Olympic weightlifter. His eyes looked like two black marbles, creating the illusion that he was perpetually squinting. Plugged into his ear was the radio receiver and a throat microphone was strapped to his neck. Tucked into the waistband of his pants was a Colt .45-caliber semi-automatic pistol, United States Army issue. The Inspector General wanted him to be sure that nothing went wrong rendering assistance to Chi. The BCV had to be returned to China. That was his assignment; that was what he would do.

But he was annoyed that he had become a babysitter for the spineless Chi. Faithfully serving the Inspector General, he would do whatever it took to see that his superior's plans were carried out—even if it meant killing Chi. A veteran of many battles, a detailed planner, and a professional killer, he had used all his experience laying the trap for the Russians. If his trap didn't work, Wa Chung was prepared to blow up the old hangar, killing everyone, including himself. In his pocket was the electronic triggering device that would set off the explosives, turning the old hangar into a giant fireball, destroying the BCV and the deed.

"You called, sir?" Wa Chung said, clearing his throat and trying to conceal his disgust.

"Wa Chung," Chi snapped, "are the men ready?"

"Yes, all is in order," Wa Chung said for the third time that day. "The men will open fire on my command. I'll be down on the first level by the power switch. When the rabbit is in the net, I'll close it. Tak Shing will be up here with you."

"Tak Shing," he said into his throat mike.

In a few seconds Tak Shing appeared and bowed.

"I want you to stay with Sang Chi. Do not leave him. Stay by him at all times. You know the plan, we want the Russians on the first floor, but if you feel it necessary to use force, then shoot them. We'll take care of the rest. They are probably wearing body armor, so take head shots," he told Tak Shing as casually as if he were giving directions to a tourist.

"Take off your coat and let them see that you are armed. That might prevent them from trying anything up here. I'm hoping to disarm them before we allow them into Chi's office. I will search them and I'm sure they will want to do the same."

Obediently, Tak Shing obeyed, bowing his head in a sign of submissiveness.

"Satisfied?" Wa Chung asked Chi. Then not waiting for an answer, he turned toward the stairs.

When Wa Chung disappeared from sight, Chi told Tak Shing to sit down. Tak Shing did not move.

"Sit down, I said." Chi almost shouted.

The bodyguard still did not move, except to bring his left hand to his ears, pressing the ear piece tight, so he could hear the orders from Wa Chung.

"Wa Chung says to tell you it is better to stand when you face the enemy. You shoot faster and you make a smaller target." With that, Tak Shing found a place by the wall to stand to face the enemy.

* * *

Gen. Zimkeroff's motorcade turned onto the perimeter road, approaching the entrance gate. Still calm and enjoying the ride, the general called Chi. Glancing over his shoulder at his men, then at Petroff, he had a good feeling as he pressed the send button.

The ringing of the phone startled Chi. Petrified, he was unable to make his trembling hand answer it. His heart pounded so hard it sounded like a beating drum in his ears. He was too scared to move.

Zimkeroff looked at the digital display to be sure he had punched up the right numbers. He wondered why Chi didn't answer.

Crack. The sound of Tak Shing's hand across Chi's face sounded like a firecracker. The blow snapped Chi's head back, stinging the side of his face.

"Answer it," Tak Shing yelled.

Still shaking, Chi brought the receiver slowly to his ear.

"Yes," Chi said, rubbing his face with his free hand.

"Is something wrong?" Zimkeroff asked.

"No, everything is fine. I was away from the phone."

"Open the gate," Zimkeroff ordered.

On the video monitor Chi saw the vans. He pressed a button on his console and the gate opened. It had started, he thought, there was no stopping the mayhem now.

When the rolling gate was open wide enough, Petroff drove through, followed by the other van. Pulling up by the side door of the hangar and jumping out, Petroff ran around to the passenger side, opening the door for Zimkeroff as the other men piled out the vans. Standing by the hangar door, Zimkeroff clutched the briefcase under his arm more tightly than before.

The metal door looked like it was rusted shut, but it opened without a sound, revealing the giant bulk of Wa Chung standing in the doorway. Not quite as tall as Zimkeroff, the massive Wa Chung blocked the doorway. All Zimkeroff could see were armed guards inside the warehouse.

"Where's Sang Chi?" Gen. Zimkeroff demanded.

"In his office," Wa Chung answered, his face emotionless.

As Zimkeroff started to push past him, Wa Chung raised his hand and pressed it against the general's chest. There was a chorus of clicks as the bolts of many weapons fell into place. Both sides were now at the ready. Zimkeroff looked at Wa Chung's massive claw on his chest. Neither man moved. Zimkeroff spoke first.

"Remove your hand," he ordered. His voice was cold; there was no hint of fear.

"Back up," replied Wa Chung in the same hard voice.

As if they had rehearsed their movements, Zimkeroff backed up and Wa Chung pulled his hand back from the general's chest. Not taking his eyes off Wa Chung, Zimkeroff said to his men: "Lower your weapons." Wa Chung gave the same order.

"Sang Chi is in his office with one other person. You, general, and one other person of your choice, may enter his office to make the exchange. I will search whoever goes in," Wa Chung said.

"Do you think I am going in there unarmed? I'll send Sergeant Major Petroff to search for weapons. Then the four of us will be unarmed."

Wa Chung calculated that even unarmed, Zimkeroff and Petroff could be dangerous. They could kill Chi, but then they would still have to come down from the second floor to exit the building. He would be able to get them then.

"Agreed," Wa Chung said, "but the rest of your men stay on the first floor."

"Agreed."

Stepping out of the doorway, Wa Chung expertly frisked the general and was satisfied he was unarmed. "Now open the case, General."

Looking inside the leather case, Wa Chung saw the vase. "Who's next?" he asked.

Petroff stepped forward, annoyed at the indignity of being frisked by some Chinese flunky. Standing at attention, he allowed Wa Chung to run his hands over him. Finishing with Petroff, Wa Chung moved aside to allow entry into the hangar. As Petroff picked up his case, Wa Chung asked what was in it.

"It's empty. We will carry the BCV in it when we leave," Zimkeroff said.

Anticipating Wa Chung's actions, Zimkeroff ordered Petroff to open the case. Petroff did as he was told. Wa Chung looked inside and, seeing nothing, he nodded his approval. Snapping the case shut, Petroff turned to Zimkeroff for instructions.

"Search them, the room, top to bottom, front to backwards," the general said in English.

"Yes, sir."

Waving his hand, signaling his men to separate, Wa Chung parted them, allowing Petroff to pass through unmolested. Pressing his microphone tight against his throat, Wa Chung spoke in English to reassure the Russians. He ordered Tak Shing to allow the Russian to search him and Chi, the room, and whatever else he wanted. He was also told to surrender his weapon and offer no resistance at all.

Making his way through the maze of boxes and crates, taking in the layout of the hangar, looking for the exits, places for cover, power switches, and counting the number of men, Petroff was a one-man reconnaissance team. He had also understood the general's signal: use reverse messages. Wa Chung hadn't picked up on Zimkeroff's deliberate poor English—front to backwards. Petroff knew what the general meant when he used the word "backwards." If it was safe, he would wave Zimkeroff away. But if there was a problem, he would wave for him to come up. The general would take the appropriate action.

As he climbed the stairs to the second floor, Petroff stopped just before the landing and looked over the hangar. He saw immediately that the hapless arrangement of boxes and crates was a planned labyrinth designed to slow them down. Son-of-a-bitch, he thought, not bad for ignorant farmers.

The design of the maze gave Petroff an insight into the Chinese plan. The boxes and crates provided cover from above. The danger would not come from Chi or anybody on the second floor firing down on them. Rather, it would come from the Chinese on the first floor. If the Chinese managed to get into the maze from the two points of ingress, they would have Petroff and Zimkeroff trapped. Each corner, each turn, could be deadly. The foolishness of such an amateurish plan made the veins in Petroff's head throb; his anger at Chi was boiling his blood.

Resuming the climb, Petroff reviewed his options, deciding which countermeasure he would employ. Looking around the second floor, he spotted the stairs that led to the catwalk circling the hangar. That was a possible escape route. Approaching the office, he assumed the glass wall was bulletproof. It was an impressive layout, he thought.

Standing in front of the metal door, refusing to knock, he would wait until Chi invited him in. It was the sergeant major's idea of an insult.

* * *

Exiting from the highway onto the airport approach road, Daniels drove past the commercial terminals and turned onto the old perimeter drive. He followed the road until he came to the CAAC hangar; then he slowed down, looking for an easy way in. By the side entrance, he saw the Russian contingent bottled up at the front of the door. He knew he had to find a way in without giving them any warning, and to do that he needed an element of surprise to compensate for the overwhelming odds against him.

The fence surrounding the building was electrified. Daniels traced the power lines to the large transformers on the ends of the building. One touch would fry him on the spot.

"Two hot boxes. Shit, shit," he muttered to himself. "This is a real professional job."

If he took out one box, there was still the other and one of the boxes fed the current into the hangar. The double row of razor wire on top of the twelve foot fence made it clear he wasn't going over. He thought about driving through the fence, but motion detectors every ten feet and rotating video cameras would announce his arrival before he was out of the truck. There was no way in without tipping off his presence—from the ground that is. But maybe he could get in from the roof. Hell, this was an airport, he thought, why not?

From the corner of his eye he saw it: A Bell Jet Ranger shooting across the sky at fifty feet or so off the ground. He gunned the truck until the spinning wheels left two black tire marks across the pavement. The smoke from the burning rubber hung in the air like a spring fog. Keeping his foot on the accelerator, he watched the helicopter as it turned eastward. Then he cut the wheel hard and the truck jumped off one road, flying onto another. Daniels saw the General Aviation area of the airport coming into view just as the helicopter dropped down behind the building.

* * *

"What's he doing?" Chi said, watching Petroff on the monitor. "He's just standing there. Why doesn't he knock? Knock, damn you, knock!"

Then he turned to Tak Shing, who had not moved since he had taken his position against the wall, and said: "Well, do something."

"What would you have me to do? This man will never knock. If you don't open the door, he will leave."

"Open it," Chi screamed. But Tak Shing didn't move, he just shook his head.

Furious at the insubordination, Chi yelled: "Do you know who I am? I said open it!"

"I know who you are. The man outside wants you, not me. It will do you no good for me to open the door. Save yourself from further shame and open it now."

Like a child being sent to his room, Chi stomped toward the door, pulling it open with a quick jerk. Petroff stepped into Chi's control center, gave it a fast glance, his eyes coming to rest on Chi's desk in the center of the room. Perfect, he thought, from there he could get a shot off to anyplace in the room. Moving toward the desk, he did not flinch when Chi slammed the metal door so hard, the sound echoed throughout the building. Placing his lethal case on the desk, Petroff decided to frisk the bodyguard first, knowing he was armed.

"What's that?" Chi asked, pointing to the case.

Ignoring Chi, Petroff motioned with his hand for Tak Shing to come over to him.

"Off with that," he said, pointing to the shoulder holster. Tak Shing obeyed, dropping the holster onto the desk. Petroff ran his hands down Tak Shing's legs and found an ankle holster. He found another gun in the small of Tak Shing's back.

"What were you expecting—a war?" Petroff growled.

Then he pointed to a spot by the wall about five feet away from the desk.

"Stand there," he said.

Tak Shing did as he was told. Turning to Chi, with a sadistic smile and burning eyes, Petroff used his index finger to call him over. He was like a magician hypnotizing a subject. The only thing missing were the words "come to me."

* * *

Parking the truck, Daniels jumped out and ran over to the hovering helicopter and watched it descend. When the Jet Ranger touched down, the copilot stepped from the left side, leaving the pilot with the aircraft. Daniels could see the pilot talking into the microphone attached to his headset. The pilot was keeping the helicopter at flight idle, the giant rotor spinning slowly. Daniels took advantage of the situation, opened the copilot's door, and jumped into the helicopter. The young pilot looked at Daniels, the surprise showing on his face. Before the pilot could speak, Daniels pointed to the ceiling of the chopper with his index finger, spun it around in a circular motion, and yelled over the roar of the giant turbines: "Spool it up."

The pilot nodded, increased the throttle, and let the huge rotor pick up some rpms. Then he increased the forward angle of pitch by pulling back on the cyclic. The rotor bit into the air and the Jet Ranger jumped off the ground. The pilot, still following orders, brought the helicopter to a hundred feet and held it steady, while Daniels adjusted his headset.

"Are you the check pilot?" the pilot asked.

Daniels understood why the pilot followed his orders without question. He was waiting for another pilot to check him out in the Jet Ranger. Daniels thought he caught a break as he heard the pilot ask him: "Where to?"

"Stay at a hundred feet, head west toward the outer perimeter," Daniels said.

*   *   *

For the briefest second, Chi felt brave enough to think about saying something to Petroff, but remembering the pain Petroff was capable of inflicting made his heart pound so hard he could hear it in his ears again. He wondered if Petroff could hear it, too. Petroff patted him down—hard, real hard. Chi was unarmed.

"Sit," Petroff said.

Chi dropped into the chair like a trained dog, watching Petroff making a meticulous search of the room. He found nothing. Picking up Tak Shing's weapons, Petroff opened the metal door and tossed them over the railing. They landed on top of one of the crates below.

Zimkeroff was standing in the doorway looking up at the second floor waiting for the signal. Petroff made a fist then began pumping it up and down for several seconds. Stopping, he then crossed both hands over his head. He then waved Zimkeroff away. Stationing himself next to Zimkeroff, Wa Chung was puzzled. Zimkeroff, however, understood the signals. Petroff had given the tanker's sign that meant *start* and *to end.* Go away meant to come up. Barking an order in Russian to Col. Kertrinkoff, Zimkeroff instructed him to hold the entrance and let no one in.

Zimkeroff stepped into the maze of boxes and crates, moving quickly through the labyrinth guided by Petroff's directions from the second floor. As the rest of the Russians moved into the hangar, the Chinese backed up, disappearing between the crates and boxes. The Russians started to place themselves where they could best cover Zimkeroff in a retreat. The Chinese took positions where they could cover the Russians. Wa Chung was nowhere to be seen. Three heavily armed Russians camped in the entrance between the crates. Zimkeroff bounded up the stairs toward the second floor. Petroff stood by, holding open the metal door.

*   *   *

The pilot followed Daniels's instructions. Once over the CAAC building, Daniels said: "Drop down to two feet over the roof of that hangar and hover there."

"What?" the pilot shouted into his microphone.

"Hover two feet above the roof and don't let it touch," Daniels said.

The pilot looked at Daniels, thinking he was crazy.

"Sir, I heard what you said, I just didn't believe it," the wide-eyed pilot said, lowering his aircraft to two feet off the roof. "What now?"

"Wait here," Daniels replied as he stepped out of the aircraft and lowered himself onto the roof. The pilot thought this couldn't be happening to him, but it was. The man whom he thought was the check pilot was running toward the end of the building.

Daniels tried to open the roof door, but it was locked. Around the other side of the doorway was a small window, but it was painted shut. He thought about breaking the window; then decided against it because it would make more noise than he wanted. Drawing his Mark 23, he squeezed off three quick rounds. The silenced gun gave off three pops no louder than finger snaps, as the .45-caliber bullets tore into the door lock. With his toe, he pushed the door open. Stepping into the small hallway, he crouched down to listen. For a full minute, he froze, not moving a muscle, just listening. He could hear nothing but the whine of the Jet Ranger's engine and the sound of the giant blade as it cut into the warm June air.

He eased himself down the stairs, pressing tightly against the wall. Two steps from the bottom, he stopped again to listen; then he let himself slide down the wall until he could see that the catwalk to the right was clear. Flipping over to the opposite wall and repeating his movements, he saw that the other side was also clear.

Stepping onto the catwalk, he kept his body tight against the wall. Slowly he worked his way toward Chi's office. From his third-story perch, Daniels could see the Russians and Chinese jockeying for positions on the ground floor. The end of the catwalk led to a small platform housing the control panel for the overhead pulleys and cranes that ran up and down the length of the old hangar. Looking over the control panel, Daniels was surprised to see the buttons, switches, and gauges were free from dirt and rust. From its condition, he guessed it was in working order.

This was great cover, he thought. Chi had picked a good place to operate. No one would question the security at this old hangar being used as a warehouse. It was all quite natural. The so-called diplomatic pouches never got to the Chinese embassy in Hong Kong. They stopped right here. He would have to mention this to Harry Saltzman.

Daniels' position at the end of the hangar gave him an unobstructed view of Chi's office on the second floor. Chi's hands were moving, swatting the air, and his head was bobbing up and down, while Zimkeroff, Petroff, and another man stood by motionless. On the desk was a black briefcase; another briefcase was on the floor by Zimkeroff's feet. Chi kept pointing down, his obvious agitation spurred on by Zimkeroff's lack of response.

In order to get a better view of what was going on below, Daniels crawled toward the edge of the platform, peering over the side at the maze of boxes and crates on the first floor. He saw the Russians and Chinese spread out in their respective positions. Looking down from such a height gave Daniels a godlike view of the dormant battlefield where men, patriotic or greedy, were about to die.

Shaking his head, Daniels realized he didn't understand the Chinese strategy. The Russians were covering the exits, which was natural, and keeping a path open for Gen. Zimkeroff to get out of there. But the Chinese were in a defensive position, which didn't make any sense to him. The Russians didn't want to take the hangar. They wanted to get out of there alive. Why weren't the Chinese out on the perimeter of the building, trying to contain the Russians, to trap their quarry. Something was wrong with this strategy.

He assumed that the BCV was in the second-floor office. Surveying the situation, Daniels knew there weren't many options open to him. There were too many combatants on the first floor, a metal door into Chi's office, and bulletproof glass. From his position, Daniels had a good field of fire and, with a little luck, he might be able to get off three or four fast shots before anybody knew what had happened. The silenced Mark 23 would be noiseless; the only sound would be the dead bodies falling.

Daniels decided he would start the battle, like he would start a race, by firing a few shots at the Russians; then at the Chinese. He hoped they would keep each other busy while he grabbed the BCV and the vase containing the deed. It was a plan, not a good plan, but a plan that at least would get rid of Zimkeroff.

As he started to crawl away from the edge, he thought he saw the back of one of the large crates moving below him.

"What the hell?" he whispered.

The crate was a Trojan horse. He watched as out of the back of the crate, through a false panel, came several Chinese carrying American-made M-4 rifles with laser target designators and under-barrel grenade launchers. Daniels let out a silent whistle, wondering where they had gotten those weapons. What the Chinese lacked in a battle plan, they made up for in firepower. This was getting very interesting, he thought. A full-scale firefight with grenades going off would create a diversion giving him a better opportunity to get away. Crawling away from the edge, he positioned himself by the control console, using it for a brace to help steady his aim. He would wait for Zimkeroff to come out.

Chi's frantic movements ceased when he seemed to give up and crossed his arms in front of his chest, doing his best to scowl at Zimkeroff. From his six-five height, the general looked down at Chi with contempt. Neither man spoke. Chi did his best to stare Zimkeroff down, but to no avail. He blinked while Zimkeroff's laser stare made Chi squirm.

Zimkeroff rested his massive hand on Chi's shoulder. To Chi, it felt like it weighed a ton, forcing him back into his seat with a loud thud. His hand still on Chi's shoulder, his vise-like grip closing in on the clavicle muscle, caused excruciating pain. Chi went through various contortions, wiggling and gyrating, trying to get out from under the powerful grip.

"Stop it," Chi demanded. "You're hurting me."

"Just a mild form of a Russian massage. I didn't mean to hurt you. Why would I do that?" Zimkeroff said, smiling slightly.

Chi wanted to get the Russians out of his office as fast as possible. Once they were on the first floor, he was safe. They could not penetrate the steel door or the bulletproof glass. He was going to watch the human slaughter on his video monitors. This, Chi thought, was going to be fun. He wished he was the one pulling the trigger.

Petroff was sitting on the desk, his arm leaning on the black briefcase, his eyes fixed on Tak Shing. He paid no attention to Chi. The sergeant major showed no movement or emotion. He just kept his eyes on Tak Shing. As soon as he opened his briefcase to place the vials inside, Petroff would come up shooting. Tak Shing would be first.

The silence in the room was shattered by Zimkeroff's booming voice.

"Where is it, Chi? Get it out. Let's see it."

Chi's chest visibly grew as he sucked in a large breath, holding it for a few seconds, then slowly exhaling. He was gathering up his courage, trying to drop his voice a few octaves: "Where's my deed?" Chi said, imitating Zimkeroff. "Where is it? Get it out. Let's see it."

Zimkeroff took his hand off Chi's shoulder and smiled at Chi's newfound bravado.

"I'll show it to you," the general said, his voice echoing off the cold electronic walls. He placed the briefcase on the desk and motioned for Chi to join him. Opening the case, Zimkeroff took out the vase and handed it to Chi.

Watching the show going on inside Chi's office, Daniels recognized the vase. It was like the ones he had seen at Gen. Xi's suite. He now had a clear view of the expensive leather case Zimkeroff had been nestling in his arms. He was a little far away to be absolutely sure, but Daniels thought he knew where Zimkeroff had gotten the deed. It didn't make sense. He could not figure out the reason, but he would have all the answers before the day was done.

As his hands touched the vase, Chi's body shook. He swallowed hard with an audible gulp. He was holding a piece of China in his hands.

Realizing he was on display, he tried to steady himself. Placing the vase on the desk, he pulled out the cork and poured the sand onto a piece of paper. And there it was: the deed to Hong Kong. He imagined himself handing the deed to President Jiang Zemin; he saw his place in the Hall of Heroes. With a reverence reserved for the most holy, Chi pulled the scroll slowly from the vase. It was real, he thought, there was no doubt about it. He had the deed to Hong Kong in his trembling hands.

Chi rolled the parchment up and placed it back into the vase. Then he poured the sand back in. He turned, looking for the cork, but Zimkeroff was holding it with his fingertips. As Chi reached for the cork, Zimkeroff palmed it.

"Give it back to me," the general demanded. He pulled it from Chi and put the cork back into the vase.

Chi was devastated. His eyes showed his emotions, his feeling of loss.

"It's yours when you give me the BCV," Zimkeroff bellowed, clutching the vase close to his chest.

Chi reluctantly nodded his agreement. This was the moment of truth. He was ready to give the Russian the bio-weapon. The door to the refrigerator was twenty steps away—the longest twenty steps Chi would ever walk. With each step, his legs began to feel heavier and heavier until he thought there were iron weights tied to his feet. This was the moment that all the planning had come down to. The slightest error would be a major disaster.

He took out two racks of vials sealed with a special safety tape and began the slow journey back to the desk. All eyes watched each step Chi made. When he placed the racks on the desk, there was a collective exhalation, followed by a genuine sigh of relief. The vials had some hypnotic effect on the four men. No one moved. Freeing himself from the unseen power of the deadly biochemical virus, Zimkeroff smiled. His smile set off a chain reaction. Petroff jerked his head back as if he had been slapped and turned his malevolent eyes on his next victim, Tak Shing. Tak Shing resumed his stoic pose against the wall, watching Zimkeroff. Chi looked at the floor.

Zimkeroff picked up one of the vials and compared the markings on the tape to the markings on the paper he had taken from his pocket.

"Wonderful," the general said, smiling.

The sight of the smiling Russian made Chi flush with anger, wishing he could tear that stupid grin off Zimkeroff's face. But he knew Zimkeroff's fate was in Wa Chung's hands. He would soon have both the biochemical weapon and the deed safely back in China where they belonged. For the present, he had to wait. But what was a few more minutes after waiting one hundred and fifty years? he thought.

"Here," Zimkeroff said, handing Chi the piece of paper.

Glancing down at the slip of paper Chi saw the serial numbers for the vials of the biochemical virus.

"Where did you get this?" Chi asked.

"It's your serial registration numbers for the vials you have here. The symbols match the markings on the tape. Just a little insurance to be sure that I am getting the real thing," Zimkeroff said, waiting for Chi's reaction. He waited for his words to sink in.

Anger filled Chi's eyes when he finally understood.

"What's wrong, Chi, didn't you know I have friends inside your science ministry? The worst of enemies may be the best of friends."

CHAPTER 40

Nothing happens until you make it happen.

— Old Chinese proverb

WATCHING from across the hangar, Daniels saw Zimkeroff pick up the vials of the deadly BCV. Remembering what Saltzman told him, he realized the general held the lives of hundreds of millions of people in his hands.

"No way," he said softly. "No way is Zimkeroff going to get out of here with that stuff." Daniels took aim. When Zimkeroff cleared the door, he was dead.

"Come on out, you miserable son-of-a-bitch, come on out," he whispered like a mantra. "Come on out."

Zimkeroff placed the vials on the desk; Petroff opened his briefcase. The deal's done, Daniels thought, spreading out on the floor, his extended arms braced against the control panel, lining up his shot at the door, mouthing the mantra "come on out, come on out."

Petroff reached into the briefcase and lifted out the 12-gauge Benelli. The barrel of the shotgun had barely cleared the case when he pulled the trigger. Tak Shing didn't have time to react as the lead pellets tore through his chest, pinning him against the wall. The semi-automatic shotgun threw back its bolt, ejected the spent shell, and loaded another into the chamber. Almost instantly, a second explosion picked Chi up and drove him through the air, smashing his broken and bleeding body against the wall. Where his heart had been was now a gaping hole. Both bodies slumped to the floor, leaving trails of blood on the wall. Petroff had been so fast that neither man had had a chance to react. They had died instantly, never knowing what had hit them.

The explosion from the Benelli was like a starter's gun. The hangar erupted; automatic rifle fire filled the first floor.

Daniels didn't take his eyes off Zimkeroff. His fingertip rested gently on the trigger, waiting to finish the squeeze when Zimkeroff's head was in his sights.

"Come on out, come on out."

Zimkeroff placed the vials into the black briefcase, while Petroff stood guard. As soon as Zimkeroff locked the case, he tucked it under his arm and nodded to Petroff, who picked up the other briefcase. Petroff led the way, the curved pistol grip of the Benelli secure in his right hand, the briefcase gripped tightly in his left.

The firefight on the first floor was picking up. Daniels heard the sound of machine gun fire, but what he didn't hear were two Chinese soldiers climbing the stairs. Daniels focused on the metal door, imagining Zimkeroff's head in his sights.

The first of the two Chinese soldiers spotted Daniels and began firing. Bullets danced in front of Daniels's face, ricocheting around him like mosquitoes. Rolling away from the direction of fire, he squeezed off several blind shots as he rolled, while trying to find cover behind the console. A quick volley of shots hit the console. Rolling again, this time knowing where the shooter was, Daniels came to his feet and pumped several bullets into his would-be assassin. The impact of the hollow point .45-caliber slugs knocked the man over the railing to the ground floor. Daniels quickly turned back toward the second-floor office, but Zimkeroff and Petroff were gone. He crawled toward the ledge and scanned the first floor, hoping to find them between the rows of boxes and crates.

The second Chinese soldier, proceeding more cautiously than his predecessor, saw Daniels and squeezed the trigger. But a bullet from below found its way into his body, making him miss the shot. Daniels turned and fired instinctively at the slumping man.

That was too close, he thought, as the Mark 23's slide locked in the open position. He ejected the empty clip and quickly pushed another one into the open handle and chambered another round. It was time for him to get out of there, he knew, but on the catwalk he would be an easy target.

One of the large crates on the first floor fell apart, revealing its deadly contents. Inside was a .50-caliber machine gun surrounded by armor plate. When it opened up at a rate of three-thousand rounds a minute, the Russians dove for cover. Daniels was as surprised as the Russians, but he had other problems. Several Chinese soldiers had seen him on the platform and were trying to signal their comrades manning the machine gun.

"Fuck, no," Daniels yelled.

As if they could hear him over the thunderous sound of the weapons, they began using Daniels for target practice, which really pissed him off. From his position he had a clear shot at three Chinese soldiers. He took careful aim and squeezed off three shots in rapid succession; all three men fell dead. The machine gun crew unleashed another burst at

Daniels. Bullets began swarming around him, pinning him against the control panel.

The crane, Daniels thought, hitting the start button. Using the remote control, he maneuvered the overhead crane into position over the machine gun. Then he let the giant hook drop behind the armor plate that protected the crew. He hit another button and the steel cable reeled in its giant fish, the armor plate. The machine gun crew was left exposed to the Russians. When his catch was at the ceiling, Daniels pressed the release button allowing the three-thousand-pound load to fall back to the floor.

The crash was deafening, but the sound of the machine gun was no more. The hangar vibrated from the thunderous explosion of the metal falling seventy-five feet to the concrete floor. The armor plate had crushed the gun crew, the machine gun, and several cases of ammunition. Bullets fired off in all directions; dust and debris filled the air, rising up like a giant brown cloud. Blinded by the choking dust, the combatants stopped shooting. The sound of gunfire was replaced with the sounds of gagging and coughing.

Because the dirt cloud had not yet reached him, Daniels had the advantage. He could look down on those who were condemned to die. Random fires began to spread, when another explosion rocked the hangar. Bodies flew in all directions and the screams of dying and mutilated men rose up to where Daniels was. No one on the first floor knew what had happened. It was time for Daniels to leave before the place came down around him.

He was up and running to the rooftop stairway. But before bounding up the stairs, he took one last look for Zimkeroff and Petroff. Maybe they were dead, he thought, although he didn't feel that lucky. Running up the stairs, he burst through the door onto the roof and ran to the side of the building where the vans were parked. Leaning over the side, he saw Petroff getting into the driver's side of the van. Aiming at the passenger side where Zimkeroff would be sitting, the Mark 23 spit out empty shell castings as fast as Daniels could squeeze the trigger. As the bullets bored through the roof, leaving neat entry holes, Daniels hoped Zimkeroff's head had the same type of holes in it.

The slide on the Mark 23 locked back. The gun was empty. Quickly ejecting the clip, he popped another one in and continued to rake the roof of the van as it drove away.

"Damn it," he said running to the helicopter still hovering over the roof.

Climbing into the chopper, putting on the headset, he glanced at the nervous pilot; then barked an order into his microphone: "Take us out of here."

The pilot adjusted the pitch on the rotor and they lifted off.

"What's your name?" Daniels asked the pilot.

"Jerry Capawitz. They call me Cappy."

"Can you fly this crate, Cappy?"

"Yes, sir." There was no hesitation in the pilot's voice.

"See that van heading toward the gate? Stop it."

The pilot spotted his target and dropped the Bell Jet Ranger almost to the ground in front of the van. Petroff's left arm came out of the driver's side window with the barrel of the Benelli resting on the side-view mirror; he fired off the deadly rounds. Cappy punched up the rpm's of the whirley bird, angled the pitch, and lifted the helicopter so the van passed underneath the landing skids by a couple of inches. Petroff was pleased he had won the first round.

"Sorry about that," Cappy said. "I wasn't expecting the shotgun. I pulled up too soon."

"Almost not soon enough," Daniels said. "Cappy, put me down on top of the van."

The pilot shot a quick glance at Daniels and laughed. He was convinced that his passenger was crazy, but he liked the idea. He was as calm as Daniels.

"Sure," Cappy said, without giving it another thought.

He moved the Jet Ranger down the road at about a foot from the ground, following directly behind the van. Petroff watched in the rearview mirror. Cappy closed the helicopter to within a few feet from the van. Then he pulled back on the cyclic and the Jet Ranger jumped up to about six feet. Petroff, guessing what they were up to, hit the brakes as hard as he could. The helicopter shot past him. The Benelli was out again and Petroff was pumping shots into the light-blue Jet Ranger.

Cappy was getting pissed. He cut the forward motion and rotated the helicopter on its axis. With its tail in the air high over the cabin, Cappy charged the van, a foot off the ground. Like jousting knights, they closed in on each other, Petroff pumping shots, Cappy's rotor whirling like a buzz saw. The distance between the combatants closed too fast for even Daniels's comfort. At the last minute, Cappy maneuvered the helicopter to the right of the oncoming van to make it difficult for Petroff to hit them from the left. As he closed the distance to the van, Cappy lifted the helicopter to about eight feet off the ground.

"Get ready," he said to Daniels. "I'll put you on the roof. Good luck."

When the helicopter was four feet from the van, Cappy swung it around, back over the van and down, with the left skid on the roof. It was an impossible maneuver, Daniels thought, but Cappy had done it. Daniels jumped from the helicopter onto the roof as Cappy pulled the helicopter up.

He braced himself on the roof rack as Petroff tried to shake him off. Daniels leaned over to open the door when several shots came through the roof. The bullets ripped through the metal skin of the van, flying past his face. He couldn't grab his weapon without letting go of the roof rack. Petroff accelerated the van; then he hit the brakes, hit the gas, hit the brakes, while Daniels hung on.

Petroff turned the van sharply to the right, driving in a tight circle, hoping the centrifugal force would throw Daniels to the left side of the van where he could get a shot at him. Knowing he would not get a second chance, Daniels let go of the roof rack with one hand and reached for his gun. As he pulled it from its holster, Petroff hit the brakes hard; then he hit the gas. Daniels pointed the Mark 23 to where he thought Petroff would be sitting. He was about to pull the trigger when Petroff hit the brakes so hard the front wheels of the van locked, causing the rear-end to come up almost off the ground. Daniels's feet came flying over his head, pulling him off the van, but instead of flying head first, stomach down, he went feet first, on his back through the air.

His back hit the hood of the van as he flew past, his momentum carrying him off the car. While still airborne, he extended the Mark 23 over his head and, looking back, he fired off several shots as fast as he could. He landed twenty feet in front of the van. Ignoring the pain, he got up with his gun pointing toward the oncoming van. He fired, but the slide locked open—the gun was empty.

Daniels didn't have time to reload; the van was coming straight at him. He was ready to die when suddenly the van veered to the right and slowed down. As it came alongside, he pulled open the door and found Petroff lying across the seat, two bullet holes in his forehead. The back of the sergeant major's head was missing. Blood covered the seat and pieces of his brain were spattered about.

Daniels shut off the engine, wondering where Zimkeroff had gone. There was no way he could have gotten out, he thought. How did that bastard get away? Had he died in the hangar? No, Zimkeroff was alive. Daniels could feel it. There was no way Petroff would have left the general's body behind.

"Where the hell were you going?" he said to the corpse as if expecting an answer

Between the bucket seats was the black leather briefcase. Daniels grabbed it, hoping it contained the BCV. Staring at the leather case, Daniels hesitated, but it wasn't what was inside that scared him, it was the gold monogrammed initials stamped on the handle. The initials confirmed his worst fears. He had figured out the who, but not the why. Daniels opened the case and saw, not the vials, but the brown glass vase.

"The deed to Hong Kong," he said, his mind racing, computing the facts. Then, snapping his fingers, he said: "That's it!"

He knew it all now. Petroff was going to bring the vase back to—

The whine of a Cessna Citation's twin jet engines made him look up. That's it, he thought. The only way Zimkeroff was going to get out of Hong Kong with the biochemical weapon was in a private jet. He now knew where Zimkeroff was. He pushed another clip into his Mark 23. It was time for Zimkeroff to die.

Smoke from the hangar was sending black clouds into the June air. Flames were beginning to flicker from the rooftop and through the windows. Daniels could hear the sounds of sirens. He had to get out of there. Looking around for a way out, he thought about using the van. But that was a driving advertisement for a police check. Instead, he started the van and wedged the Benelli shotgun between the seat and gas pedal causing the engine to rev. Then he put the van in gear and aimed it in the direction of the hangar. It sped off, racing toward the blazing inferno. He picked up the briefcase and was walking away when Cappy dropped the helicopter down in front of him.

"Thanks," Daniels said climbing into the Jet Ranger. "Glad you were in my neighborhood."

"I'd hate to live in your neighborhood," Cappy said. "Too dangerous."

The chopper lifted off the ground and climbed to five hundred feet when a giant fireball erupted out of the old hangar.

"What the hell was that?" Cappy asked.

"Don't know, don't care. By the way why did you come back, Cappy?"

"Well, I wanted to see how you finished your ride on that van you just sent into the blazing inferno. More important, and please don't take any offense at this, I need someone to explain the bullet holes in this beautiful flying machine. Got any ideas?"

"I think I can help you. Drop me off at General Aviation, please."

"GA coming up," Jerry Capawitz said. He had flown the flight of his life.

The Bell Jet Ranger flew across the airport passing over the fire trucks, ambulances, and police cars madly rushing to the CAAC hangar. Daniels was upset with himself for letting Zimkeroff escape, but he remembered that nothing happens until you make it happen. He would make it happen.

CHAPTER 41

A journey is not over until the last step is taken.

— Old Chinese proverb

FOR years prior to the Hong Kong International Airport's construction, the planners had argued over the best means of mass transportation between the terminals. It had become a favorite topic in the papers as each group argued the value and worth of one method over another. The American consultants recommended an aboveground monorail as the most efficient way to move passengers from terminal to terminal. The British consultants had other ideas. They favored a subway modeled on the one that worked so well in London. The bickering went on for years until local governmental authorities settled on an underground monorail. It was known as the URN for underground rail network.

The URN at Hong Kong International Airport was a complex system of lines that crisscrossed the airport, running beneath the many terminals and parking lots and connecting to the trains that traveled to Kowloon. The URN was a marvel of modern technology, run by computers, without the benefit of engineers or conductors. The sleek, silent electric trains moved quietly and quickly between stops and it was the preferred method of traveling to the airport by millions of tourists each year.

Looking like any other passenger riding the URN, Gen. Zimkeroff sat with his deadly cargo stored in the leather briefcase propped on his lap. He watched the signs for his stop—the General Aviation terminal. Private aircraft owners were not allowed to use the commercial terminals to pick up or discharge passengers. They had to use the General Aviation facilities. Parked outside the terminal were the multi-million-dollar private jets painted in a variety of company colors and decorated with corporate logos on their tails. There were no lines, no crowds, and no luggage search. Privacy was ensured.

When the shooting started, Zimkeroff had dashed down the stairs, headed for a rear door that opened onto a large fenced-in storage area with no visible means of escape. Anyone foolish enough to be out there would be trapped. That's why the Chinese hadn't bothered to cover the exit. A meticulous planner and a survivor of many battles, Zimkeroff knew there was an emergency escape hatch located at the end of the storage area. Had there been a problem on the URN, passengers could escape by any one of a number of emergency exits located throughout the system. Zimkeroff had opened the hatch, climbed down a few steps, and had walked about a half mile until he came to a station. Then he had waited patiently for the train.

As Zimkeroff had planned, Petroff would exit from the side entrance of the hangar where they had entered. His part in the escape was to distract the enemy, a role Petroff gladly accepted. If Daniels had looked over the other side of the building, when he was on the roof of the hangar, he would have seen Zimkeroff running across the open storage area. But he, like everyone else, was tracking Petroff.

Sitting comfortably on the URN, Zimkeroff was pleased the first phase of his plan had worked so well. Chi was dead, Zimkeroff had the bio-weapon, and Petroff had the vase with the deed to Hong Kong. The second phase of the plan was underway: Petroff would deliver the deed and the general would take off in a private jet to meet up with the others. Thinking about the third phase of his plan brought a smile to his face. He would sell the weapon, destroy the United States, and retire to a life of leisure. The only thing bothering him was that his two trusted officers, Bresneyev and Kertrinkoff, were in the building when there was a tremendous explosion from inside the hangar. He had wondered what it was, but hadn't stopped to look back. They had to be dead, he thought.

The URN rolled along, stopping at various stations, its doors opening to anxious travelers trying to make their flights. After they had passed the major airlines, and most of the riders had gotten off, Zimkeroff found himself alone. The signs over the car door started to flash in Chinese, French, Spanish, and English, announcing the arrival at the General Aviation terminal. As the doors opened, he stepped out of the car, looking both ways, being cautious and not taking anything for granted. His strides covered the distance to the escalator in a few seconds; he rode the escalator to the street level.

Once outdoors, he squinted until his eyes adjusted to the bright sunlight; then he looked around to get his bearings. The large blue letters *GA* were painted on the windows of the blue-and-white building, which housed the reception area. Zimkeroff almost gave a sigh of relief. He wanted to relax, but his instincts wouldn't allow it—he wasn't safe yet. Finally, feeling comfortable enough, he released the leather briefcase from under his arms and held it by the handles.

The atmosphere in the reception area was warm, quiet, and very rich—not at all like a crowded commercial terminal. Soft music filled the room and the walls were decorated with photographs of jet airplanes. Plush couches, desks, chairs, phones, and faxes awaited the owners of the multimillion dollar toys. At the front counter a pleasant young lady stood to greet him.

"Good day, sir. May I help you?" she asked.

Her English was accent-free. She was either British or American, he thought.

"I am General Alexis Zimkeroff. Is my plane ready?"

"Yes, General. Shall I call a porter for your bags?"

"That won't be necessary, thank you. I just have my carry-on bag," he said, lifting the black leather case for her to see.

"Very well, sir. Your pilot filed a flight plan from here to Australia. Do you have your passport?"

"Of course," he said reaching inside his coat pocket, handing it to her.

She very casually looked it over and returned it to him.

"Sir, I'll have a porter escort you to your plane out on the tarmac. Your pilot is onboard and ready. Have a pleasant flight. Porter, porter."

Zimkeroff followed the porter down a long hall through double glass doors to the outside parking area where the planes were tied down.

"Please stay within the blue-striped lines, sir," the porter said. "It's for your own safety."

As Zimkeroff walked passed the cockpit, the pilot nodded to him, and gave him a half-hearted salute. When he entered the plane from the rear port side, he heard the starboard engine start up. Making his way up the aisle past the bar and dining table, he placed the black briefcase on a window seat, securing it with the safety belt through the handles and strapping it in tightly. Taking the aisle seat next to the briefcase, Zimkeroff sank his massive frame into the soft leather. Pulling the seat belt tight, Zimkeroff picked up the intercom phone connecting him to the pilot. As soon as heard the pilot acknowledge him, Zimkeroff ordered: "Let's go."

The port engine began its slow whine to life and he heard the flight steward close the cabin door. The plane began to move down the taxiway, and finally, he thought, he could relax. He had made it. If all went well, he would meet Petroff and the others in Australia where they would stay for a few days before flying off to meet their buyers. Feeling quite satisfied with himself, he let out a long breath.

"Steward," he said loudly. "Bring me a tall glass of your best vodka."

Sitting on the runway waiting for clearance, the pilot leaned hard on the brakes as he pushed the throttles in. The engines were winding up to take-off rpm, beginning to scream; the aircraft began to shake. Over the roar Zimkeroff heard a voice say: "Did you forget this?"

Zimkeroff's head turned sharply. Standing there was Mac Daniels, holding the briefcase containing the vase. Zimkeroff froze. Daniels was alive, but he couldn't understand how. He had been told Daniels was dead; it was taken care of.

"What's wrong, General, did you see a ghost?"Daniels said, throwing the briefcase on an empty seat."Let's have a little talk before I have the pilot turn this plane around. There are a few questions that need answering."

"The only ghost I see is you,"Zimkeroff yelled, reaching for his pistol.

Standing over the seated Zimkeroff, Daniels had the advantage. He used his body weight to pin Zimkeroff's arm back against the seat. With his free hand, he gave Zimkeroff a vicious backhand across his face.

"Don't be so anxious to die, General," Daniels said. "Sit there and don't move."

The side of Zimkeroff's face turned as red as the blood running from his nose and lip. Zimkeroff showed no sign of pain, his fingers tightened around the armrest, squeezing it so hard that his knuckles turned white. His black eyes narrowed and his nostrils flared. He was going to kill Daniels. With his weight still pressing on Zimkeroff, Daniels reached into the general's jacket, pulled out the pistol, and tossed it aside.

"Now let's talk."

When the tachometer showed takeoff power, the pilot nodded to his copilot, and released the brakes. The jet lurched forward, racing down the runway. Daniels lost his balance, falling back and hitting his head on the corner of the dining table. In one fluid motion, Zimkeroff unbuckled his seat belt and jumped out of his chair. Before Daniels could recover from the fall, Zimkeroff was on top of him, furiously pounding him with his club-like fists. Still dazed, Daniels tried to ward off the punishing blows. Twisting, turning, and trying to force Zimkeroff off him, Daniels could not get enough leverage. It was useless. In desperation, he smashed Zimkeroff's head with his own. The sound of the two skulls knocking together made a loud thump; it was painful to both men.

Zimkeroff stopped punching for a moment, trying to clear his head. His adrenalin racing, Daniels swung a right roundhouse that landed squarely on Zimkeroff's jaw, knocking him backwards. Daniels slowly climbed to his knees as did Zimkeroff. They swung at each other, but neither could get enough leverage to deliver the knockout punch. Their arms locked and they managed to stagger to a standing position.

As the plane picked up speed, the nose wheel came off the ground at a hundred and fifty knots. The pilot pulled back sharply on the stick and the jet jumped off the ground, rocketing upwards at a thousand feet per minute. Unlike a commercial airliner, a private jet was not regulated and the angle of climb was at the discretion of the pilot. The sixty-degree angle caused both men to fall toward the rear of the aircraft. Daniels rolled backward until he slammed into the bar. Zimkeroff managed to grab onto a leg of a seat, stopping himself from falling farther to the rear of the plane. Using the seat to steady himself, Zimkeroff rose to his feet; Daniels was still pressed against the bar. Rolling over, Daniels managed to rise up on one knee when, from the corner of his eye, he saw Zimkeroff's size fourteen foot coming at his face.

Zimkeroff's foot passed over his head into the bar. Reaching for Zimkeroff's other leg, Daniels pulled it with all of his remaining strength, knocking Zimkeroff down. Then he got up and braced himself for the general's next attack. From a kneeling position, Zimkeroff threw a right that landed in Daniels's stomach, causing him to double over. Picking up Daniels like he was a rag doll, Zimkeroff threw him onto the bar. Then he took one of the lead-weighted ashtrays and brought it down trying to smash open Daniels's skull.

Rolling off the bar, Daniels fell behind it, knocking down an assortment of bottles just as the ashtray crashed near his head. As Zimkeroff came after him, Daniels wheeled a bottle into Zimkeroff's knee. The general went down. On his feet Daniels brought a right hand into Zimkeroff's face, breaking the general's nose. Blood poured from Zimkeroff's face, but he was indifferent to the pain, which seemed to fuel his ferocity. Zimkeroff bounded to his feet and blocked Daniels's next volley; then he managed to get his massive hands around Daniels's neck and lifted him off the floor, squeezing the life out of him.

Using his last bit of strength, Daniels delivered a double chop into the sides of Zimkeroff's neck. Dropping Daniels, Zimkeroff stepped back. With a little distance between them, Daniels used the bar for leverage and swung his legs up catching Zimkeroff in the ribs, knocking him against the cabin door. Wiping his face with his sleeve, Zimkeroff stared at the man he hated. Snarling, he reached for the cabin door lever; with a hiss the door began to open. Because it wasn't high enough, the plane was not yet pressurized, so there was no suction from the open door. With unbridled fury, fed by his pain and hatred, Zimkeroff charged Daniels, grabbed him in a bear hug, and picked him up to throw him out of the plane.

"Time to get off the plane," Zimkeroff hissed.

"Fuck you."

The control panel in the cockpit lit up with red lights indicating that the plane was not capable of being pressurized and that the cabin door was not secured. The pilot banked the plane into a tight right-hand turn, causing Daniels and Zimkeroff to fall to the other side of the cabin. Zimkeroff lost his grip on Daniels and grabbed the bar to catch himself. Daniels hit the floor. The general's face was a puddle of blood and his right eye was swollen shut. Daniels did not look much better. He was losing his strength quickly and if he didn't stop Zimkeroff soon, he would be dead.

When Zimkeroff tried to pick him up again, Daniels delivered a vicious right hand to the general's temple, followed by a quick left. Then, reaching back and mustering his last bit of strength, he punched Zimkeroff square in the face, knocking him into the open door. The general grasped the door frame, preventing himself from falling out of the plane. Daniels had given it his all; he was amazed that Zimkeroff was still standing.

Physically drained and fighting just to stand up, Daniels's hand hit something—a bottle of vodka. He took it by the neck and threw it at Zimkeroff's head.

"Here's your fucking vodka. Drink it in hell."

The bottle smashed into Zimkeroff's bloody face and bounced back toward Daniels as the general fell from the aircraft. Daniels stared at the open cabin door, watching the bottle rolling toward him. Twisting off the cap, he took a long hard swallow; then he poured the rest over his face. He wasn't sure which burned more, the vodka he drank or the vodka he poured on his face. He hurt. He hurt all over.

The copilot ran to the rear of the cabin, a horrified look on his face. He hit the lever, closing the door.

"Where's Gen. Zimkeroff?"

"He got off. The vodka must have gone to his head," Daniels said.

* * *

"Harry, I've got the deed, the biochemical weapon, and Zimkeroff is dead," Daniels said on his cell when he was back at the airport.

"Thank God," Saltzman said. "Are you on your way back to the hotel?"

"No. I have one stop to make. See you later."

"No, Mac," Saltzman said, his voice rising. "Get back here now. Don't take any chances. You have a very valuable cargo onboard."

"I'll be back, Harry, but I have something to do. Something very important to me," he said, hanging up on a spluttering Saltzman.

He drove the Suburban slowly out of the airport, on his way to see Johnny Leng at the Hi-Jinks Club. He had a score to settle. He had no idea how many people would be there, but it didn't matter. The Lengs were going to pay for Kelly's death.

Parking the truck, he took the black leather briefcase holding the deadly vials of the biochemical weapon. Time for a real test, he thought. Payback was going to be a bitch.

Surprised that the club was packed at such an early hour, he made his way through the crowd and found a seat at the bar. The two men sitting next to him stared for a moment; then they moved as far away from Daniels as possible.

"You run into wall or something?" a topless Chinese bartender said, giving him a disapproving look.

"Vodka on the rocks with a twist."

"Run a tab?"

"What's the damage?"

"Five American dollars."

"Keep the change," Daniels said, handing her a twenty.

Did she have a sucker here? she wondered.

"Hey, why don't you clean up and pick me up when I'm done. We have some fun, no?"

He took a fifty-dollar bill and waved it in front of her like a matador. She lunged for it like a bull. Then she came over the top of the bar and got as close to him as she could, waiting to hear what he had in mind.

"No. No fun now. Maybe later," he said. "Is Kelly here yet?"

"Don't you like Chinese girl?" she asked, disappointed. "Kelly have big boobs, but they fake."

Daniels took a drink.

"These," she continued, cupping her breast in her hands and pushing them into his face, "are real. You wanna touch? Chinese girl know how to make man very happy."

"I'm an old friend of Kelly's. I have to give her this," he said pointing to the leather briefcase. "Where is her dressing room so I can drop it off? Then I'll come back for you. Here's fifty now, a deposit for later."

"You need the combo to get in," she said. "Press four-one-five-eight-five and you're in. I'll be off at midnight."

"Thanks," he said, "see you later."

At the back of the club, Daniels entered the combination and opened the door leading to the performers' changing rooms. Walking down the long hall, he came to a door with a star on it and the name *Happy Holiday* in big bold letters. The door was unlocked, so he opened it. In the room, he could feel her presence. On the corner of the dressing table he saw the little stuffed dog he had given her a lifetime ago. Around the mirror were photos—Kelly's life in pictures. There was an old college shot of him and Dick; another one with the three of them; one of him and Kelly alone. His anger overcame his remorse and again he vowed revenge.

Staring into the mirror, he understood why everyone in the club had given him funny looks. His face was crusted with dried blood and one eye was black and blue. His face was red and bruised, his hair was messed, and his clothes were torn. The sight of himself made the pain more conscious—not the physical pain, but the emotional pain. He should be dead, not her, he thought.

After washing his face in the sink, he ran his wet hands through his hair, finger combing it into place. The cool water made him feel better. There was nothing he could do about his clothes, but he didn't care. It was back to business.

Remembering the peephole Kelly had told him about, Daniels carefully examined the wall and found it between two paintings. He placed his eye up to the peephole and there was Johnny, Jeff, and several other men having some type of party. He wondered what they were celebrating, but it didn't matter—they were all going to die.

Daniels hoped the bio-weapon was as bad as it was supposed to be, so that the Lengs would die horrible deaths. For a second, Daniels wondered if he should use the Mark 23 on the Lengs instead. He had an extra clip and a few rounds left in the gun. But even with surprise on his side, there was always the possibility that Johnny could escape. That was not an acceptable option. No, he was going with the bio-weapon. He had to be sure.

From Ron Haig's lecture on the weapon, Daniels decided that the best way to use it would be in its liquid form. Finding an empty ice bucket, he filled it with cold water and placed an empty sealed vial in it. Within minutes, the cold water began to cause the gas to condense into a liquid. So far so good, he thought, just as advertised. Haig had been right about the deadly substance: A clear gas that easily changed into a clear liquid.

Picking up Kelly's phone, Daniels dialed the club operator and ordered a bottle of the best champagne. Then he checked on the vial. There was more liquid in it now. He began to wonder if all the gas had condensed. If not, a lot of people, including himself, would die. The knock on the door forced him not to think about the vial.

"I'll get the door, Kelly," he said in a loud voice.

He took the ice bucket, bottle, and glasses, and gave the waiter a ten-dollar tip. Kicking the door shut behind him and locking it, he popped the cork on the champagne. Taking the vial out of the cold water, he decided to play it safe. He pushed it into the ice that surrounded the champagne. When the liquid began to solidify, he felt reasonably comfortable that all the gas had condensed. Carefully tearing off the safety tape, then very gently twisting the rubber stopper from the vial, he allowed one tiny drop of the liquid to fall into the bottle of champagne. Quickly replacing the rubber stopper, he put the vial back into the champagne bucket and replaced the cork.

"Party time," he said.

Daniels found some paper and wrote a note to Jeff Leng. Then he called the operator again and asked her to send a waiter to Kelly's room. In a few minutes there was a knock on the door and he repeated his performance pretending Kelly was in the room. He handed the waiter the tray with the bottle of champagne, a twenty-dollar bill, and the note for Mr. Jeffery Leng.

A moment after the waiter had taken the tray, Daniels heard him knocking on Johnny Leng's office door. He placed his eye to the peephole and saw a burly Chinese man take the tray from the waiter and bring it to the desk. He popped the cork and poured the champagne while Jeff read the note.

"Enjoy the fruit of the victory. It couldn't have been done without your help. Looking forward to seeing you," Jeff read in English.

Daniels saw Jeff talking to his grandfather, pointing to the note, and he wondered if he had hit a nerve. The burly man, who had answered the door, handed Jeff and his grandfather each a glass of the lethal champagne. All the men in the room stopped talking, their eyes were focused on Jeff Leng, holding up their glasses. Jeff raised his glass: "To the Hong Kong of my grandfather. To our Hong Kong, now and forever."

They all drank except Johnny Leng. Daniels shook his head and reached for his Mark 23. His eye still pressed against the peephole, he watched as all the men in the room began to convulse; then vomit. They doubled over in pain. As hardened as he was, even Daniels was taken aback by the horrifying results of one tiny drop of the weapon. He shuddered to think what a bottle full could do to a reservoir.

While Johnny Leng watched, his grandson Jeffery shit himself, vomited all over his suit, and convulsed so hard, he was thrown from his chair. With the blood flowing from his nostrils and suffering agonizing pain, Jeff Leng died less than a minute after drinking the champagne.

Johnny Leng was confused and abjectly afraid. Fear held him hostage and he was unable to move. What had happened? he wondered. No poison acted that fast.

Daniels closed the frames and wrapped the open vial in a cold wet towel before placing it back into the leather briefcase. He was nervous that the contents of the opened vial would return to its gaseous form and escape. It was time to finish his personal assignment.

With the case in hand, like a doctor making a house call, Daniels opened the door to Johnny Leng's office. The stench of vomit and feces filled the room. Those who had taken large swallows were dead; those who had taken little sips were still dying. This biochemical weapon was more deadly than he had imagined.

"Destroyer!" Johnny Leng screamed when he saw Daniels, the man he thought was dead.

Daniels found Jeff Leng on the floor, lying face down. He pushed the body over with his foot. Then he placed his lethal bag on the desk and pushed the Mark 23 hard up under Johnny's chin. The old man's eyes closed. He was ready to accept his death.

"Not that easy, Johnny," Daniels said. "They're all dead now. Take a look around."

He forced Leng to view the horrific sight. Then he drove the Mark 23 hard into the old man's stomach. Leng doubled over, gasping for breath. Daniels threw him on the desk and poured the rest of the champagne into his gaping mouth.

"That was for Kelly," he said.

Daniels stepped over the dead bodies and crossed the room. He could hear Johnny Leng's last agony, but for Daniels it hadn't lasted long enough. Leng was dead by the time Daniels got to the door. He left the club.

Walking toward the truck, he thought the journey is not over until the last step was taken.

CHAPTER 42

When anger rises, think of the consequences.

— Old Chinese proverb

THE ride from the Hi-Jinks Club to the Peninsula Hotel should have taken no more than twenty minutes, but for Daniels the journey seemed to last an eternity. At every red light, he found himself looking at the leather briefcases on the front seat next to him. They were harmless in appearance, yet one held death and destruction and the other the deed to Hong Kong. It didn't fit, he thought. The pieces of the puzzle still didn't fit together. There was still something missing. He just couldn't put his finger on it. Approaching the hotel, he opened his satellite cell phone and called Harry Saltzman.

Pacing back and forth in his office, a bundle of nerves, Saltzman jumped on his phone, answering it on the first ring. The caller ID indicated it was Daniels.

"Mac, are you all right?"

Even over a cell phone, Daniels could hear the concern in Saltzman's voice. "I've got a throbbing headache and I don't look too good, but other than that...." His voice trailed off. The sight of the Peninsula coming into view reminded him of what he still had to do.

"Where are you now?"

"On my way to the hotel. Meet me at my suite."

"All right."

"Harry," he said, his voice showing fatigue, "this shit really works. I opened one of the vials and ran a little test. Just thought I'd tell you."

"Jesus H. Christ, are you crazy? You're certifiable. Do you have any idea what that could do? Is it secure?"

"I think so. I certainly hope so."

"I'll see you at the hotel. Be careful, please."

As their phones shut off simultaneously, Saltzman made a series of calls, frantically dialing one number after another. They had to be ready.

Daniels decided to use the underground parking garage to avoid going through the lobby. He was sure it was full of British watchdogs waiting for him and the last thing he needed was to run into Montgomery. Parking the truck, he rode to his floor in an empty elevator. When he stepped out into the long hall, he knew he was beginning the last steps in a long journey. Each step had brought him closer and closer to facing the chilling truth.

Standing before the door of his suite for a few seconds, staring at it, he let out a long breath before letting himself in. He heard voices coming from the sitting room. The long hall suddenly seemed longer and his stride grew shorter. He was emotionally as well as physically exhausted.

He heard Astrid's soft drawl and the voice of a man with a Chinese accent. The man's back was to the door, Astrid was facing him, and they were engaged in animated conversation. When she noticed Daniels, her hand went to her mouth in surprise. Seeing Astrid's reaction, Gen. Xi stood up.

"Oh, my poor darling," Astrid said, running to him. "What happened to you? Should I call a doctor?"

Not waiting for an answer, she grabbed him by the arm and led him to a chair. Daniels didn't resist her efforts, but instead of sitting down, he placed the two briefcases on the seat and propped himself on the arm of the chair.

"You," Daniels said to Gen. Xi. "Sit down."

Xi sat.

"You, too, Astrid. Please sit down. We have to talk."

She didn't move.

"I said, sit down, Astrid, we need to talk," he repeated, standing up, towering over her, his voice rising.

"Mac," she protested. "What's the matter with you?"

She sat down on the couch.

There was pain in Daniels's face and hurt in his eyes. His voice trembled.

"Why, Astrid, why?"

"Why what, Mac?"

"I figured most of it out, but there are a few gaps. How about you filling me in?"

"Mac, you're not making any sense. What are you talking about?"

Before Daniels could answer her, Gen. Xi reached inside his coat for his gun, but he was much too slow. Daniels's hand flew to the Mark 23; it was pointed at Xi's face before the general's hand reached his holster.

"Go ahead, give me an excuse to shoot you. One more won't matter," Daniels said.

"You're crazy," Gen. Xi said, slowly moving his hand away from his coat.

"I'm crazy?" Daniels said, pushing the Mark 23 back into its holster. "Did you think you and Zimkeroff could get away with this? Zimkeroff was going to trade the deed to Chi for the biochemical weapon, but Chi wanted to bring the deed back to China. That wasn't in your plans. You needed the deed to sell to the British."

Turning to Astrid, he said: "And you provided Zimkeroff with the deed to Hong Kong. Why?"

"No, Mac, it's not true. I didn't give anything to him."

"When I was in Zimkeroff's hotel suite, I noticed the sweet smell in the air, but I couldn't place it. When I returned here, I realized it was your perfume. I wanted to believe it was coincidence, but I don't believe in coincidences. I couldn't figure out why you would be seeing Zimkeroff, so like a lovesick fool, I let it go. But now it makes sense, you were working with him. He knew you were going to deliver the deed to him. How did you find it?"

"You're wrong, Mac. I met Gen. Zimkeroff as part of a story I was doing. I didn't give him any deed. Please. You're scaring me. Stop this," she cried.

"How did you find the vase with the deed in it? Your buddy here," he said, pointing to Xi, "couldn't find it. You were in Inga Holm's room. The security guard, Frank Shen, saw you at the elevator and described you perfectly. He thought you were just another contestant. And you never showed up for your meeting with Harry. Why? Why!"

"You have it wrong. Please listen to me," she pleaded.

"If I have it wrong, how do you explain this?" he said, patting the briefcase. "The one with your initials A. R. on it—the one I gave you as a present."

With Daniels so emotional, Gen. Xi thought he had another chance and his hand slowly started to move again, inching its way up his coat. Daniels pointed a finger at him; it was enough to stop Xi in his tracks.

"You little fuck, you sold out your country, you let Zimkeroff get the bio-weapon. You tried to have Chi killed at the Water Street warehouse, but I stumbled into your trap. You didn't trust Chi, so you had to be sure he was out of the way. Your buddy Zimkeroff took care of that little detail for you. Petroff was on his way here with the deed to give it to you as planned, except he had an accident—he ran into several .45-caliber slugs. I relieved him of the deed; it's right here," he said pointing to the case.

"My men will be here soon. The deed is mine," Gen. Xi said, his voice a growl.

"They're all dead," Daniels said. "You wanted a little insurance, so you had them at the hangar in case Zimkeroff tried to double-cross you. But

I saw it all. Your men are dead. The only deed you'll get is to a Chinese cell."

Turning back to Astrid, he said: "The only way Zimkeroff could have gotten out of the country with this stuff was on a private jet. Since you provided him with the deed, I figured you would lend him the plane to make his escape. That's where I found him—that's where he dropped dead."

"Mac, I don't know what you are talking about. What stuff? I didn't give anyone the plane. You're wrong," she said.

"If I'm wrong then tell me who gave Johnny Leng my picture from the newspaper files. Who?" He didn't wait for her answer. "Did you have Jeff Leng try to have me killed? He sent a couple of his goons to hit me, only it was Kelly who got killed. Unfortunately for her and fortunately for me, she overheard Leng planning my exit party. She saw Leng had my picture, the file photo from the archives, the one you gave to him."

"Are you crazy? I love you," she said, the tears streaming down her face.

"So tell me why? Why did you do it? Yes, that's it, Jeffery Leng. The Lengs get to run their empire without interference from China or is there a merger with Reed Worldwide? It doesn't matter. They're all dead, too. You know Xi, that BCV really works."

Astrid was sobbing.

"If you can't tell me why, then tell me who gave the Lengs my photo."

"I, I love you, you ass," Astrid said through her sobs. "All I ever wanted was you—nothing else."

"Then who gave them the goddamn fucking photo!" Daniels yelled, his anger rising, not caring about the consequences. "You set me up, Astrid. You wanted me dead—and you killed Kelly."

Astrid put her hands over her face and sobbed.

"I gave Jeff Leng your picture," said a voice from the hall.

CHAPTER 43

Sometimes the shortest distance
isn't the shortest course.

— Old Chinese proverb

HARRISON Reed walked into the room, a small revolver in his hand. He pointed it at Daniels.

"Daddy," Astrid cried.

"Reed," Daniels said.

"Perfect timing," said Xi.

"So you're the architect of all this," Daniels said.

"I was quite impressed with your deductions, Mac. You almost had it right," Reed said. "Astrid had nothing to do with any of this except for finding the vase for me. I knew you would find it and, in a way, you did. It was your pictures of the Galaxy contestants that did it. I also wanted you where I could watch you. I have been in Hong Kong all the time. In fact, I'm in your room. I had the hotel cancel it, forcing you in here with Astrid. I worked with the Lengs, not Astrid. I gave them your picture. I couldn't take a chance with you on the loose. But I underestimated you. You were too good, so I asked Jeff to eliminate you. I took Astrid's brief-case for the vase and delivered it to Zimkeroff. He, Gen. Xi, and I had it all planned. It was so simple, but you had to fuck it up. Astrid knew nothing about the biochemical weapon. That was strictly Zimkeroff. Astrid, tell Mac how you found the vase for me."

Astrid sat back down in the chair, wiping her eyes, feeling somewhat vindicated.

"Dad told me a story about a deed when we were back in the States. I thought it was crazy, but I agreed to come here because of you. Then Dad called me and told me that the vase with the deed was here. It had been sold by a tourist shop to one of the Galaxy contestants."

"Sorry I lied to you," Reed said. "If I had said something, you might have told Mac."

"Why didn't you tell me your father was here, Astrid?" Daniels asked.

"She thought I got here last night," Reed said. "I arrived right after you two landed. I told Astrid that I wanted to surprise you. I was going to make you an offer you couldn't refuse, an interest in the company. She wanted to believe that you would marry her. Anyway, finish telling your story."

"I knew one of the contestants had the vase," Astrid said. "Dad said the Chinese authorities believed that one of the blondes from the beauty pageant might have it. After looking at the pictures, I knew it was one of two. It was either the Miss Sweden, Inga Holm, or Miss Ireland, Tara. If you had looked at the photos carefully, you would have noticed that Inga was carrying two pocketbooks. One was hers and one must have belonged to a friend. If you weren't a man, you would have realized that no woman would carry a plaid purse with a striped skirt.

"So I searched the other photos until I found a woman wearing the right outfit. It was Miss Ireland. In fact, the outfit she was wearing was made of the same material as the purse. I went to Inga Holm's room first, planning to buy her vase, but she was not there. The door, however, was open and I found the vase, but it was empty.

"Later, I went to Tara's room under the pretext of interviewing her. Sitting there on her dresser was the vase. I offered to buy it from her, but she told me I could have it only if I spent the night with her. That's not my style. I told her I was with you and that made her mad. She went nuts. After calling you a few names, she told me she would never sell the vase to me. She saw how upset I was getting and told me that you were on your way and she was going to fuck you. I just wanted to get out of there. When I left her, she was alive. I called my father and told him where the vase was. That's the night you saw me coming in late."

"I went up to visit the young lady," Reed said. "I tried my best to fill in for you, Mac, but I wouldn't do. When I mentioned the vase to her, she became suspicious. She was going to open it. Fortunately, the champagne arrived and diverted her attention. I slipped a few pills into her drink. You know the rest."

"That answers some of the questions, but why?" Daniels asked.

"Why? That's the easy question," Reed said. "Greed! Pure and simple greed. Once the deed was given to the English by my good friend Gen. Xi, the turnover would be delayed until the legal ramifications could be worked out. Eventually, I would have made my claim and the English would have had to recognize that the Island of Hong Kong was given not to their government, but to General H. R. Powell—that's Harrison Richard Powell, my great-great-grandfather, my namesake. It was his land grant.

"After his death, his sister took care of his children. The children took the name of their aunt, which was Reed. When things had settled down,

I would, out of the goodness of my heart, have given the deed back to the Chinese for the cable rights to China. You have no idea what that's worth. Think of it: Twenty-five percent of the world's population in one country. Do you have any idea just what ten percent of the market is worth at just a dollar? It is over two hundred million a month. At ten dollars, it's two billion a month. China is the fastest growing economy in the world. Oh, I originally liked the idea of having my own country, but an extra ten or twenty billion seemed much better. And I have you to thank for this, Mac. Here's your payoff."

Reed pulled back the hammer of the snub-nose .38-caliber revolver, squeezed the trigger, and a shot rang out.

Astrid jumped up screaming: "No!"

Xi tried to grab her, to pull her back, but he missed.

Daniels fell back onto the chair, but he wasn't hurt. Looking at himself, he saw that there was no blood. He was all right. How could Reed have missed at such close range? he wondered.

"Astrid!" he screamed. But although she was shaking, he didn't see any blood on her either.

Then he looked at Reed and saw a massive red stain where his heart should have been. Reed hit the floor trying to scream, but death took him first. Astrid fell to her father's lifeless body. Standing in the doorway was the Inspector General, the smoke still rising from his Daewoo.

"Your arrival has been fortunate," Xi said, rising to his feet.

"Not fortunate for you. You are under arrest and will stand trial for treason," the Inspector General said with obvious disgust in his voice. "I believe those briefcases belong to me, Mr. Daniels."

The sound of the front door slamming caused the Inspector General to turn. Xi thought this was his chance and drew out his gun. The noise from the hall also caused Daniels, who was on his knees beside Astrid, to look up and, seeing Xi's movements, he quickly fired off two shots in rapid succession. The first found Xi's heart, the second his brain, and the impact knocked him back over the chair. The general was dead before he hit the floor. The Inspector General whipped around, his gun pointed at Daniels, whose Mark 23 was pointed at him. Rising to his feet, his weapon still pointed at the Inspector General, Daniels said: "I think those briefcases are mine. It's up to you, what's next?"

"You better put those guns away before someone gets hurt," Admiral Charko said, entering the room.

"Good idea," the Inspector General said as he holstered his weapon. Daniels holstered his Mark 23 and dropped back to comfort Astrid, who was sobbing uncontrollably.

Behind the Admiral were Saltzman and two other men. Daniels recognized one of the men from the park, the cleaner. He knew what had to be done. Astrid couldn't witness what was about to happen. Daniels nodded toward her; Saltzman understood and said something to the cleaner, who took out what appeared to be a fountain pen, but was really a hypodermic needle, and pressed it against Astrid's arm. Her body fell limp. Lifting Astrid in his arms, Daniels carried her to her bedroom. Gently laying her down on the bed, he pulled the covers over her.

"I'm sorry," he whispered to the sedated Astrid. "I love you."

Leaning over, he gently kissed her.

Back in the sitting room, the cleaner was already working on Xi's body. The Admiral, Saltzman, the Inspector General, and the unidentified man were huddled together. As Daniels approached, they stopped talking.

"Somehow I expected you, Admiral, but not the Inspector General," he said. "How are you, General?"

"Compared to the way you look, I'm doing fine," the Inspector General said.

"I don't know what brought you to Hong Kong, sir, but I'm glad you're here," Daniels said.

"Lucky for you I came down here to pick up that traitor, Xi. You're also very lucky I showed up when I did. This is the second time today we have saved your chestnuts."

"When?" Daniels asked.

"Well," Saltzman, said, "I think we have some business to finish up here before Mr. Montgomery comes busting through the door."

Daniels picked up the two briefcases and handed the case with the biochemical virus to Saltzman.

"Be careful. One of the vials is open," Daniels said.

Saltzman gingerly passed the briefcase to the other man, who disappeared down the hall with it. He handed the one with the deed to the Inspector General.

"Here, I believe this is what you want. Now tell me how you saved my chestnuts?"

"It wasn't me. It was Wa Chung."

"Wa Chung?" Daniels said. "I haven't seen him since Taiwan."

"He saw you," the Inspector General said.

"Where was he? "Daniels asked.

"He was at the CAAC hangar where I had sent him," the Inspector General said. "You were on the top floor when one of Chi's men was coming up the ladder—a sitting duck up there. Wa Chung was below and, seeing you were occupied, he took the gunman out for you. He said you were a one-man wrecking crew. You almost killed him when you dropped the armor plate—very ingenious. He was lucky to escape alive after you burned the building down. Very good, Mackenzie Daniels. You know, you're a real cowboy. E. J., you had better fill him in. I have a loose end to deal with—Col. Miu. Then I must get back to Beijing."

The Inspector General shook hands with Daniels and nodded toward the bedroom where Astrid was sleeping.

"It looks like you're going have your hands full," he said.

Then he handed the Admiral the briefcase containing the deed.

"Take good care of this," he said. "Thank you."

"No, thank you, my old friend," the Admiral said.

For the first time in his life, Daniels was mad at the Admiral. As he watched Inspector General Lee Kem leave as quietly as he had come in, he said: "Admiral, you owe me an explanation."

"I do," the Admiral said. "Harry, stay here with Ms. Reed until the rest of the crew arrives. I'm going with Mac to his room."

"What's this about?" Daniels asked, closing the door to his bedroom.

"What I'm about to tell you, no one, not Saltzman, not Haig, no one on our side, knows. The president, after he had returned from his London trip, called a combined joint chiefs and National Security Agency meeting. After the meeting, I told him what I am about to tell you. We had received word from Lee Kem about the biochemical virus. The initial reports were staggering. An attack by the Chinese would have virtually destroyed the United States. Lee informed us that the Chinese Central Planning Committee would not authorize the use of the BCV because they feared they couldn't control the airborne virus. We had to get a sample before the Chinese figured out how to control it. That was vital to our very existence. Lee and I devised a plan to trade the deed to Hong Kong for a sample of the BCV."

"Don't tell me," Daniels said, interrupting the Admiral.

"Yes, you figured it out. We needed a deed, so we created one. It's fake."

"A fucking fake!"

"The story of the land grant has been around for a hundred years. It was probably started the day after the Treaty of Nanking was signed. All Lee had to do was give it a jump start to revive it. We had to have something to trade for the bio-weapon. The biochemical virus was top secret—so secret that even Lee was barred from the project. We desperately needed the formula, but Lee couldn't get it for us, so we used the infamous deed to Hong Kong as bait. Once we leaked it to the British, the word spread like wildfire. With a loose cannon like Sang Chi running around, the story became even more real. Lee had his Free China Society working overtime, sending out false information. We managed to get the word to Gen. Zimkeroff about the BCV. His desire for revenge was the spark. Gen. Xi's greed added fuel to the fire and Reed put it all together. The power of greed combined with the lust for power is a deadly combination. Lee suggested that the BCV be turned over to Sang Chi to trade for the deed. That was the hard part, but Lee pulled it off. By the way, his life was on the line for this one. Lee convinced his higher ups that he could get the BCV back.

"The deed was to be delivered by the Chans, then to Gen. Xi, who would have given it to Zimkeroff, but the deed got lost. I needed you to find it, to complete the circle, so the trade could be made for the BCV. Somehow the deed ended up with the Galaxy contestants and you know the rest of the story."

"A fake," Daniels said, stunned at what he had heard. Kelly came to his mind. "This whole thing was a fucking fake, a show. A lot of people died because of a fake piece of paper, Admiral."

"You got it wrong, Mac. A lot of people will live because of a fake piece of paper. We have the BCV and we hope to create an antidote. We did what had to be done. Sometimes the shortest course isn't the shortest distance. But it's over."

Daniels took the vase out of the case, held it up, and admired it.

"Sure looks old, Admiral. What are these characters on the bottom?"

Without looking, the Admiral said: "It's probably a name, the name of the man who owned or made the vase."

Daniels popped the cork, poured out the sand, and removed the parchment. He unrolled it and shook his head. It was unbelievable. Then he lit a match and hesitated for a moment. Blowing out the match, he rolled the parchment and placed it back in the vase, pouring in the sand.

"What are you doing?" the Admiral asked.

"I decided that this belongs to Kelly, Admiral. I'm going to put it on my mantle to remind me of her and what she did. You don't think anybody will care, do you, sir?"

"No, Mac. Keep it."

* * *

Christopher Patten, the last Royal Governor of the colony, boarded a Royal Air Force jet at Hong Kong International Airport and buckled himself into a plush seat for the long ride home. The special priority aircraft had been cleared for immediate takeoff. The plane lifted off the runway at exactly eleven fifty-nine, leaving Hong Kong before the British flag was run down.

It was over.

CHAPTER 44

It takes the last piece, no matter how small,
to complete the puzzle.

— Old Chinese proverb

Atlanta, Georgia, July 7, 1997

THE story was on the front pages of all the papers, the lead in all the evening newscasts, and a nonstop marathon on the World News Network. The Reed publications carried their founder's picture, trimmed in black, detailing the life of the media giant who had died suddenly of a heart attack while in Hong Kong. As the *Atlanta Press* said: *Friends and foe alike are mourning the death of Harrison Reed; his friends will miss his company, his foes will miss his fight.*

The Georgia state police estimated that more than five thousand people had attended the funeral services.

The *New York Times* lead story read: *The great headquarters building of the World News Corporation was dark today as Harrison Reed was laid to rest. The mourners were led by Astrid Reed, his daughter, President Clark, and the First Lady.*

Also attending the services were the governors of several states, a dozen United States Senators, and the CEO's of many major corporations.

The *Washington Post* ran the story of a man whom the world held in high esteem, a man who was larger than life. The stories made great reading and the public relations spin was impressive.

An editorial in *The Wall Street Journal*, after acknowledging Reed's many contributions to the world, ended its story by stating that his daughter Astrid would be running World News Corporation. It said: *Miss Reed, an executive at World News, was at her father's side when he died. She is a bright young woman, but will the market support her in her bid to run her father's empire?*

* * *

292

Washington, D.C., August 25, 1997

Admiral E. J. Charko sifted through the reports on his desk, speed reading them, and placing them in the appropriate boxes for filing or further action. Then one from China caught his attention. He saw the handiwork of Inspector General Lee Kem in the report. It stated that Sang Chi was posthumously inducted into the Hall of Heroes for giving his life to save state secrets. He had died along with another great Hero of the People's Republic, General Xi, in a fire at the CAAC hangar at the Hong Kong International Airport. The fire had destroyed the entire facility; nothing had been saved from the blazing inferno.

Charko was pleased that the Inspector General had found a way to keep the secret—that the BCV was in American hands. Lee had accomplished his mission, according to the Chinese government. The vials of the BCV and the deed had been destroyed in the fire, along with the bodies of Chi and Xi. Lee Kem was safe for now and so was the United States.

* * *

London, England, September 24, 1997

An announcement in the *Times* of London read: *Mr. Michael Montgomery and Miss Elizabeth Browning were married today at Saint Paul's Cathedral. Mr. Montgomery, who recently retired from Her Majesty's Secret Intelligence Service, met Miss Browning in Hong Kong where she was a customs officer. Miss Browning was attended by Ashley Williams and Lu An Adams. The groom's best men were Winston Williams and Col. Leslie Adams, both returning from Her Majesty's service in Hong Kong. The three couples, all old friends, will be living in London.*

* * *

Hong Kong, September 30, 1997

A large photograph of the new Chief Executive Tung Chee-haw on the third green of the exclusive Royal Hong Kong Golf Club was featured on the front page of the *South China Morning Post*. The caption read: *Golf's Newest Devotee. Chief executive seen with American entrepreneur Tom Camarow and the new Miss Galaxy, Pa Ti-kay.* The paper went on to report that Camarow had the inside track for opening several golf clubs in China. Ms. Pa told reporters: "Tommy and I are looking forward to crowning another Miss Galaxy next year."

* * *

Long Beach Island, New Jersey, November 26, 1997

The wind whipped across the dunes, picking up the fine grains of sand and spreading them over the streets like snow. Daniels pulled up his collar and kept his back to the wind, his arm around Astrid, holding her close. The early winter cold front made them shiver as they looked at the grave marker. It read simply: *Kelly Brook, died so that others may live.* Daniels placed flowers on the grave stone. There were no words he could offer, only silent prayers.

They left the little shore cemetery at Saint Lucy's Church, walking arm in arm. Astrid held him tight as if she were afraid he would blow away.

"A storm's coming in," Daniels said. "Time to go."

"Yes," she said, "time to go."

Astrid was quiet as Daniels headed for the mainland. He was driving her to the Atlantic City airport, where the Reed corporate jet was waiting for her. Each could read the other's mind. She wanted him to stay; he had to go.

At the airport Daniels walked with Astrid to the jet's doorway.

"Come with me," she begged, as tears streamed down her cheeks. "I love you, Mac, I always have."

"Don't cry, please. We both need a little time, especially you, my love. You've been through a lot and you have a big company to run. I have an assignment, something I have to do," he said, wiping away her tears.

"We love each other. It's not fair, Mac. Why can't they send someone else?" She didn't wait for an answer. She knew. "Mac I'll always love you. Please, quit the agency. Help me run the company. Give it a chance, give us a chance."

He loved her, but he was not ready to sit behind a desk. It would be unfair to her to be married to a man who would be here one day and gone the next, and not be able to tell her where he was. They were from two different worlds at this time; maybe the next time. He took her in his arms and held her tight. Ever so gently their lips met; no words were necessary. A kiss of love was a promise to return.

Daniels closed the cabin door. The clunk of the lock securing the door was a pain in his heart. With a sad smile, he gave the thumbs up sign to the pilot. The pilot nodded and the jet moved slowly off the tarmac and onto the taxiway. He could see Astrid's face in the window. The jet taxied to the runway, the engines whined and picked up power. Daniels watched it disappear into the evening sky, becoming just another star.

Back inside the terminal, Ron Haig was there waiting as Daniels came in from the cold. He handed Daniels a briefing book.

"Yeah, I know," Daniels said wearily. "If I read it, it might save my life."

"Ah, fuck it," Haig said. "I'll buy you a drink."

* * *

New York City, May 25, 2000

Regis Philbin, wearing a dark blue shirt and matching blue silk tie, was cool even under the hot studio lights.

"Are you ready?" he asked.

The contestant was nervous; perspiration formed on his forehead. But after taking a sip of water, he said he was ready.

"For one million dollars," Philbin asked calmly. "Who was the last Royal Governor of Hong Kong? Was it: *A.* John Major. *B.* Christopher Patten. *C....*"

EPILOGUE

Sometimes mistakes turn out for the best.
— Old Chinese proverb

IT was a warm spring day almost eleven months after the turnover. The beautiful weather had brought out the masses in Beijing. The parks were crowded. Even the Inspector General left his office, saying to his new secretary that he was going to the Monument of the People's Heroes. He was glad to have gotten rid of Mi Ler; it had made life difficult having a spy in his outer office. Although she didn't know it, Mi Ler had helped bring about the downfall of Gen. Xi by supplying him with information that the Inspector General deliberately leaked to her.

The park was a few short blocks from the Great Hall and the Inspector General walked slowly toward the monument, allowing the sunshine to warm his face. It felt good to be outside. Walking along, he thought about his creation, the Free China Society, and about how he had used it for years, never realizing how important it would be in keeping the balance of power between the United States and China. The Society, the Water Street warehouse, the Chans, Zimkeroff and Xi had all been entangled in the web of deceit he had created.

Surrounding the monument was a park with picnic tables where many Chinese ate in the presence of those who had given so much for the Great Revolution. Crowds gathered around the marble obelisk paying their respects to the names chiseled in stone. The Inspector General stayed away from the crowd. There were too many names on the public tombstone, he thought, that should never have been there. Two immediately came to mind—Chi and Xi.

"Nice day, Inspector General," the voice said.

The Inspector General didn't turn around. He recognized the voice of Jong Le-til, one of his most trusted agents. Although he had served the Inspector General faithfully for fifteen years, Jong had been just another player caught in the web of deceit. He had no idea of the part he had played in the game.

"Yes, it is. At my age every day is a nice one, Jong."

The Inspector General moved toward the tables and picked one that was being used by a young family. He noticed that they were almost finished eating. Perfect, he thought. They would leave soon and Le-til would take their place.

"May I sit here?" he asked. It was common for strangers to share their tables. The man gestured with his hand.

"Please be seated."

Taking an apple from his pocket, the Inspector General brushed it against his sleeve, shining it. The family had no sooner left when Le-til sat down across from him. As was the custom, both men nodded to each other. Had anyone been watching, it would have appeared as if two strangers were sharing a table.

"Do you play chess?" asked the Inspector General.

"I do."

The Inspector General took out a cloth chess field, opened it, and ironed it flat with his hand. Then he took the chess pieces from his pocket and the two men set up the game. But the Inspector General had more on his mind than chess.

Several minutes into the game the Inspector General spoke.

"You have served me well, Jong. Thank you. But you have served China far more than you will ever know."

"Thank you, sir."

Le-til's mission had been to find an old parchment and to hand it over to another agent, Mr. Chin, an expert forger, who was to create the false deed to Hong Kong. After that, Le-til was to see that the vase with the deed was delivered to the Chans.

The Inspector General took one of Jong's pawns.

"Sir, I was given this by the curator of the Chinese Revolution Museum. He said you had an interest in the Opium War and he thought you might find it interesting," Le-til said.

He handed the Inspector General a manuscript. The label read: *Journal of Lord Ti Lu Chou.*

"Do you know what this is?" asked the Inspector General.

"I don't know, sir, it's written in an old dialect that I can't read."

The Inspector General nodded, pleased that Le-til couldn't read the ancient writing.

"I think I know what this is. I found the first part and this may be the rest. Let me take a minute to see."

Flipping through the pages, the Inspector General stopped to read for a moment.

On April 15, 1843, as the English would date it, Major General H. R. Powell was in his London sitting room basking in glory. The carriage ride that morning had been like Caesar's triumphant march through

Rome. The crowds that had lined the route to the palace were enthusi-
astic, waving and shouting. Little girls had thrown flowers in his path.
His men had led his carriage, their brass buckles glistening in the sun,
their drawn sabers shimmering in the light, the plumes on their shakos
blowing in the wind. A barbaric spectacle, my men reported.

The weather had been perfect and even the horses had cooperated
by trotting in unison. The closer he had gotten to the palace, the larger
the crowds had grown and the louder they had cheered. Queen Victoria,
herself, must have heard the noise from the streets below. When the
carriage had stopped, his men had formed a guard line from the carriage to the entrance to the palace. Powell, his medals shining, his chest
puffed up, was ready to receive his knighthood from the queen.

The afternoon party at Powell's residence was a success. It had been
truly a splendid day for him being surrounded by his officers and their
wives, his children, his sister Elizabeth, and her husband Charles Reed.
After most of the guests had departed, he called those few officers
remaining, those he truly considered friends, into his study. He opened
a bottle of cognac and poured a portion for his men. One of the senior
officers raised his glass and said: "To Sir Harrison." The room resounded
with cries of "Hear! Hear!" Someone else demanded a speech.

Powell was glad to oblige them. "My fellow officers, my brothers in
arms, my friends, our queen this day has done me honor, an honor that
I gladly share with you," he said. "For without you, I would not be here
today. I thank you for giving me the privilege of leading you in glorious
battle for queen and country. It is always an honor, always a privilege,
to be a Royal Marine. God save the queen."

"The queen," rang out a chorus of voices. Raising their glasses, they
drank. Then a senior officer spoke: "Sir, speaking on behalf of your officers and men, I say without reservation, we are honored to follow."

"No," Powell said, "the honor is mine—and that's an order."

The remark brought laughter. After a few healthy swallows of
cognac,
Powell continued.

"Men, tomorrow I shall notify Her Majesty that I am retiring from
the Royal Marines."

Several voices at once rang out: "No! No! No!" The atmosphere in the
study immediately turned gloomy. The men whispered among themselves, their concern all too evident.

"You must be jesting," an officer said.

"I jest not, but I want to share with you my plans," Powell said. "I will
spend the next six months putting my affairs in order. Then I will return
to Hong Kong where I plan to develop the island into an empire for all
of us. I believe a fortune awaits us. I say 'us,' gentlemen, because we will
all share in the bounty."

As he walked over to his desk, the men gave way for him, their eyes following his every move. He found a large map and unrolled it on the desktop.

"Look," he said, pointing to Hong Kong Island. "It is the gateway to southern China, a natural harbor, the port of entry—our port of entry. Each of you will be given a piece of the island, a share in the business."

All this was reported to me by men, who had taken up residence in Gen. Powell's house, posing as his servants.

Turning a few more pages, the Inspector General took Jong's rook and continued reading.

On the night of the celebration, my men were worked like slaves.

"Fu Shan, come quickly. Tai Ding where are you? Lazy yellow dogs," Powell had growled.

Fu Shan came into the room first, followed closely by Tai Ding, their queues flying behind them. They stood with their hands tucked into the white sleeves of their uniforms as Powell barked orders and insults at them. They ran out of the room as fast as they had run in. A few minutes later, the sound of their sandals on the floor preceded them as they arrived with trays of food, wine, and tobacco. The party lasted far longer than it should have, not ending until dawn. All night my men were abused by the Red Devil.

"Goodnight or should I say good morning," Powell said as the last of his guests staggered away. He shut the door behind him and leaned on it for support. The children and Charles Reed were sleeping, but Elizabeth was in the library reading her Bible. She heard Powell enter, but she didn't look up. She continued to read, asking him: "Are you really going to retire, brother?"

"Sister, were you listening at the door?"

"Of course not, you talk loudly when you are with drink. Will you please answer my question, Harrison?"

"Yes, I am," he said.

Her face showed her pain. She and Charles had not been fortunate enough to have their own children. After Powell's wife had died, Elizabeth had taken her barren state as a sign from God that she had to take care of her niece and nephew. She was as devoted to the children as if she were their natural mother. The children were very attached to her and Charles, and the thought that they were going to Hong Kong without her was too much to bear.

"Why the sad look, sister? You will enjoy living in the East."

She dropped her Bible and flew to her brother, giving him a hug. "When do we leave?" she asked.

"Soon enough. You didn't think I could separate you from the children. Lord knows you've spent more time with them than I. Elizabeth, I have fought too many wars and I missed so much, it's time for me to come home. Just remember, if anything happens to me, take care of the children."

"Nothing is going to happen to you," she said. "We are going to have a good life in Hong Kong."

"No, not Hong Kong. Powell Island."

"No," she said. "Reed Island."

She shared a laugh with her brother and went to wake the children. Powell went back to his office. He took the vase from the mantel, opened it, and poured out the sand until a rolled piece of parchment was visible.

Unrolling the parchment, he stared at the document while my men watched him from the hall. His fingers caressed it. This was the future for him and his family. The crackling of the logs in the fireplace must have interrupted his thoughts. He rolled the parchment and restored it and the sand to the vase before putting it back in its position of honor on the mantle over the fireplace.

The Inspector General was suddenly lost in the middle of the nineteenth century. The sunshine, the park, and the laughing families all evaporated for him. He was in foggy, rainy London. But he did manage to take one of Jong's bishops before he started reading again.

It began a few days after the party, a slight stomachache, not much to be distressed about, a little uncomfortable, perhaps, but Gen. Powell thought he would survive. Elizabeth thought the cause was too much merriment, too much drink, too much fun. Powell let it go, continuing on with his busy life. But the pain persisted; it got a little worse; then dysentery set in. Several days later, Powell was running a high fever and finally allowed his sister to call the family physician. The doctor diagnosed the ailment as a stomach disorder and prescribed tea, toast, and plenty of rest.

As difficult as it was for an active man like Powell to confine himself to bed, his weakened condition forced him to follow the doctor's orders. My men kept the teapot full. Every day he grew a little worse; every day he suffered a little more. The pain then grew severe and constant. He found he couldn't stand up, he was severely dehydrated, and his breathing was labored. To reduce the fever, the doctor had tried blood letting, but it didn't work. It only seemed to make him weaker. Powell was eventually confined to bed.

My men enjoyed seeing him deteriorate before their eyes. They knew I would approve.

All London mourned the passing of Major General Sir H. R. Powell, my servants reported. The queen herself attended the services. The men with whom he had served acted as a guard of honor. They were brave men, who showed no emotion on the battlefield, but that day they had tear-stained cheeks.

Powell's parade mount Lance led the procession with the general's boots placed backwards in the stirrups. The big horse kept turning its head, looking for his rider. The eerie sound of barbarian bagpipes filled the air as Powell's sister and his children marched behind the flag-draped casket toward their family tomb.

The Inspector General stopped reading and rubbed his eyes. He was about to put the manuscript away when he noticed a sheaf of papers of a different shade at the back of the bundle. Curious, he flipped to the slightly darker paper and it said: *Report to Lord Ti Lu Chou From His Most Faithful Servant, Fu Shan.* The writing was different from Chou's and the grammar and syntax was a bit difficult for the Inspector General to read, but he was intrigued to find a first-hand account.

Several weeks after Gen. Powell lay dead, my friend Tai Ding and I were in the middle of the Atlantic Ocean trying to weather the rolling ship as it made its way westward. We would land in Panama and cross the isthmus by horse; then board another ship bound for China. And home!

We ate in our cabin, trying to avoid all contact with the Westerners. There was nothing much to do on the ship, so when Tai Ding brewed and poured us tea, it set my mind racing, remembering what we had done together, Tai Ding and me.

I thought about how we had poured tea for Gen. Powell back in London. Every day, we poured him his tea and every day we stood waiting and watching. Powell had treated us like dogs, never showing us any kindness. But we never complained. On the last day of his life, the general could hardly drink his tea and he had lost the ability to speak. It was on that day that we finally spoke to him.

"Lord Chou has his revenge," I said to the Red Devil in English.

Powell heard me, but he hadn't quite understood. His lips had quivered as he had tried to say, "Chou." But no words had come out.

"Yes, the great and honorable Lord Chou, our master. He instructed us to place a Chinese herb in your tea—a little bit every day. Just enough to make you sick, but not enough to kill you all at once. Each day we put a little more poison in your tea. You had to suffer before you die. Now you will die. There is nothing more to do," I said to him.

Gen. Powell tried to reach for his pistols hanging from the bedpost, but his arm had no strength. He was too weak to lift his pistols from their holster. He had let out a long breath. He would never speak again.

I said to him: "Remember the old Chinese proverb: That which is taken wrongfully is never owned."

That was the last thing the Red Devil heard before dying.

Days later, as the waves broke against the bow of the ship Tai Ding opened his trunk and sorted through his possessions for the simple hand-painted vase that once stood on the mantel in Powell's house. *Taking it out and handing to me, he said:* "Let us throw it to the fishes."

"No, we must bring it back to China," I told him. "It is not for us to destroy. This vase belongs to Lord Chou. See, his name is on the bottom."

Putting down the manuscript, the Inspector General knew he had to ask a question. "Tell me what you did?" he asked, taking Jong's other bishop and moving in on the king.

"Well, sir, after the vases were delivered to me, I went to the Museum of Chinese History. Where else to find old parchment? But I couldn't find anything there that was the right age. When I asked the curator, I discovered that the materials on the Opium War were kept at the Chinese Revolution Museum.

"I managed to get into the old basement storeroom one night when the museum was closed. I was trying to find a parchment from that era when I came upon a closet that held a vase exactly like the ones I had. I took it, figuring it was authentic, not a cheap copy like those sold at the House of Chan. Inside the vase was an old parchment with plenty of blank areas for the forger to use, so I delivered it directly to Mr. Chin."

"What did Mr. Chin say?"

"That was the surprising thing, sir," Jong said. "He looked at it and told me it was a good forgery and why was I wasting his time when he had so many other things to do."

"What did you do?"

"I had the parchment and the vases sent to the Chans," Jong said. "If Mr. Chin approved the forgery, I thought it would be all right."

"Sometimes mistakes turn out for the best," the Inspector General mumbled, not lifting his eyes. His hands had a slight tremor.

"Sir, I'm sorry. I didn't hear you, sir."

"Checkmate," the Inspector General said, moving his queen.

"You win, sir. The game is over."

"Yes, the game is over."

There were many people in the park that day, but the Inspector General had never felt so alone. He had created a devious web of deceit, only to have been caught in it himself.

A chill came over him as he realized what had happened. The deed to Hong Kong wasn't a myth, after all. It existed and he had sent it out of the country. The consequences were staggering. If something had gone wrong with his plan. . . .

His only comfort was knowing that the Admiral had destroyed what he thought was the fake deed. He looked at the monument and whispered, "Thank you, Lord Chou."